DESIRE'S BARGAIN

"Please, I need to find passage to New Orleans," said Alexandra, casting the captain an imploring look.

"Don't," Jake said gruffly, his blue eyes turning icy. "A coy look doesn't fit you at all. Leave that to the experts — Southern ladies. You'd better play straight with me."

"I need to go to New Orleans," she repeated directly.

"You have money for passage?"

She had lost everything she had brought with her from New York — all her fine clothes, all her money — on the schooner. In fact, for the first time in her life she was dependent on someone else. She hated the feeling.

"Captain, I have nothing to offer that's worth anything."

Jake hesitated a mo___ ___ ___ spell. "You're wrong ___ ___ was tall and powe___ couldn't remember ___ shoulders before.

"With no possessio___ ___ still have a great deal to offer — if you're willing . . ."

JANE ARCHER

TENDER TORMENT

PINNACLE BOOKS
WINDSOR PUBLISHING CORP.

PINNACLE BOOKS

are published by

Windsor Publishing Corp.
475 Park Avenue South
New York, NY 10016

First Pinnacle Books Printing: March, 1993

Printed in the United States of America

For Dean

The true adventurer goes forth aimless and uncalculating to meet and greet unknown fate.

—O. Henry

TABLE OF CONTENTS

Prologue

i

The moon shone brilliantly in the dark sky, spreading its soft silver light over the night-darkened New York City. It was an unusually cold night for early April and people hurried about the streets, pulling their coats tightly about them, anxious to finish their business and gain the warm security of their homes. Even those who had no warm cozy home awaiting them hurried, for it was a night of deep shadows, whistling winds, vague murmurings. The crisp clip-clop of horses' hoofs upon the cobblestones seemed to hasten them on their way like a clock ticking off the seconds to a deadline while clouds of frozen breath drifted from the noses of the steeds.

But inside the stuffy, smoke-clouded library of Stanton Lewis' modest home no notice was taken of the rising wind or the biting cold. If the four men there felt anything at all, it was that the night matched their own cold, turbulent feelings.

"I say kill Olaf Thorssen, and the sooner the

better," Stanton Lewis said bitterly, as he turned away from the window to pace the narrow, over-heated, book-lined room.

"But we've tried to avoid this, Stan," Winchell Clarke said, pulling at his elegantly groomed and patiently grown full set of whiskers as he regarded the man who'd been more like a son to him, to them all, than a nephew.

"Look, I tell all of you that we either kill the man or lose the fortune, and I for one have no intention of losing that money. I've waited too long," Stan continued, seating himself in a creaking leather chair.

"Well, we've given Alexandra every chance to make a good marriage, one that we can all agree on, and frankly, I don't understand her rejecting our boys," Wilton Clarke said, drawing irritably on his expensive cigar as he thought of his handsome, twenty-four-year-old son.

"Damn the girl!" William Clarke exclaimed. "*I* understand her. She's just like her father. It's that damn Clarke pride and stubbornness all over again. No one could ever tell Alexander Clarke a damn thing, and no one can tell Alexandra anything either."

"Isn't that the truth," Winchell said. "I'll never forget Alexander walking into the Magee ball cool as you please, like he owned the damned place. He took one look at Deidre Magee and walked straight over to her," he continued, his face turning livid as he thought back over the years.

Wilton groaned, sharing the hated memory.

"Walked straight over to her," Winchell went on,

12

"smiling that self-assured smile and strutting like a peacock. He never did walk normally."

"Hell no!" Wilton agreed, slapping his hand down on the polished wood of a shelf, making a small cloud of dust rise from the long ignored books resting there.

"Walked straight over to Deidre Magee, just like *we* hadn't been courting her for months and just like *he* hadn't been away at school for years, and said, 'You're the most beautiful girl here and I'm going to marry you,' " Winchell finished, choking suddenly.

And as his coughs filled the room, Wilton and William glared at each other, still infuriated twenty years after the incident, for it wasn't the only thing about Alexander Clarke that had angered them over the years.

He had inherited the family shipping firm. *They* had been given jobs with the firm. And all because Alexander's father, being the first born son, had inherited over their father, the second born. The unfairness inflamed them yet. And Deidre Magee, the beautiful daughter of the firm's partner, had been *stolen* from them by Alexander. *He'd* married her and it outraged them to this day, for not only had she been the most perfect, most desirable woman they had ever known, she had also been the key to inheriting equal control of the shipping company, the company which should have been theirs to begin with. If only Deidre had chosen one of them. If only —

"I never could understand what Deidre saw in him," Winchell grumbled, lost in his thoughts, breaking the angry silence which had settled over the room.

"She deserved better," William declared.

"She was such a beauty," Wilton said wistfully. "A woman never breathed that was so perfectly beautiful and sweet."

Stan Lewis had been patiently listening to his uncles' self-pitying conversation, but finally he had had enough. There was the present to worry about. He decided to smash the old men's dreamy memories of lost love and opportunity.

"Obviously there was one big flaw in the perfect Deidre," Stan said dryly, grinning derisively. The three heads jerked toward him, disbelieving his blasphemy. Stan smirked a moment longer then exploded, exasperated at their blindness. "Irish! Her father was Irish! Deidre was Irish! All Irish!"

The three men, with eyes riveted on Stan's face, at last acknowledged that truth, a truth they preferred to ignore, and nodded their heads in mute agreement. Then Stan continued.

"And in her daughter, too, there flows an Irish streak a mile wide. Couple that with the Clarke pride and stubbornness and gentlemen, you have a problem, a big problem—a problem named Alexandra Clarke," Stan said coldly, analytically, his wintry gray eyes boring into each old man like a drill, satisfied that he finally had them back on the track of the business at hand.

Wilton shook his head sadly. "I'd hoped she'd be like her mother, then she would have been sweet and done exactly what we wanted of her—"

"I really think you men have a mistaken idea of

14

the character of the long departed Deidre," Stan cut in, determined not to let the subject stray back to the supposedly angelic Deidre. "After all, she married the man you hated and if he was half as bad as you say, that must have taken a lot of courage." Stan laughed cruelly.

"We never said she didn't have courage," Winchell said, bristling.

"Of course not," William agreed quickly.

"She was just so sweet that she couldn't hurt Alexander Clarke by turning him down," Wilton said, nodding his head vigorously, wishing he could really believe what he said.

"That's right. She'd probably never have stayed with him if they'd been married longer," Winchell said, repeating the personal fantasy he had used to console himself for so long.

"No, she'd have learned of his devious ways in no time," William agreed.

Stan rolled his eyes toward the ceiling in frustration, realizing they'd escaped him again, their old minds drifting away down the paths of their memories. It was the same overly discussed subject to which he had been forced to listen for too much of his thirty-nine years. He had a plan, a plan to right all their supposed wrongs and get the company back in their control. But the old men seemed able to do nothing but mourn the long lost Deidre. True, they had never been men of action. No wonder Deidre Magee had preferred the dashing, progressive Alexander Clarke, Stan thought, as the raspy voices droned on.

"He killed Deidre, of course," Winchell said angrily. "He was never satisfied with the way things were. He was always upsetting everyone, including the company."

"He *would* insist that she accompany him on the test run of that crazy new ship of his," Wilton said, biting off the end of his cigar in his agitation, then angrily spitting the end into the fire.

"We didn't need any new ships. The old ones were perfectly good. After all, they were good enough for our fathers. If Alexander wanted new ships, he could have had new ones built just like the old, good ones," William said earnestly, joining in the gratifying anger at unalterable events long passed.

"Well, he killed her, all right. They all went down with that foolish killer ship," Winchell said.

"I'm just sorry that their only child wasn't with them," William added, his faded gaze suddenly gleaming wickedly, thinking of Alexandra.

Stan eagerly caught the reference and determined to try again to get to business. "Yes, she's been nothing but trouble ever since they died. You should have had control of the company then. And you *could* have made it your own, but the clever Alexander Clarke put it all into trust for Alexandra, their darling daughter," he said savagely. "And for eighteen years you've been battling Olaf Thorssen," Stan hurried on while he still had their attention. "He was the only man Alexander trusted with his company and his daughter. The one person Alexander made trustee of his estate and guardian of his daughter until she reached the tender age of twenty-one. And that sea captain has

16

turned out to be one hell of an opponent, hasn't he, gentlemen?" Stan asked coldly, rubbing salt into their long open wounds to keep their minds alert.

"Gentlemen," Stan continued, his voice now cajoling and soft, "you must remember that our time has run out. Alexandra Clarke will soon be twenty-one. On the third of August, 1867, barely four months from now, she will be twenty-one. Twenty-one! We want her married to our man and in control of her estate before she reaches her majority. Thorssen has advised her too long, protected her too long—always against us. Agree with me and he'll never advise her again. Then she'll *have* to turn to *us*. I'll kill Thorssen," he whispered harshly, "and gladly."

"But," Winchell said weakly, "how do we know that you'll see things our way, when, when—"

"I'm your nephew. Surely you haven't forgotten," he laughed conspiratorially. "I've *always* been one of you. Also, I need your help in running the company," Stan added, dropping his voice to a lower key, lulling the men into the safety of his desires. "Anyway, it's not like you didn't give her a choice, is it?" Stan pushed them ever nearer to agreement.

"We *did* give her every chance for a happy life, a long life—with children. And Thorssen could have been with her like always if she'd agreed," William said, as if he'd personally done all he could to make Alexandra happy.

"Indeed, we did," Wilton joined in. "Didn't all three of us go to Alexandra and tell her that she

17

could marry any one of our sons? Yes, we did! They were all near her own age, well educated, well dressed, all of them handsome young men. Any other young lady in New York City would have been anxious to marry them, but they all waited for Alexandra, just like we three once waited for — Deidre."

"Yes," Winchell agreed. "She could have had her pick," puffing on his cigar, the smoke and stale air swirling around him. "But she was quite ungrateful, even became upset and said she would never marry *any* of them, actually even complained that we'd kept her from meeting any other eligible young men by not letting her have a coming-out ball. Imagine! The nerve! The ingratitude!"

Stan chuckled low in his throat. He had them at last. "Well," he began, "all you've said is true, gentlemen. Are you now ready to right wrongs, to do what is best for yourselves — and the company?"

"We've always done what was best for the company," Winchell insisted irritably.

"Of course, gentlemen, you've always done that," Stan quickly agreed to soothe their offended pride. "And I've gone along with your plans to marry Alexandra to one of your sons, but now she's seen and rejected them all, even after your persuasive hints about Thorssen's continued good health."

"I can't understand her. Just can't," Winchell mumbled, pulling at his beard, images of Alexandra and her mother, Deidre, mingling in his mind.

"Now, you do all remember our bargain?" Stan

18

asked. "I will marry the little heiress," and for more reasons than the money, Stan added to himself, a vision of the beautiful Alexandra waiting sweetly for him in their marriage bed flitting across his mind. "Yes, I will marry Alexandra — after I've disposed of Thorssen and I'll take *that* responsibility completely upon myself. All I want is your agreement that after I marry Alexandra, I will share your control of the company." Stan stared hard and insistently at each man in turn, carefully avoiding the rest of his plan to eventually take complete control for himself.

There was a silence in the room. Each old man thought his own thoughts but eventually each man decided what Stan had skillfully led them to decide — that control of the company must be gained at any cost. Alexandra Clarke must not be allowed to marry out of the family.

Three pairs of cloudy eyes began to clear until finally they glinted evilly and assuredly at Stan. Their decision was made. He could read it in their faces. "Well, gentlemen?" he asked, urging them to the final, overt commitment.

Each head nodded and each voice agreed.

Suddenly Stan stood up, furious energy flowing through him, readying him for action.

"The company will be ours — yours — at last," Stan assured them. "Just leave matters to me. Whatever happens, act surprised. I will take care of Thorssen *and* Alexandra, but you must all play your parts, too."

Once more they nodded, wanting now only to be done with the formalities so that they could go back to discussing the virtues and beauty of the perfect Deidre Magee, forgetting entirely that she was the mother of Alexandra whose fate they had just signed away to the greedy Stanton Lewis.

"Then the deed will be done. And soon," Stan promised ruthlessly, a burning eagerness spreading through his veins as his passions for riches, for power, and for the beautiful Alexandra Clarke edged ever closer to a final fulfillment.

ii

Alexandra Clarke paced the floor of her upstairs sitting room nervously as she awaited the return of her old friend, Olaf Thorssen. He was late in arriving from his daily afternoon walk, and she was unaccountably apprehensive. When he had not arrived on time, she had come upstairs so that she could look for his familiar figure coming jauntily down the street, but he had not yet appeared.

She was frankly worried for Olaf. Recently, her three second cousins, William, Winchell, and Wilton Clarke, had made scarcely veiled threats against the old man, and she had not been able to shrug them off as Olaf did, or at least pretended to do.

Olaf had warned her to marry only a man that she could love, and she could hardly even stand to be in the same room with the dutiful, pompous boys that her three cousins had presented to her as eligible young men. Marry one of them—bah!

Yes, she was worried about Olaf. He had

scoffed at her suggestion that he should have someone with him all the time. For even at seventy, Olaf was a strong, bull of a man and would not be intimidated.

Where was Olaf? It had been much too long. She jerked back the drapes and her heart jumped strangely in her breast as she saw a crowd gathered in the street at the intersection less than a block away—the place where Olaf always crossed the street when returning. Panic gripped her, but she would not believe the scene below had anything to do with Olaf. Her nerves were to blame. They had been so strained of late.

Yet, with a white pinched face, Alexandra threw the drapes back, ran quickly across her room, grabbed her cape, and hurried down the stairs to the front door of her mansion. She would never remember the steps that took her to that bizarre scene in the street, only the wild pounding of her heart and the urgent desire to be with those people, see for herself that it was not Olaf.

The crowd was steadily growing as she pushed them back roughly, trying to gain the center of the circle. The hurriedly gathered group parted for her as they saw her pale face and haunted eyes, knowing that she was connected with this somehow. Finally, Alexandra pushed aside the last person and a small whimper came from her throat as she saw what she had known would be there and yet had denied to the last moment.

"Olaf." She knelt by his strangely contorted body covered in dust and mud. "Olaf, I'm so sorry. It's all my fault," she said chokingly as her tears formed two paths down her cheeks. She lifted his head to her lap and for the first time saw that he looked old, tired, and at last, mortal.

"Alexandra," he whispered hoarsely.

She pushed back his hair, stroking his temples, as she leaned down close to his face.

"Alexandra, you must flee. Do not delay. They'll kill you, too, or force you to marry one of them. Beware of Stan—Lewis. He's deadly," Olaf rasped, then coughed weakly. His face was becoming grayer by the second, but yet she could not believe that he would really leave her. He was all she had, had ever had.

"I've loved you like my granddaughter, like the grandson I never got to know. Go, Alex, go to New Orleans. Find my daughter, my grandson. Perhaps they'll be able to help you. Go, while you still can. Hide from the family at least until you come of age," he whispered weakly, his eyes glowing feverishly in his head.

She could hardly see him for the tears clouding her eyes, but she knew she would forever hear his words.

"Promise, promise me you'll go. Now. Go to New Orleans and find my family. Tell them that I always loved them and that I was . . . was a stupid old man."

"No! No, Olaf, you were never stupid, and I, I promise—anything, only don't leave me."

"Don't wait for my funeral, Alex. Go now. Flee while you can, before they can snare you, make you one of them. Prove that you're your father's daughter. Prove—" he started, but his breath seemed to die away and his eyes lost their brilliance, slowly losing their focus. Then he was still and lifeless against Alexandra. She hugged him to her, sobbing in her anguish.

Although her heart felt like ice, her mind was on fire with his words. They had killed Olaf — killed him to gain control, she thought. Well, she would show them. She *would* go. She would flee to New Orleans. If Olaf had used his last moments to ask her to promise him something, nothing in this world could keep her from that promise.

Yet how would she find two people she had never seen, who had been gone from New York for twenty-five years? But she *would* find them. She had promised. And she was glad that Olaf had at last forgiven his daughter for marrying a Southerner and then following him to Louisiana. Olaf had once explained to her how his only daughter, Eleanor, had fallen in love with a Southern gentleman named Jarmon from Louisiana when he had been on business in New York City. They had married almost immediately, even though Olaf had not approved of her choice. But they had been so much in love that nothing could stop their happiness, or their determination to be together, until Jarmon received word from his plantation in Louisiana that his father was sick. He was needed at home. He was afraid for Eleanor to travel with him since she was now pregnant, and so she agreed to stay in New York with her father until the child was born. Then her husband could return and take them to his plantation near New Orleans.

Eleanor had bravely accepted their separation,

24

consoling herself with thoughts of their child and their future together. She moved in with her father and waited for word from Jarmon. She received no letters and no replies to her own letters. Time passed and her child was born, a son, but still there was no word from her husband in Louisiana. Olaf told her to forget the man who had so abandoned her, but she finally became desperate and, after arguing with Olaf, fled, taking her infant son, Jacob, to Louisiana to find the man she loved. Olaf never heard from any of them again, and his pride had kept him from seeking them in the South.

And now, after all these years, after the bloody Civil War, would they even still be alive? Would she be able to find them? Alexandra pulled Olaf's body closer to her, thinking that if he wanted her to go to them, find them, then she must. And Olaf's death would not go unpunished. She would have her revenge. She would—

Suddenly Alexandra was jerked up roughly by strong hands. She whirled around, her eyes flashing dangerously.

"Stanton Lewis," she said, surprised. "What are you doing here?" Seeing him there reminded her suddenly of Olaf's words concerning this strange, cold man—beware, deadly. She would indeed be wary of him, but then she had never trusted Stan Lewis.

"I was coming to see you, Alexandra, when I saw the commotion in the street. I came over to offer my services, but found you. And Olaf," he said slowly, without emotion.

25

Alexandra eyed him unsurely. His answer was too pat, too ready. She didn't trust him.

"Olaf. I don't know—" she began, feeling her tears dry and a numbness invade her body. She did not feel warm and vibrant any longer, but cold and lifeless like Olaf. Still, she had a mission and she must be very careful, cautious if she were to carry it out.

"I will take you back to your home, Alexandra. You shouldn't be out here in the street with all of these people. It is lucky for you that I came along."

"But Olaf—"

"I will see that all is taken care of. There is nothing more that you can do for him now," he said authoritatively, as he pulled her away from Olaf, out of the ring of spectators, and toward his carriage.

"But what happened? I didn't see—"

"You didn't see what happened?" he asked quickly.

Alexandra thought she heard a note of surprise, a pleased sound in his voice, but she couldn't be sure. They stopped by his carriage and he continued speaking.

"It's best that you didn't see, Alexandra. He was run over by a carriage and its team of horses."

"Oh, no. Did they tell you that?"

"That's what the spectators saw. The driver never stopped or returned to help. We'll never know now."

"No," she said vaguely, really believing that her friend had been murdered by her own family.

26

Stan Lewis helped Alexandra into his carriage, then jumped in beside her. They rode the short distance to her home in silence. He helped her out, hurrying her up the steps and into the large, imposing house with a proprietary air that she didn't think necessary. After escorting her into the dimly lit parlor and carefully seating her on a small settee, he rang for service. Alexandra didn't like his taking charge, but she remained quiet.

Soon the maid returned with two drinks on a heavy silver tray. Stan took them from her and came to Alexandra, sitting down beside her on the settee. The maid discreetly shut the door, leaving them alone together.

"Here, Alexandra, drink this," he said softly, handing it to her.

"I don't really want—"

"Drink it. You need it."

She took the crystal glass and touched it to her lips. It burned. Brandy. She drank a little more. It was warm and comforting. She began to feel more like herself, but even the brandy could not warm the coldness in her heart.

"Now, Alexandra," he said, leaning toward her.

Alexandra looked up and was surprised to find his face so close to hers. His gray eyes were burning with an intensity she had not thought possible. She shrank back from him, not recognizing this Stan Lewis.

"Alexandra," he began again, "you needn't worry about Olaf. I will take care of the funeral. You needn't worry about anything—anymore."

Alexandra quickly looked away from him, her

27

heart beating faster. She knew he was going to say more and she didn't want to hear the words. Intuitively she had never trusted Stan, never, not even before Olaf had told her about him: about how he was the illegitimate son of Celeste, the sister of the Clarke cousins; about how she had been raped at fourteen; about how his birth had killed his young mother.

Under the circumstances, the Clarke family had walked the middle road, giving the child the last name of Lewis, his grandmother's maiden name. But Stan had always been an outcast, an underdog, determined to improve his lot and to prove himself more worthy than other men in order to compensate for his socially inferior status. He had worked harder than others, learned faster, risen through the company ranks quicker until at last he had been Olaf's right-hand man, helping to manage the company. But still, though Olaf could understand what drove Stan and motivated him to such extreme exertions, the sea captain had always felt there was something disturbing and basically dishonest lurking just under Stan's hard-working, conscientious veneer. And Alexandra had felt it, too, even as a little girl. Perhaps his gray eyes were too intense? Had they watched her too closely then, just as they were doing now?

She made a move to get up, but suddenly found herself stopped by the iron grip of his hand. She looked down at it and then up into his determined face. It was a face strangely without lines, the smooth pale skin drawn tightly over his prominent bone structure. The only concession he seemed to

28

have made to age was the silver gray hair blending in with the natural sandy color. Still, as long as she could remember, his hair had been that silver-sandy mixture, giving him the look of a wolf with his piercing gray eyes.

"Please, Mr. Lewis, you're hurting my arm," she said softly.

"I'm sorry, Alexandra. I've no wish to harm you," he said as he loosened his grip, yet kept his hand on her arm. "I only want to help you, as I've always tried to do. This is not the best moment to discuss what I'm going to tell you, but our lack of time makes it imperative."

"Oh," she said, hardly aware that she had spoken.

"I will see that the funeral takes place in three days, Alexandra. In four days we will be married."

"What?" She jerked roughly away from him. "Are you mad? No! No! A hundred times no," she screamed, her fists clenched as she stared at him with furious eyes.

"Don't reject me so soon, Alexandra," Stan said, ignoring her fury, his voice lulling, reassuring as she stood there, her breasts heaving in her agitation. He could not help but think of how her smooth, warm flesh would feel when she at last lay beside him.

"Don't reject you? I *am* rejecting you — now and for all time! Get out of my home," she hissed, her eyes glinting with fury.

God, she was beautiful, he thought, then said, "I know what has happened between you and the Clarke boys. I don't blame you for not wanting to marry them, but you must marry someone of the family. You know that. I will be a good husband to you, Alexandra. I'm not so old that I can't make you happy and I will be gentle with you, if you allow me to be. You will have no worries. I'll handle everything for you. You could not ask for a better husband, and I've been determined to have you since you were a child. I understand you. I can make you happy."

"You've planned all of this, haven't you—in your cold, calculating way?" she asked, understanding dawning on her.

He laughed harshly, smiling. "I'd do anything to get you, Alexandra, and now my chance has finally arrived. You have no choice, dearest."

She paced the room several times, trying to calm herself enough to think how to get rid of him, then finally turned, facing him. "Mr. Lewis, even if we are to be married, we could not possibly wed the day after Olaf's funeral."

"Call me Stan. It's only fitting since I'll soon be your husband. The gossip will die down. That doesn't worry me."

"You won't be my husband as Stan or Mr. Lewis," Alexandra cried angrily as she stamped her foot on the expensive, imported rug.

Stan smiled smugly as he walked over to her, putting his hands on her shoulders. She tried to shrug them off, but he tightened his grip mercilessly. She bit her lower lip in pain, furious with his presumption. "I am the one for you, Alexandra. The others are too young to appreciate you,

30

and besides, I'm giving you no choice. You *will* marry me in four days."

As he bent his head toward her face, she pushed against him, desperate in his tightening embrace. "You're wrong, Mr. Lewis. You have no rights where I'm concerned, and you can't force me to marry you."

"Don't fight me, Alexandra. Don't make me hurt you. I'm going to have you one way or another," he said hoarsely as his mouth came down hard on hers.

Alexandra grew rigid in response to her first kiss, automatically clinching her jaws desperately. She felt stifled and her mind flew to thoughts of escape. She couldn't travel on one of her own ships. She would have to rent some small schooner to take her down the coast and then around to New Orleans. A boat that could not be traced; one on which Lewis would never think to look. She would have to get money from her bank, pack her clothing, rent the schooner. All in three days. But it could be done. It must be done!

In frustration and irritation, Stan Lewis finally raised his face from hers, his eyes glittering dangerously as he held her rigid body away from him. "I know you're not that cold, Alexandra, for all that you're inexperienced. Perhaps you simply need lessons. I'll be happy to give them to you," he said, his silver eyes glowing with passion. "Would you like your first one now?"

Fury and disgust washed over Alexandra at his words, his insults, and she slapped him hard across the face with all her strength. She was glad to see

31

the white imprint there which slowly began to turn red. Then she glanced into his eyes, the eyes of a mad wolf, and she stepped back — frightened of him for the first time. He didn't seem human any longer as his eyes suddenly raked over her body.

He grinned, showing white teeth, and said, "That was really quite stupid, Alexandra. I suppose now I will have to teach you more than one lesson. I am your master and you will learn to obey me in all things no matter what your feelings are. And never — *never,* ever strike me again. I might not be able to control myself as I am today, and I might hurt your lovely body seriously. But then, we don't know just how lovely it is, do we?"

Alexandra did not retreat any further, determined not to show her fear. "You're mad. Absolutely mad. Get out of my house and never come back."

He laughed, a sound almost like a wolf howling, and turned sharply on his heel. She watched him distrustfully as he hurriedly crossed the room, then stopped before the door. The lock clicked into place, the noise seeming to fill the room. Alexandra felt helpless, a feeling that she had never encountered before. She hated it, and him even more.

Still grinning his wolfish grin, he turned around and started back for her. Darting in front of him, she reached for the bell rope. Her servants would answer her summons. But he was there before her, stopping her desperate bid for help.

"Now, Alexandra, you don't seem anxious for

your lessons. Aren't you interested in learning something new?"

She tried to squirm out of his hands, shaking her head back and forth. "You can't do this. Get out of here. Let me go, you brute."

But her fury seemed only to excite him all the more, as if he would rather tame a wild cat than toy with a gentle kitten. He pulled her hair, clutching both her wrists with one hand in an iron like grip, and soon the golden-red curls cascaded down all about her shoulders, falling heavily down to her hips. His eyes glowed as he stared at it, almost mesmerized, then he lost his hand in its thickness. She tried to kick out at him, but became tangled in her skirts, losing her balance and falling against his chest.

"That's better, dearest," he said, his voice muffled as he buried his face in her rich, luxurious hair.

"Let me go, you monster," she cried, trying to pull away from him for his body heat seemed to reach through her clothing to her bare skin beneath. His very nearness was stifling, hateful.

"I'll never let you go, Alexandra. You're mine and I'll prove it now — once and for all. Then you'll truly be mine, all mine."

"No! No, I hate you," she cried, helplessly caught in his arms and her clothing, but struggling with all her might. Pushing at him, kicking at him, she finally knocked them both off balance and they fell heavily to the floor. She tried to roll away from him, fighting furiously, but he threw himself on top of her, jerking her arms up over her head.

She was now pinned under him and incapable of escaping, but still she struggled, writhing beneath him helplessly.

"Stop it, Alexandra," he said angrily, his face a stern mask of passion and determination. "Be still."

"No! Never!" she cried out, tossing her head back and forth.

A loud crack sounded in the room, and pain flooded Alexandra's face where Stan had hit her hard with his fist. Stunned, she watched him, feeling almost detached from her body, as his gray eyes raked her limp body in triumph. There was no longer any need for him to hold her hands for she was incapable of moving after his devastating blow.

Ripping her bodice apart to expose her full, tantalizing breasts, he panted over her, his breath coming in quick gasps. He grabbed her breasts savagely with his hands, cruelly squeezing them before he hungrily covered them with his mouth.

Dazedly, Alexandra could feel his teeth biting her suddenly taut nipples in his frenzy; it was like a nightmare in which she was a spectator. It couldn't be happening to her.

Then Stan moved still lower, pulling the offensive skirt and petticoats completely off her and tossing them across the room. Only her chemise was left to cover her nudity. He ripped it open and his panting increased as he ran his hands over her naked body, plying, pinching, feeling every curve and valley. He was leaving nothing, no spot untouched.

She shivered automatically, still stunned from his blow, as her soft, virgin body was explored by a man's hands for the first time.

There was a low moaning in his throat as he roughly pulled her legs apart, spreading them wide with his knees. He was like a wild man, or a starved brute, as he grasped her hips, pulling her roughly upwards, then caught her softness with his mouth, plying it with his lips until he suddenly plunged his tongue into her moist warmth.

Alexandra gasped, realizing she could still feel. Too much. Disgusted, furious, afraid, she tried to push him away, but her body no longer obeyed her commands.

Suddenly he drew back, then lifted his body over hers, pausing only a second before plunging his hard, pulsating manhood into her softness. Alexandra caught her breath, then gasped out loud. Stan's silver-gray eyes, dark with desire, mesmerized her now open green ones, as his hot, rigid organ pushed repeatedly, as if demanding acknowledgement, against her maidenhead. He smiled wickedly at her, pleased with himself, then said, "You see, Alexandra, you belong to me." Then he drove in deep, tearing through her natural defenses to make her a woman. And as she screamed out in pain, he covered her mouth with his, driving his tongue into her, filling her completely with himself. In a few quick, yet furious movements, Stan spilled his seed in Alexandra, leaving his mark deep within her.

When he stood up, quickly fastening his trousers, Alexandra lay in agony on her parlor floor, sick at heart with what had just occurred, in her own home. And by Stan Lewis, a man who had been born from the rape of his mother. How could he have done it?

She did not even have the strength to cover her nakedness. She felt lifeless, absolutely without feelings, as if he had taken more than her virginity—as if he had stolen her soul.

"You see, my dear, you are indeed mine," Stan said. "I should hope that our next lesson will be accepted by you more reasonably, but always remember who is the master in this family and know that I will take what I want from you with force if necessary.

"Go," Alexandra whispered weakly.

"Soon, my lovely Alexandra. Your body is even more beautiful than I could have imagined, and I will never let another man touch it."

At his words, Alexandra tried to cover herself, but his foot came down brutally on her hand. She whimpered in pain. "Not yet, my beauty. I'm not done looking."

"Please go, just leave me alone," Alexandra said, feeling the coldness that had begun with Olaf's death penetrate her entire body.

"Now, listen to me and listen to me good. We *will* be married the day after Olaf Thorssen's funeral for there's not another man of respectability who would marry you now. They would all expect and demand a virgin. You are no longer that, dearest."

"Get out. Get out, you brute," she hissed, sitting

up slightly as her strength and anger began to return.

He smiled at her sardonically. "I'm going now, as you wish, but remember—you are mine, Alexandra, and never forget it." With those words he strode across the room, unlocked the door, then shut it quietly behind him as he left.

Alexandra collapsed miserably on the rug, but no tears would come to bring her relief. She couldn't cry, she couldn't feel anything any more. But determination rose out of her cold anger and she said out loud to herself, "No, Stanton Lewis, you do not yet know your woman. I am not yours, not now or ever. I will never marry you, nor any man—not this way."

Part One

The Deep Blue Sea

Chapter One

Alexandra Clarke sat huddled in her tiny cabin aboard the smelly fishing schooner, *The Charlotte*. She watched the flickering oil lamp sway with the motion of the boat, wondering if the nightmare she had been living through the past several days could really be true.

In her strange coldness born of Olaf's death and Stan's rape, she had handled the problems of the trip with a kind of detached efficiency. She had cleverly withdrawn a large sum in cash from her bank, then she had sought transport to New Orleans. This had not been easy, especially as she had been so short of time, but surprisingly her cousins and Stan Lewis had not kept the close watch on her that she had expected. She could only attribute this to the fact that they had believed her so overcome with grief that she would do nothing until after the funeral—then it would be too late. But her heart was too cold for grief. She could not mourn her old friend, but she could and would keep her promise to him.

Unfortunately, that entailed hiring this horrible little fishing schooner, but she could not have booked passage on a regular steamer. She had to pay the nasty Captain Sully a huge sum of money to persuade him to make this special trip to New Orleans. She had felt vaguely uneasy about him from the beginning, but she had dismissed her suspicions in her determination and need to get out of New York. Now, she wished she had heeded her feelings.

From the first moment she had arrived at the quay, there had been trouble. Captain Sully had insisted that she had too much baggage. She had insisted that she was paying him handsomely for herself *and* her belongings. Captain Sully had finally taken Alexandra and her trunks on board, but not without a lot of arguing, muttering, and oaths. Her cabin was hardly large enough for herself, much less all her baggage, and she'd had to be satisfied with only one trunk in her cabin — the trunk which held her money and necessities. The others were stacked and piled all over the schooner, and she doubted if she would ever get the fishy smell out of them. But even that she could have accepted had it not been for the captain himself.

After they were down the coast and the sun had risen on the first day, she had felt the need of fresh air so she left her cabin. Once on deck, she quickly realized what it was like to be a woman alone on a schooner with only a doubtful captain and his motley crew for companions. The sailors were dirty, rugged, and considered the trip more of a vacation than work. That in itself made her uneasy, but soon the captain left the running of the schooner to his men and came to her side. She had easily read the leer and obvious passion on the man's weather-hardened face, and the intentions of his hands when he had placed them around her waist was all too clear. She had pushed him away, then fled below. And she had spent the rest of that day and the next two in her cabin with her door locked and her trunk against it. Food and water were left outside her door at certain hours, always accompanied by the sniggling laughter of the cook's mate.

Although the schooner had continued on its course down the coast since that first day, the sailors had paid less and less attention to their job and more and more attention to their drinking, joking, and continuous remarks about the passenger hiding in her cabin.

And as Alexandra sat there now, the noisy party above deck, which had kept her awake as the night had progressed into morning, continued. The sailors had gotten worse as the trip lengthened until now she didn't know how they even kept the schooner on course, reeling drunk as they must be. Also, she had gradually become more and more worried about the weather for she could hear the loud crack of thunder and her cabin grew lighter fitfully as lightning brightened the sky. Perhaps they should dock somewhere if a storm was brewing, but she dared not go on deck to check with the captain.

Suddenly the noise above stopped. She soon

heard the stumbling yet determined steps of the crew making their way to her cabin. She clutched her cape more closely around her, a poor excuse for protection, she well knew.

There was nowhere to go, no place to escape. Voices began to call to Alexandra from outside her cabin door, making loud, obscene remarks. They beat upon the door, rattling it as they tried to get in. She recognized Captain Sully's voice as it rose above the others in command.

"Open the door, my beauty. We're lonely men who wish the pleasure of your company on a cold, lonely night," he said, his voice slurred.

She shrunk further back into her berth, realizing that her worst fears were upon her. She could only regret that the captain and his men were not drunker—so drunk that they would be unable to move. Instead, they had had just enough to feel capable of anything and were determined to satisfy their lusts.

"Go away, Captain Sully. You and your men are interrupting my sleep. Go away," she called out to them in as strong and assured a voice as she could muster.

Drunken laughter was their reply. Then the strong shoulders of the sailors began striking the thin door which separated them from their quarry.

They were not long in breaking down the door. The whole group came falling into the cabin as they tripped over the trunk. Alexandra looked down at the jumbled, smelly heap and shook her head as if to clear away her nightmare. But when she looked again, it was to see the men picking themselves up in triumph.

Captain Sully disentangled himself, then took the few steps that brought him close to her bunk. Leering down at her, his legs wide apart, he said, "You're right where I want you, beauty. Now, all we need to do is rid you of those unnecessary clothes."

"You must be mad, Captain Sully. You forget that I am a paid passenger on your schooner and *you* should be at its helm," Alexandra said coldly, trying to make him remember his station.

He threw back his head and laughed heartily, his sailors joining him. "I could make this run in my sleep. I did it often enough — when there was better profit to be made. Right, sailors?" he asked. They agreed with him vigorously.

"And I have an idea that you just might be a little hot contraband, too, my pretty, classy lady," he said, leering at her as he moved still closer.

"You're drunk and have no idea of what you're speaking," Alexandra said quickly, realizing that this man must be talking about blockade running during the Civil War. Some of the most daring and ruthless of men on both sides had been involved in that lucrative business, she had heard, until the blockade had grown too tight toward the end of the war.

"Sure I'm drunk. We're all drunk, but not that drunk, beauty, not too drunk to take advantage of what God gives me," he said, laughing wickedly as his cruel eyes ran over her body.

"Frankly, I doubt if God even admits you're one of his flock."

"Makes no matter who claims me—God or the devil. I'll accept whatever comes my way and, my sweet, you're here so—"

There was a loud clap of thunder. He glanced up quickly, frowning.

"Damn it all to hell. I'm sure going to have you now, beauty. If I have to outrun a storm, I'm going to have something to remember while I'm at it."

"Don't touch me, you brute," she cried desperately as he lunged for her in the bunk, catching her in the folds of her cape, gown, and petticoats as she tried to escape. She felt suffocated by his huge, stifling body, his clawing, searching hands.

"Now I've got you, my pretty. Wait your turns, mates. She's mine first," the captain bellowed as he ripped Alexandra's cape off her, throwing it to the group of men who grabbed it, tearing it apart in their frenzy.

"No! You're all madmen," Alexandra screamed as Captain Sully, his eyes glassy, reached for her. She kicked out at him savagely, striking his most vulnerable area, and as he doubled over, cursing her, she sprang from the bunk.

The other sailors quickly turned on her, and she heard her gown tearing as she pushed, shoved, and clawed her way toward the doorway through the seemingly endless sea of groping hands, hands which caught at her and ripped more and more of her clothing away as she struggled stubbornly onward, thankful for the liquor that made them weak and uncoordinated. At last she leaped over the trunk and through the doorway to freedom. But when she suddenly felt the cool night air caressing her bare skin, she glanced down and realized in horror that she was nearly naked, clad only in her thin chemise. She ran frantically up the stairs onto the open deck, and despite the obvious hopelessness of her dangerous predicament she vowed to herself never to give in voluntarily to the passions of the drunken men.

Desperately she ran around the deck, stumbling into trunks, over ropes as she tried to find some place to hide or at least something she could use as a weapon. But before she could do either, the captain and his men were on deck searching for her. Captain Sully held a torch high so that they could better find her.

"There, there she is," one of the sailors bellowed, catching sight of Alexandra. The others turned toward her, catching scent of their quarry, and began stalking her in earnest.

Alexandra shivered with cold and fear as she began backing away from the sailors who slowly pressed closer, sure now of their ultimate victory. She stumbled, and looking down, saw a large oar that someone had misplaced. Hope swelled in her breast as she quickly knelt and picked up the weighty, bulky wooden oar. This, then, would be her weapon and she would clout any man who dared to come near her. She held it out away from herself in defense, but brought it closer to her body when she felt its weight tearing at the muscles in her arms.

But still the men stalked, grouping together now.

She backed away again—into the railing. She could retreat no further. A flash of lightning splashed over the schooner, revealing the sailors' leering faces to her. She glared angrily at them as they formed a semicircle around her, laughing at her desperate attempts to fend them off with the heavy oar. Thunder crashed, drowning out their degrading taunts.

Suddenly, one of the sailors rushed her. She struggled with him, pushing with the heavy oar until she lost her balance. She felt herself going over the side, falling down, down toward the cold waters of the Atlantic. Clutching the oar desperately, she hit the water, plunging into its depths, into its dark oblivion.

Chapter Two

The captain of *The Flying J* stood on the bridge of his ship watching the gathering storm with a frown creasing his forehead. He had raced through these waters many a time with the Yankees hot on his tail when he was blockade running during the war, but this was the first time he had raced a storm. He had won the other races, but he did not think victory would be his this time. The storm was gathering so fast that he had little hope of making port in Nassau before it broke.

Hell, he hadn't planned to stop in the Bahamas this last trip at all. There was nothing to say to Caroline that he hadn't said before, although, and a smile spread over his face at the thought, there was still plenty he wouldn't mind doing with her. But that all belonged to another time — when he was younger, when she was younger, when Nassau had been the hottest port around, and when money had been tossed around like waves on water because the sailors were making at least triple wages.

He frowned again, the smile wiped suddenly from his hard, determined face. A lot of things had been different then, different before the South had gone down in its final agony of defeat. Yet, it had been much more than defeat. It had been the death of a way of life, a way of thinking, and even though he had been able to see the end long before most of the others, he was still shocked when confronted with the ruin and destruction that was now the South. The Bahamas had ridden the high crest of the wave of blockade running, but it had gone down with the South when the war had ended.

He shook his head remembering the yellow fever that had ravaged Nassau and Wilmington that fatal summer of 1864. A fourth of the residents of Wilmington had died and Nassau had not fared much better when the blockade runners had carried the disease back and forth. But Nassau had felt that less because of the influx of money and people than the disasters of 1866 when the money had gone and the people, too. Not only had typhoid ravaged the islands in that year, killing almost half of what was left of the population, but a hurricane had hit New Providence Island, destroying many of the new buildings that had gone up during the war, as well as more of the people. Nassau had suffered, of course, and there had been no recovery in the islands. No, 1867 had seen no new recovery from the depression that had hit the Bahamas, and the captain of *The Flying J* was not anxious to make port there. He had seen enough ghosts in the South to last him forever.

There would have been no need to stop in the islands if the storm hadn't been brewing for he had planned to make it to New Orleans with all haste. There was no dallying around once his mind was made up, and he had decided to sell *The Flying J* to the highest bidder in New Orleans. He could get the best price there, and he would need all the money he could get once he returned to Texas.

Thoughts of Texas brought fire to his blood as he remembered the wide open spaces where a man could breathe free and easy, and make what he wanted out of his life. He had chosen it a long time ago over the South, even though he appreciated the quiet beauty that it once had been. But a man couldn't live in the South now—not anymore. A man could only starve there on his half-forgotten dreams. Texas was the place, a place where a man could build an empire, make a fortune, and make his own laws. He loved the sea, but Texas was like the ocean—vast, endless, ever-changing, ever-challenging. Yes, Texas was where he would put down his roots, deep in its rich soil.

"What the hell?" he swore under his breath as his thoughts were pulled abruptly back to the present.

There was something ahead in the ocean, but

he couldn't be sure what it was. Straining his eyes, he began to make out a shape.

"Cap'n? Cap'n Jake? Is—is it a mermaid?" The rough voice of the old sailor sounded hollow as it pierced the heavy, silver-gray dawn, followed by lightning and a loud clap of thunder.

The busy sailors stopped their activity. There was a moment of absolute silence broken only by the creaking of *The Flying J* as the sailors gazed down at the eerie, beautiful sight in the water.

Against the dark opaqueness of the ocean, the shimmering white body framed by long, golden-red hair seemed scarcely real to the journey-tired sailors who stood gaping at the apparition which grew steadily closer.

The spell was broken suddenly as the old sailor asked hesitantly, "Is—is she dead?"

"We'll see."

The brusk reply was followed by several quick orders from the captain which sent two men over the side and slowed the ship to near stop.

Silence once more hung heavily over the deck of *The Flying J*. The men looked up uneasily at the sky, then back down at the dark water with the unnatural being floating atop its depths. The approaching storm which held the sun at bay was bad enough, but this being from the sea lying in the path of their ship brought all their superstitions rapidly to their minds.

The two sailors swam swiftly toward the form. When they got close to the body, they approached her cautiously, treading water by her side. They saw that she had draped herself over a heavy, wooden oar. That could easily keep a tiny thing like her afloat they knew, but how had she come to be in the ocean all alone and with only the oar to keep death at bay? They had never seen one so lovely, or so close to death.

One sailor gently pulled her from the oar, making sure her head stayed free of the water, and began swimming toward the ship. The other grinned wryly to himself and brought the oar, thinking that he never had any luck. But then perhaps his luck would be that he had never touched the lady for surely she now belonged to the water spirits, and would they let such a prize be taken from them so easily? He looked up at the leaden sky, wondering if their time had come at last. Would the ocean take them all to regain its prize?

He reached the ship before his mate, who swam slowly, gently with his delicate charge until the ship was within reach. Standing at the bottom of the rope ladder, the sailor looked once more as his friend pulled the young beauty from the ocean, water falling away from her form as in a soft waterfall to reveal the full curves of her body. His own body tightened at the sight, and he cursed slightly at himself as he swung hastily and clumsily up the ladder, the vision of her forever imprinted on his mind. The other sailor hoisted the young woman over his broad, strong shoulder as carefully as possible, then followed his mate up the ladder.

53

Just as the two sailors reached the deck, the storm broke. But the men on board scarcely noticed it for all their attention was on the scantily clad young woman who was now placed gently at the feet of their captain. They all seemed mesmerized by the gentle rise and fall of her breasts outlined by the sheer, wet silk fabric. She was alive.

They formed a circle around her prone body, shutting out the harsh wind that had begun to rage around the ship. Slowly, Alexandra began to regain consciousness. Her red-gold hair clung to her head and body, away from the perfect oval of her face, revealing full, pale lips that were growing pinker as she revived. At last she opened dark fringed eyes and gazed at the tall, looming figure of the captain, then around at the circle of sailors. An involuntary gasp came from her mouth.

The sailors stepped back from her in confusion and consternation.

One muttered, "Red hair."

"Green eyes," another growled.

Another, "The fates preserve us."

It was then that the full impact of the storm and the beauty from the ocean hit them, and they looked questioningly at their captain. With her on board, could they survive? She seemed to read the expression in their faces, and put her pale, slim arms around herself as if in protection. The movement was not lost on the captain.

He gruffly commanded his men to their stations, then turned to the old sailor at his side.

"Take her below, Morley. Lock her in my cabin. Then come back up. We'll need all hands to weather this storm."

The old sailor nodded, then leaned down to pick up the frightened Alexandra, but she stuck out her chin slightly and on trembling limbs lifted herself to her full height, well below the two men standing over her.

"I —" She cleared her throat. "I'm quite capable of —"

But her sentence was never finished for a huge wave splashed over the deck as the old, tough sailor caught her in his arms and ran for protection below. The impact of his lunge and the wave had been too much for her slight strength, and the sailor carried her unconscious into the captain's quarters.

He paused momentarily as he placed her in the narrow bunk, then hurriedly stripped the wet clothes from her body. He could not control his sudden intake of breath as he saw her in complete nudity, for she was as perfect a woman as he had ever beheld. He quickly covered her up, then hurried back outside onto the storm-ridden deck.

Chapter Three

A sound awakened Alexandra. Her mind began to clear and she remembered the horrible nightmare of the storm raging all around her. She had been locked in the cabin, sure of her death when the ship sank to the bottom of the Atlantic. And she had been sick, sicker than ever before in her twenty years of existence. Now she felt weak, but grateful for the calm, gentle rocking motion of the ship. She glanced around the room, then gasped as she noticed a man dressed in torn, sea-stained clothes, staring at her in a cool impertinent way.

And as she looked at him in horror, unable to move in her terror, she saw his eyes rake her face, then move lower, appraising the full curves of her body as a pirate would his prize. She felt a blush of red travel from her breasts to her neck then explode in vivid color over her face. For she now realized that the covers had fallen down around her hips, and she was naked.

Furiously she jerked the covers up around her shoulders, glaring at the insolent man standing casually before her, who had the audacity to smile, showing even white teeth.

"How dare you?" she said in an unsteady voice.

"Dare I what?" he mocked, his lips curling slightly.

She blinked several times, trying to understand his words. They seemed to have been drawn from his throat in a slow, lazy manner. She realized that before her stood a Southerner, a real Southerner, even a former Confederate perhaps. She had never seen one before and looked at him more closely.

He was tall, stooping down slightly beneath the low ceiling of the cabin, and powerfully built. She couldn't remember having ever seen such wide shoulders before. The sea-stained clothes, pulled taut over his hard body, barely concealed the raw strength of his muscles. But his face was what intrigued her the most for it was tanned and in contrast to the sun-bleached blond hair and the blue eyes with fine lines at the corners as proof of his life in the sun. She could only hope he was a gentleman for there was a cool recklessness in the sharp, angular features of his face.

"How dare you?" he asked sarcastically.

"Oh," involuntarily came from her lips. She blushed scarlet. She was as bad as this man.

She certainly had better manners than to stare so openly—especially at a man.

"Well, my little drowned rat—" he began, moving toward her.

Her green eyes darkened as she edged back against the bed, pulling the covers tightly up around her chin. "I'm not your anything and I'm no rat!"

"So the lady has a fiery spirit to go with her fiery hair."

"I—I think you should leave," she said with as much conviction as she could get into her voice.

"Leave? But where would I go? I'm the captain and this is my cabin," he stated, gesturing around the room.

"Then, then *I'd* better leave," she said softly, glancing around the room for her clothing. None seemed to be in evidence and she glanced uneasily back at the rugged face watching her intently.

"You didn't have much on to begin with, and they were wet so—"

She blushed again until her skin seemed to blend in with the roots of her hair. "You—you didn't—" She couldn't finish her statement.

He smiled wickedly, letting her believe the worst.

"I need something to wear. There must be something on board."

"Now, why would you want to cover up a body like yours with clothing?"

"Oh, do stop! I won't be treated like this. I won't be talked to like this."

He raised an eyebrow mockingly, then grinned sardonically. "Is the choice yours, my dear?"

She shuddered involuntarily, feeling suddenly exhausted. The room swam about her and his face began to fade. She heard him murmur something as consciousness slipped from her once more. . . .

Voices forced her awake this time. She could hear them in the hall—sailors talking among themselves. "He's still got her."

"Yes, and locked in *his* cabin."

"Won't give her up. She caused the storm. She caused all the trouble."

"But she's mighty pretty."

"No matter. Fate's against us as long as she's with us."

"What's this?" the captain's voice boomed in through the door.

The sailors muttered among themselves as they hurried away.

A key turned in the lock and Alexandra stared apprehensively at the moving door. The large body of the captain filled the opening for a moment as he came through, then behind him came the slighter body of the old sailor, carrying a tray. The sailor smiled warmly at her, then set the tray down on a small table.

The old sailor came over to her, smiling. "I'm Morley, miss. You've been mighty sick, and you must eat now to get better. If you need anything else, you just tell old Morley here."

She nodded at the smiling sailor, feeling her stomach gnaw at the smell of the food. She was hungry.

Morley glanced down at the clutched covers in her hands, her reddened face, then back at his captain. "Clothes. She's got to have something to wear, Cap'n."

The captain growled, but turned to dig through his trunk. He finally pulled out a fine, hand worked shirt and threw it at the old sailor. Morley grinned, then handed it gallantly toward Alexandra.

She smiled slightly, and took the garment. She looked about her, then stared pointedly at the two men, saying, "If you don't mind."

Morley quickly turned his back to her, but the captain still watched her with amused interest. Finally Morley cleared his throat and motioned to his captain who finally turned around, slowly and reluctantly. Alexandra jerked her arms into the long sleeves, pulled the huge shirt, which reached to her knees, around her, then hastily began to button the shirt.

The captain turned back again, continuing his hungry search of Alexandra, as Morley busied himself with the food, wanting to help the beautiful lady as much as he could. But the

60

captain soon dismissed him. Morley left reluctantly after giving Alexandra an encouraging smile.

When the door had closed, leaving them alone together, the captain's attention focused on her once more.

"Better eat while the food's hot," he said.

Wanting the food more than the security of her bed, she slipped her feet over the edge of the bunk, aware that he could see at least half of her legs. She blushed again, desperately wanting more clothing to shield her body from this man. But there was nothing she could do about that and she had to eat. She walked unsteadily across the small room, holding on to whatever was handy until she lowered herself carefully onto the chair in front of the table of food. It smelled delicious, and as she began to eat the thick seafood soup, she forgot the captain's presence.

Soon she could feel strength returning to her weak body and she hungrily pushed more food into her mouth But her benefactor, if he were that, was not to be ignored for his voice broke the stillness of the room. She hastily looked up to see that he had moved to stand closely beside her. She could read the questioning look in his hard, sun-weathered face and realized that he must have asked her something.

She stopped eating. "I'm sorry, I didn't hear you."

61

"What do you call yourself?" he drawled in his low, commanding voice.

Alexandra froze. This was the question she had been dreading. No one must know her true identity. She could trust no one with the truth for if her relatives ever found her, it would surely be death, or, worse, marriage to Stan Lewis.

She glanced up into the clear blue eyes of the captain and decided that she could tell him at least her nickname. That way she would not be confused when someone called her by that name.

"You may call me Alex."

"Alex!" he chortled. "That's no name for a woman, even a Yankee woman. But then maybe Yankees give their women male names since they can't tell the difference."

Fury washed over her. Her green eyes blazed and she tossed her hair back like a horse's mane. If he had known her better he would have recognized the uncontrollable anger that was about to descend on him, but he didn't know her and he wasn't used to the spirit of a Northern woman. A Southern lady would have held her temper with a sweet smile on her face, but made sure that he paid for his remark later—in a back alley if necessary. But Alexandra never controlled hers so she let its full force fall upon him.

She picked up her bowl of food and with all

her strength threw it at him. He easily dodged it, much to her dismay. She flung herself bodily against him and began to pummel his chest with her fists. Intent upon his destruction, she did not realize for some time that she was having no effect upon him at all. When in confusion she looked up into his face, he winked at her.

This was too much. She began to throw anything loose in the cabin at him. He dodged all the missiles, making his way carefully toward her to stop the further destruction of his cabin. As he got closer, she began to run out of weapons and finally stopped to glare angrily at him, her chest heaving as she gasped for air.

He held out his hands and said softly, "I'm not going to hurt you, Alex," as he continued to approach her.

She backed away, determined to find some means of escape, the desperate scene with Captain Sully vivid in her mind.

"What has someone done to frighten you so badly?"

He still didn't know his woman. At the word frighten, her chin jerked up and her eyes flashed dangerously at him again, but not as desperately as before.

"I'm not frightened," she said softly, evenly between her teeth. "And I will not be treated meanly."

He smiled, pulled a chair around, and sat

down before her. "I haven't meant to treat you badly, Alex. You're my *guest* while on my ship, but you are also under my protection."

Suddenly her legs felt weak. She gestured toward the bed. He sat between her and its comfort, and she wanted his assurance not to be molested in getting to it. He nodded, but as she passed closely by him, he reached out and touched her softly. Yet he did not detain her. She hurried by and sat down on the bed, pulling the covers up around her shoulders for security as well as warmth.

"Frankly, I can't devote as much attention to you as I'd like right now," he said, grinning again, "but perhaps we can take care of that later."

She frowned at him and tossed her golden red hair.

"All I want to know is how the hell did you get in the Atlantic with just an oar? You must realize that I saved your life. I'd always thought there was some special reward for such a deed."

She looked thoughtfully at him, calculating if he was teasing her again. She couldn't be sure. "I do appreciate your getting me out of the ocean. I'm sorry I haven't thanked you properly before. Thank you for your help. I would naturally offer you money, but—" She bit her lip remembering that she wanted no one to know about her or her position in life.

"But your life isn't worth much, or my saving it isn't worth much?"

He was teasing, she thought, but still trying to learn more about her. "Not that either is worth little, but I have nothing to offer that's worth anything," she said and turned her clear green eyes to his.

He hesitated a moment as if caught in some spell. "You're wrong there. With no possessions at all you have a great deal to offer—if you're willing."

It took a moment for Alexandra to understand his message. She blushed and looked quickly away. "You don't treat me with respect," she said unhappily.

"On the contrary, my dear lady, I have treated you with a great deal more respect than I would have most women whom I found in my bed. But then, perhaps I'm too tired today to be fully appreciative of your charms. Another time perhaps."

"Please, I must—I need to find passage to New Orleans," she said intensely, looking at him imploringly.

"Don't," he said gruffly, his blue eyes turning icy. "A coy look doesn't fit you at all. Leave that to the experts—Southern ladies. You'd better play straight with me."

"I need to go to New Orleans."

"You have money for passage?"

She had lost everything she had brought with

her from New York—all her fine clothes, all her money—on the schooner. She couldn't risk contacting her bank to get more money because Stan Lewis would immediately come for her and she had no way to defend herself. No. She had no money, no clothes. In fact, for the first time in her life she was dependent on someone else. She hated the feeling.

"Do you have a name?" she asked.

"Jake."

"Captain Jake?"

"I'm the captain but the name's Jake. Don't tag anything else on to it," he commanded harshly.

She caught just a flash of what his anger could be like if it was ever directed at her; she hoped never to see it. She knew she had a temper, but she had a feeling that in comparison to his it would be tame.

"Call me by my name," he said softly, urgently.

She glanced at his face and caught a warm glint deep in his eyes that she couldn't quite understand, but it suddenly made her stomach tighten, made her legs seem weak and heavy. She looked away and whispered, "Jake."

"I didn't hear you."

"Jake," she said loudly and looked deep into his hard blue eyes, her own green ones glinting strangely.

He was silent a moment and his voice was

thick when he again spoke. "What were you doing in the Atlantic and who are you?"

She swallowed, thinking fast. "I must beg of
you to let me keep my identity a secret, at least
for now. Surely it can't matter to you, and for
me it is—it is a life and death matter."

She spoke so earnestly that he raised his
brows in surprise, quietly deciding. "All right.
Have your secrets. You want to go to New Orleans. Do you know where you are now?"

She shook her head.

"We are, unfortunately, in the Bahamas so—"

"Bahamas! But—"

"We are in the Bahamas so I would assume
that your original destination could have been
New Orleans. The storm has not only blown us
off course, but has done damage to my ship as
well. All in all, it is not a fair day for either of
us."

She shook her head, then looked up suddenly
at him. "The sailors—"

"Yes?"

"I overheard them talking. They think I'm re-
sponsible. You won't let them—" She shivered.

He watched her closely. "Cold?"

"No."

"They are superstitious about women on
board ship, especially a ship like this. But they
won't dare harm you. You are safe—at least for
the moment," he said, grinning wickedly.

Somehow she didn't feel as reassured as she

should have. She just wasn't used to coping with a man like this; he seemed so wild, untamed.

"Thank you for the small measure of comfort," she said icily.

"You're quite lucky I picked you up, by the way."

"Really? I was beginning to think that I would have been better left in the ocean."

"Never think that. As a matter of fact, I have a few friends here I made during the war — well, never mind that, but I've already sent for supplies and for a conveyance to a plantation that's not too far away."

She looked up at him in surprise, then quickly around the cabin. So she wouldn't be forced to stay here after all. She breathed a sigh of relief.

"I didn't realize you were so unhappy with your accommodations."

She waved her hand abstractly. "It's not that. I'll just be glad to be on dry land again."

He grinned. "I know what you mean. My friend has a sister, about your size I suppose. I'm sure she'll be happy to help you out of your predicament."

Alexandra smiled up at him for the first time — a smile of happiness and gratitude that was dazzling in its beauty and sweetness. He caught his breath for a second, then hurriedly got up, turning his back to her.

"I've got work to do," he said gruffly. "I want you to stay in here. I'll lock the door. When the carriage comes, we'll go to the plantation." And he walked quickly from the cabin without another word.

Chapter Four

The day was turning to dusk when the key turned in the lock again. Jake hurried into the room, looking quite pleased with himself, and strode over to the pale young woman sitting in his bunk, the covers pulled up around her neck.

"Hurry, hurry, my dear. We're on our way."

"But I can't go anywhere. I have nothing to wear."

"Well, I can't think what to do with you except wrap you in a blanket and carry you outside. What do you think of that?"

She turned horrified eyes on him, imagining her entrance to one of the genteel plantation homes in that manner. "Never," she spit out.

"You really have a very bad attitude considering your situation, my dear," he went on quite cheerfully, digging around in his trunk until he came out with a large, woolen blanket in garish colors.

"Now, I believe this will do quite well," Jake said as he came toward her.

"Don't you come near me with that thing," she cried and made as if to jump from the bunk.

But he was too quick for her and rolled her neatly in the blanket before she had time for any more protests. Huge, glaring green eyes reproved him, but he only grinned.

"Perhaps this is the safest way to keep you," Jake said, sitting down in a chair and holding her on his lap.

"How can you treat me this way," she sputtered in fury.

"You know you might be quite pretty if we ever got you cleaned up. You should see yourself. You're quite a sight. But then it's said that many men find their treasures in the ocean," he finished almost thoughtfully, then leaned forward and kissed her lightly on her small, straight nose.

She wrinkled it at him in disgust which brought deep laughter from him.

"I must say, my dear, you are certainly no Southern lady."

"Thank goodness for that!"

"Let's save your opinions for another time. At the moment we must be on our way. We're expected, you know."

"How can you take me somewhere looking like this?"

He grinned down at her as he stood up and, carrying her, walked to the door. "I'd take you anywhere, anyway, Alex."

He fumbled with the latch on the door, and was finally aided by Morley, who held the door open so that Jake could carry his captive outside.

"Do something with my cabin, Morley. She took a fit earlier and left the place a mess. You wouldn't think she'd have so much strength."

"No, you wouldn't, Cap'n. She doesn't look too well, and that's the truth. See that they take care of her right up there," Morley said earnestly, then smiled encouragingly at Alexandra.

"Oh, they will. They will. Caroline's there—"

"Better get somebody else," Morley muttered almost to himself as he went into the captain's cabin.

"Never could tend to his own business," Jake murmured as they went up on deck.

For the first time since the storm, Alexandra could smell the cool, clean air and see land again. It felt good. She was glad to be out of the bowels of the ship.

As Jake carried her across the deck, she drew the attention of all the sailors. An almost ominous quiet settled over the ship and a shudder went through her. She remembered the intensity of the words that she had overheard concerning herself, and she wondered just how safe she really was.

"Are you cold?" Jake asked.

"No—no. Just, are you sure the men—"

"They have their orders. You'll be safe with me."

She nodded and laid her head against the strong muscles of his shoulder. For some reason she did feel safe in his arms as he carried her toward the rope ladder. In the water, a small boat awaited their departure.

Jake stood for a moment by the railing, looking over the edge at the sailor steadying the boat. "Now, don't be afraid, Alex. It's not really that far."

Before she could realize what he meant, he dropped her into the arms of the man below. She was unharmed, but furious. She watched Jake climb nimbly down the rope, then jump into the boat beside her.

"Now that wasn't really so bad, my dear, was it?"

She was too angry to speak; she turned her eyes away, studying the horizon.

"Look at the water, Alex. Have you ever seen any so clear, so beautiful?"

Reluctantly, she looked down into the calm, placid water reflecting the last of the dying sun and smiled as she saw what Jake meant. It was beautiful. Her anger left as quickly as it had arrived. "It's as if one could see forever in it."

"Perhaps one can," Jake said softly.

They were not long in gaining the shore and

Jake leaped into the shallow water, then once more picked Alexandra up as if she weighed nothing. There was a carriage awaiting them, with an old coachman patiently sitting in the driver's seat. He silently got down and helped them into the carriage. Soon they were slowly moving down the packed dirt lane.

Inside, the carriage was cool and dim, and they seemed to be enclosed in a world of their own.

"Your ship—is it badly damaged?" Alexandra asked.

"Bad enough."

"How long do you think it will take to repair it?"

"Long enough."

"Really, Jake. How long will we be here?"

"Probably too long."

She did not try to pursue a conversation, his obvious taciturnity advised her that it would do no good.

Night had fallen by the time they reached their destination, and she had only caught glimpses of a lush, green island with strange smells and sounds all around her. It was like nothing she had ever known before, and yet it did not feel hostile to her. Would she at last be safe?

When the driver stopped the carriage outside a large, dark building, Jake got out, then leaned in to take her in his arms. But she hesitated, pulling back from him. How would she be received? How *could* she be received in her state?

But Jake was not going to let anything stop him in his decision, and he jerked her almost roughly into his arms. As he walked toward the mansion carrying Alexandra, he whispered in her hair, "I won't let anything harm you, Alex. Remember, you're under my protection."

She shuddered against the warmth of his chest, then steeled herself for what would come.

Whatever she had expected it was not the beautiful woman who ran off the veranda of the mansion and toward Jake.

"Jake. Jake, darling, at last."

The woman stopped abruptly several feet away, unable to understand the body Jake carried in his arms. Her lovely dark eyes clouded and her full, sensuous lips formed a pout.

"You said you would bring someone, Jake, but I hardly expected—"

"Now, Caroline, don't say a word to me until I get this taken care of. Then I'll explain. But if you say a word now, I'll never tell you a thing."

She shut her mouth abruptly, and followed, half running to keep up with his long strides.

Alexandra hid her face in Jake's shirt, feeling embarrassed and confused. But it was only the beginning. As Jake mounted the wide steps to the veranda, another figure came out of the shadows. This one held a tall drink.

"Jake. Glad to see you, old boy. Sorry about your trouble, but glad you turned to us. What the—" he exclaimed as he caught sight of Jake's bundle.

"Don't say a word, Hayward, or Jake will never tell us," Caroline said softly as she caught up with the two men.

They all hurried into the house. In the foyer, Jake looked up at the long flight of stairs.

"Is everything ready like I ordered?"

"Of course, Jake darling," Caroline said in a voice dripping with honey.

"Good, then I'll take care of this myself."

"You'll what?" Caroline asked, more disturbed than shocked.

Jake took the stairs two at a time. "Just have a drink ready when I come down."

Jake found the door he wanted, kicked it wide, then strode into a large, ornately furnished room. Sitting in a rocking chair was a large dark woman.

"Hello, Leona," Jake said familiarly as he approached her with his burden.

"Well, if it ain't Mister Jake himself. I've been waiting myself for your secret," she said, grinning at him while trying to see Alexandra better. "You always was one for secrets. Yes sir, you sure was."

"I need your help. I fished this surprise right out of the ocean, and it's special."

Her eyes grew large and she looked askance

at Alexandra. "You done drug this out of the ocean? It's no sea creature, now is it, Mister Jake?" she asked worriedly.

"Not in the least," he said pleasantly, then promptly set Alexandra on her feet and unwound the blanket.

Leona gave a little cry as the golden red hair came tumbling all about and the green eyes looked at her coolly, appraisingly.

"Never seen hair that color before," Leona said, as if disbelieving her eyes. "This creature ain't natural, and that's for sure. You best take her back where you found her, Mister Jake."

"Now—please," Alexandra began. "I fell in the ocean and Jake saved my life. That's all. I'm perfectly normal, or at least I will be if that's a bath I see over there."

The question seemed to remind Leona of her responsibilities. "That it is and you need it, that's for sure. What happened to your clothes, child? That's a man's shirt!" She rolled her black eyes toward Jake and a thunderous look came over her face.

Jake spread his hands wide and began backing away. "No fault of mine, Leona. No fault of mine. If you'll just repair the damage, I'll be happy."

"Be gone with you. We've got woman's work to do."

With that Jake was pushed out the door, and Leona turned her attention to Alexandra.

"You're sure a sight, child. Now, get in that bath while I see what I can do about clothes. You're taller than Miss Caroline so I'll have to let somethin' out."

Alexandra stepped gratefully into the bath, delightedly feeling the warm, fragrant water swirl up around her hips then over her breasts. "I'll be happy to wear whatever can be spared," she said.

"No *lady* can go down with her gown too short, and that's a fact, Yankee or no Yankee."

There was no answer to that so Alexandra turned her attention to her bath, scrubbing her skin until it glowed pink and healthy again. Then she washed the sea water from her hair until it shone brilliantly. When she emerged from the bath, she was feeling her old self again, except for the unaccustomed weakness from her sickness and the coldness that had invaded her heart.

"Be through in a minute, honey. You sure look better. Before you looked like a drowned rat. This is one of Miss Caroline's second dresses, but we didn't know what to expect so we'll find something better later."

"This will be fine. I don't need much."

They both continued in silence for a time. Alexandra dried her hair while Leona hemmed the pale green dress. Alexandra was pleased that the gown was of a style and color that would look good on her. For once she really wanted to look pretty. The woman downstairs was certainly lovely, and seemed to know Jake very well. For some reason, she did not like that at all.

Finally, Leona broke the silence by standing up and saying, "This is ready so we'll just get you into it, child."

There were soft cotton undergarments for Alexandra to put on. They were not the sheer silk ones she was used to, but they were comfortable and serviceable. She was grateful for anything to wear. Leona expertly dressed Alexandra, then led her to a full-length mirror.

Alexandra was a little taken aback by her appearance for she was unaccustomed to seeing herself in such soft, revealing garments. She had always worn high necked, heavy silk dresses in New York, but this gown was of thin cotton and cut low to reveal the swell of her breasts. Also, her hair hung down in riotous curls to her hips, still damp and drying in the air, giving her a sensuous look that she had never connected with herself before. The contrast was even greater because her skin was so pale and finely drawn over her bones from her illness that her eyes appeared large and luminously green in the soft light of the room, giving her the look of an enchantress.

"You're sure a pretty thing. No wonder Mister Jake took such special attention with you," Leona said behind her. "But remember, child, he's Caroline's man, and she'll take no one coming between her and her man."

Alexandra whirled abruptly to look closely at the woman, but there was no trace of expression on the soft dark face.

"I—I hardly know the man, and I have no plans to know him any better. He is merely doing a stranger in distress a favor."

Leona chuckled to herself, then motioned toward the door. "They're waiting for you, honey."

"Thank you. You've been very kind," Alexandra said before leaving the room and the older woman behind.

Chapter Five

Alexandra followed the lights and laughter to a room just off the foyer. She stopped just within its entrance, watching the occupants of the room. Jake was leaning against the fireplace. He had changed clothing and looked much more the Southern gentleman than the ship captain that she had known before, but still there was that feeling of carefully restrained energy about him, like a tightly coiled steel spring.

For the first time she looked closely at her host and hostess. Jake had called them Hayward and Caroline. They were both handsome people, having soft dark eyes and hair. There was a calmness about them which contrasted sharply to the intensity of Jake's presence.

Her thoughts abruptly stopped when she realized the group had noticed her and was staring at her intently. She smiled at them, then stepped into the warm light of the room. Hayward gallantly escorted her to a seat by Caroline on a settee near the fire. She smiled gratefully at him, then sat down by the lovely woman.

Alexandra felt frankly disturbed by the look she had caught on each person's face when she had realized they were watching her. Jake was openly pleased with her transformation, as was Hayward. Caroline's expression had turned hard, calculating, almost filled with dislike, but it had lasted only a moment, then it became soft and lovely again.

"Alex," Jake said, breaking into her thoughts. "I believe this is the quietest you've been since you were seasick."

She smiled softly at him. "I'm afraid I've just not adjusted to land yet."

Their eyes held for a moment and she felt a shattering inside herself, a weakening, and hated herself for it. His eyes were too blue, too piercing, she thought angrily, and turned from him to stare into the fire.

"Let me introduce you, Alex, to two dear friends of mine. This is Hayward Graves and his sister Caroline."

"I'm delighted," Alexandra said graciously. "And I do want to thank you for your generous hospitality."

"Think nothing of it," Caroline returned, her smile edged with ice.

"We're only too glad to be of help," Hayward

said, holding her gaze with his warm brown one for a long moment.

"And," continued Jake, "I can only present my ward as Alex."

"Your ward?" Caroline asked, too quickly.

"That seems to be the way I must think of her."

"Whatever do you mean, old boy?" Hayward leaned forward.

"I did promise them a tale, Alex. What shall it be?"

She looked down at her hands, then raised her clear green eyes to his. "Really, Jake, you know perfectly well that anything you say will be as much as I know," she said innocently, sweetly. Then she turned to her hostess. "I remember nothing."

Jake laughed out loud, then quickly agreed by saying, "And that my friends is our plight. She has no memory. And since I saved her I must see her to her destination. Isn't that right, Alex?"

Her eyes glinted mischievously in the firelight as she looked up into his handsome face. "Yes, Jake. You see," she said, turning toward Hayward, "Jake actually fished me out of the ocean."

"And what I catch, I keep, or so the saying goes," Jake mumbled but loud enough for the others to hear.

"I had nothing with me—nothing. I was desperate until Jake helped me. And now the two of you are being so kind. I can't thank you enough."

"We are delighted to help you, darling," Caroline said. "Such a terrible story. You must have been a pitiful sight when Jake brought you in."

Jake laughed deeply. "For once you're absolutely right, Caroline."

Alexandra flushed and turned her back on Jake.

"But how did you come by the name Alex?" Hayward continued. "It really doesn't seem to suit you."

Alexandra smiled at him. "It seems to be the one word I do remember."

"Ah, perhaps it's the name of your fiancé, or husband?" Caroline asked, then glanced quickly at Jake.

He finished his drink, no expression on his face.

"Why, that is interesting, Caroline," Alexandra said, "though somehow I don't think so."

"But you don't know?"

"No."

"Wait," Hayward said excitedly. "Suppose it's a shortened version of another name."

Alexandra sat very still. The others waited attentively as Hayward struggled in his mind with names.

"I've got it. Alex—Alexandra! Now that is a name that fits you perfectly. Alexandra." His eyes glowed as he regarded her intently.

She paled slightly, then turned a bright pink.

"Is that it, Alex?" Jake asked, watching her closely.

She didn't dare look at him, but instead kept her eyes on the floor. "I don't know. I can't remember."

"Well, we'll call you whatever you want, Alex," Caroline said as if she would be done with the subject, obviously used to being the center of attention, especially Jake's attention.

Alexandra looked up at her quickly, but before she could say anything, Hayward continued, "Well, I'm going to call you Alexandra. Nothing could be more perfect."

"Alex is really fine, but you may call me Alexandra if you like, Mr. Graves."

"You must call me Hayward, otherwise I shall be deeply hurt."

Alexandra laughed for the first time and all their eyes were drawn to her brightened face. "Well, I certainly don't want to hurt you, Hayward, especially since you and Caroline have done so much for me already."

"Not nearly as much as we'd like to do," he said solemnly.

"Oh, my brother is such a helpful man." Caroline tried to lighten his words. "He'll help anyone, any time. Isn't that right, Jake?"

"Undoubtedly, Caroline. Undoubtedly he has great heart."

Caroline laughed lightly, then continued, "Do you ride, Alex?"

"Yes. I—I'm not sure."

"Well, we love to and always do when Jake is here. Perhaps we can find out tomorrow. One never knows how long he will be here so we must take advantage of the opportunity."

"Don't make any plans for me, Caroline," Jake said. "The ship was hit hard, and I'll have to be there most of the time."

Caroline pouted. "You must save some time for your old friends, Jake."

The conversation was then interrupted by the announcement that dinner was ready to be served. Hayward quickly jumped up to give Alexandra his arm, while Caroline took Jake's arm.

Alexandra was able to get a better look at the house and she saw that while the furnishings were lavish, they seemed to be in a state of disrepair. She was disappointed to see this, and wondered about the financial state of the Graves' family. She had known that the plantations begun in the Bahamas by the English and Tories had not worked out as well as expected, but perhaps it was worse than she had realized.

They were led to a sumptuous dining room and seated at a long table with Caroline and Hayward at either end. Alexandra and Jake sat in the middle facing each other. She admired the beautiful silver, china, and crystal, but still felt that the whole setting had a feeling of degeneration.

The meal was delicious, the wine superb, and the company witty and sparkling. Alexandra was enjoying herself completely. Her only uncomfortable moments were when Jake's eyes would settle on her, seeming to burn into her very being as if probing to find answers to unvoiced questions. Yet most of all she hated her own strange, unaccustomed feelings toward this suave, arrogant man. It was something she simply could not understand, especially after what she had suffered at the hands of men.

After dinner they went back to the drawing room, and Alexandra settled into a cozy chair. The warm room, the delicious meal, and the wine all began to tell on her tired, overwrought body. She could hardly follow the conversation, and finally, unable to keep her eyes open any longer, fell asleep.

She awoke with a start, turning rosy with embarrassment when she realized that someone had been speaking to her.

"I think the lady is exhausted and it's no wonder," Hayward said indulgently, smiling at Alexandra.

"I'm terribly sorry I'm such poor company tonight," she said regretfully, "but it has been a trying day."

"Of course, how thoughtless of me," Caroline said, standing up. "I'll just take Alex up to her room, then go on to mine. You men can stay and talk if you like, but we women need our beauty rest, don't we, Alex?"

"Indeed," Alexandra said, standing up.

The men rose, too. Hayward bowed over Alexandra's hand, then lightly touched it with his lips. "Please consider our home yours for as long as you would kindly grace it."

Alexandra smiled, thinking that this was the pose of the Southern gentleman she had imagined. "Thank you, Hayward, but I would not impose on your hospitality for long."

"Please—it is an honor."

Jake walked over, and Alexandra's eyes were drawn up to his as if by a magnet. "Sleep well, Alex," he said with concern. "Don't rise early. The day will be yours to rest."

"Oh, Jake, you do talk like her guardian. I never thought to hear the day," Caroline taunted.

Jake merely laughed, not taking her bait.

"Good night," Alexandra said. "Thank you for your kindness."

Caroline hurried Alexandra into the foyer and up the stairs as if wanting to get her away from Jake and Hayward. "Here is your room, Alex. You don't mind if I come in for a quick chat, do you?"

Tired, but aware that she could not deny her hostess this request, Alexandra said, "Please come in."

They settled into chairs near the fireplace where the low flames crackled faintly, casting strange shadows over the room.

"Is the room to your liking?" Caroline asked.

"Oh, yes, everything is quite wonderful. Thank you."

"I'm so intrigued with your story. Of course, you aren't from the South. Your accent tells us that much."

"Yes."

"You know, a lot of ships sail around the Bahamas. Not as many stop now as they did during the war so it's really quite easy to keep track of which ships are in port, at least on New Providence Island."

"Yes, it must be," Alexandra said sleepily.

"Take, for instance, just before the storm hit only one schooner docked."

"Oh?"

"I believe the name of that schooner was *The Charlotte*," Caroline said softly.

Alexandra's drooping head jerked up. Fatigue left her instantly at the mention of Captain Sully's schooner. If Caroline saw any sign of the new interest in her story, she didn't show it. She continued talking just as before.

"Yes. I was talking with the captain—"

"You were speaking with the captain of *The Charlotte?*"

Caroline nodded, her eyes glittering in the dimness of the room. "Oh yes. He's an old acquaintance of mine from several years back. He was telling me how lucky he was to reach port just before the storm hit. Unfortunately, Jake was not so lucky."

"Unfortunately," Alexandra said, almost in a daze, her thoughts whirling in her head.

"I thought you might be interested if you needed passage somewhere more quickly than Jake could take you. If you like, I could speak with the captain."

"Oh, no. No. I'd like to rest first. I'm not quite well enough to travel."

"But of course, darling. Take all the time you need for we're delighted to have you here. Perhaps you'll soon regain your memory."

"I hope so."

"You might like to talk with this captain. He may be able to help you with your identity. After all, his was the only schooner that docked just before the storm, and you were probably lost at sea about that time."

"I wouldn't want to bother him."

"No bother at all. In fact, since he's an acquaintance, I'll invite him over for dinner tomorrow night. You could talk with him then. We might *all* learn something interesting, don't you agree?" Caroline asked, probing deftly.

Alexandra looked quickly about her as if some answer would appear to save her from this confrontation, but there seemed to be nothing she could do to prevent it.

"As you say, Caroline, we may all learn something interesting."

"Excellent. I couldn't be more delighted." Caroline stood up and started for the door.

Alexandra followed her, dimly trying to stay unaffected by the woman's words, but dreading a meeting with Captain Sully.

"And Alex—" Caroline began as she paused at the door.

"Yes?"

"Since Jake will be so busy, why don't you just rest in the morning. I'm sure you need it, and we can ride another day."

"Yes. Yes, that will be fine. Good night."

"Good night, and sleep well."

Chapter Six

"Miss Alexandra. Miss Alexandra," called Leona as she drew back the drapes, letting the warm afternoon sun flood the room.

Alexandra awoke, struggling out of her sound sleep, and for a moment couldn't place the deep, soft bed with the ornate hangings, or the bedroom with the slow moving dark woman. Gradually her memory returned and with it the problems, frustrations, and horror that had filled her recent life, but she determinedly pushed these from her mind as she sat upright. She hadn't slept so well since long before Olaf's death, and she felt refreshed, ready to face whatever was necessary to complete her promise to that old friend.

"Miss Alexandra, you done slept through half the day," Leona said, almost scolding. "Course, Mister Jake said not to disturb you on no account. And, *after all,* now Mister Hayward, he said get you up after noon so you could go rid-

92

ing with him when he came home. So that's
what I'm doing. Can't please them all, all the
time—" Leona's words trailed off as she set a
breakfast tray across Alexandra's lap.

Breakfast in bed! What a luxury for Alexandra after the days in the cramped cabin of the
schooner.

"Do you know if Captain Jake is here?"
Alexandra asked, almost shyly, hating to admit
her interest.

Leona grinned knowingly. "That's some man,
ain't he? A girl can't resist him—"

"Oh, no. It's just—"

"I know, honey, but remember he's Miss Caroline's man while he's here."

"That's fine with me. I'm certainly not interested in him—that way. I merely wanted to
know how his repairs were coming."

"He's been gone since daybreak out at his
ship. Seems to me he's in some hurry to get
out of the Bahamas. I can remember the time—
but we'd best get you dressed if you're finished
eating."

Alexandra would liked to have heard what
Leona had been going to say, but she stilled her
impulse to question her further.

"This here is the best we could do on such
short notice. It's one of Miss Caroline's old riding habits, and I must admit it's seen better
days. Still, it's all there is. I altered it slightly,
but it's a little short."

"It'll be fine, Leona. I really appreciate what you have all done for me."

In fact, Alexandra thought that Caroline had purposely chosen a habit completely out of style and one that would not look good on her, but she would simply have to wear it. She thought longingly of her trunks of fine clothing, but dismissed them as being lost to her. Yet, if Captain Sully were coming to dinner, she might be able to get her things returned. She shuddered at the thought of being with him again, of having to ask for her things. What would he do? What if Captain Sully decided to tell them that she came from New York? He knew she had money, but that was all he knew. Alexandra breathed a little easier; the captain of *The Charlotte* couldn't really identify her.

After she had dressed, she surveyed herself in the full-length mirror. The outfit accentuated her curves, making her realize that she was indeed a full grown woman. She had been isolated for so long that she had never given it much thought until Stan Lewis and Captain Sully had made it obvious that they thought she was a woman, a woman to be desired.

"I'm working on another gown for you to wear this evening, Miss Alexandra, to the dinner party," Leona said.

Alexandra felt chilled, remembering Caroline's words of the night before. Yet, she needed her trunks. How was she to get them back if she didn't face Captain Sully? Anger and necessity gave her more courage as she thought of her treatment at his hands. If he came, she would have to approach him, she decided.

"I'll look forward to this evening and the gown you're preparing for me. Do you suppose Hayward is waiting for me now?"

"I suspect he is, honey. That one's powerful eager to see you again," Leona said.

Alexandra left the room, pleased that the gentleman found her attractive. Yet she was concerned with his interest. Before her encounters with Stan and Captain Sully, she could have enjoyed a man's attentions more easily. Now she had begun to suspect them all of wicked, ulterior motives. Could it be so difficult for a man to like a woman just for herself and not because of her wealth or her body? She didn't quite know what to think or believe anymore. She should hate all men, and yet something strange happened to her in the presence of Jake. But no, she wouldn't think of him. She would go riding with Hayward and try to put all of this out of her mind—for the present.

"Alexandra," Hayward said graciously as she reached the bottom step leading to the foyer. His brown eyes glowed warmly with pleasure. "You look even more beautiful today."

She smiled at him. "Thank you. I suspect that a good night's sleep in such a comfortable bed would work wonders for anyone."

He led her out the front door. She was impressed with the lush, tropical growth that covered the island, held at bay only by the diligent work of gardeners. There was a warm, lazy quality about the island that was in great contrast to the climate of New York.

Hayward led her to the front lawn where two horses were being held by a groom. Alexandra had never before been around so many Negroes and she was curious about them although she tried to keep her interest to herself.

"I chose this mare for you, Alexandra, because she is gentle but yet not a nag."

"Oh, she looks perfect. A real beauty."

"I fear that one of my passions is horses, and I devote myself to them a good deal of the time."

Hayward mounted his horse, then waited as the groom assisted Alexandra into her saddle. When she had settled herself, arranging her skirts, they walked slowly away from the house, then turned down a narrow dirt path leading deep into the lush growth of the island. Alexandra found her mount easy to handle. In fact she preferred a faster, more spirited animal for she loved to race on the back of a fine horse, feeling the wind in her hair. This slow, ambling pace was not exactly her idea of fun, but she could hardly gallop away from Hayward; besides it being rude, she would undoubtedly get lost.

This man with her seemed to blend in with his surroundings, becoming a part of the slow, unchanging rhythm of the island. He would never blow hot or cold, she thought, but would remain constant in whatever he did, whatever he felt. He would probably not even have much of a temper, or would control himself if he did. He was a handsome man, but his easygoing grace did not seem to touch her. He left her entirely without feelings for him.

She shook her head, trying to push her thoughts away so that she could simply enjoy the beauty of the island and the feel of the horse under her. Why did she have this sudden interest in men, especially after what had happened to her? Why was she suddenly noticing the way they moved, their voices, their bodies — oh, yes, their bodies. It seemed to have begun on *The Flying J* when she had first seen Jake standing over her, looking so powerful, so masculine. She mustn't think of him. She couldn't trust him and he made her body feel traitorous, as if he communicated directly with it, bypassing her mind.

"What do you think of this, Alexandra?" Hayward asked.

"What?" she asked, glancing around quickly. Lost in her own thoughts, she had hardly noticed their progress deep into the island. Now she realized that he had led her to a clearing, with soft grass as a floor and the branches of trees meeting overhead to form a roof over them. In the center was a clear, dark pool of water. It was so perfect a setting that she could hardly believe it was real. New York City had always been her home and this abundance of natural beauty was almost too much to be true.

"Oh, Hayward, it's lovely, truly beautiful," she said as he dismounted and came to help her off her horse.

"I'm glad you think so. It's a special place of mine."

"I can see why."

They left the horses and walked slowly toward the pool, surrounded by the sounds and smells of the island. They sat down by the still water. Hayward moved close to her. She stiffened slightly.

He noticed her movement. "Don't be afraid of me, Alexandra. We don't know what your life has been like or how men have treated you, but I wouldn't harm you for the world. Please believe me."

He sounded so sincere that she turned her dazzling gaze upon him, wanting to trust him. She could not help noticing that he seemed almost to lose himself in her nearness, as if there were nothing else alive for him except her. It gave her a strange feeling of power and she began to be aware of her innate feelings of femininity. A woman did have power, she thought, but of a different sort than a man. A pleasant thrill went through her as Hayward continued to be lost in the spell that seemed to bind him to her.

"Have you lived in the Bahamas all your life, Hayward?"

He grinned boyishly. "Yes, I was born here. Caroline was, too. But that is about all we've ever had in common. She would like nothing better than to leave the islands, while I think I would be lost anywhere else. About the only time you couldn't have gotten Caroline away from here was during the war. Oh, but you're from the North—"

"Yes, it seems so, but that's all over now," she said warmly, wanting him to go on.

He flushed slightly, then continued. "Well, that was the wildest time ever and I think she thought it would go on forever. You see, the South was staying alive by blockade running and the Bahamas got almost all of that trade. It was rough then, and the islands were crowded with tough men and women. They came here to make money, fast money, and most of them did. Of course, they spent it just as fast as they made it, and that's where the islands should have made their fortune. You see, the money was spent here—no one stayed in the South."

"Yes?" Alexandra encouraged him. She had never heard this side of the story before.

"Well, I suppose I was just as much taken in

as Caroline. I thought the prosperity would never end, and I guess she thought the good times would never end."

"What happened?"

"Well, of course, the war ended, then it was worse here than ever before. The people left and they took the money with them. I guess the islanders didn't hang onto their part, or either they spent it. So they were left with little when it was all over."

"I'm sorry."

"No, it's my own damn fault. I should have looked far enough ahead, but I've never had a business head. None of my family ever has. You see, my ancestors were Tories and came here to build a cotton plantation when the rebels won the war for independence. Well, they built the plantation all right. You've seen the house, but what with one thing and another, it failed. All the rich cotton plantations failed. It just wasn't right here."

"Could nothing be done?"

"No. They hung on, though, just like we have. I had the money during the war, but I built warehouses in Nassau. It seemed a good investment. We even own part of the Royal Victoria Hotel there, the grandest hotel in the Bahamas, and also the emptiest. We can't sell it now, can't give it away. We even lost some of the warehouses in the hurricane that hit us in 1866, as if losing the war hadn't done enough destruction to the islands. So, my dear Alexandra, I own an unproductive plantation, a rundown mansion, empty warehouses, and part of a hotel that goes begging for customers."

"I'm truly sorry, Hayward," she said, feeling uncomfortable with his open confession. She could understand his being upset over his fate, but she couldn't sympathize with his failure to make more of his life.

"No, no," he said, waving his hand as if to push away her concern. "We are far from destitute. I have hopes that the Bahamas will become important in shipping once more, and when it does I'll be here—ready."

"But what will you do in the meantime?"

"Oh," he said casually, turning soft brown eyes on her, "what we've always done here in the Bahamas. Most of the schooners you'll see in the waters around here are wreckers."

"Wreckers?"

"Yes. I own several myself. The islands are hard to maneuver around and frequently ships crash. The wreckers salvage what they can and get paid handsomely for their service."

"Oh," Alexandra said, thinking that it sounded gruesome.

"Wrecking is the business of the Bahamas, and it can pay off handsomely. I usually handle the business end of it, but occasionally I go out on my schooners if it's an interesting or especially profitable wreck."

Alexandra could hardly believe he was so casual about this horrible business. It was hardly an honorable occupation, but if it was all that kept them going, she should not condemn his actions or attitude. Yet, she was repulsed by the idea.

"You don't think badly of me over this, do you, Alexandra?" he asked, as if reading her mind.

She shook her head and tried to smile warmly at him. "No. No, the people on the islands must live."

"That's right," he agreed quickly. "And someone must bring in the wreckage. Of course, the islanders are terribly upset that the authorities want to put up more lights."

"Lights?"

"Yes, of course, to mark the dangerous points for the ships."

"You mean they'd rather have the ships wreck than go on in safety?"

"That's it, I'm afraid." He paused, then leaned closer. "I've told you all this for a reason."

She felt instinctive alarms go off all over her body but she didn't move, didn't speak.

"Alexandra, you can't have failed to notice my interest in you since the first moment we met."

She shook her head, not wanting to hear the rest of his words. Yet she could not run away.

"You're so beautiful I can scarcely believe it, and so sweet, so kind."

"I, I—"

"No, let me continue. I've always dreamed of someone like you, never hoping she really existed or that I could hope to meet her. Yet, you arrive suddenly, all alone and with no memory. Your past doesn't matter to me. Do you think, could you possibly want to live here in the Bahamas—permanently?"

"This is so quick, Hayward," she said, stumbling over her words. "I am very honored by your words, naturally, but it is so soon. I cannot say, I do not know—"

"That is enough. It is enough for now that you do not reject me and my island. It is enough that you will give us time to know each other. I feel," and here he touched his chest over his heart melodramatically, "that we belong together."

She could scarcely believe his words. Could he possibly mean what he said? What did he quite mean anyway? Was he thinking of marriage? Did he love her? So quickly?

"I'm not rushing you, Alexandra, but I feared you might leave me before we had time to know each other. I'd not normally have spoken so soon. You understand, don't you, darling?"

He slipped strong hands around her waist, pulling her into his arms as he leaned forward, his lips seeking hers.

Surprised, she didn't respond even though his mouth was urgent on hers, trying to entice her to passion. His hands cupped her breasts, frantically trying to open her bodice. But other men, other places flashed vividly across her mind and she pushed him from her. She saw his flushed, surprised face as she jumped up and ran from him. He was a man, she thought, just like all the others. She couldn't trust him.

Hayward hurried to follow her as she quickly covered the distance to the horses. "Alexandra, I'm sorry," he cried. "Please don't be mad. It's just that you're so beautiful I can't help myself."

Once more, she felt her power surge through her. She turned to face him. "You rush me. I can't make any decisions, much less know my own mind until I can remember who I am, what I'm doing here." Realizing she'd spoken too sharply by his crestfallen face, she softened her voice and touched his sleeve. "Let us get to know one another while I'm here, Hayward, then we can speak again."

He brightened instantly. "Thank you, Alexandra. I'll do anything to make you happy."

As he helped her into the saddle, she thought that this kind of man displeased her almost as much as Stan Lewis' cold calculation. She knew instinctively that she did not want a man she could control or command, yet she did not want one who would hurt her.

They rode back toward the house as leisurely as before, only now Hayward hummed happily to himself, or pointed out points of interest, plants with unusual names, any number of things to gain her attention. She thought he acted like a young school boy trying to impress her, but still she liked him for he was a pleasant companion and wanted to please her in any way he could.

The afternoon sun was fading as they arrived at the plantation. The first sight to meet their eyes was Caroline coming toward them.

"Have you had a pleasant afternoon? When I awoke from my nap, Leona told me you two had gone riding. So you can ride, Alex?"

"Oh, yes. Yes, indeed. We had a lovely afternoon. The island is gorgeous. I've never seen anything like it."

Caroline shrugged. "If you like islands—"

Hayward laughed. "You can never be satisfied with anything, or anyone, Caroline."

Caroline's eyes narrowed a moment before she said, "Oh, you're wrong, Hayward. There's someone who could make me completely happy—if he would."

Alexandra immediately thought of Jake. And Leona's words—Caroline's man. So Caroline wanted Jake to marry her and take her away with him, away from this island life. But would he?

"I'm so glad you two are enjoying each other," Caroline said pointedly. "You know,

Alex, there aren't that many young ladies on the island anymore who are appropriate for Hayward. He's quite particular, and of course, you're well bred for all that you can't remember."

"Now Caroline—" Hayward began.

"Oh, Hayward, it's obvious you two belong together so there's no reason to hide it," Caroline said positively.

Alexandra blushed, hardly knowing how to cope with Caroline's forwardness. She is pushing us together, Alexandra thought unhappily. But why?

"Caroline, you've embarrassed Alexandra. You must give her time to understand us and our ways. She's not used to your outspokenness."

"Oh, I'm so sorry, Alex. It's just that I want everyone else to be as happy as Jake and I are," she said smugly.

Alexandra looked into her soft brown eyes quickly, feeling suddenly nauseous, then back at Hayward questioningly.

"Now, Caroline, you shouldn't be too quick to speak for Jake. He's—"

"Nonsense. He's here, isn't he! That proves what I've been telling you. He returned for me and that's why we should be so happy, shouldn't we, Alex?"

Alexandra swallowed, then nodded, "Yes, indeed. I'm very happy for you and Jake, Caroline."

"Thank you," Caroline said, her dark eyes burning hotly.

"Caroline, since you're dressed for dinner, shouldn't Alexandra change now?" Hayward asked, concern in his voice.

"Oh, of course, and you should hurry. People could be arriving any time now."

Alexandra was only too grateful to escape them. She went quickly into the house, telling herself that it didn't matter in the least that Jake had returned for Caroline.

Chapter Seven

Alexandra floated down the magnificent staircase on a wave of soft silk, rustling petticoats, and sweet perfume, assured of her beauty. The gown Leona had made over for her was in a soft apricot color that accentuated her golden red hair perfectly. She had pulled her hair back into a simple knot at her neck, giving only a hint as to its true luxuriance. She had never felt more beautiful, or more feminine.

The soft murmur of voices wafted on the sweet smelling breeze from the verandah that was softly lit by moonlight. She could hear crickets, frogs, and the soft droning of insects in the distance. She paused at the entrance.

Hayward seemed to sense her presence. He looked up quickly, stopping his conversation with an elderly gentleman in mid-sentence.

His heart pounded loudly in his ears as he became aware of nothing save the dazzling beauty framed by soft moonlight in the doorway. Alexandra stood there casually as if she belonged, as if she would belong anywhere for everything must seem a backdrop for her radiating presence. Her pale skin seemed almost glowing in the eerie light and her hair almost on fire, as if drawing color from her soft, clinging gown. He could think of nothing except burying his face in the soft warmness of her full, high breasts. He had never wanted anything as much as this woman standing so causally before him. He must have her—and soon.

His gaze never wavered as he covered the distance between them, feeling himself to be in a dream. He drew her close to him so he could smell her sweetness and feel the warmth of her body. "You are exquisite, Alexandra. More beautiful than anything I have ever beheld."

Alexandra scarcely heard what he said for when her eyes had become accustomed to the darkness, she had seen Jake. Her heart had given a strange flutter which had instantly turned to cold pain when she realized that Caroline leaned over him, her voluptuous breasts almost falling out of her low-cut gown. Caroline was wantonly willing Jake to love her, Alexandra thought coldly, suddenly determined that she would never make such a display for a man. Of course, Jake was probably used to women throwing themselves at him and actually expected such action from them. Well, he would certainly never see her approach him like that. After all, she was a Northern woman and a Clarke as well. She would never grovel to any man — for any reason!

Jake felt her eyes on him. He wanted to smash in Hayward's face when he saw them standing so closely together. He gripped his glass, almost shattering it in the sudden fury that washed over him. Alex had been on his mind all day and thoughts of her soft body had plagued him more than his damaged ship. Hell, what was wrong with him? There'd never been a woman he couldn't love and leave, forgetting her completely, and this woman he had never even touched yet. Still, he could almost feel the soft, smooth texture of her skin; how her nipples would harden at the touch of his hands and mouth; how her lips would burn with a sweet hungry flame.

Caroline saw the direction of Jake's gaze. Containing her fury behind a cold smile, she mumbled something to him about playing the proper hostess, and walked over to the young woman who was too beautiful for her own good.

"Alex," she said with a tight smile, "you look lovely this evening. I see the gown suits you."

"Yes, thank you," Alexandra said quickly, determined not to let her true feelings about Caroline and Jake show.

"I'd like you to meet our other guests," Caroline said as she pulled Alexandra along with her. Hayward followed.

"This is Doctor Elder. He's an old, dear friend of ours, and practically keeps the islands going single-handed," Caroline said with warmth in her voice.

"How do you do," the elderly gentleman said as he touched his lips quickly to Alexandra's hand.

"I'm glad to meet you, sir. You are a medical doctor?" Alexandra asked hesitantly, her heart beating faster. Could this man tell that she had not lost her memory?

"Oh, yes," Caroline answered for him, looking slyly at Alexandra. "He's the only doctor in the Bahamas and we all pay homage to him, don't we Doctor Elder?"

"My dear Caroline, you've never paid homage to anyone since I first brought you into this world," he said, chuckling.

"Well, we couldn't get along without him. Perhaps he can help you, Alex."

"No rush, my dear," Doctor Elder said to Alexandra. "Caroline has explained about your loss of memory. There's nothing that can be done. Sometimes it returns, sometimes it doesn't. But I'll be happy to check you over some time so that we can be sure that's the only injury you suffered."

"Thank you," Alexandra mumbled and then

in a stronger voice continued, "I'd be grateful for your service. I'll try to come to your office in a few days."

"When you feel up to it. I'm usually in Nassau, but if I'm not my office will know where I am."

"Thank you," Alexandra said again, noticing that Caroline looked somewhat disappointed. She could appear so sweet and helpful, but Alexandra felt sure that Caroline wanted to hurt or expose her in some way.

"What's this about losing memories?" a voice boomed out behind Alexandra.

She whirled around, instantly recognizing that voice. Captain Sully was advancing on her, grinning at her expression of dismay. Her mind whirled in every direction, trying to think of some means to escape, but she couldn't do that. She had decided to demand her trunks from this man and she would.

"Captain Sully, you haven't met Alex yet, have you?" Caroline asked pleasantly.

Alexandra caught the malicious glint in her eyes. What was Caroline trying to do to her? And why? She seemed determined to learn the truth about Alexandra. First, the doctor and now Captain Sully. Well, she would not let Caroline frighten her, or force her to reveal the truth.

"I'm very glad to meet you, Captain. Are you another *friend* of Caroline's from the war?

Hayward has told me how much you all enjoyed making port here."

Captain Sully's smile slowly faded as he realized that Alexandra was not going to be quite so easy to intimidate as he had thought. He wanted to give her away, tell them all that he knew of her, but he couldn't afford to have these people know that she'd gone over the side of his schooner and that he'd left her for dead.

What kind of games was she playing? First, she had insisted on hiring his schooner for a trip to New Orleans. She would give no name, but she seemed to have plenty of money. Now she was pretending that she had no memory, but he had seen the quick rush of recognition in her eyes when she had first seen him. He had decided from the beginning that she was probably a fancy whore who had been run out of New York City. Seeing her dressed now in the clinging soft gown confirmed his suspicions. The little bitch wanted her trunks back because a high-priced whore needed the tools of her trade. Well, he would let her have them, all right, but for a price. A sampling of the wares for free—that's what he'd charge.

Jake watched Alex carefully, wondering how she knew Sully, for it was obvious that the captain—whom he'd known and disliked during the war—had met Alexandra before. If she had escaped from Sully's schooner, then Jake knew

113

why, if Sully had already molested her, he'd kill the man.

"I do believe it's time for dinner," Caroline said, stopping Sully from answering. "Please follow me into the dining room."

The dining room was lovely in the soft candlelight that masked the encroaching decay of the house. There was a beautiful floral arrangement in the center of the table composed of gorgeous tropical flowers that Alexandra had never seen before. It could have been a perfect evening if she had not felt that she was losing control of her life. Hayward was like a fawning puppy dog; Sully was a vile man who would go to any length to hurt her, she felt sure; Caroline was playing a malicious game of cat-and-mouse for a reason she could not fathom; and Jake — Jake was awakening in her emotions she did recognize and could not deal with.

Hayward sat at one end of the long table, while Caroline held court at the other. She had placed Jake at her right and Captain Sully at her left, while Hayward had seated Alexandra at his right and Doctor Elder had sat down at his left. The space that separated the two groups at the same table seemed to be more than just a matter of feet for Caroline was determined to ignore everyone except the two men beside her.

As the dinner progressed, Hayward, Doctor Elder, and Alexandra could hardly pretend not to notice the separate party at the other end of their table. For as the wine flowed freely, Caroline had imbibed more and more until now she was in her own curious state of euphoria. She leaned toward each man in turn, displaying her charms until her heavy breasts were almost falling out of her gown. It was as if she wanted to play one man against the other until they erupted in violence with passion for her and jealousy of each other. But this night, her ploy did not seem to be working and it was making her progressively more blatant about her desires. Alexandra had decided that at any moment she might get up, strip, and dance on the table. Caroline would surely gain their full attention that way.

"Caroline," Hayward said finally, "is a woman who needs constant reassurance of her desirability. During the war, she had no end of admirers, but since then—"

"I—" Alexandra began, trying to cover his embarrassment.

"No, I understand her. She needs a husband, a strong man—like Jake. She plans to marry him, but—"

"Of course, she'll marry him, Hayward," Alexandra said quickly. "You can see how fascinated he is with her."

Both Hayward and Doctor Elder looked at her questioningly, as if they knew the blockade runner better than she did and they knew he had never yet been faithful to one woman, much less marriage to Caroline.

Hayward, Doctor Elder, and Alexandra struggled through the long meal uncomfortably. The food was delicious, but Alexandra could not eat. She felt a deep depression take hold of her as she tried to keep her eyes on her plate. Yet at the same time she felt a rising excitement within. She was beginning to acknowledge the fierce drive of desire as her eyes kept slipping to the others. She felt something responding in herself, something awakening that she had not known existed. And she wished she had not been so well brought up, or that she had so much icy control at all times, or that she had been raped. What would it be like to enjoy feeling a man's hard naked body against her own? What would it be like to forget all else except the moment, the man—Jake.

She suddenly found her gaze locked with Jake's, and there was an answering fire in his eyes, a yearning for her. She blushed furiously, forcing her gaze from him.

When Alexandra thought she could endure the spectacle at the table no longer, the meal finally ended. She had drunk more of her wine than she had intended and she felt slightly lightheaded when Hayward helped her out of her chair. She found herself leaning heavily against him before she quite knew what was happening, and looked up to see Jake staring at her with barely concealed anger in his face. He grabbed Caroline and pulled her out through the front door. Alexandra could hear Caroline's sultry laughter as she let Jake lead her down the verandah steps.

Captain Sully hurried after them. "Hey, Jake. Let's share the bounty," he called out.

Hayward led Alexandra down the hall to the parlor, and the doctor joined them.

"I fear the others may not be joining us," Alexandra said, smiling.

"One never really expects Caroline to join the party after dinner," Doctor Elder said. "She usually makes her own. This is not unusual for us, but I do hope it doesn't alter your opinion of Caroline. She is really a lovely lady, but she simply has this need for reassurance."

Hayward nodded agreement.

Alexandra could only wonder if they really believed what they said. She was the closest thing to a whore that Alexandra had ever seen for she sold herself to any man for compliments and reassurance. But, remembering her companions, Alexandra would not let these two men see her true opinion of Caroline.

After several weak attempts at conversation, the doctor excused himself. When he had gone, Hayward got up and came to sit close to Alexandra. With her new heightened sense of femininity and her slightly dizzy feeling from too much wine, she was very much aware of his presence as a man, a handsome young man who desired her. She knew she should move, or make him go away, but a kind of lethargy seemed to steal over her and she remained immobile, awaiting his next move.

"Alexandra," Hayward said passionately, "I, I want you to marry me. I love you. Could you ever, could I hope that you might some day marry me, love me?"

He held both her hands in his, leaning toward her, his breath warm against her face, his brown eyes puppy soft. She felt paralyzed, helpless, trapped. She couldn't marry this man. She felt nothing for him. Her senses, her emotions no longer seemed hers to control. They were caught up with another man.

"Tell me, Alexandra. I must know."

"It's too soon, Hayward. Please," she cried, pushing him away from her and jumping up.

He stayed where he was, looking completely dejected.

"It's not that I don't like you," she said, trying desperately not to hurt him. "It, it's too soon. I hardly know you."

He watched her closely, a strange gleam beginning to glow in his eyes. "You know, dearest, I have Caroline's dislike of being rejected. Neither of us would care to be thrown over for someone else."

"There is no one else."

"But you have no memory, or do you? Is this

118

all some kind of game to you? Do you play at collecting men's hearts? Do you, Alexandra?"

He had risen, and stood over her now. She could not fail to mistake the savage gleam of passion in his eyes, or the jealous leer on his handsome face.

"Am I so repugnant that you would not even give me a kiss this evening, after all I've done for you?" he asked, putting his hands on her shoulders and drawing her slowly to him as his eyes tried to mesmerize her to his will.

"I will not play the whore for my room and board," Alexandra said angrily, having done with being nice. "Let me go. I'm going to my room."

But his hands only gripped her harder, pulling her to him, his mouth groping for hers, finding it, closing on it in possession. She struggled against him, but he ignored her efforts as he savagely kissed her. He tried to force a response from her as he loosened his grip so that his hands could play over her body, finding her soft, yielding curves. With one hand around her waist to support her, he boldly thrust the other inside her gown, finding her warm, quivering flesh and her hard nipples. Groaning, his wet lips left her mouth to travel down her neck to the deep valley between her breasts where he paused, his lips burning, his need real and potent.

At last Alexandra saw her chance to escape,

and jerked back, surprising him. She slapped him hard across the face. "You insult me, sir, and you are obviously no gentleman," she said hotly before turning and stalking from the room. As she hurriedly walked away, willing herself not to run, she condemned all men for their brutality.

Hayward put his hand to his cheek, silently cursing his stupidity for rushing Alexandra, but at the same time the throbbing in his groin demanded release. He watched her body move gracefully, seductively from the room. He had to control himself not to rush after her, pull her into his arms and carry her to his room where he could lose himself deep within her. But he wanted her more than once, he wanted her permanently. He had never wanted any woman as much as he wanted this fiery eyed vixen. He had to have her.

Alexandra rushed up the stairs, determined to make the security of her room before he could follow her. Was everyone in this house mad with lust? She slammed the door to her room, then locked it. There would not be any intruders into her room this night, she decided. She had to get off this island, away from these men.

Chapter Eight

As Caroline slowly undressed before him, Jake tried to keep his mind from wandering to Alexandra. What was the matter with him? Caroline was one of the best women he had ever had, and here she was, eager for him. Forget the Yankee bitch, or think of her as Caroline. One woman was the same as another, once in bed, he told himself sternly, trying to enjoy Caroline's sensual beauty. Anyway, if Alex was going to play with that poor excuse of a man, Hayward, he was going to push her from his mind with Caroline.

Caroline, now naked, walked slowly, tantalizingly toward him. He sat on her bed, fully clothed, and looked at her closely. Her long, dark hair hung down around her shoulders, making a frame for her smooth skin. Her breasts were large, rounded, the nipples dark against her pale skin. Her rounded hips demanded attention, promising hidden delights to any man. He felt his blood stirring as she came to him. He pushed her back onto the bed, burying his face in her voluptuous breasts as he brought his knee up between her thighs.

She groaned at his touch, pulling him closer. "Oh, I've missed you, Jake. I've needed you. Don't ever leave me again."

"From the way you played with Sully, I'd not have known it," he said dryly as he sought her pink nipples with his experienced tongue.

"It was only to make you jealous. I got rid of him when it was time, didn't I?"

"Did I need to become jealous to want you?"

"I should hope not, my love."

"And how do I know that he won't come to you later?"

"Because you'll be here with me all night." She tugged at his jacket. "Take this off, Jake. I want to feel you against me."

He quickly got undressed and turned back to her. The pale light fell on her soft, feminine body and his manhood stirred, but it was not Caroline he thought of as he covered her with his body for he saw golden-red hair and fiery green eyes. He covered her mouth with his hungrily, trying to quench the fire that burned in him, branding his need for Alexandra. Caroline returned his kiss with a passion that equaled his own. Suddenly he stopped, his body completely still.

She groaned, trying to pull him to her. "What is it?"

"Shhhh. I heard something. Be quiet."

"So—I thought you'd come to me, my lovely lady," Captain Sully said lazily, his voice coming from the garden.

"Of course, even though you were brazen in calling up to my bedroom window. I must have my trunks back. I need them," Alexandra said sharply.

"I know you need them and I know why you need them," he said, as if he knew all about her.

"What do you mean you know why?" Alexandra asked, fear in her voice.

"You had to get out of New York City fast without anybody knowing, but you insisted on bringing all those trunks full of clothes. Now, the answer is obvious."

"Is it?" Alexandra didn't see how that could have led him to the truth of her identity.

"Don't try to play the innocent with me. I doubt if you've been innocent for a long time."

"I really don't know what you're talking about," Alexandra tried to sound calm.

"Now look, all I ever wanted was a little of what you've been spreading around, but you've played so hard to get—"

"What!"

"Lord, you're a cool one. I know they ran you out of New York for being a high class

123

whore, but whore you are in my books no matter what kind you are."

"A whore!" Alexandra said, laughing harshly. "You fool! I want my trunks. That's all I want from you. I've already paid you well. I—"

But she never finished, for his heavy hand came crashing down across her face, knocking her to the soft, damp ground.

"You dare call me a fool, you little slut. I'll just show you what kind of man I am," Sully growled as he began to unbuckle his trousers.

"Leave me be," Alexandra moaned, unable to move.

Cursing, Jake leapt from Caroline's bed. He quickly donned his pants. As he rushed from the room, Caroline called after him, "You heard. She's a whore. There's no need to protect her. It's what she wants."

But Jake was already halfway down the stairs when she finished her words. Caroline began hurriedly dressing. Jake was hers and she intended to fight for him.

Jake took the stairs two at a time, fury driving him in cold-blooded determination. Sully was just pulling Alexandra's gown up, exposing her long, lovely legs while she whimpered, hitting out at him helplessly, as Jake rushed up to them.

"What the hell are you doing, Sully?" he demanded, his voice deadly as it broke the still, island night.

Sully jerked around and was on his feet in an instant, obviously ready for Jake. "I'm taking what's mine. It's none of your business. Go back to Caroline. You're the one she wants tonight. I've got a right to take my pleasure where I can."

"You've got no rights where Alex is concerned, Sully."

"Listen, big man, you don't carry no weight around here. This one's mine. She's a whore. You don't want her."

Jake struck Sully full in the face with his fist, catching him by surprise. Sully went down heavily. When he began feebly trying to get up, Jake put his foot on the man's broad chest. "Stay down, Sully, if you don't want more of the same. I'm taking Alexandra with me. Don't try to follow. She belongs to me and don't you or any other man forget it."

Jake took Alexandra's hand, jerking her to her feet, then pulled her behind him. She ran, stumbling after him as they quickly crossed the mansion's plush lawn. Just at the edge, where the native island growth began, she looked back. Sully was angrily getting to his feet, and Caroline was now with him.

Alexandra was glad to be getting away from them, but she was not very sure of Jake either for he pulled her roughly into the thick underbrush of the island, having little concern for her thin slippers and sheer gown.

125

They plunged deeper and deeper into the dark, dense vegetation, and she fought the clinging vines and clutching brush as she half ran to keep up with Jake's long strides. He was not hampered with a full skirt that threatened to be torn off at every turn, she thought angrily. She tried to pull her hand free from his grasp, but he only tightened his grip, jerking her along. She stumbled, almost losing her balance, then caught at his back with her free hand to steady herself. Why couldn't he slow down? Surely they wouldn't be followed. Her breath was coming in gasps now. There were pebbles in her slippers and her feet hurt with every step. Would he never stop?

Finally, after what seemed an endless time, he halted, and she collapsed at his feet. Exhausted, disheveled, dispirited, she hardly cared what happened to her next. She just wanted to rest.

Jake knelt beside her. "It's all right now, Alex. They won't follow us here, and the ship's not far away. We're all alone. You're safe."

Trying to control her ragged breathing, Alexandra looked up into his face made sharp and angular by the moonlight, and did not feel at all safe alone with him. In fact, she suddenly became very aware of his body so close to hers, his bare chest with its thickly matted hair, his hands coming toward her, touching her arms, pulling her towards him. And she was incapable of fleeing. He raised her to her feet, putting his arms around her, pressing her against him, giving his warmth to her. His body was hard, muscular, lean. She could feel the heat of his naked flesh as her partially exposed breasts strained against him. When his head bent toward her, she moaned slightly, afraid of being hurt again and yet unable to escape the emotions that bound her.

His lips covered hers possessively. She pushed against his chest, trying to pull free before she was completely lost, but he captured the back of her head with one hand so that she was unable to resist the hungry demand of his mouth as it pressed urgently against her own, forcing her lips to part. His tongue darted swiftly inside, plunging deep, deeper into her in his greedy search. His hand caught at her hair, pulling it until it tumbled down her back, free. His other hand held her tightly to him and she could feel the hard muscles of his thighs pressed against her, unrelenting.

Oh, but what was happening to her in his crushing embrace? For suddenly she found herself returning his kiss, and her arms moved weakly up his back until they found the soft hair at the nape of his neck. She had never felt this way before. It was as if there were nothing else except the fusion of their bodies and the hot pounding in her ears. Then his lips left hers and she was hardly able to stand as he placed small kisses down her throat to the hollow place where they lingered, burning her. His hands caught at her bodice, unfastening it expertly, then slipping his hands inside to cover her breasts with hot, urgent movements. She leaned against him, soft moaning sounds coming from her throat as his lips found her taut, straining nipples, teasing them with his tongue until a hard, warm core began to ache in her belly. What was he doing to her? Her mind couldn't seem to focus except where he touched her, leaving her skin on fire. She mustn't let him do this. She mustn't!

Gathering strength, she pushed away from him, failing to see the surprised, then angry look cross his face as she rushed away from him. She found herself on the soft sands of the beach. Moonlight turned the incoming waves a phosphorescent silver as she hesitated, not knowing where to turn. The ship and the house—she could return to neither, but before her was the ocean and behind her Jake. Then she heard him close to her, and with a soft cry she ran desperately toward the ocean, scarcely knowing what she was doing. She couldn't reason any more. She was blinded by fear, fear of feelings she couldn't understand, didn't dare accept.

But Jake easily covered the distance between them, catching her just at the water's edge. She twisted, jerking from his hands and they both fell into the shallow water, splashing noisily as he tried to bring her under control. But she was almost wild with despair.

"I won't hurt you, Alex. What has made you so frightened of me? I've never hurt you, now have I?"

His words made sense, but she wouldn't listen to them, hitting out at him in her desperation, for she could not forget another man, another time. Had Stan Lewis ruined her for all pleasure with men? She was afraid.

Finally, Jake caught her to him, feeling her soft body quiver against him as the waves rolled in over them. Pulling back from her slightly, he looked over her body. She was beautiful, he thought, savoring how the wet clothes molded to her curves, how her bare breasts were taut with desire. Her eyes opened slowly as he made no move to hurt her and she rapidly blinked salty drops of water away before the pale green orbs focused on him in confusion, fear, and anger. Their gaze met. And then their lips came together hungrily. Instantly a flame flashed through them, urging them on. She found her hands in his hair, pulling him to her, wanting something she could not understand, but knowing that she must have it. He kissed her gently at first, then more roughly as the flames began to kindle, devouring them with it.

"Alexandra, Alexandra," he murmured as his lips left hers and found their way down her throat. Moving quickly, urgently, he slipped the wet gown off her, then removed his trousers. He lowered himself to her, covering her body with his own.

She shivered as his warm body touched hers, for she could feel his hard manhood pressing between her thighs.

"No, no, Jake. Please—" she began. But he covered her mouth with his own, his tongue artfully bending her to his will as his hands explored the soft curves of her body. Soon, she could protest no longer and lay weakly in the sand, feeling the cool, salty water hit her skin, then run swiftly around her body, outlining it, searching for its release.

His strong hands moved over her breasts as he tore his mouth from hers to follow the pattern of his hands, searching the ripe fullness that was his to take. His tongue lightly plied the taut nipples that seemed to reach out to him, offering their sweetness. Then his lips moved lower, leaving a trail of searing kisses.

She moaned, unable to control the deep shudder that went through her body. She hadn't known it could feel like this—a fire growing in her depths, demanding release.

His hands stroked her. "Open your legs for me, Alexandra," he whispered urgently.

"Oh, no, Jake." But her legs spread of their own accord, the need within her too great to be denied.

Gently, deftly, he slipped inside the moist

warmth of her. Moving deeper, deeper, probing, searching, but not finding. A frown marred his face. He looked up quickly, but her eyes were closed and her hands clutched the sand convulsively. Hell! Fury washed over him. Someone had stolen her virginity before him. Who had she given it to? He should have been the first — and the last.

Angrily he jerked out, causing her to start up in fright. Seeing the frozen blue eyes staring angrily at her, she cried out in real fear. What had happened? He gave her no time for thought as he grabbed her roughly, pulling her up towards him, then in one furious, revengeful plunge, drove in deeply. She gasped, not so much in pain as in despair. He wanted to hurt her. Tears slipped from her eyes.

But even in his overwhelming anger, Jake was determined to burn out any trace of the man who had gone before him. He slowed himself, determined to give Alexandra something to remember, something to make her forget that other man. Controlling himself, he moved in her slowly, reassuringly, determined to bring her with him.

She opened her eyes in wonder, suddenly aware of the change, but stifled her cry when she looked into his hard, blue eyes, bright slits of anger. Oh, what was he doing now? Her thoughts were wild, distorted, frightened, then slowly they began to focus on the mounting tension within her. Was there no release? She couldn't stand much more. Her body had broken out in a fine film of sweat. As he kept moving within her, she reached out, drawing him to her, wanting more, demanding more until finally the raging fire exploded and she rushed into oblivion, taking him with her.

He fell on top of her heavily, sweat trickling down onto her breasts, as his breath came in great heaves, drowning out her own gasps.

As their breathing stilled, she became aware of the waves crashing in upon the shore and the cool water swirling up around them, outlining their bodies as one. But it was a momentary oneness for as the water receded, there was nothing left to prove that it had once formed the shape of two people joined together. Suddenly Jake moved, rolling from her, and she was cold, alone, vulnerable as never before. Would she ever be the same again? No, she knew now. She knew how it felt to be joined with another in supreme bliss, to be one with Jake. The water swirled up around them again, but this time it outlined two separate bodies. She felt sad, as if she had lost something that should have been treasured and kept always.

"Who was the first one, Alexandra?" Jake asked, lying on his back in the soft sand, his voice hard as flint.

"What?"

"Who was he?"

132

"Oh!" Alexandra sobbed, rolling over on her stomach as if to hide, to forget what had happened before him. And what right did he have to know? He condemned her without knowing. That was what had happened when he first began making love to her—he had discovered she was not a virgin. Stan had been right. No other man would want her once he had taken her. Oh, how she hated him, and she hated Jake, too, for condemning her so quickly.

"Tell me, Alex." He gritted his teeth as he grabbed her wrist, squeezing it painfully.

"No. You won't believe me. You'd rather think I was a whore," she sobbed, refusing to look at him.

"Damn it, Alexandra, tell me his name." He knew he was hurting her for her face blanched as he pressed harder, knowing how easy it would be to snap her tiny wrist, but still he wanted to hurt her, punish her for her unfaithfulness.

Controlling her tears, but feeling the coldness in her heart returning, she glared at him with green eyes like bits of glass. "All right, if you must know. I was raped by a man who wanted to marry me. He told me that once I'd lost my virginity no other man would ever want me. I hadn't thought it would make so much difference, but I can see that I was wrong."

"Rape?" Jake said softly, wondering if she spoke the truth.

"Yes, rape. But you'll never believe me and I don't care. I really don't care. Just leave me alone," she said coldly, determined to retain as much of her dignity as possible.

Could she be a whore who played a virgin as Sully had suggested? Jake thought. Had she played him for the fool? Had she played them all for fools? "His name, Alexandra. I want to know. Tell me."

"There's no need. You'll never meet him."

"Tell me his—" Jake began, but suddenly stopped, gripping her wrist even harder as his eyes quickly scanned the dark, shadowy wall of palms which bordered the silver sands of the beach.

She watched his face questioningly. What did he see, or hear? He had stiffened, like an animal sensing another presence, but what was out there?

"Get dressed, Alex. Then slowly walk toward the ship. Whatever you do, don't look back, and act natural," he hissed, his eyes still searching the shadows.

"But what—"

"Shhhhh. Don't ask any questions, just do as I say." He squeezed her wrist in warning, then let her go.

She felt her heart beating rapidly as she got up unsteadily from the clinging sand. This unknown enemy was even more terrifying than something she could have seen. She picked up her gown—torn, dirty, salt stained now, and quickly slipped into it. She put on her sand-filled slippers, ignoring the gritty feeling on her feet in her concern to get away from the beach.

Not looking in any direction, she started walking as quickly as she dared down the moonlit beach. She had taken only a few steps before Jake fell in beside her. He was wearing his trousers. He didn't look at her, but put his arm comfortingly around her waist.

Suddenly shots rang out and sand splattered in front of them where the bullets drove deep into the soft sand. Jake didn't hesitate. He pulled Alexandra with him as he broke into a run. She could hardly keep up with him, and as more shots rang out, she stumbled, falling to one knee. He jerked her up, pulling her more fiercely after him.

Suddenly he stopped dead still. She looked at him in surprise, then in the direction that he gazed. She gasped, instinctively moving closer to him. Directly in front of them stood Caroline, a long, black whip dangling from her right hand, with Hayward and Sully on either side of her, guns in their hands.

"Did you really think we were so stupid, Jake?" Caroline asked softly, gently flicking the whip over the sand like an undulating snake.

"I thought you were smarter than to tangle with me, Caroline. We would have gone in peace. I don't want a quarrel with you," Jake said, his voice tightly controlled.

Alexandra stood there, intensely aware of the malevolent expressions on their adversaries' faces and the hard tenseness of Jake's body touching her own.

"Give her to us, Jake," Hayward said coldly, his face like a mask of death as he glared first at Jake then at Alexandra.

"Give us what belongs to us, Jake," Sully said as he leered obscenely at Alexandra in her wet, clinging gown.

"Yes, we want her, Jake," Caroline said, almost purring.

Alexandra shrank back, her hands clutching Jake for protection. She had thought there could be nothing worse than the three Clarkes trying to run her life. But they wanted to rule her in life. These people wanted to rule her in death.

"All three of you know Alex is mine. I found her. I keep her. I've made her mine."

"But, my darling double-crossing love," Caroline said coldly, letting her whip flick toward them, "you are unarmed. Give her to us, or they will shoot her now. Do you want her dead?"

The guns were trained on Alexandra for an instant. Jake shoved her behind him.

"You think you're clever, Jake?" Sully asked. "That won't work. I only have to walk around behind you while Hayward guards you from the front. Give her to us."

"Stop playing with them," Caroline said sharply, suddenly losing her patience. "I want that woman!"

She snapped her whip once, twice, then sent it reeling toward Jake in a vicious snap at his eyes. But he was ready for her move and caught it in his hand. He jerked the whip, and Caroline fell, still clinging to the weapon. He took the few steps to her. As his foot crushed mercilessly down on her hand, a sharp, commanding voice rang out in the soft stillness of the night.

"Drop the guns — slowly."

Alexandra glanced up in surprised relief to see several brawny sailors under Morley's command, all armed with rifles which were trained on Hayward and Sully.

Jake jerked the whip out of Caroline's hand, then threw it far away into the surf. He gazed coolly at her sprawled form, then stepped back and took Alexandra's hand.

Caroline struggled to her knees, then stood up in all her feline magnificence and glowered at Jake and Alexandra. "You may have won this time, Jake, but don't ever set foot in the Bahamas again," she warned angrily, her brown eyes hard.

"Don't worry. I have no plans for that. There doesn't seem to be any reason now."

He smiled down at Alexandra, but it didn't

extend to his eyes. She wondered if he did it to taunt Caroline. She would not soon forget his earlier anger, or hers either. He had unfairly condemned her, and she knew instinctively that it would be something not easily worked out between them.

"I have no need for more bloodshed," Jake said. "There was enough of that in the war. Alexandra belongs to me and let that be the end of it."

He bowed curtly, then turned to give instructions to Morley before taking Alexandra by the arm. He led her toward his ship which she could now see anchored not far away. It was a welcome sight after what she had just been through, and it would have looked like a safe haven if not for the hard, unforgiving man who walked by her side.

Part Two

In the Land of Cotton

Chapter Nine

Alexandra paced the captain's cabin on *The Flying J.* They were in the port of New Orleans, but she was virtually Jake's prisoner. Although they had only been together a few days since leaving the Bahamas, Jake had decided to keep her with him. He would not listen to her pleas that she had to stay in New Orleans, that she had business in the city. He was going to Texas and he was taking her with him, one way or another.

Jake quickly settled their relationship once he had her on his ship. When he wasn't on deck, commanding his ship, which fortunately had been most of the time, he was in his cabin with her, teaching her the art of love. She fought him, for she could not give in to a man who treated her as a high class harlot. She never succumbed without a fight, but still he was so strong and somehow, her own body always turned traitor in his arms. She was furious with herself for responding to his desires, yet when he came to her, her own body would rise eagerly to join his until she lay exhausted and satisfied in his arms.

She could not understand herself. She had never felt about anyone as she did Jake. He outraged her with his demands and his assumption that she would be glad to stay with him, doing anything to be with him. Well, he was wrong. She was her own person. She had her own life. And she would not allow herself to become prisoner of the strange power he seemed to have over her body. She would escape him. She *had* to escape him!

And then, there was her promise to Olaf which she was determined to keep. She was in New Orleans. She had come a long way and through a lot to get here. She would not allow herself to be whisked away to some barbarous place in Texas by a man she didn't even like, much less trust. No, she had to get off Jake's ship and out of his life.

Her first problem was clothing. She had the one gown that she had worn from the Bahamas—and no underthings. It was embarrassing, but she simply had nothing else, except the garish shawl that she had found in Jake's trunk. At least that would hide the bodice which was cut much too low for the daytime, exposing half her breasts.

She had no money. She could not risk contacting her bank in New York for as surely as she did, Stan Lewis would know exactly where to find her. She would have to slip away from the ship, and make inquiries in New Orleans for the Jarmons. She was determined to find Olaf's family and perhaps they could help her. She was certainly in no position to help them at present, she thought unhappily.

Jake had left the ship early that morning. He had told her not to leave, or he would hunt her down. His hard blue eyes had threatened her and she knew his temper would flare if she did escape, but it made no difference. She was determined to leave. He had also told her that he would be gone several days, and when he returned, he would bring her new clothing and take her on a tour of New Orleans. She had decided that he must actually believe Captain Sully's taunt that she was a whore fleeing to New Orleans; why else would she come to the city? And then, why mind going with a man to Texas? Fool! She would show him!

All of *The Flying J* sailors had been given leave, except Morley, who was in charge of her, with strict instructions from Jake to keep her locked in his cabin. The old sailor had been kind to her on the trip from the Bahamas and she had grown fond of him so she felt a little guilty for what she would have to do to him to escape, but it was necessary. She had been waiting impatiently all day for Morley to bring her dinner. It would be her best chance to escape since he would have to unlock the door and come in. She was just sorry it was getting so late in the day. She would much rather have been venturing into the unknown city in full daylight.

Then she heard the knock on the cabin door that she had been expecting. Morley, at last. Determination turned her eyes a hard, glittering green. She must not think of Morley's past kindness to her, or of Jake's fury with him when he discovered her gone. She had to escape no matter what. As the knock came again, more urgent, she picked up the nearly full whisky bottle Jake had left on his desk. It was the best weapon she could find and it would have to do. She tiptoed to the door, positioned herself behind it, holding her weapon ready.

The knock came again, louder, more persistent. Morley called out in concern, "Miss Alexandra. Miss Alex. I've brought your dinner. I went into New Orleans and bought you fresh fruit and vegetables. You'll enjoy the change. Are you asleep? Well, I'll just be coming in then and leaving the tray."

A key turned in the lock. Alexandra tensed, ready with the bottle. Morley pushed the door open. Just as he stepped into the cabin, she brought the bottle down on his head with all her strength. It broke, spilling its contents down the man and spraying her as broken glass flew from the force of the impact. Morley's knees buckled and he crashed heavily to the floor, the dinner tray spilling its contents all around him.

Alexandra quickly checked to see that he was still breathing, then she grabbed up the shawl and a blanket from the bunk. She threw the blanket over the old sailor, wrapped the shawl around her shoulders and left the cabin, closing the door tightly shut behind her.

As the soft April night fell over New Orleans, she stepped onto the quay, pulling the brightly colored shawl more closely about herself, acutely aware of the stench of whisky that had soaked her gown. Although the day had been warm, she could feel the cool, damp evening air penetrating her clothes and curling the soft hair that had escaped the knot at the back of her neck. She smoothed down her skirts, then looked about. Nothing was familiar, of course, and she didn't know which way to go, for she knew nothing of New Orleans. But she knew she must do something quickly. She walked determinedly away from the dock, heading for what appeared to be the main part of the city. Perhaps she could find a church there and make inquiries, or at least find a place for the night within its safety. She had no money for a hotel, and she certainly did not want to be out alone at night.

She plunged into the narrow streets of New Orleans. It was darker here for the buildings blocked out the dying rays of the sun, and she pulled the shawl more closely to her body, as if in defense of the eerie, deepening shadows around her. Without realizing it, she moved toward the sounds of people, deeper into the dark

145

labyrinth of streets, and closer to what she hoped would be safety.

But as she continued her fast pace along the dimly lit streets, turning first down one and then another, she grew more and more confused and steadily more aware that she was not approaching a church. For as she hurried along, more sailors passed her, calling to her, and from dark, shadowy doorways, shapes beckoned, calling her to them.

As dusk turned into night, street lamps spread their pale luminous glow to the buildings and people, Alexandra realized that she was not in the best part of town. She hurried even faster, feeling her heart grow cold with fear as she tried to find a better section of the city. Suddenly a stranger grabbed at her shawl, suggesting things in a low voice that she could not believe he said. Where was she?

Finally, out of breath from her frantic pace, she stopped and looked around. She was on a narrow street lined with two and three storied buildings. Light streamed from the open doors of each building, and loud, tinny music blared from them all. The sounds of high pitched women's laughter and the low, mellow sounds of male voices chimed with the music of piano and fiddle to fill the street with a chorus of raw noise. Alexandra stared at the rough, coarse, crude-looking people about her, and knew that she had somehow stumbled into a *very* bad part of New Orleans.

What was she to do? As she pondered her problem, another brawny sailor stopped, pulling her roughly to him. She pushed at his broad, hard chest desperately.

"Where's your place, honey? You're a frisky little thing, aren't you?" he said loudly as his hand reached down boldly and fondled her hips.

Alexandra cried out, trying to hit him. But he merely caught her fists, laughing.

"Yes, you're a hot-tempered one all right. That's the way I like you ladies. Don't worry, I've got money. Just been in port a few hours. You make it worth my while, and I'll spend it all on you," he said, his hands roving over her body until they reached her full breasts, then quickly darted under her shawl for better contact. "Oh," he moaned, "you're a beauty, a real beauty."

As Alexandra struggled to free herself, he held her close, one hand at the small of her back, while the other kneaded her breasts, trying to get to her bare flesh.

"Let me go!" she cried sharply, hardly able to believe the man was pawing her in the streets.

"So you like to play games, do you? Suits me. Now, where's your place?"

"I don't have a place, you—you slime!"

"No? With your looks, I'd have thought you'd have your own room. Well, for you I'm not adverse to a carpet. Where is it? You want to put it down right here, or you got an alley somewhere staked out?"

147

"No!" she cried, savagely jerking away from his embrace. She began running down the street. Her long gown hampered her so she pulled it up around her knees as she ran on, bumping into people, being caught by lecherous hands ready to feel any woman, until finally she fell over a drunk sprawled across the street. Picking herself up, she hardly noticed her raw, scraped hands in her desperation. She ran on, her breath coming in ragged, burning gasps.

She could still hear pursuing footsteps behind her, and she knew the lusty sailor must surely be following her, or another equally horrible man. How could she get out of this labyrinth of terror? The street was seemingly endless, and men and women in various stages of dress lined the block, as well as the barrel-houses and dance-houses on either side. She had never seen such a place before or even dreamed it existed, and she was beginning to know the stark terror of fear.

Suddenly several large hands clamped down on her from all around, stopping her in mid-stride. She shrieked, horrified, and lost her balance, falling into what seemed to be a huge group of sailors, laughing and grinning down at her.

Ogling their prize as they hurried her along with them, the lusty sailors pawed her trembling body as she tried to knock their hands away. They slipped her in between buildings into a back alley, then shoved her to the ground.

She shrank back from them, not knowing how to escape.

"You can't get away, my pretty, as if you really wanted to. Since you seemed to need some subduing, I called for my mates. They'll be glad to share you. Didn't I tell you she was a looker?" the sailor asked the others and they quickly agreed, coming closer.

"Please, please, you don't understand. I'm lost. I don't belong here," Alexandra cried out desperately.

"Didn't I tell you she liked to play games? You like a little fight? Is that right, honey?"

"No! No! Stay away from me. I'll scream."

The sailors all laughed as they advanced on her. Then one said, "Won't do you no good, girlie. There's plenty of screams go on in Gallatin Street all the time. No one will care, and there's no police here. They don't dare come into Gallatin Street."

There were three of them, she saw. Big, brawny sailors who could tear her to pieces if they had a mind to, but a hot, fierce fury was growing in her. She was determined that they never touch her. As the first sailor knelt over her, she slapped him hard across the face, crying, "Leave me be, you brute!"

He growled, rubbing his jaw, then leaned toward her again, but he stopped suddenly as a hard, feminine voice rang out in the dark alley.

"Now, you boys don't have to go forcing the ladies of Gallatin Street. I've got a place with soft beds and willing women. Come on, sailors, don't waste your time with this one. Come with me."

Alexandra hardly breathed, anxiously awaiting the sailors' reaction. Would they leave her to go with this woman? All three men had turned to look at the curvaceous body silhouetted in the soft glow of the street lamps. There was a moment as the men hesitated, trying to make up their minds.

"Now, come on, boys, I ain't got all night, neither have my girls. Gallatin Street's busy tonight so you'd better find your spot early."

This seemed to decide the men. After glancing at Alexandra once more, they quickly followed the woman back onto Gallatin Street, the last one giving Alexandra a final pinch before throwing her a few coins and laughing as he left her alone on the dirty, littered ground of the alley.

She huddled there for what seemed a long time, trying to collect her thoughts, her courage. She had come so close to being raped that she still felt weak. How could a place like this exist? Would she have been better off having stayed in New York City? This could never have happened to her there. But yet she *had* been raped there, in her own home. She thought longingly of Jake for a moment. He would never hurt her. But no, she wouldn't think of him. He was gone from her life forever. What she had to do now was get out of this place called Gallatin Street

150

and to a church somewhere without being raped or molested.

She felt the coins that had been thrown into her lap, then laughed harshly. Well, she had been paid, paid because they had thought her a streetwalker. Nevertheless, she was no longer without funds!

Silently she vowed that she would not succumb to the terror and weakness that threatened to overcome her. She had been pursued by men ever since she had left New York City, but she would take care of herself. She was a Clarke and she would do whatever was necessary to survive. Her green eyes turned hard as she clutched the coins in her hand and stood up. She would learn the rules of this cruel world and play the games that had been thrust upon her.

Reaching down for her brightly colored shawl, she understood that it, the low-cut gown, and the smell of whisky that clung to her branded her as a streetwalker. All right, then, she thought, if that is what she appeared to be, she would play her part, but only up to a certain point. She would do whatever was necessary to get out of this dreadful place called Gallatin Street. And throwing the bright shawl over her shoulders, flinging her riotous curls back from her face, Alexandra stepped out boldly onto Gallatin Street, determined to survive.

There was a horde of streetwalkers, sneak thieves, garroters who openly carried their deadly strangling cords, and footpads with sling shots looped about their wrists who swooped down on the country men, sailors, and steamboat men seeking women and diversion in Gallatin Street. She walked among them all, calling back to the men who propositioned her in a friendly, easy way, but always saying no — regretfully. She was popular, a radiant beauty among the street's throng, and she began to feel her power as a woman again.

Her plan was working well, for she was accepted as a streetwalker, and she was even beginning to grow accustomed to the noise, the pinching, groping, and jibes that she received everywhere. And since she was taken for one of the street's own, she was not molested or hurt. As she made her way down the street, hoping to soon find her way out, a man grabbed her, jerking her into his dance-house.

She blinked blindly into the light after the half darkness of the street as he whispered urgently to her, "Business is brisk tonight, baby. You're lucky. We can use a good looker like you in there. You know the rules — ten percent of the drinks and all the tips you get, and I'll bet you get plenty. If you do well tonight, I might take you on permanent." He leered at her with small, beady eyes, his sour breath warm on her face.

"I — I — "

"Don't thank me. Business is good, and we can use a looker like you to give the place class. But remember, you got to pay for the room upstairs in advance. All the girls do. I'll take it now. You'll have a man later I've no doubt." And with those words he grabbed the money from her hand and shoved her into the room.

Alexandra started back toward the door, anxious to get out of the place, but as she did, a greasy, dirty man grabbed her around the waist and began hauling her across the room. She was not given a chance to say no, or to escape, for the man was strong and held tightly to his prize.

As he hurried her across the room, she had a chance to look around. It was her first glimpse of the inside of a dance-house. There was a long bar running the length of the front room and behind it, on high stools, sat the bouncers. There were four or five of the giant rough fellows armed with clubs, sling shots, knives and brass knuckles on both hands. She had never seen such a sight before and gawked in astonishment as her partner pulled her by the bar and toward the back room. One of the huge bouncers nodded at her, his eyes raking her body in evaluation and obvious approval. She looked quickly away, afraid that the great brute might take an interest in her.

The back room, she soon discovered, was the dance-hall where music of a sort was being made on a tinny piano, a fiddle, and a dented trombone. The dance-house women wore knee length calico dresses, slippers which were badly scuffed and rundown at the heel; their hair was worn long and loose. They were dancing, if the rowdy movements they performed could be called dancing, with scowling, black-bearded, red-shirted men who presented such a motley throng that she could imagine them as part of a pirate crew in Lafitte's day.

There was a sort of grim determination set on their faces that she found interesting. She wondered if these people ever laughed, ever really enjoyed themselves. The women might have been pretty at one time, she thought, but now they were dirty and rough looking. The men seemed quite satisfied though; perhaps it was all they expected.

"Here, honey," said the man who had brought her into the dance-hall. "This'll make you dance like a dream. What's your name?"

"Alexandra," she muttered under her breath, hoping he hadn't heard and wishing she'd given another name.

"Lannie. Nice name. Here now, down your drink. You know the rules."

He put the drink in her hand, then tilted her arm toward her face. She wasn't going to resist or struggle. That would only get her hurt. She would play their game the best she could, then escape. She put the offensive smelling drink to her lips, worrying how clean the glass was. He nodded encouragingly, his slightly glazed eyes watching her closely, then threw his head back as he downed his glass in one swallow. She tried to do the same, but as the fiery liquid slid down

154

her throat she choked, coughing in misery and confusion.

He was soon slapping her on the back, saying, "It wasn't that bad, honey. Same as any other liquor in these dives."

Finally, when she managed to catch her breath, feeling as if her throat and stomach had been burned, she gasped, "You like it?"

He almost smiled. "Like it? Never thought about it. Who drinks it for taste?"

She nodded in dumb disbelief as she felt the raw alcohol spread through her veins, leaving her flushed and relaxed.

She had no way of knowing that her floor length gown, bright shawl, and gleaming hair was causing a sensation in the dance-hall, and it was not the men who were most concerned. They enjoyed the sight. The strumpets had a strict dress code and any woman not adhering to it was asking for trouble from the others. Without realizing it, Alexandra had broken the code and it was only a matter of time before the other women decided to take action against the newcomer.

As the man started to pull Alexandra out onto the dance floor, one of the roughest, toughest-looking of the women working for the dance-house walked up to Alexandra. She stopped in front of her, hands on hips, feet wide spread. Alexandra's partner seemed to fade away, for he had obviously seen this kind of trouble before and he knew better than to get involved.

After looking Alexandra up and down, the woman said, in a deep, loud voice, "I'm Wanda. You new here, honey?'

Alexandra looked around uncertainly as the other dancers stopped and formed a circle around them. "Yes. I'm — Lannie."

"Lannie, is it? Well, Lannie, how come you think you can get away with wearing clothes like that?" Wanda asked, snorting derisively.

"It's all I have," Alexandra said, sensing that the woman wanted trouble. Yet, she felt no fear and wondered if it were the unaccustomed liquor in her body, or just a belated reaction to all the recent violence.

"Ha! Don't give me that trash, girl. You don't need this pretty shawl," Wanda cried, tearing it from around Alexandra's shoulders to throw it high in the air. It landed midst the crowd and there was an immediate scramble, then it was ripped apart and thrown back to Alexandra.

She looked at the tattered remains on the floor beside her, then back at the woman. She said nothing, her heart pounding wildly in her chest as she held onto her temper.

Wanda was grinning, a harsh twist of her mouth, "See, honey, you didn't need that. You don't need that fine long dress either." She reached out, ripping Alexandra's gown at the shoulder.

Suddenly Alexandra had stood all she could. Her anger finally boiled over. She shoved the woman back from her. Wanda growled and

156

glared at Alexandra like a wildcat after its prey. They paced each other warily. Alexandra was too angry to feel any fear. The crowd surged around them, calling out to the women. Sides were taken. Bets were placed. Some called out for Lannie, as they thought of Alexandra, but most of them called out for Wanda for she was a well-known fighter on Gallatin Street.

Wanda was a tall, large-boned woman with long, heavy straight blond hair, sharp blue eyes, and large red lips. Her Germanic heritage showed in her buxom breasts and ample hips. She could have been a Valkyrie as she lowered her head and charged.

Alexandra stood still a moment, hesitating as Wanda plunged toward her, the large strong hands outstretched. At the last moment, Alexandra ducked back just as the woman reached her. Wanda turned around, frowning as she found Alexandra again, closer now. She jerked out, clasping Alexandra's small wrists, and pulled hard. Alexandra fought against the woman, struggling back from the massive breasts, but her strength was not nearly as great as Wanda's force.

Alexandra was suddenly snapped against the strong chest and squeezed until the breath left her. Anger swept through her as she gasped for air and in her fury, she kicked out savagely at Wanda's shins, causing the woman to scream in pain as she let go. Immediately, Alexandra flew against the woman, scratching, clawing at the fair skin. Wanda fought back, grabbing Alexandra's hair and jerking it fiercely. Alexandra moaned with pain and began pulling at Wanda's long hair.

They struggled, straining against each other, until Alexandra grabbed Wanda's bodice, pulling until the fabric gave way, exposing one huge breast. Growling in rage, Wanda let Alexandra go and reached up to rip Alexandra's gown clear to the waist — both breasts glistening naked in the light, their taut rosy peaks an invitation. The men groaned, straining closer to see more of the exposed women.

Then, facing each other once more, the two opponents threw themselves bodily against each other, fury overriding any other emotion in their attempt to be victorious. They went down, falling heavily to the dirty, littered floor, struggling in each other's grasp, rolling over and over against the feet of the watching crowd. As they fought on the floor, pulling each other's hair, scratching, biting, tearing at their clothing, neither could seem to gain supremacy. It was obvious to the crowd that neither had any intention of giving up.

But just as Wanda drew back her arm, her fist clenched, to give Alexandra a stunning blow, it was grabbed by one of the bouncers. She turned on him and hit him in the stomach instead, then turned back to Alexandra, who took the opportunity to land a well placed fist in Wanda's eye. She screamed and began clawing at

158

Alexandra. But the bouncer summoned help. Now, two brawny men got between the struggling women much to the dismay of the crowd. The crowd knew better than to oppose the huge bouncers, and grumbling, went back to their dancing.

Alexandra felt her anger cooling as one bouncer held her tightly, dragging her up the stairs to the second floor of the establishment. She looked wide-eyed at the small rooms where the harlots did their private entertaining during the day. She tried to struggle against the iron-like grip of the bouncer, but he simply tightened his hold until she could hardly move.

Suddenly they all stopped before one of the rooms. The door was opened and Alexandra and Wanda were pushed inside. One bouncer looked Alexandra up and down. She clutched the tattered remains of her gown over her breasts, determined to fight him off if he approached her.

Instead he turned to Wanda. "Give her a dress. Hers is ruined."

"What!" Wanda exclaimed. "Do you think I'm made of dresses?"

"Shut up, slut," he snapped. "Give her a dress. The boss wants her back down on the floor. He's got a special interest in her. He thinks she's classy. Get her the dress, then come on back down. You know it's a busy night." He glared at them in warning, then slammed the door shut, enclosing the two women in the room.

Alexandra could hear the bouncers' heavy footsteps retreating as she and Wanda eyed each other warily. She did not know what to expect next.

Finally Wanda shrugged. "Well, honey, you may be new, but you're not a bad fighter. With a little more experience, who knows?"

Alexandra felt a surge of relief that she would not have to fight again.

"We'd better get you dressed," Wanda went on. "I've got a gown that'll about fit you." She pulled two rumpled dresses from a drawer, then threw one at Alexandra before shucking her torn gown and methodically putting the other one over her naked, dirty body.

"Is there a place to wash?" Alexandra asked hopefully.

Wanda laughed harshly. "Hell, honey, nobody washes here. Forget that. Won't make no difference later anyway. You'll just have a man up here, and they never notice."

"Well, I really don't think —"

"Sure dancing's hard work, but you paid for a room, didn't you?"

"Well, yes —" Alexandra began, slipping off her torn dress then hurriedly putting on the other.

"Then you'd better get your money's worth. Pick out a rich looking man. And if you need any help later getting his money, call on me. I know how to handle a man who doesn't want to be parted with his money."

"I can well imagine."

"Come on, we'd better go down. The boss wants us out there."

Alexandra tried to push up the bodice of the low cut gown for it barely covered her nipples, but nothing could be done about that or the short length. She would just have to endure the evening.

As they went out the door and started for the dance-hall, Wanda pointed downstairs. "Make those men pay for anything they get, honey. It's the only way to survive."

Chapter Ten

Wearily Alexandra sat down on the lumpy bed and pulled off her badly worn slippers. She sighed deeply, rubbing her red, swollen feet. Never in her life had it felt so good to sit down. She wondered if her feet would ever be the same again after a night of trying to dance on them while avoiding the clumsy, booted feet of a score of men. What she wouldn't have given for a basin of hot water to soak them in, but she knew that water was almost unheard of in the dance-house. Here no one even drank it!

What a night, or rather what a morning. Nothing had shut down until dawn and then most of the men had paid to share a woman's bed and come upstairs. She had been offered money to share her own bed, and it hadn't been easy to say no and not simply be carried off. But the boss had kept an eye on her so she hadn't been molested.

The boss hadn't cared what happened on the dance floor as long as the brawls didn't damage his furniture. In fact, dancing was hardly what anyone did as the night wore on, for the women drank more and more of the mind dulling liquor and soon they began discarding their clothing. Alexandra had been horrified when she'd noticed that several of the couples were dancing completely naked. And many of her partners had tried to remove her own clothing. It hadn't been easy to remain sober, clothed, and unmolested throughout that endless night. In fact, many of the naked couples had finally had to be thrown out by the bouncers when what they were doing could no longer be considered dancing, or even close to dancing. And she had no doubt that the couples finished their frenzied lust on the street or in an alley. Anything was possible on Gallatin Street, she now knew, and she also knew that she had to get off Gallatin and out of the dance-house during the day when everyone was sleeping off the night.

The boss had decided to take her in as a permanent dancer, with a hint that she would be servicing him, too. She had not been forced into his bed yet because there had been so much business the night before. She had to escape while she could before she was dragged down into the mire of this life and could no longer find the strength to escape. For, with dancing at night and being used by men during the day, a woman would soon have no energy or will left *to* escape. She could now easily understand why the women that worked here looked so tired and worn out. They were aging before their time at the hands of these insatiable men. She would have to leave, and soon. But she needed rest first and she felt sleep claim her.

A bloodcurdling scream brought Alexandra out of her deep sleep. Chills ran through her body as she looked quickly around her small, cramped room. There was no one with her. How long had she slept? She was completely disoriented and had no idea what time it was.

Suddenly the quiet was again shattered by hollering, cursing, and fighting in the room next to hers, then out into the hall. She recognized Wanda's deep, resonant voice. She got up and ran over to her door to open it slightly.

Two of the bouncers were dragging a man down the hall as he screamed, "I've been robbed. She took everything I had, the bitch! I demand she give it back! Return my money!"

The man was causing so much noise that one of the bouncers knocked him out with one mighty blow. The man hung limply between the two bouncers as they dragged him down the stairs.

Alexandra noticed that Wanda was watching her. She winked, then motioned for Alexandra to come to her room. She did, thinking that perhaps Wanda could help her get out of the dance-house and off Gallatin Street.

"Sit down, honey," Wanda said, motioning to her rumpled, filthy bed as she tightened the belt around her sheer dressing gown. It concealed very little of her voluptuous body, but she didn't seem to notice, or care.

Alexandra still wore her dance-house dress since she had nothing else. She sat down on the bed as there was nowhere else to go. She watched Wanda as she poured a glass of liquor, then motioned toward Alexandra with her glass.

"No thanks."

"This isn't that rot gut stuff they serve those poor bastards downstairs. This is good. Buy it myself."

"No thanks," Alexandra repeated.

Wanda shrugged, then came to sit on the bed beside Alexandra, fluffing the pillows up behind her back and leaning against the wall before she said, "That fool. He ought to know better than to bring that kind of money with him to Gallatin Street. If I hadn't relieved him of the burden, someone else would have and then he might not be so lucky to still be alive. 'Course, now I'll have to share with the bouncers, but I suppose it's worth it. I thought he was out cold. He came to when I was searching his pockets. Damn the luck!"

"You do this to all your customers? I thought they paid you for your—services."

Wanda grinned. "Sure they pay me, but I try to pick the ones with money. I'll take anything a man has on him. We all do. You'll learn, too, if you plan to stay here." She glanced up at Alexandra with those words.

Alexandra was beginning to realize that perhaps Wanda didn't want her around; did not want the competition. Good. That would suit her plans perfectly. "To tell the truth, Wanda, I just needed a place for the night. Now—"

"You paid for it last night, but you didn't get your money back. You could have had any of the rich ones. How come you didn't take a man?"

Wanda looked genuinely puzzled, but Alexandra didn't want her to know the truth yet so she shrugged her shoulders.

"Come on, honey, I know your game. The boss. Sure, he has an eye for you, but take my word, he's not one to stick with a woman after he's had his fill and that don't take long—don't take long at all. He may set you up in a room here, but believe me you'll pay more trying to please him than if you worked straight like the rest of us. You see, the boss's girl has to service his special customers. You don't want that, honey. I've known too many who didn't live through one of those nights. You wouldn't live long. You're too delicate. Anybody can see that. Now me, it'd take a hell of a lot to kill me, but still I don't cater to the boss's type of affair."

Alexandra watched the woman closely, not quite understanding what she was trying to say about the boss, but Wanda was sincere, she felt sure. "And you'd as soon have me out of here just in case the boss might take to me permanently?" Alexandra asked, hoping that she understood Wanda correctly.

166

Wanda said. "You're sharp, honey. You don't belong on Gallatin Street. You could be a fancy whore for some man. You see, the boss is mine. He can have other women for his affairs, but when it comes to a permanent woman, I don't plan to let nobody take my place. You got that?"

"That's fine, Wanda. Look, I don't want a row with you because I'd come out the loser. But if you want me out of here, you'll have to help me."

Wanda's eyes narrowed. "You'd leave?"

"Sure."

"Good. I can get you out."

"Well, I'll need a little more than that."

Wanda frowned, her face hard and unrelenting.

"Not only do I want out of this house. I want off Gallatin Street."

Wanda nodded again. "I understand. You want to be set up in a parlor-house in the *Vieux Carré*. Why shouldn't I just bash your head in and drop you in the river, or the gulf either?"

Alexandra's heart thumped hard. Wanda could do exactly that and she had no doubt the dancer would if it suited her. She'd have to be careful. "No reason, Wanda. I could use your help, that's all. I don't demand it."

"You damn right you don't demand it. Nobody does! Well, I kind of took a liking to you. You got guts and you got brains. I'm not set to

167

see you out of this life. But I don't part with no gold and that's a fact."

"I don't expect that. I thought you might introduce me to someone."

Wanda nodded. "That could be done. Soon be late enough. But, mind you, I don't want to see you back on Gallatin Street. I'll kill you if I find you here again."

Alexandra nodded quickly. "I won't be back if we can get this set up."

"It's a deal then."

Wanda thrust forth her large, strong hand and clasped Alexandra's firmly, her eyes holding the gaze of the tired green ones for a moment as if to make Alexandra understand the importance of their bargain. It could not be broken, but that suited Alexandra fine.

"I'll give you a shawl," Wanda said, standing up. "That dress is all right for the dance-house, but you're going to *Place d'Armes,* Jackson Square, and it won't do there. A shawl will make you acceptable. After all, you're a whore same as any other."

Alexandra knew that if she didn't get off Gallatin Street Wanda's words might soon be true. There was little else for a woman to do here.

Wanda grabbed two shawls from a drawer and threw one of the filthy, ragged garments to Alexandra. She pulled it around her shoulders and held it firmly in front to cover her low cut dress.

Wanda went to the door, eased it open, then

looked both ways in the hall before motioning
for Alexandra to follow. Once out of the room,
they walked quickly, turning down several halls
before finally coming to the back staircase of
the dance-house. Again, Wanda stopped, motioning for Alexandra to remain quiet and where
she was, then she continued down the stairs to
the bottom. In a moment she was back, motioning for Alexandra to follow her. They crept
down the stairs, through the back door, then
were out in the alley, which was littered with
garbage and drunks sleeping off the night's
liquor. Some of the men had cracked heads,
blood congealed on their matted hair. All had
their pockets turned out.

Alexandra carefully tried to avoid the bodies
as well as the litter as she walked, but it was not
easy and she stumbled, almost falling several
times. They walked this way silently for perhaps a
couple of blocks.

"We'll soon be out of Gallatin," Wanda said
thoughtfully. "I don't like coming out like this.
Ain't safe for me. Police out here."

They walked only a short distance more before
Wanda stopped abruptly. She jerked her head
rapidly to either side, searching the cross street,
then, satisfied, turned to Alexandra.

"Look, honey, this is the end of Gallatin
Street. Now, you follow my instructions and go
to the *Café du Monde* in Jackson Square. Order
a coffee, or whatever. Wait there until a woman
comes for you. She's a real beauty, Madame

LeBlanc is. Has a place—real fancy—on Basin Street. I'll send her a message about you. She'll be good to you and you can meet the rich Yankees through her. They've got the money now."

Alexandra nodded, looking anxiously around her. Yes, she could see the difference past this point, but she was amazed that Gallatin was such a short street for last night it had seemed endless. At last she would get off Gallatin!

"Thank you, Wanda," Alexandra said, glancing at the woman who had first fought her, then helped her.

"Here's a few coins, honey. Buy the coffee, something to eat, then wait like I said. She'll come out about dusk, I'd imagine. Now, take care. Don't back talk to the police if they give you trouble. They can be mean except on Gallatin Street. They're afraid to come here. They don't get out alive. No sir," she said, smiling suddenly. It changed her entire face, revealing that she had once been a young, pretty girl, but fate had long since changed that.

"I'll be all right," Alexandra said with more conviction than she felt.

"Sure you will, honey, but remember our bargain. I don't want to see you here ever again."

"You won't," Alexandra promised and after listening closely to the directions Wanda gave her, smiled and walked away, turning her back on Gallatin Street.

Alexandra trudged hurriedly forward on tired, aching feet, determined to make Jackson Square

170

as quickly as possible. At least this area of New Orleans had police and she would feel safer. She had no intention of meeting this Madame LeBlanc, but she could do with some food and perhaps she would see a church in the area.

As she walked through the *Vieux Carré,* or French Quarter, she could not help noticing the beautiful houses. There was gorgeous wrought iron everywhere, used as gates, on balconies, set around windows. She could easily see the French influence, although the buildings seemed built to conceal their beauty rather than expose it, suggesting interior courtyards in all the homes.

There seemed to be an assortment of houses, restaurants, and businesses along the streets so that she could not tell exactly what kind of district it was. There were not many people about and the sun had begun to go down. She simply had to find a church before it was dark.

Following Wanda's instructions exactly, she at last came upon a large square surrounded by various buildings. This had to be Jackson Square. She walked to the beautiful center of the square, a park with deep grass, ancient trees, flowers, and benches. She sank down on a bench gratefully. At last, she felt safe. Now, how to go about finding a church? But that was quickly settled for as she looked around, she saw a large, magnificent cathedral.

Delighted, she got up and started toward it, smoothing her skirts. Then, remembering her clothing, she looked down in dismay. Hunger gnawed at her as she tried to smooth her hair and straighten her clothes. But it did little good. She looked like a streetwalker and she knew it. What if they wouldn't help her in the church, or even let her inside looking as she did? Well, she would eat first and then try to clean her face and clothes. She knew she would be stronger and more sure of herself if her stomach weren't empty.

Her decision made, Alexandra went into an outdoor café. She realized too late that it was the very one Wanda had suggested, the *Café du Monde*. Well, she decided rationally, since it was early, she would be gone before this Madame LeBlanc arrived. Besides, she was too tired and hungry to go on. She sat down gratefully on a small, wrought iron chair at a tiny round table under the bright awning of the outdoor cafe, then gave her order to a reluctant and snooty waitress.

Could she look that bad, she wondered, pushing her long hair back. The only answer could be yes from the way people were staring at her as if she didn't belong and shouldn't be there.

The young waitress quickly brought a steaming cup of *café au lait* and hot *beignets* to the table. Alexandra handed her the money and got back very little in change, not enough to eat again, she quickly realized. Wanda had not been *that* generous. She sipped the coffee and nibbled the sweet French doughnuts, wanting to lengthen her pleasure. She hadn't realized how really fam-

172

ished she was, or how completely tired. But sitting there, safe for the moment, all her problems came flooding back. As she completed her meager meal, she leaned her head tiredly on her crossed arms and closed her eyes.

"Excuse me, mademoiselle. Would you be Lannie? I see the hair and surely there could not be two such colors in all of New Orleans. I am Madame LeBlanc," a strangely accented voice said softly so that only Alexandra could hear.

Alexandra jerked her head up, stumbling to her feet. Madame LeBlanc! She looked wild-eyed into the large black eyes of a beautiful woman, one of the most unusually beautiful women she had ever seen. Madame LeBlanc was petite with a perfect figure, and a mass of luxurious black hair was piled high on her head. But her skin was her most striking feature, for it was a warm, mellow shade that seemed kissed by the sun. And her clothes were expensive, exquisitely tailored, and worn with natural grace and style. Alexandra had never seen a woman like her before.

"May I join you, mademoiselle?" Madame LeBlanc asked politely.

Alexandra looked hesitantly around, not knowing quite what to do, then nodded. "Yes, please do."

The woman gracefully sat down, motioning for Alexandra to be reseated. Alexandra did so, feeling too tired to think, or go anywhere else. She had never seen a real madame before and

173

this intriguing woman carried herself like a lady, looked like a lady. Alexandra was relieved to at least see this.

"Chérie, Wanda did not tell me that you would be such a rare beauty. Your hair alone is worth a fortune and I'm sure your body is perfection itself, although I will, of course, want to see more before we agree to anything."

Alexandra looked back at her, stupefied.

"Ah, but I rush you. I see you've eaten, but please be my guest to more. I do so hate to eat alone."

Alexandra just continued to stare with large green eyes, bewildered and confused.

Madame LeBlanc's order was quickly set on their small table and the plate heaped high with hot *beignets* was pain to Alexandra until she could put one to her mouth. As she ate, still watching Madame LeBlanc closely, the woman pulled a small container from her reticule and poured a golden liquid into both their cups of coffee.

"I believe you need something stronger than coffee, *chérie,"* she said. "You look exhausted. How did you ever end up on Gallatin Street? It's hardly safe for anyone, especially a young lady like yourself."

The kind words and the coffee laced generously with brandy began to restore Alexandra's spirits as well as strength. She smiled hesitantly at Madame LeBlanc.

"I do appreciate your coming, Madame, but I

174

fear you have made a trip for nothing."

"Oh?" Madame LeBlanc asked.

"You see, I accidentally walked into Gallatin Street and, well, I'm only too grateful to just be out of that place."

The woman laughed shortly, showing small, perfect white teeth. "No wonder, *chérie,* that place is hell itself. I often wonder why Wanda insists on staying there, but I think I really know. You are lucky to be alive, *ma chère.*"

"Yes, I realize that now."

"But how could you possibly have wandered there?" she repeated.

"I'm not from New Orleans. I arrived yesterday at sunset and not knowing my way, ended up there."

"A young lady, unescorted? You are obviously not from the South by your accent. I find this odd. If you are not looking for employment in a brothel, what are you doing in New Orleans, and how do you possibly think you can survive?" she asked as if Alexandra might very well be mad.

Alexandra smiled, finishing another *beignet.* "I came here looking for the relatives of a close friend of mine who died recently. I became lost from my companions."

Madame LeBlanc's perfectly arched brows rose slightly. "I see. That, of course, can happen, and much as I'd love to have you in my house, I will help, if I can, to find your friends. Their name?"

175

"Jarmon," Alexandra said softly.

Madame LeBlanc's eyes widened, showing more emotion over this one word than anything else Alexandra had said. "Jarmon! Did you say Jarmon?"

"Yes, that's the family name. I believe they have a plantation, or did before the war."

Madame LeBlanc smiled, a gleam in her eyes. "Oh yes, they did and still do. I know the Jarmons well, quite well, especially the two sons."

"Really?" Alexandra asked, feeling relief flood through her, the mention of two sons not registering. "Are they in New Orleans? Could I see them soon?"

Madame LeBlanc raised her hand to stop the flood of questions. "They live on their plantation now. I do not see the Jarmon boys as much as I once did, but that is as it all is. The war has left nothing the same," she said sadly. "We all do what we must to survive."

Alexandra looked into her eyes, now dark liquid pools of sadness. "I'm sorry. I—"

"No, mademoiselle. It is all over now. Our wounds will heal, or we will die, as our South has died."

Alexandra did not know what to say. She had never thought much of the South after the end of the war. It obviously was dreadful for the Southerners and she only now began to realize it. They really hadn't been affected in the North, except that business had boomed, especially her shipping firm. There was no end to the North's need of ships, and her fortune had increased greatly during that time. But these poor people had been left with little when it was all over. She dreaded to see the once magnificent plantation. Would it be in ruins? But at least she knew the Jarmons were still alive.

"Now, do you want to rejoin your companions here in New Orleans—those from whom you were lost last night?"

Alexandra knew the madame hadn't believed her and it was a weak story anyway. "I came alone. I lost all my trunks in a storm near the Bahamas."

This time Alexandra saw a sparkle of deep interest in Madame LeBlanc's eyes instead of disbelief. "Wanda mentioned that your name was Lannie, but it is not, is it?"

"No, it's Alexandra, or Alex if you prefer."

Madame LeBlanc smiled like a contented cat, and Alexandra began to feel alarmed.

"Alexandra, of course. This grows more interesting all the time, mademoiselle. You say you want to visit the Jarmons, but they are not your kin?"

Alexandra did not want to tell her more, but she felt that the woman would not help her if she didn't give her some type of story. "As I said, they are related to an old friend of mine who died recently. I decided to come here to visit them and tell them of his death."

"Just which of the Jarmons did you plan to visit?"

Madame LeBlanc was making this difficult, Alexandra thought, but surely the woman had no way of learning her true identity by this little bit of information. "Well, I'm planning to visit Eleanor Jarmon and her son, Jacob Jarmon."

Madame LeBlanc smiled, a self-satisfied movement of her lips. "So you are Alexandra who appeared in New Orleans last evening on your way to visit Eleanor and Jacob Jarmon. *Ma chère,* you positively have made my day, my week, my lifetime."

Alexandra watched Madame LeBlanc's eyes glow with some emotion she could not define. She grew more apprehensive. Would a woman like this help her? Had she ever helped anyone except herself? She must get to the Jarmon plantation with or without Madame LeBlanc's assistance.

"Yes, that is all true. I must see them soon. I will be fine if you will tell me where their plantation is." Alexandra adjusted her tattered shawl.

Madame LeBlanc laughed, a tinkling sound that chilled Alexandra. *"Ma chère,* you obviously have lived in a city all your life. You have no idea of the acres and acres that a plantation can cover and the miles that you must travel to get there. Also, there are all kinds of riffraff roaming the area. You could not possibly walk that distance by foot, even if you were properly attired, and you could not hope to arrive there unmolested, if alive."

Alexandra blanched, having been unaware of

the facts. Was it really so bad in the South? If only she could send for money, then all her problems would be solved.

"I had no idea."

"Obviously. Now what will you do for me if I help you get to the Jarmon plantation?"

Alexandra's face turned even paler, her eyes grew wide, but not in fright. She hadn't realized that she must pay this woman for her help, but of course, she would want that.

"I have no money now, but when I get some I could repay you."

Madame LeBlanc sniffed. "That will never do, *ma chère*. I will not have you in my debt—that would not be profitable."

"I'm sorry, but I have nothing, absolutely nothing now."

"You are no virgin, are you?"

"No." Alexandra said slowly, afraid of what she would hear next.

"Wanda told me that you were very popular at the dance-house last night, but that you sold yourself to no one later. That's really not smart, *chérie,* but you obviously have much to learn."

"I'm not a harlot."

Madame LeBlanc smiled. "Don't be absurd, *chérie.* All women are, even if they are married. Women sell their bodies for many things. They have no choice. But we professionals sell our wares for cash. It is an infinitely better situation, I believe."

Alexandra tried to keep her surprise to herself,

179

but she could see that Madame LeBlanc had read her expressive face. It was a viewpoint she had never thought of before, but perhaps this woman was right. If she had married Stan Lewis, he would have taken her body and in exchange she would have had security, children, no worries. But she didn't want a marriage like that, although she knew that a lot of women did, indeed, marry men for their money, their position, what they could do for them. But did they have a choice? She was lucky to have a fortune that allowed her freedom from necessity. She wanted to marry for love, and if she couldn't, she would never marry at all. In love, there was only giving and receiving, and that was the way it should be.

"I'd never thought of it like that," Alexandra said finally.

"You're not married?"

"No."

"Good. I don't propose that you play the harlot while in my house unless you want to, only come there, stay a few days, and entertain. Nothing lewd, of course, but surely you sing, play the piano. We are very discreet in my house. You would have no troubles with the men. They would simply admire you and word of your extreme beauty and unusual hair would quickly pass through New Orleans. It would bring more business my way. That would pay me, and then we could see that you had a decent gown and underthings to wear when you go to the Jarmons. I would send you in my personal carriage.

"Now, that is a good deal. You would be foolish to turn it down. After all, you've spent the night dancing in Gallatin Street. You would only end up there again tonight and perhaps worse would befall you. And the church? They would not even let a woman who looked like you past the doors. The government? You would be raped there most likely. You see, *chérie,* my offer is very good, even if I asked you to work one of the rooms for a few nights. What do you say?"

Alexandra did not have to think long on it. Singing in a brothel was unbelievable to her, but it was infinitely better than another night on Gallatin Street. And she believed Madame LeBlanc about the church and government. Besides, how could she possibly arrive at the Jarmon plantation in her condition? The decision was out of her hands.

"I accept your offer. I do sing and play the piano, but unfortunately the songs I know will be Yankee songs."

Madame LeBlanc laughed. Her dark, intelligent eyes roamed over Alexandra, considering the possibilities. "Perfect. You don't really think Southern gentlemen, what there are left of them, could afford LeBlanc's girls? Hardly. We cater to Yankees, *chérie,* and are well paid for it."

"Oh, I hadn't realized."

"The Yankees have been here a long time. We

are used to their ways, although they will never be accepted."

Alexandra nodded, lowering her eyes as she realized that she was one of the hated Yankees. When she looked up there was a large dark man dressed in livery standing beside their table. He bowed briefly to both women.

Madame LeBlanc glanced at him, then spoke to Alexandra, "This is my driver, Jonah. He will escort you to my carriage. Wait there for me. I will be with you shortly."

Alexandra stood up, feeling completely lost, and walked ahead of the huge man with as much dignity as her clothing would allow. The carriage was sumptuous, expensive, and surprisingly not garish. The driver held the door open for her to enter and she sank gratefully down into the cushions.

Chapter Eleven

Relaxing in a hot, steaming bath, Alexandra felt as if she might really be alive after all. She made no attempt to wash herself yet. She had no desire to move any part of her body. All she wanted to do was rest and let the water erase all the pain and memories of her recent past. Of course, she knew the memories would still be with her, but the hot bath was helping to ease the pain of them.

She let her eyes roam around the sumptuously appointed bedroom. The fireplace and mantel were of white marble, and the furniture, upholstered in rep and damask, was of highly polished solid black walnut, as was all of the woodwork. The floors were covered by richly colored Oriental carpets. The hangings of the huge bed, even the mosquito bar, were of lace, and an exquisite basket of flowers hung suspended from the tester of the bed. Around the

walls were hung chaste and costly oil paintings. It was a magnificent, although gaudy,
room. She had never seen its like before, but
was well aware that it must have cost a small
fortune.

She sighed, hardly able to believe that she
was actually in a brothel, a bordello, an assig-
nation house, whatever one wanted to call it.
She was actually in a place where women sold
their bodies for money. Of course, they had
done the same in the dance-house, but there it
had been a different atmosphere entirely. Madame LeBlanc had explained on the way from
the coffee house that she ran an expensive
brothel of extreme elegance and formality. She
encouraged only high-class trade and rowdies
who occasionally invaded the house were
promptly ejected. Her girls wore evening
dresses, and bawdy talk and behavior were not
allowed. They were all ladies and they were
treated as such. She also explained that she de-
pended principally on the carpetbag politicians
for her business, and while they bled the city,
she was making her money from them. It was
the only way to survive the aftermath of the
Civil War.

Alexandra had never before realized that such
a life for women really existed, or at least it
had never seemed so real before. When explained from Madame LeBlanc's viewpoint, she
could understand why some women had turned

to this trade to survive. Had many of them really been given another choice? With so many of the men dead after the war, and probably a lot of the women raped, the women were left with no way to survive without a man to support them. Some had been forced to turn to the oldest profession. She realized that in her own case, if she had not had her own money, after being raped, she might have made the same choice. If a woman were not a virgin, she had little chance to marry.

As the water began to cool, she ran the scented soap over her body, reveling in the simplicity of being clean once more. She had never realized what a luxury it could be. As she washed her arms and legs, she noticed scratches and bruises turning purple on her pale skin. Gallatin Street had left its mark on her both emotionally and physically, and it would be some time before she was free of its reminders.

She washed her hair thoroughly, lingering over the marvelous feeling of suds in her hair. Finally, when she felt clean, she rinsed, then picked up the soft linen and wrapped it around herself as she stepped from the gilded tub. As she began to rub herself dry, the door opened and Madame LeBlanc walked into the room. She hurriedly covered her body, embarrassed by her own nakedness.

Madame LeBlanc stopped a short distance from her, smiling. "You shouldn't be so shy,

Alexandra. A body is a beautiful work of art. You should be willing and happy to share what is your gift to the world."

Alexandra smiled back, amazed that this woman's viewpoint could be so different from everything she had been led to believe and yet still make sense. "I'm just not used to being naked with others."

"Well, you must grow up. Now, remove that cloth so I can see your body."

Alexandra shyly removed the fabric and held it away from her, embarrassed as the madame's experienced eyes looked her over as one might check a horse for sale. She felt a sudden stab of apprehension, but pushed it from her mind.

"Lovely, truly lovely, *chérie*. You could make a fortune if you decided to work here. You could command the highest price — at least twenty dollars an hour. You have so much class, so much style. You are a rare beauty all over. It's a pity you're ashamed of the idea of using your body, but perhaps you'll change your mind," she said, her eyes hard as bits of coal.

"I, I don't think so, Madame LeBlanc, although I thank you for the compliments."

"Hmm, yes, well, we'll see. Now, I must find you something to wear tonight. The men will begin arriving soon and I would like you to entertain them later. You are in my suite, but I will find you a small room later where you may sleep — alone."

Alexandra began rubbing her hair dry as the madame threw open the doors to her wardrobe, revealing rows of expensive evening gowns. She thought back to Captain Sully's words that an expensive whore must have a fine wardrobe. At the time she did not understand his reasoning, but it was all painfully clear now. And although she might try to understand this business, she could never become a part of it, she knew.

Flipping through the gowns, Madame LeBlanc pulled out a soft green one. "I believe this will fit," she said. "I keep gowns in several sizes in case a girl arrives just as you have. One must always be prepared." She laid the gown on her bed, then went over to pull out sheer silk underthings, hose, and finally a pair of green slippers. Placing everything on the bed, she turned back to Alexandra. "Would you like me to help you dress, or shall I send in a maid?"

"I believe I can do it myself," Alexandra said, wanting to be alone.

"All right, *chérie*. I will send a small tray of food up to you. You will be drinking later and I don't wish you to become sick or tipsy. When you have eaten and dressed, please join us below. And don't be afraid. It should be an interesting experience for you."

Alexandra lifted her chin, determined to make the best of the situation and determined not to act like a child again. Smiling, she nodded at Madame LeBlanc. "I appreciate your hospitality

187

and I will enjoy the evening, I'm sure."

Madame LeBlanc laughed shortly. "I believe you would make a renowned lady of the night, Alexandra, if you would unbend some. One must take their pleasures where one can and inhibitions only prevent this. I'll look forward to seeing you later," she said softly in her emotionless voice, then shut the door tightly behind her.

Shivering in the cool air, Alexandra began to dress. The undergarments were very risqué and the chemise was cut low, barely covering her nipples. She walked over to the full length mirror and looked at herself. Her thick, curling hair fell all around her in disarray and with the transparent chemise, she looked too sensual to be a lady, yet her bearing demanded respect. She sighed as thoughts of Jake suddenly came to mind. What would he do if he saw her dressed like this, in a room like this? She laughed, a soft low sound. There was no doubt what he would do. Shivers ran over her body as she recalled Jake's hands on her, his mouth, his hard body pressed to hers. He had awakened something in her that she had not known existed and now, now she wanted more.

Thrusting these thoughts from her mind, she walked hastily back to the bed and pulled the soft, green silk gown down over her body, pulling it into place. It fit like a second skin, clinging to her soft curves. Fastening the bodice, she walked back to the mirror. She was amazed at what she saw.

There was no young, innocent girl looking back at her, but a woman, with a woman's hips and breasts, full and soft and inviting. Madame LeBlanc certainly knew what she was about, she decided as she put on the soft slippers.

A timid knock came at the door, and a tawny-colored Negro girl walked in, carrying a tray. Her eyes grew large at the sight of Alexandra in her clinging green dress. She hesitated, then set the tray down, "You're sure the prettiest girl I've ever seen."

Alexandra laughed. "Thank you. Do you, uh, work here, too?"

The girl's eyes grew wider. "No, ma'am. White women and dark women can't work in the same house. Madame LeBlanc says that soon I'll be able to work the men at one of the other houses. I think she'll teach me when it's time."

And before Alexandra could say another word, the girl was gone.

A mere child and already she plans to become a whore, Alexandra thought in amazement. And the girl was pleased, proud. But then, what kind of life would she have otherwise? She shook her head, very much aware of the different world she had entered.

Looking at the food, she realized that the coffee and doughnuts had long since left her and she was ravenous again. Raising the silver covers on the expensive dishes, she saw a feast that would have delighted even the most snobbish of women. Madame LeBlanc must have a very fine French chef indeed. As she ate, savoring the delicious French cuisine, she knew she was really very well off, for her surroundings, the food, her clothing were better than anything she had known of late. If she hadn't been in a brothel, she would be perfectly content until she could reach the Jarmon plantation.

Finishing the delicious meal, Alexandra leaned back in the delicate chair, thinking that now she had no excuse not to join the others below. Standing up, she smoothed out her gown, and left the room. She entered a long, carpeted hall and followed it in the direction of low laughter, voices, and soft music. Stopping briefly on the landing, she gazed in wonder down into the foyer. There were two statues representing some obscure divinities holding lighted flambeaux. She continued down the stairs, her eyes roaming over the sumptuous interior of the house. She paused in the entrance to the drawing room, noting the expensive paintings in gilded frames, the plated mirrors, the delicately-tinted furniture.

The conversation seemed to drift away, finally stopping completely as the occupants of the room discovered Alexandra. She stiffened, raising her chin slightly, while keeping a slight smile on her lips, and entered the room. Her green gown softly flowed around her legs as she walked gracefully, elegantly into the room which contained perhaps fifteen beautiful young women in glittering, form-fitting gowns with several men standing and sitting around.

"Alexandra," Madame LeBlanc said softly as she approached, looking beautiful in a shimmering white gown with a deep decolletage. She took Alexandra's hands in hers. "How nice of you to join us. Please come and meet our guests."

Alexandra followed until she was in the center of the room, surrounded by the others. "I want you all to meet Mademoiselle Alexandra. She will be here for a while to play the piano and sing for us. She has lately arrived from the continent and is considering making New Orleans her home—so please make her stay a happy one and perhaps she will grace our home permanently."

There was a general murmur of agreement, then one man said in a soft, Southern accent, "Please allow me to buy champagne for everyone in Mademoiselle Alexandra's honor."

This suggestion was quickly accepted and soon a Negro boy was passing around sparkling champagne in crystal glasses on a heavy silver tray. Alexandra accepted her glass, while wondering at Madame LeBlanc's lie that she was from the continent.

The man who had bought the champagne came over to Alexandra and stood closely by her side as he raised his glass in a toast. "May the most beautiful woman in New Orleans stay with us long enough that we may know her better, much better," he said loudly for everyone to hear.

Alexandra blushed, and the man smiled warmly at her, then said for her ears alone, "You are indeed a rare beauty, and such delicacy—a blush. I have not seen one in a long time. It is indeed a pleasure, Mademoiselle Alexandra."

He clinked his glass with hers and the rest of the company raised their glasses in a salute to Alexandra. She drank quickly, covering her embarrassment, feeling as if she were the show before she even sat down at the piano.

The man standing beside Alexandra was handsome, or rather beautiful. There was nothing rugged about him, yet there was a masculine sensuality in his perfectly carved features that a woman could not ignore. He was only a bit taller than Alexandra, and slender. Helplessly, she compared him to Jake. There was nothing similar between them. This man had luxurious black hair and unfathomable black eyes that now regarded her with a mixture of desire and curiosity. She became uncomfortable under his scrutiny and lowered her gaze.

Madame LeBlanc approached them, a glass

of champagne in her hand. "I would like you to meet Giles Beaumont, of the New Orleans Beaumonts. I see Mademoiselle Alexandra has gained your interest quickly, Giles." She patted his arm familiarly.

"*Enchanté*, Mademoiselle Alexandra. Your beauty and elegance surpass any that I have had the pleasure of encountering before."

His soft, low voice was tinged with a hint of the Creole accent that Alexandra remembered from Madame LeBlanc's voice. In fact, there was something vaguely familiar in his features, but she couldn't place it.

"You are from Louisiana, Mr. Beaumont?" Alexandra asked.

"Please call me Giles. I think we will be great friends."

Alexandra blushed, afraid of his implication. "Of course, thank you — Giles."

"Yes, I am. I own a plantation near here."

So not all of the South was destitute, Alexandra thought. "That must be very nice for you. It's lovely here."

A look of pain flashed across his dark eyes, then was gone, quickly snuffed out. "Yes, I suppose, but you should have seen it before the war."

"Please, don't mention the war," Madame LeBlanc said. "It brings back too many memories."

"Would you be so kind as to play for us,

Mademoiselle Alexandra?" Giles asked.

"Indeed, I would be delighted. Madame LeBlanc?"

"Please do, *chérie.*"

As Alexandra walked across the room, she noticed that there was a wide assortment of men in the room. All had the look of success and money—their clothes and stance bespoke this, but none of them had the air of the natural born aristocrat as Giles Beaumont had, she decided. It was something that could not be bought, although it could be acquired by a few special people. For the most part, it had to be inbred and these men simply did not have it and never would. She decided that these must be the Northern carpetbaggers that Madame LeBlanc had mentioned. What a difference in these men and the celebrated Southern gentlemen one had heard so much of before the war—a man like Jacob Jarmon's father, the man Olaf's daughter had fallen in love with, a real Southern aristocrat. She wondered if men like that would ever be seen again, except rarely.

The women were all lovely, beautiful in every sense of the word and in every variety, also. A man could have his choice of any type of woman here and perhaps any nationality. There was no doubt that they were all dressed like ladies and in the drawing room acted as such. And for the first time Alexandra wondered about the word, *lady.* She had always thought it meant a woman of gentle birth and breeding, but these were harlots who acted and looked like ladies. She could not even tell herself what they really were. They all had beautiful carriage and manners. What did, indeed, make a lady?

Two small men dressed in black bowed to Alexandra as one left the piano and the other put down his violin. They both disappeared into another room, leaving the music to her. It was an expensive, well-tuned piano, she realized, as she began playing a light, airy tune that had been popular in New York when she had left. Soon she added her own clear, sweet voice to the music of the piano, and when she finished the first number, she was surprised to see Giles standing by her side.

"Beautiful, *chérie*," he said smiling at her. "Please, play more for us."

Alexandra was happy to play since she felt more hidden behind the piano, but she wished that Giles had not chosen to stand beside her for he made her nervous and too aware of herself as a woman.

As she sang and played a variety of numbers, she noticed that Madame LeBlanc was approached first by one man and then another. Madame and the man would leave, then presently return. She would then speak with one of the girls, who would smile coyly at the man and join him. Soon they would leave the draw-

195

ing room and go upstairs. It was very delicately handled, she thought. The pattern repeated itself several times as she played, and she was only thankful that she was not a part of it all.

After a while, Giles left her to join Madame LeBlanc, and she watched them apprehensively before they left the room. When they returned, Madame LeBlanc left Giles and came over to Alexandra.

"You must be tired, *chérie*. Please join Giles and myself for a drink."

Alexandra could not refuse and nodded agreement. As she left the safety of the piano, the musicians returned and began playing soft, slow, dreamy music. She and Madame LeBlanc walked over to Giles. He rose, helping Alexandra to sit down at a small table, then sitting down himself. Madame LeBlanc leaned over and smiled encouragingly at Alexandra.

"Alexandra, Giles is a regular customer of mine and most impressed with you. I thought you two might like to become better acquainted," Madame LeBlanc said, then nodded before walking away as another guest was announced.

"*Ma chère,* I do hope you won't consider me presumptuous or rude if I tell you that I was struck with your beauty and grace the moment you entered the drawing room. So much so that I have been unable to look at another woman since. Can you be so cold-hearted that you would deny me the pleasure of your company for at least one hour, or an entire night if you would be so kind?"

Alexandra blushed furiously. No matter how delicately he put the words, his intentions were the same. It was much better than being thrown down and raped, but still, *still* it was the same thing in the end.

"Ah, you have blushed for me again. How very charming. You needn't fear me. I would be very gentle with you. I approached Madame LeBlanc and she told me that you were unavailable by your own request, but can you be so hard-hearted to a man who adores you as I do?" Giles' dark eyes softened as he looked entreatingly at her.

She felt herself weakening. Could it mean so much to him? But no, she could not sell herself this way. She would not be used like this. Her green eyes, soft and dark in the muted light, turned harder. "No, I'm sorry, sir. I appreciate your great compliment and interest, but I'm here tonight to play music and that is all."

Watching her closely, he smiled. "It would be worth a great deal to me, Miss Alexandra. Say, fifty for an hour."

Alexandra's eyes opened wide, knowing what a great deal of money that was for a woman. Then she smiled, feeling a sudden power sweep through her. "You do me more honor than ever, but truly, I am not available tonight except in the drawing room."

Surprisingly he appeared not the least perturbed. "Madame LeBlanc said you were a prize and a most unusual lady. I must have you, no doubt about it!"

Alexandra could not keep herself from gasping. The man spoke with such determination and finality. "I, I—"

"Never mind. Name your price, or your night, Mademoiselle Alexandra, for I am available to you at any time and for any amount."

Alexandra realized that she could not say no to this man—he did not understand the word. "You honor me greatly, sir, with your suggestion, and yourself, but tonight is not the night for us."

He smiled broadly, then raised an eyebrow knowingly at her. "You want to make it special, yes? Good. I can wait. It will only be all the better when we're finally together," he said as he covered her hand with his own strong one.

Alexandra steeled herself not to jerk back from his searing touch and smiled into his black, determined eyes. "You say, sir, an entire night at any price. That could be very expensive. Are you sure I would be worth it?"

He laughed lightly. "Indeed, yes. You'd be worth any price, my beauty, but don't make me wait too long. I can become an impatient man and I shall touch no other woman until you, *ma chère*. But now, I must go because being with you without being able to hold you in my arms can not be long endured."

Alexandra held her smile as he squeezed her hand, then got up, calling for a bottle of champagne to be served to Mademoiselle Alexandra. With a last penetrating look in her direction, he left the establishment.

She breathed a sigh of relief and even took the glass of champagne that was offered her by the Negro boy who expertly set the bucket of champagne down on her table. She took a long drink, hoping it would relax her after her experience with Giles. He was a disturbing man, a handsome man, a man obviously used to having his way with women, but he didn't touch her deeply. And she did not trust him—he was too smooth, too sure. She knew she would have to get out of the brothel and to the plantation before he became more demanding and insistent. She frankly didn't think she could keep him at arm's length for long—especially here.

She smiled as she saw Madame LeBlanc coming toward her, graceful and beautiful in her gown.

The madame sat down and poured a glass of champagne for herself. "You've certainly impressed Giles, and he's a hard man to please. Did you know that this champagne costs a customer fifteen dollars a bottle?"

Alexandra's eyes opened wide. "So much?"

Madame LeBlanc nodded. "It's part of the

profit. They're expected to buy it for everyone in the room, but he really outdid himself tonight."

"You know what he wanted?"

She nodded. "I knew you would be an instant success, *chérie*. All of the men have asked for you, but accepted my word that you were not available. Now, Giles is a most determined man. He offered fifty an hour for you. That is quite extravagant and you can be sure that he would return frequently. You could make a lot of money this way, *ma chère*. Won't you reconsider?"

Alexandra shook her head. "He offered that to me first, then offered any price I named for a night."

Madame LeBlanc's eyebrows rose dramatically. "Really? He's more smitten than I realized. I've never heard a better offer than that. Did you turn him down flat?"

"He doesn't seem to take no for an answer and seems to think that I'm just waiting to make special plans of some kind."

Madame LeBlanc laughed low in her throat. "That sounds like Giles. Ah well, perhaps you will yet change your mind. Why don't you come with me now. You might be more agreeable if you understood this better."

Madame LeBlanc stood up quickly, as if making a decision. Alexandra got up also, following her out of the drawing room and back up the stairs toward the bedrooms. They went back into Madame LeBlanc's bedroom, across it, through a sitting room, then stopped before a closed door.

Madame LeBlanc turned to Alexandra, putting a finger across her lips, as a warning to be silent. They walked into a dark, closet type area. Alexandra stood very still, feeling quite strange and uneasy while the madame sat down on a small stool and pulled back a tapestry on the wall. Then she put her eye up to the bare wall. Satisfied, she motioned for Alexandra to take her place.

Reluctantly, Alexandra did. From the peephole, she could see directly into another bedroom in which one of the harlots was entertaining. She was a plump blonde with pink white skin and huge, ponderous breasts that were now dangling down freely toward the face of a man who was lying on his back across her bed. Both were completely nude. Alexandra jerked back, suddenly aware of what she was doing. She looked up at the madame who frowned as she pushed Alexandra back to the wall. She had little choice except to obey or make enough noise to bring the lovers down on them. It was over as quickly as it had begun. The harlot got off him and casually moved away, throwing on a sheer negligee.

Alexandra pulled back from the peephole and Madame LeBlanc looked closely at her face, then nodded approvingly. She led Alexandra out of the closet and back into her bedroom.

Alexandra felt ashamed and embarrassed. Why had Madame LeBlanc insisted that she watch that? What did she really want of her?

"Alexandra, it is time you learned more of life. There are many ways to please a man other than the traditional way of which you are probably aware, but we will not go into that at this time. I have chosen a room for you. A lovely room near my own suite so that you may contact me quickly if the need should arise."

She led Alexandra out of her bedroom and down the hall until she opened a door. Alexandra entered, but Madame LeBlanc did not follow.

"You needn't come back downstairs. Remember, what you saw tonight was quite normal and accepted. You must learn these things if you're to be a complete woman."

And with those words Madame LeBlanc turned and walked back down the hall. Alexandra quickly shut the door, locked it, and looked wonderingly at her ornate, ostentatious bedroom with its overshadowing bed. Did Madame LeBlanc really plan to let her go in a few days, or did she plan to keep her here and make a fancy harlot of her? She was worried and realized that she had better make plans for escape, if she could. But first she was going to rest. She was exhausted mentally and physically.

Chapter Twelve

Almost a week had passed since that first night at Madame LeBlanc's brothel, and Alexandra was most anxious to leave. She had not been forced into any liaison with a man, but she did entertain every evening and speak with the men who came. Giles still continued to be a most persistent visitor and for the moment he seemed content to wait, but she didn't know how long that would last. Somehow she knew that he expected her to want him and that by being patient, he would gain her. But it would not be that way, she knew.

Last night she had confronted Madame LeBlanc about leaving. She had spent enough time at the brothel and had told the madame she was anxious to go on to the Jarmon plantation. Surprisingly, Madame LeBlanc had told her that tonight would be her last night at the brothel, and that tomorrow she would see that Alexandra was at the Jarmon plantation. Madame LeBlanc had brought her a pretty, simple dress with lovely underthings, matching shoes, and a cape to take with her. There was also another gown more elegant for the evening. There was even a small valise in which to carry it all. It was ideal and she could have been much more pleased if she had understood the situation and Madame LeBlanc's motives. But she could learn nothing from Madame LeBlanc and there was no one else to ask so she planned to get through the evening as quickly as possible.

The others were down in the drawing room and the men had begun to arrive, Alexandra knew, but there was no reason for her to join them yet. She would have plenty of time to entertain them later. Leisurely, she took off her negligee and looked at her naked body critically before the mirror. The bruises and scratches she'd gotten on Gallatin Street were not as noticeable and she'd put on a little more weight. Still, she was thinner than usual. Yet she didn't think it unbecoming for her breasts were still round and full. The skin was stretched more tightly over her face, but she looked pretty in a more mature, refined way.

Suddenly, she glanced hurriedly around the room. She felt that someone was with her. Again. She had the same feeling almost every evening when she dressed or undressed—as if someone were watching her. Always the memory of the other peephole came to her mind, but Madame LeBlanc had assured her that her room had none. She had examined the room, but had found nothing. Still, the feeling persisted.

She hurried over to her clothes and slipped into her underthings. This chemise was more revealing than any she'd worn before and it was in a sheer fiery orange to match the gown that Madame LeBlanc had given her. She slipped on the gown and walked over to the mirror. What she saw looked more like a harlot than anything she had yet worn. Her hair seemed almost on fire as it reflected the color of the gown—the shimmering, red-orange seemed almost to have a life of its own. And this dress was not modest in the least. It was of the sheerest silk, molded to her breasts and waist, then falling loosely to the floor in yards of the filmy material. And it was cut low, barely concealing the pink of her nipples, so that if she leaned over in the least one could see their points. Why had Madame LeBlanc chosen this dress? A man's first thought could only be to tear off the gown and take what it concealed, making it his own. But there was nothing else to wear. Madame LeBlanc would be furious if she wore either of the two country dresses, and she could not afford to anger the woman at this point. Well, she would go ahead and see the evening out.

Alexandra's eyes hardened defiantly as she walked down the hall. Nothing could make her less than the lady she was, she decided, not even entertaining in a brothel. She followed her usual route down to the drawing room and saw the same beautiful harlots with a group of men. These men were rarely the same, although a few of the faces had become familiar.

Upon seeing Alexandra, Madame LeBlanc hurried to her. "You look superb this evening, *chérie*. I had the gown made especially for you, and it was well worth the cost now that I see you in it."

Alexandra smiled, her green eyes suspiciously watching her benefactress. "Thank you. It is lovely, although perhaps a bit revealing."

Madame LeBlanc laughed. "Not on you, *chérie*. They will love you even more tonight. They already have named you the Ice Maiden."

Alexandra raised her brows. "Ice Maiden? With this hair and gown?"

"That's what is so confusing to them and also so challenging," Madame said, looking as sensual as usual in a clinging gown of pale blue.

"But it's of no consequence to me. I'll soon be gone and they'll forget me quickly."

"And Giles?"

Alexandra shrugged.

"Are you sure you will not change your mind, and join our little group here as one of the girls?"

"No. I must get on to the Jarmon plantation. I will sing and play as usual—for tonight only."

For a moment Alexandra thought she saw the

dark eyes of Madame LeBlanc narrow in hate, but it lasted so brief a moment that she felt sure she must have been mistaken.

"As you wish, *ma chère.*"

Alexandra then walked over to the piano which the musicians had vacated for her, knowing the pattern by now.

She sat down, but before she could begin playing, Giles was at her side. "You are perfection itself tonight, *chérie.* I can hardly stand to be with you without taking you in my arms. But we'll save that for later, *oui?*"

Alexandra looked up at him, and started to give him his usual no, but he was already gone, ordering champagne for everyone. She shrugged her shoulders, glad that she was getting away from him. He was becoming more forward and demanding all the time. Then forgetting where she was, she began playing. Tonight she didn't play strictly the popular tunes, but more of the classicals—those which were her favorites.

Finally, when the evening had worn on into the early hours of the morning, Madame LeBlanc came to her holding a glass of bubbling champagne. She handed the glass to Alexandra.

"I know you must be tired, *chérie.* Why don't you drink this? It'll help you sleep, then go on up to bed. You can use the rest, I'm sure, before starting your journey to the Jarmon plantation."

"Thank you." Alexandra took the glass and sipped the liquid. She didn't really want the champagne because she'd already had so much, but Madame LeBlanc stood there watching her.

Pushing the piano bench back, she stood up, anxious for the privacy of her bedroom. She set the glass down on the piano. Madame LeBlanc picked up the empty glass and walked with her to the foyer. There, the madame smiled, but it did not extend to her eyes for they were cold and hard. Alexandra shook her head slightly, wondering why she suddenly felt so strange, so lightheaded, but attributed it to too much champagne.

"Good night, Alexandra. Have pleasant dreams," Madame LeBlanc stroked the glass.

"Good night," Alexandra said, then started up the stairs, carefully holding onto the banister.

With great relief, she found the door to her bedroom and shut it tightly behind her, clicking the lock into place. She felt quite strange. Her body felt hot and she was beginning to tingle and burn all over; nothing seemed quite clear any more. She sat down on the bed, the effort to undress almost too much for her.

As she struggled to undo her bodice, a sound made her turn her head. Giles was walking toward her, a smug smile set on his face. She stared at him, vaguely wondering how he had gotten into her room. She had not heard the door open. She also wondered why she felt no surprise at seeing him there and why she was not demanding that he leave. But for some reason she was very aware of his body, and of the fact that she did not want him to go. Languidly, she stood up, feeling desire growing in herself like a power over which she had no control. She felt hot, flushed, and she wanted, needed what this handsome, desirable man could give her. She held out her arms and he pulled her tightly against his hard chest; his hands were warm and exciting through the sheer fabric of her gown.

Downstairs, Madame LeBlanc smiled smugly to herself. The man she had been awaiting had arrived. Her timing had been perfect, but then she knew this man well, at least as well as any woman could ever know him. He strode easily into the elegant drawing room, making the furnishings look suddenly too feminine, too gaudy. He overpowered the room, making it seem small and crowded, where before it had been intimate and cozy.

There had never been another man like him, Madame LeBlanc thought. In all the times they'd been together, he had never tried to please her or even begin to love her. No, he was a man who took *his* pleasure, enjoying a woman for the moment. He was not a man to commit himself and yet, yet she had wanted him to love her, need her. He was the man she had always wanted. He was the only man who could satisfy her completely. Giles was good, but he was a gentleman and eccentric in his lovemaking. He could not fulfill her needs. This man could, but he had needed no one except himself until—now.

Madame LeBlanc watched his powerful, lithe body move toward her, his hard blue eyes quickly surveying the room. He was always aware, like the animal he was. Yet, he was well educated, a gentleman when he wanted to be. He was so like a hard, lean, young lion on the prowl with his tawny hair and spectacular body, but tonight she would tame the lion. He would finally feel the feline's claws, she thought, jealousy tearing at her. What did the little redhead have that attracted him so? She was nothing but a Yankee slut giving herself fancy airs. Well, he would know that soon enough now.

"Jake, *chérie*," Madame LeBlanc purred as the tall man stopped before her.

"Looking as lovely as ever, I see, Bella, and from your expression as calculating as ever, too."

She frowned, then smiled coyly up at him. "You always temper your compliments, don't you, Jake?"

He laughed. "Only when necessary, my dear. Now—"

"I thought you'd return earlier," she said as she guided him toward a table and poured him a glass of champagne.

"Do you have the clothes, Bella? I'm short of time. I've been busy ever since I got back. It's the first chance I've had to stop by."

"Then you haven't been to the ship?"

"No. Why?"

"I think I might have a little surprise for you."

"Damn, Bella! I don't need any surprises."

"Do you plan to spend the night here with me, Jake?"

"I haven't got time. You know that."

"You just used me to buy clothes for your woman, that Alexandra."

Jake frowned, his face menacing, and she knew she had gone too far. Jake had a devil of a temper. He had killed men for angering him. "I'm sorry, Jake. It's just that I'm jealous of any other woman with you."

His face looked only a little less severe as he shook his head. "You've never been jealous in your life, Bella. There's only one person you're concerned with and that's yourself. Don't try to make me think otherwise. We've known each other too well, too long for that."

She pursed her pretty lips, pouting. "Why don't you take me with you now, instead of that—"

"I'm going to Texas, Bella—permanently. You don't belong there. It's too wild, untamed. You like all this; you need it," he said, his eyes sweeping the opulent room.

"So, I can't help it if I was born a quadroon in New Orleans."

"No, but you made plenty of it. And now with the carpetbaggers you're doing quite well, aren't you? They don't know you're quadroon, do they, Bella?"

She shrugged. "Why should they?"

He nodded his head and smiled sardonically.

"You won't tell them, will you, Jake?" she asked, suddenly anxious.

"No, I'm going to Texas. It'll be awhile before I get back."

She pouted again. "I could make it in Texas. You just won't marry me because I'm quadroon, but I could pass as white—you know that. And I'm more beautiful, more skilled than any white woman, even that Alexandra. I could have gone up North and passed like the other quadroon did. They had little other choice when their protectors went off to war, but I've stayed, Jake, waiting for you to finally realize how good we are together."

Jake frowned. He had never known Bella to talk like this before. She had always taken the times they had together in as much fun as he had, but she had never asked anything of him. Marriage? She would make a terrible wife and she would never survive even six months in Texas—unless she was pampered in a brothel. She wasn't strong like Alexandra, or a fighter. No, Bella was a Southern quadroon, a beautiful

212

ornament, born and bred to be a Southern gentleman's mistress. There was nothing else she could, or would even want to do.

"Look, Bella, you knew from the first that we'd never marry. I'm not a marrying man."

"What about this Alexandra?"

"What makes you think I'll marry her? I want a woman in Texas. There are few enough there, and she's strong and determined enough to make it. Stay where you belong, Bella. Don't come to Texas. Now, where are the clothes?" he asked, suddenly eager to be gone as he thought of the golden-red hair and furious green eyes that he'd left locked in his cabin.

He had been too long without Alexandra. Even for all her fighting him, in the end she had wanted him as much as he wanted her. Damn! He had never wanted a woman like he wanted this one. He knew nothing about her, but that didn't matter. She belonged to him and he'd never let another man touch her. He became furious every time he thought of that Yankee raping her, using her to force a marriage. He should have been her first.

Thinking of her made his blood stir and he cursed to himself, wanting to be rid of Bella and New Orleans. He wanted Alexandra and Texas now more than anything. He didn't love her, but there was something about her that made him forget other women. No, whatever the reason for his desires, he didn't love her. That was

213

impossible. She was a wildcat and hated him. That made him laugh to himself. She hated and yet wanted him at the same time, although she would admit nothing except her hatred for him. Well, it would be fun to tame the wildcat. She and Texas would go well together.

"Do you want to see my surprise, or are you going to stand there with your trousers bulging all night? You know, other women can relieve that besides that redheaded bitch," Bella said sharply. She'd never seen Jake like this before. Her revenge would be all the sweeter.

"I don't have time for surprises, Bella."

Madame LeBlanc smiled her inscrutable smile, knowing that her revenge soon would be complete. Like all white men, Jake had never understood her, the quadroon woman—part French, Spanish, and a little Negro—whose heritage was steeped in the dark African jungles as well as sophisticated Europe. They were complex in their heritage, resorting to the use of either past to gain their end. Men loved their dark, sensual beauty carefully wrapped in European civilization, but they had coveted and lusted after their wild, uninhibited African blood. Bella would use whatever came her way, employing voodoo as well as Christianity to secure her revenge. Jake and Alexandra must be kept apart at any cost and she had made her plans well.

"You *have* time for this surprise, Jake. Come upstairs with me. The clothes are there and something else—" she said, letting her words trail off as she led him up the stairs.

Reluctantly, Jake followed. He only wanted the clothes and to be done with Bella. He was done with the South, too. There was nothing for a man here and when the carpetbaggers had finished taking everything, there would be nothing left for the Southerners except poverty and death. He hardly noticed Madame LeBlanc's sensually swaying body as she led him up the stairs and into her suite. Smiling smugly at him, she led him through several rooms to a small dark closet. Before going in she turned to him.

"You say this Alexandra has most unusual hair—reddish-blonde and is quite beautiful?"

Jake hesitated, then looked at Bella more closely. She was full of tricks, but what now? "That's right."

"That's very interesting," she said, her large black eyes shining. "I'd like you to see the couple in this bedroom. I don't know, of course, but I think you might be interested."

Jake frowned, his anger growing, "All right, then no more games. I'm in a hurry."

They went into the small dark closet and she pulled the tapestry back for him. She'd had him watch these performances before, but they did little for him. He was a man of action. Putting his eye up to the small hole, he had a clear view of the bed, a close view.

There was a fiery orange gown on the floor with a matching chemise and a man's clothing, too. He grinned to himself as he watched the couple. Bella had really gotten a wanton with this woman for she was fairly consuming the man.

Suddenly, he started. The covers had been partially concealing their faces. He let out a string of oaths as he realized, hardly daring to believe, that Alexandra was wrapped in Giles' arms, welcoming him, begging him for what she had always rejected, fought against, from him. There was no doubt that it was them. Anger and hate flared in him until he saw their writhing, sweaty bodies in a red haze of fury. Yet, he could not tear his eyes away as Giles pulled Alexandra up toward him while she moaned, clutching, demanding his body, then thrust deeply into her. Something seemed to tear apart inside of Jake and he turned blindly from the peephole, knocking Bella aside.

She glanced once into the room, confirming what she knew to be happening, then followed Jake's long, angry strides across her suite. Finally, she caught up with him in her bedroom and grabbed his arm, hanging on as he tried to throw her off.

"Well, Jake, could that have been the lovely Alexandra?"

She abruptly dropped his arm, stepping back in fright as he stopped and looked down at her.

She had never seen a man so full of cold, unrelenting rage in her life and it was now directed at her. She was afraid. What had she done? Had she gone too far?

Controlling himself, Jake said coldly, precisely, "You are not mistaken, Bella. That is, indeed, Alexandra and Giles. How she came to be here with him, I don't know, or care. I am sure that you have somehow managed it, but not without their cooperation. The lovely Alexandra will not go with me to Texas."

He turned and strode angrily from the room. Madame LeBlanc did not follow him. She was too afraid. He was quite capable of killing someone in his present rage. Then she smiled wickedly to herself. Her plans had worked. Jake would forever hate Alexandra as a deceiving whore. Her revenge was sweet, very sweet, but still it was only the beginning. Perhaps, sometime soon she might consider a brothel in Galveston. She knew they did well there and she knew several of the madames for she had procured girls for them frequently. Yes, now that Alexandra was out of the way, she could consider her plans for Jake once more. Laughing to herself, she stretched out languidly on her bed. Life was good, very good indeed.

Alexandra had never felt so strangely in her life. She knew that Giles was thrusting deeply within her, and that she needed him, wanted him with a strange burning that she had never felt before. She clawed at his shoulders, moaning in desire and frustration as he continued his deep penetrating movements. But she could not seem to get enough and yet it all seemed hazy, foggy as if she were not on the bed with a man she'd never wanted before, had never even allowed to touch her before. Now, suddenly, this evening, she accepted everything he did to her, wanting only more, and nothing could seem to satisfy the ache that burned inside her. Oh, what was happening to her?

She heard Giles groan with ecstasy, then saw his black eyes gleam in triumph. He got up and left her. She lay in the bed, aching with frustration and unhappiness that could not be satisfied. *Jake.* She wanted Jake. He could stop the pain deep within her. Tears burned her eyes. She blinked them away. No. She had a promise to keep. Nothing more.

Giles came toward her as if in a dream, completely nude, with a glass in his hand. She drank. It was thick, sweet, and faintly bitter. He took the glass from her. She thought she saw evil in his yes, but even as she tried to shake away the image she felt herself grow dizzy and tired. Finally she slipped into dark oblivion.

Chapter Thirteen

Alexandra lay in bed, not daring to move for fear the dizziness in her head and the nausea in her stomach would overcome her. Gradually, as she lay still, the feelings passed and she began to think clearly once more. The last she remembered was her strange passion for Giles. She was unable to forget her boldness and desire — hardly believing it had happened. Now she felt only disgust.

She had to leave the brothel. She could trust Madame LeBlanc no longer. She had obviously helped Giles get into her bedroom. How much had Giles paid for her body, she wondered.

Deciding to test her strength, she started to lift herself from the bed. She gasped with shock. She wasn't in the brothel. She'd never seen this room before. It was a bedroom, true, but it was done in pale, harmonious colors and elegant taste, although everything about the room suggested a slow decay.

"It's all right, dear. Don't be afraid," a soft voice said.

Alexandra looked around. A small woman sat in a rocking chair near her bed, smiling softly. The diffused sunlight came in through windows behind the woman, casting a golden glow on her still body. A soft, moist, warm breeze moved the sheer white drapes back and forth in front of the windows. And it was absolutely quiet. There was no sound to be heard. She shuddered. It was an eerie place to her, a place that didn't seem quite alive and yet not quite dead. Where could she be?

"Welcome to Jarmon Plantation, Alexandra," the soft voice continued.

Jarmon! Alexandra quickly focused on the woman. She was small, shrunken, her skin clinging to her bones, and yet there was a trace of beauty about her still. She was not old, but she was no longer young. And there was something familiar in her features. Most of all, the woman looked sick, as if constantly in pain.

"Jarmon Plantation?" Alexandra asked, looking in confusion around her. How had she gotten here? The last she remembered was being with Giles in the brothel.

"Yes, we're glad to have you, of course. It's not like it once was, but you're welcome here," the woman said in that same soft voice. She pushed back a strand of gray-blonde hair with

220

a thin, work-worn hand. "I understand that you came to Louisiana looking for Eleanor and Jacob Jarmon."

Alexandra leaned toward her. "Yes. Yes, indeed. I must see them. I've come a long way."

"You look a great deal like your father, Alexandra."

Alexandra's eyes widened in wonder. "My father? I—I don't understand."

"I'm Eleanor Thorssen Jarmon. Please call me Eleanor. And you *must* be Alexander Clarke's daughter?"

Alexandra smiled, nodding at the woman, breath escaping from her lips in relief as she leaned back on her pillow. "Eleanor Jarmon. I'm so glad."

"I'm very happy to have you here, but I, frankly, don't understand. Giles didn't tell me anything except your name and that you were looking for me and my son."

Alexandra frowned suddenly, sitting up again. "Giles? Giles Beaumont? What does he have to do with this?"

Eleanor looked a little confused. "But Giles brought you. Giles Beaumont Jarmon."

Alexandra stared at her a moment, utterly shocked. "Giles Beaumont Jarmon lives here?"

"Indeed. He's Jacob Jarmon's half brother. Giles Beaumont Jarmon III was my husband's first son by a New Orleans woman of high Creole lineage."

221

"Yes, I see," Alexandra said slowly, indeed beginning to see that Madame LeBlanc must have contacted Giles when she first learned of her desire to go to their plantation. But why?

"I'm sorry that my own son isn't here. You did wish to see him, too, isn't that correct?"

Alexandra looked at her sharply. "Yes, that's it. He isn't here? I don't understand. Isn't this his home?"

Eleanor sighed deeply, then began a faint coughing which increased until her entire body shook. She drew out a cotton handkerchief and pressed it to her lips. When at last the seizure subsided, she leaned back in the rocker, weak and pale. The handkerchief she hastily tucked away.

But not before Alexandra had seen the blood on it. She looked at the woman more closely, realizing she was quite sick. "Can I help?" she asked hesitantly.

Eleanor shook her head, unable to speak.

Alexandra looked away, embarrassed, confused, not knowing what to do, or how to act.

"It's all right, Alexandra. I'm fine," Eleanor finally said.

Alexandra looked back at her and saw that the tired, pain-ridden blue eyes watched her with much interest.

"You have come here, inquiring of me and my family, but you have not yet told me why."

Alexandra blushed. "I'm sorry. I suppose I

222

appear the ill-mannered Yankee."

Eleanor laughed gently. "No, my dear. You must remember that I, too, am a Northerner. I've never become used to the South and its strange ways," she said, her voice lonely and haunted.

Alexandra spoke quickly, not realizing how she emphasized her Northern traits with her quick speech and blunt tongue, reminding Eleanor of her lost home and family, and so hurried on with her story. "I'm sorry, Eleanor, but your father died a few days before I left New York City," she finally said.

The small, thin body shook with silent sobs as Eleanor buried her face in her lap.

Alexandra looked on in sympathy. She'd never yet cried for the one man she'd loved more than any other. She couldn't cry, not even now with his daughter. Her heart was like ice. Too much had happened for her to still feel anything but loathing for any man.

At last, Eleanor looked up and dried her eyes. "You came to tell me that?"

"More than that, Eleanor. When your father died, he asked me to come here to tell you that he was sorry and that he'd loved you always."

Eleanor's eyes brimmed over with fresh tears. "I loved him so, Alexandra. He was all I had until I met my husband. It almost broke my heart to leave him, but I had to—I loved my husband so dearly. And then, I wanted Jacob to have his father's inheritance. I wanted what was best for my son. I wanted him to inherit his father's plantation. Only, only—"

"Yes?" Alexandra prompted.

"Only," Eleanor said, trying to control her tears, "he was dead when I arrived here. *Dead*. I came all that way, quarreled with my father, to find my husband dead and buried when I arrived. He never even got to see his son. He'd been killed instantly—thrown from a horse."

"Oh, I'm sorry. How horrible. But why didn't you go back to your father?"

Eleanor raised her chin slightly. "Pride. I was too proud to say I was wrong, to say I was sorry, and then I still thought that Jacob should be with his family even after I'd learned that—" she hesitated slightly before continuing.

"It was such a shock to learn that my husband had been married before. He'd married a beautiful Creole lady from New Orleans. She died in childbirth. He'd loved her before me. I never really knew then if he'd loved me as much as I had him. He left me pregnant in New York to hurry back here when his father became ill. He said he had to run the plantation, but I wonder, I've always wondered. I suppose I always will."

"Of course, he loved you. He married you, didn't he?"

Eleanor smiled faintly. "Yes, he did, and I

224

had nothing to offer him—not money, not a fine family name like his first wife. He must have loved me, mustn't he?"

Alexandra nodded. "Of course, and you were very beautiful, too."

"Yes, I was. He adored my blonde hair and blue eyes. He was so used to the dark Creole beauties that he was fascinated with my fairness."

"Then," Alexandra said hesitantly, "all has been well with you, after all?"

"In some ways it has been all right. In some ways it has not been well at all. You see, the plantation and everything it stands for will go to the first son, nothing for the second. That's the way it always has been in this family. And there will not be much for the first son if the taxes continue to rise."

"What do you mean?"

"I mean that if we can't meet the carpetbaggers' exorbitant taxes, we will lose the plantation."

Alexandra's eyes widened. "You can't make a living on this good land?"

"No. The South is broken and I doubt if it will ever recover," she said sadly.

"But the land, the cotton?"

"We have the land, but what good is it without the slaves? There is no cotton because there are no slaves to plant it, pick it. Don't you see? Without all those workers, there is no more South. I hated the slavery, but yet it was a beautiful life for the few."

Alexandra nodded, hardly comprehending. "And your son?"

Eleanor smiled softly, thoughts of her son altering her face completely. She became almost beautiful again. "Jacob has won in the end. He doesn't need this burden of the South. He chose another life long ago when he was little more than a boy. I think he always knew. No, nothing of this will ever go to him. It will all go to Giles when his grandfather dies."

"He's still alive?"

Eleanor laughed harshly. "Of course. It would take a lot to kill that old man. If anything, the war only made him stronger. He will leave everything to Giles, the first son, just as his father left everything to him, the first son. You know, he had a younger brother, Lamar. There was nothing for him so he left years ago. He went to Texas."

"Texas?" Alexandra asked, the word reminding her of Jake, but she pushed the thought from her mind.

"Yes, he got a land grant under the Mexican government and has kept it through everything, even the wars. He's never made a fortune and life has been rough for him, but he has the land and his dreams. That's where my son lives. He went to Texas some time ago to join his uncle, Lamar Jarmon. He wanted me to go with him, but it was no place for a woman and I haven't had the strength for such a rugged life in years. Now it is too late."

"Too late? What do you mean? If you want to go to Texas, we'll go."

Eleanor looked at Alexandra sadly. "No, my dear. I'm not well. I don't have long. Life has been too hard, and the climate here is too moist for my lungs. But soon it will all be over."

"Oh, but no! I've just found you. I, I—"

Eleanor shook her head. "Your coming here is a great gift—to know that my father still loved me and forgave me when he died will ease my own passing. I always felt guilty and sorry, more so as I grew older. I won't feel that any longer, and I thank you for that."

"I'm only happy to have helped, but still—"

"You could have seen my son, too. He's only been gone a day. He came to visit me before he went back to Texas. He wanted me to come with him. It is better there now he says, and he and Lamar have big plans for Texas and their ranch. They'll do well, I know. But I couldn't go. I couldn't take the trip."

"I'm sorry I missed him. His grandfather loved him very much. I want to see him, too. I promised."

"Of course, but it's a long way to Texas and it's not so civilized there, although the South is not what it once was either. It has become quite unsafe here for a woman alone. I'm surprised you even made it here. It's so lucky that you happened on to Giles."

"Yes, isn't it," Alexandra said coldly, determined to confront Giles with his charade at the earliest moment. She had no desire to stay under the same roof with that man, but she couldn't leave Eleanor yet, not yet.

"I'm glad you're here, Alexandra. It's lonely here for a woman. I wish, though, that you could have met Jacob. I feel that you two would have liked each other. He's a brave man. I believe you have the courage and also the pride that Jacob has. But let's not talk of it now, let's just enjoy each other. It's been so long since I've talked to a young woman like yourself."

At that moment, there was a knock on the door and it swung open, revealing a large dark woman, carrying a tray.

"Ebba, do come in," Eleanor said with obvious warmth in her voice.

The woman came into the room, a broad grin on her face as she carefully placed the tray of food across Alexandra's lap.

"Here, child. You eat up. Bet you're hungry by now," Ebba said as she stepped back and crossed her large arms across her ample bosom.

Alexandra smiled. "Thank you. It's very

thoughtful, but you needn't have gone to so much trouble."

"Don't get that much company anymore, child. Course, there was a time—"

"Before the war it was all different," Eleanor broke in. "This is Ebba, Alexandra, and Ebba, this is a close friend of my father. He was her guardian. This is Miss Alexandra Clarke. She brought me news of home. My father is dead now. I have no more family except here." Sadness crept into her voice.

"I'm sorry, Miss Eleanor, sure sorry, but you got a fine son. That Jacob Jarmon is a fine man."

"Thank you, Ebba. Alexandra wanted to see him, but she's just missed him, hasn't she?"

"Sure has. That's a shame."

"I'm sorry I missed him, but surely he'll be returning. I want to spend some time with Eleanor. That's why I came," Alexandra said, thinking that she couldn't leave Olaf's daughter, wouldn't even want to. Jacob Jarmon was all right—she knew that now, but Eleanor was not. She would stay here and help Eleanor all she could.

"Thank you, my dear. And Jacob will be returning, although one never knows when."

Alexandra began eating the large bowl of thick soup. It was delicious and the thick slice of cornbread that Ebba had served with it made a tasty meal. She hadn't realized how

229

hungry she really was and ate hurriedly. She couldn't help noticing, after the ostentatious opulence of the brothel, that the bowl and spoon were items that should be found and used only in the kitchen. Times must be very hard indeed in the South.

After she finished eating, she looked at both women. "I want to tell you both now that I'm quite ready and willing to do anything that needs to be done. I may not be good at chores, but I'll gladly help. You can be sure of that."

"We're delighted to have you visit us, but you're our guest. We wouldn't think of your working," Eleanor said.

"But I intend to help. Didn't your son?"

"Of course. Jacob always does what he can when he's here, but—"

"Then think of me in the same way. I feel like I'm part of the family."

Tears streamed down Eleanor's face. "You are so good, my dear, to want to help, but truly—"

"Now, Miss Eleanor, this has been too much for you. I'm going to take you to bed," Ebba broke in. "Miss Alexandra, you just stay here and I'll be back for your tray."

Ebba helped Eleanor up from her chair and across the room. At the door they turned around. "Thank you for coming, my dear. I'll feel much better later. It has all just been too much for me, I fear," Eleanor said.

They left the room, closing the door behind them. Alexandra sat in the great bed, wondering at the plight of these people. Ebba had reminded her of the dark woman she'd known in the Bahamas and wondered why she had stayed on after she was free.

There was a light tap on the door, then Ebba hurried in, a conspiratorial look on her face. As she came close to the bed, she said, "Child, I'm glad you come at this time. She's failing fast and insists on working. That Mister Giles won't hardly lift a finger. Always gone to New Orleans gambling. Mister Jarmon holes up in his library going over his books, figuring out all he lost in the war. That leaves poor Miss Eleanor to do all the planning and she's hard put to make ends meet. I cook and clean, but my joints aren't what they should be. We've got no man here to do the hard work."

"How do you get by?"

"Ain't easy, child. Ain't easy. Mister Jacob just left so we're fixed up fine now for wood. He repaired things for us, got some other things to working again. He's some worker, but I don't expect him back for a time. He was awful upset that Miss Eleanor wouldn't go back with him. It almost tore her heart out to appear so well and happy with him here and all the while knowing that she'd probably not see him again."

"Not see him again?"

"Doc said she's on borrowed time. Could have lived longer in a dryer climate and if she hadn't worked so hard the past few years. That war's killed her sure as a bullet through her heart."

"I'm so sorry," Alexandra said sadly.

"You can see she's not well, and almost killed herself doing for Mister Jacob and proving that she was as strong as ever."

"And he believed her?"

"Sure. He didn't want to know how sick she was. And she didn't want him worrying none about her. Also, he was in a hurry and she didn't want him wasting time here with her, waiting for her to die. Course, he'd never have left if he'd known. He never was one to stay long, though. He don't get on with his brother and grandpa.

"Child, you're not going to leave Miss Eleanor, too, now are you?"

"No, Ebba. I'll stay here as long as I'm needed."

The older woman let out a sigh of relief. "That's a heap of worry off my mind. When she goes, I'll go, too. I got friends up North. I've even got my fare to get there, but I'd never leave Miss Eleanor here alone with those two men. You see, I took care of Mister Jacob when he was a little one, just like I did Mister Giles, but I can tell you now, Mister Jacob was my favorite. Mean little devil, but loving, too, when he loved. Always in trouble, but he was out in the open with it. That Mister Giles is the Creole and when he was in trouble, he'd weasel out of it somehow. Never could trust his handsome little face." She shook her head, smiling to herself. They'd been her children and always would be.

"Look, I've no experience, but I'll do whatever I can to help. If you'll just show me what to do, I'll do it and gladly if it will keep Eleanor in bed."

Ebba nodded her head slowly, then grinned. "I'm sorry you missed Mister Jacob. I got a feeling in my old bones about you two—yes, perhaps you will go to Texas. He needs a fine, strong woman like you."

Alexandra blushed. "I'm not looking for a man, Ebba. I came to keep a promise to Olaf Thorssen, that's all."

Ebba said nothing more, but raised her brows and clucked to herself for a moment. "Well, child, I can sure use the help, but there's not a lot you can do for this old place anymore. They've sold off the china, the silver, and soon they'll start on the furniture, the paintings, either that or sell the place. It'll never be the same again, but with your help we can at least keep a few of the rooms clean and usable."

"Are my things with me?" Alexandra asked.

"Mister Giles brought a valise with you. Sure funny him meeting up with you in New Orleans. Something fishy about it all, but don't quite know myself. Never can tell with Mister Giles, never could."

Alexandra averted her eyes, afraid that Ebba would read too much in them. Giles! How she hated him!

Chapter Fourteen

Panting, sweat dripping down her face, Alexandra lifted the heavy tray of food to carry to the mansion. She had never worked so hard in her life as she had that afternoon in the kitchen. The room was large, old-fashioned, and had once been tended by many servants. Now, there were only Ebba and Alexandra. Of course, there weren't so many people to cook for, either, but still there was plenty to do. They had cooked and cleaned all afternoon, and she realized for the first time the vast amount of work required to run a home. She glanced down at her red, sore hands, and knew they were no longer the soft white hands of a lady. But somehow, it didn't seem to matter. These people needed her help and she was only too glad to give it to them.

It had been intensely hot in the kitchen. She'd never felt such humidity before and it seemed to stifle her very breath. How Eleanor had lasted this long, she did not know.

As she stepped out into the cool night, the beautiful mansion loomed large before her as the last rays of the sun bathed it in a golden glow, masking its decay and slow destruction. She could imagine how it had once been with soft voices floating on the sultry air, and singing coming from the fields and slave quarters. It must have been a beautiful life if one had not looked beyond the house into the shanties behind it, or to the long rows of slaves working in the fields under the hot, southern sun.

The kitchen occupied a separate building from the mansion so that the heat and smells would not intrude on the people living there. Now, it would not have mattered so much, and the walk between the two buildings seemed unnecessarily long to Alexandra, who tottered along on tired feet under her heavy burden. Although there was no reason any longer, proprieties were still followed by Mister Jarmon, and Ebba and Eleanor had to follow his desires no matter how much more work it made for them. He was still head of Jarmon Plantation and they worked for him, as the women always had before them.

Ebba had stayed in the kitchen where she made her home now. It was big enough and warm in the winter without the constant draft of the main house, and then she was Negro. Mister Jarmon would never allow her a room in his home, no matter that she was no longer a slave. The past had not died for him and the future he ignored.

Alexandra was a little anxious about meeting him for she had seen no one except Ebba and Eleanor. They had told her about him and she wondered how he would accept the sudden appearance of another woman in his home. Well, she would certainly not be an expense to him for she was working for her keep.

She dared not let herself think of Giles. She could hardly believe that he was really a Jarmon. Why had he kept this fact from her? What more did he and Madame LeBlanc plan for her, or had they already accomplished what they wanted? She couldn't understand them, or their motives, but she was determined to find out soon. She would confront Giles at the first opportunity. She wasn't afraid of him, only confused and curious, and full of loathing.

Following Ebba's instructions, she hurried into the mansion, shutting the wide door behind her. There was no need of such a wide door now that women no longer wore the wide hoops under their skirts, but the doors remained as a reminder of what once had been.

Her arms aching, she found her way down the dimly lit hall to the room that Ebba had told her was the main dining room. Balancing the tray on one hand, she pushed wide the door and entered. The light here almost

237

blinded her and she had to stand still a moment while her eyes adjusted.

Finally she was able to see, and ignoring the gazes that she knew were fastened on her, she quickly approached the huge table and put down her heavy burden. Wiping her hands on the rough cotton apron around her waist, she looked at the faces around the table. Eleanor smiled warmly, looking stronger and more rested. Giles looked quite amused and his brows quirked upward as their eyes met. Mister Jarmon was frowning down his nose at her over his spectacles.

Breaking the heavy silence, Mister Jarmon asked, "Is this the girl, Eleanor?"

"Yes, this is Alexandra Clarke, Mister Jarmon, the young lady I told you about."

"Doesn't look like much. How come she's dressed like that? I thought she was a relative of yours."

"She, she is helping—"

"I've been working all afternoon in *your* kitchen, *Mister* Jarmon. Someone has to do the work and Eleanor is obviously too sick." Alexandra was shocked by her words but the explosion came unbidden. She was tired, angry, hurt, and Mister Jarmon's arrogance was too much for her.

Mister Jarmon looked away as if she were a distasteful spectacle. "Yankees are all alike. No class or respect for their elders."

"Mister Jarmon," Eleanor began.

"Well, if she wants to act like a servant in my home, then so be it. I suppose that's all these damn Yankees understand, anyway," he said, still not looking at Alexandra. "Well, serve the food before it cools, girl."

Alexandra could not believe her ears. The nerve of this old man. She wanted to throw the food at him and walk out, but instead she took a deep breath to gain control and began lifting the covers from the food.

"I'll help you, Alexandra," Eleanor said, beginning to rise from her chair.

"No, no, please, Eleanor. I'd rather that you didn't. Your setting the table had been enough already. You need to rest."

"Let the girl serve if she wants, Eleanor. Anyway, we can't afford to feed another Yankee for nothing," Mister Jarmon growled, now watching Alexandra closely.

Alexandra saw Eleanor look down at her lap. What she must have endured at the hands of this proud, unbending family was beginning to become painfully clear. She did not think that she could have stood being treated as an inferior Northerner—for any reason. But then here she was, silently accepting this man's unkind words and attitude. Yes, there were reasons that could make a woman stand this type of life.

She set the food down in the middle of the

239

table. She wasn't about to serve everyone individually. She was too tired and there was no need. Fortunately, everyone was sitting at one end of the long table. It was a beautiful room with heavy, dark wood furniture that still gleamed brightly from Eleanor's determined polishing, but there was no fancy silver or china to grace the table anymore. They were using the simple utensils from the kitchen.

When Alexandra had set the food on the table, then seated herself at the empty place by Eleanor, she paused to look around the table. Everyone still stared at her, as if expecting something more. "There's no need for me to serve. I'm tired and we can just pass the bowls—there aren't many."

"Of course, dear," Eleanor said quickly, picking up a bowl and handing it to Mister Jarmon.

He took it, glowering at her. "If it's not too much trouble, we will pray like all good Christians."

Eleanor looked quickly at Alexandra, indicating that it was the custom, so she bowed her head. She had no objections to this, but she had to be told the customs of the house. Mister Jarmon went on so long that she was certain the food would be cold before they would eat. Finally, the prayer ended and the food was passed. It was good, though simple, and she thought wryly that the whores in Madame

LeBlanc's brothel ate better than the genteel plantation families. The old aristocracy of the South must surely think the world had been turned upside down.

There was little conversation at the table. Eleanor ate in small bird-like bites, as if afraid of eating too much. Alexandra ate heartily, aware of the old man's glowering eyes frequently watching her. Giles seemed singularly disinterested, and this puzzled her. She ignored him, too, for she didn't want Eleanor to know that they had ever known each other more than casually. But Eleanor seemed beyond noticing anything at the table. In fact, Alexandra realized that she was very uncomfortable and anxious to get away. Perhaps, if she carried a tray to Eleanor's room where she could eat alone, Eleanor might eat more. It was certainly worth a try. The atmosphere here was oppressive, and Mister Jarmon and Giles did nothing to help it.

When the meal was finally over, the men quickly retired to the study for cigars and brandy just as if the war had never been and as if they weren't on the brink of poverty. Alexandra was amazed at their attitude. In their place, she would have been desperately trying to save what was left of the life she had lived. But casting their problems from her mind, she began gathering the dishes. Eleanor started to help her.

241

"No, Eleanor. You must go back to bed. Rest and perhaps tomorrow you'll feel more like doing something."

Eleanor smiled sweetly, with a touch of sadness. "Thank you, Alexandra. You've helped me so much by being here. Tomorrow I'll be more my old self again and I'll help you and Ebba."

"We'll see how you feel then," Alexandra said as she continued to stack the dishes on the heavy tray.

"Good night then," Eleanor said as she bent down and kissed Alexandra gently on the cheek. "It's just like having my very own daughter, my dear. I'm so glad you've come."

Alexandra returned the dishes to the kitchen where she and Ebba cleaned up. Stepping outside to go to her room, she looked around. Night had descended on the plantation and she could hear the night calls of the insects and animals. She shivered slightly, not knowing what made the sounds, and walked hurriedly, aware of the strange shapes all around her that seemed to grow and move in the moonlight. She was unused to the country and the quietness seemed loud to her, filled with menace.

Not looking ahead, but watching the ground, she suddenly gasped as she became tangled in the low hanging moss that clung to all the trees. Trying to knock it away, she only became more entangled, feeling its soft, clinging moistness enclosing her, trapping her in its strength. Moaning, she finally wrenched loose and ran toward the house, away from the moss filled trees with their branches turning down toward the ground as if they grew away from the sun. She'd never seen such a place, or such trees. If not for Eleanor, she would never stay.

As she ran, she looked desperately ahead for the light which should have been coming from the door to the house, the door she'd purposefully left open in order to find her way back, but there was no light. Had someone closed the door? Then she tripped on something in the darkness and fell to the dew drenched ground.

"Alexandra, *chérie,* allow me to help you up. You seemed to have stumbled."

Stifling a cry of alarm, Alexandra gazed up at the dark shape standing over her.

"What are you doing here?" she asked hotly.

Giles chuckled. "I was indoors, *ma chère,* but the night beckoned me. Isn't it lovely outside in the moonlight? A perfect time for wooing a lovely lady, wouldn't you say?"

Alexandra began to rise, but Giles quickly helped her up, putting his strong hand under her arm.

"Leave me be, Giles. I must be going inside."

"Must you? I think not, Alexandra," Giles said firmly as he began leading her away from

243

the house and toward the dense growth of trees.

"No. I won't go with you. I'm going inside."

"Don't we have some things to discuss, *chérie?* Don't you have some questions for me?"

Alexandra hesitated. She did want to speak with him, but not out here in the dark, all alone. "I, I don't know."

"Well, I *do* know. Come, pretty Alexandra. I will not harm you. Have I ever?"

"Yes, I believe you have."

He laughed softly again, still guiding her away from the house. "Come with me, my little dove. We have much to discuss and I don't want to be overheard, do you?"

"Surely there is a room—"

"No, there is not. The old man wanders the house at night, looking into corners, disturbing old ghosts. He will not let the past die," Giles said harshly.

Alexandra was afraid of this man, this man who had used her body, or had it been that she'd given herself to him? She didn't know for that night was still hazy in her mind, unreal, impossible to believe. But her resolution was shaken. She wanted to talk with Giles and yet she didn't. She hated him and yet she didn't.

He took her back toward the trees, then into the dense growth holding back the clinging moss so that she could pass ahead of him. It

244

was close in the trees, clammy. It was a heavy, muggy feeling, leaving her listless and lazy. She could feel lethargy creeping over her as they walked further back into the trees, toward a gazebo. It had been lovely once — its wood painted white. In the moonlight it still looked pretty and romantic. But as they approached, she could see the fallen planks, the peeling paint, and once more she felt the death and decay of the South strongly upon her. She didn't want to stay in this place, surrounded by the clinging trees, the cloying smell in her nostrils, and the dampness penetrating her body. No, she did not like it here. She wanted to escape, to run away and forget this feeling of helpless death.

But Giles held her arm firmly. He wanted something of Alexandra and he was used to getting his way on the plantation. Once he had hundreds of slaves at his beck and call, and he would never forget the power and importance that had been his then. He planned to have that once again, and if he couldn't control one single woman, he wasn't much of a man. When he thought of the slave girls in all colors, shapes and sizes, his blood grew hot again. He'd been master then and they'd dared not disobey. His teeth flashed white in the darkness as he thought of the things he'd made them do for him, to him. Yes, that had been the life — all the money and power he could want, all the women he could handle. For not only had there been the slave girls, but the delightful Bella LeBlanc had awaited his pleasure in New Orleans, too. He had owned her as surely as he owned his slaves when he set her up in the Quadroon Quarter, but she had always been unfathomable to him, always keeping a part of herself from him. He'd beaten her for that, but he soon learned that it did no good. There had also been Jacob. He'd seen Bella's eyes on Jacob, and he'd known what he'd not wanted to know. Since he'd never had any proof he had pushed it back in his mind, but it haunted him even yet.

Eventually he would have taken a wife to bear him children and run his plantation, but the war came before that. The war had changed everything, but now he had another chance to regain his power, money and a woman, a woman he wanted. He looked down into her wide green eyes and grinned a wolfish grin.

Alexandra was suddenly reminded of Stan Lewis. She shrank back from Giles, but he pushed her into the gazebo.

It was dark there, lighted only by the fitful moonlight that seeped in through the softly swaying branches of the trees, and she thought she heard the soft rustling of small creatures all around her. The cloying, musty smell was stronger here, invading everything, even herself.

She could hardly breathe for the air was thick and she felt herself grow pliant, losing any desire for control—until she felt Giles' hands on her.

She jerked away from him, determined that he not touch her again. But he was even more determined and pushed her up against the gazebo's wall. He stood closely in front of her, blocking any escape.

"Don't touch me, Giles. You said we would talk," Alexandra said desperately.

Giles smiled. "I won't hurt you, Alexandra. But how could I forget our night together. You were eager for my arms then, my caresses, my kisses—"

"No! No. I don't know what happened that night."

"But you do admit it happened?"

"How can I not?" she asked miserably.

"Indeed. You enjoyed me then. Why shouldn't I hope for more of the same? I brought you here to my home so we could share it. Do you suddenly find me so unpleasant, my home unsatisfactory?"

"I, I—"

He put his hands on her arms. She felt stifled, but stilled her impulse to run. "Now, that's better. We're going to get to know each other well, very well indeed. We are good together. We've already proved that, haven't we?"

"I don't know what happened that night,"

she whispered, her eyes glowing like twin green lights.

Giles laughed softly close to her ear. "I do, *chérie*. Sometimes a woman needs a little extra stimulus—"

"What?" Alexandra asked sharply.

"I tried. I really tried with you, *chérie,* but you didn't seem to grow in affection for me as I did for you. I'd never had trouble before. I couldn't understand it. Bella, Madame LeBlanc, who's wise in these ways, suggested something for your drink that might help stimulate you."

"Oh! You monster!" Alexandra hissed, trying to raise her hand up to slap him, but Giles blocked the blow.

"Easy, my dear. It is not so unusual. And Bella was determined that I should have what I wanted."

"You're *both* monsters!" Alexandra cried, her fury rising.

"Not at all. We merely have extravagant tastes that we are determined to satisfy."

"Let me go, you, you—"

"Don't provoke me, Alexandra," Giles said, jerking her arms behind her. "I do want to talk with you, too."

His voice had become thick with passion as he felt her body struggling against him. Grasping her to him, he forced her face up to his, then captured her soft lips with his mouth. She was so sweet. Biting into her tender lips, he heard her cry out in pain and at the same time her mouth opened, allowing him to plunge inside. He thrust deeply, exploring the depths again that he had so recently discovered. Yes. Yes, she was just as wonderful as he remembered.

Still holding her hands behind her, he adjusted his grip so that one hand could touch her, feel her delights, but he kept her mouth locked with his to satisfy his mounting desire and to keep her quiet. His hand moved around her shoulder down to the peaks of her ripe, full breasts. Quickly he undid the front of her bodice and boldly thrust his hand against her warm, bare flesh for she wore nothing under the dress. She struggled against him as his hand greedily fondled her swelling mounds, and it excited him all the more. Tearing his mouth from hers, he glanced down to see her two white breasts bathed in silvery light, the peaks dark and hard. He caught her tightly to him, his excitement mounting.

"Let me go, Giles," she moaned against his chest. "Don't do this to me. I'm not strong enough to fight you." And truly she felt her strength ebbing away in face of this man's desires. She didn't want him to touch her and yet she couldn't seem to fight him. Where had her strength gone?

"You don't want to fight me, Alexandra.

You want me to make love to you as I did before, as I will again. Let me love you, let me touch you all over, feel your glorious body against me. Come love, remove your gown. You don't need clothes here. The trees protect us. No one will ever know. I'll make you want me as you did at Bella's place."

"No! No, Giles. Take me back. I don't want you to touch me. You've said yourself that I was given something that night."

"Only something to bring out your natural inclinations," Giles said as he undid her gown. Then, releasing her hands, he let the dress slide down her body to fall in a heap on the gazebo's floor.

The cool damp air touched Alexandra's body. She shivered but proudly did not try to cover her nakedness with her hands.

"No, Giles! Tonight I'm not your plaything." She reached to pick up her gown, but he kicked it aside.

He was deaf to her words, greedily drinking in the beauty of her lush body. He grabbed her to him, but she stayed stiff, cold in his arms, under his demanding caresses.

"Alexandra, Alexandra," he moaned against her soft hair, "why can't you love me? I've loved you since the first instant I saw you. Why must you make me hurt you?"

But his words were so soft that Alexandra was hardly aware of their meaning. All she could think of was the pain, the humiliation, and the hatred inside her that spawned a burning desire for revenge.

"No!" With a strength she didn't know she possessed, she thrust him from her, grabbed her dress, and ran for the house.

Chapter Fifteen

Alexandra sat by the bed, a frown puckering her forehead as she watched Eleanor struggle to breathe, wracked almost continually by coughs now. The weather had become warmer and muggier as April had turned into May so that as she sat there, hoping for more breeze, or perhaps a cooling rain, she constantly wiped the sweat that seemed to always be trickling down her body. What a place to live, she thought unhappily. How had Eleanor stood it? She now understood the reason for the slow Southern speech and movements—there was no other choice in this type of climate.

Had two weeks really passed since that dreadful night in the gazebo with Giles? She'd given him no further chance to molest her, but he was constantly there—watching her with his knowing black Creole eyes. She wanted desperately to be rid of him, but she could not in good conscience leave Eleanor. When she was not working with Ebba, she was in the room with Eleanor. She even slept there now for she didn't want to leave the failing woman alone. Giles had not approached her again, although his dark, watchful eyes saw everything.

A few days after she had arrived, Eleanor had become worse and a doctor had been sent for. He had shaken his head, mumbled under his breath, and said that there was no hope. They could only make her comfortable and happy in her last days. There was nothing the doctor could do. Alexandra had become desperate, insisting that she would take Eleanor back to New York to finer, younger doctors. But the old doctor had merely shaken his head, saying that he had seen the illness before. There was no cure. The lungs simply gave out. A trip to New York would only be painful for the sick woman and would probably cause a quicker death. Alexandra had had no choice but to believe him and had kept Eleanor in bed ever since, watching her become weaker, thinner, and less aware. She had come to love Eleanor and her pain was Alexandra's pain. Death walked with them every day and they could only await for it to finally claim Eleanor.

Another thing that had also affected Alexandra strongly was the sudden and definite decline of Mister Jarmon. It had begun soon after the doctor had been to visit Eleanor and had become worse until now he never left his room. He looked bad, his color was pale, and his appetite

253

was almost nonexistent. She had argued with him that the doctor must be sent for again, but the old man said that the doctor had more important cases to handle and that he would only waste the man's time. And as she fought to save his life, she gained a new respect for the old Southerner for he never complained, but only waited, as if he would welcome his release from life.

It finally came down to her running the plantation, or what was left of it. She had risen to the responsibility, surprising even herself. Giles came and went, hardly letting the death and decay touch him. His mind was set on another path and the life around him was no longer a part of him.

As she sat there watching the fitfully sleeping Eleanor, she was suddenly shaken by loud voices downstairs. She jumped up, alarmed, and ran out of the room to the landing above the foyer. Looking down, she saw several burly men walking around, their dirty, booted feet marking the worn, imported carpet.

She rushed down the stairs, completely unaware of her disheveled appearance — golden-red curls escaping around her face, a smudge of dirt on her cheek, and her gown unbuttoned to reveal the valley of her breasts. "What are you men doing in here? Leave this house at once!" she shouted.

When she reached their level, she had to look

up at the men for they towered above her, grinning at the unexpected pleasure before them. "Get out of here immediately!"

Finally one of the men recognized the authority in her voice and her haughty manner. "Sorry to disturb you, ma'am, but we got orders," he said, looking her over as if she were a fine filly.

Giles entered, dressed meticulously as usual. In one glance he took in the situation. "Gentlemen, may I present my fianceé, Miss Alexandra Clarke." He walked across the foyer to stand closely beside her.

Alexandra's eyes opened wide at his words, but she knew better than to speak out now.

"Please continue, gentlemen, while I escort my fianceé upstairs. I'm sure you've frightened her. It's usually so quiet here in the country."

The men looked at Alexandra one final time, then turned reluctantly away.

Giles took a firm hold of Alexandra's arm and forced her back up the stairs. She stumbled along beside him, not knowing what was happening, but worried all the same. She didn't want to go with him, be with him at all. Once they reached the landing, he jerked her into the hall, away from the eyes of the workers below. Pushing her up against the wall, he stuck his face close to hers, his black eyes snapping as he hissed.

"What the hell do you think you're doing downstairs? Do you realize that if I hadn't come in just then, they all might have jumped on you, raped you, and who knows what else?"

Alexandra blanched. She'd never thought of that. She had been determined to protect the mansion.

"You fool! Do you have any idea of how you look with your dress unbuttoned half way to your waist. For God's sake, Alexandra, I know it's hot, but those are red-blooded men down there."

Alexandra blushed. "I didn't think. I was surprised to hear them and just went down. What are they doing here, Giles?"

He laughed, a mocking sound that seemed to be wrenched involuntarily from his throat. "They're doing to this home what has been done to many others. They're buying the furniture. It'll bring a fine price in New Orleans and if I don't get it sold now, the government will take it all, including the land for taxes. Do you understand that, my pretty heiress?"

"How, how did you know?" Alexandra gasped.

I know that you are Alexandra Clarke, a wealthy young heiress, for Eleanor had spoken of your family long ago. What you're doing here working like a servant, or what you were doing in New Orleans acting like a whore is no concern of mine. I *am* concerned with your money. I have need of it. I would make you a good husband, and so you shall marry me."

"Never!"

Giles went on as if she had not spoken. "Yes, I plan to marry you and gain your fortune, but I won't sink that fortune in a worthless plantation. The South is gone, Alexandra, and so is that type of life. I'm not fool enough to try and revive what is dead. Grandfather will never admit to his loss, but I did a long time ago. The past is past, but I plan to make a future with you. Now, no more about this. I'll leave enough for us to set up a beautiful, gracious townhouse in New Orleans with part of the family's heirlooms, but the majority will go to buy that house. Houses are going cheap in some sections of New Orleans at the moment so I'll invest well and have the furniture moved there. You see, I plan well, *ma chère,* and you are part of my plans."

"Never, never!"

"You're going to marry me, Alexandra, whether you want to or not. Now, go back to the sick ones and stay there. This will take most of the day and I don't want to see you out again. You'll be safe in the room with Eleanor."

Giles stepped back, his dark gaze raking her body quickly before he pushed her away toward Eleanor's room.

Alexandra went, glad to be away from him. He was so sure of himself, so determined to have things his own way. Well, she'd never marry him, that was sure.

The long day wore on with the sound of the workmen echoing throughout the mansion. Giles had moved Eleanor to Alexandra's bedroom since he wanted to keep that furniture and sell what was in Eleanor's room, explaining that he was keeping only the very best pieces for their townhouse in New Orleans. But she didn't care what he did, for as she sat with Eleanor and watched her strength slowly fade, something of herself seemed to die, too. She no longer felt young. She felt as old and tired as the South.

The shadows were growing long when Giles finally came to her room again. He walked over to her, looking a little tired and dirty himself. Many of the rooms had not been cleaned in years and he bore the dust of those hopeless years. He stood by Alexandra a moment, looking down at Eleanor. "How is she?"

"Not well, Giles. I don't know how much longer she will be with us. She's not been really aware all afternoon."

He nodded. "They've taken everything. They'll store it in New Orleans until I can get the highest bid. It's a better time to sell now than just after the war when the others sold to the Yankees. I should get a good price. I've kept the best pieces for our home. You'll like it in New Orleans, Alexandra. I'll show you a different side than you saw before."

Alexandra didn't answer him. She didn't care. They would never share a home.

Presently he left, shutting the door quietly behind him. She breathed easier knowing the men were gone and that Giles would not bother her for a while. Soon Ebba would bring the trays with dinner. She would have helped, but she didn't want to leave Eleanor in case she needed anything.

A little later when the last rays of sunlight had faded, Ebba knocked hesitantly on the door. Alexandra quickly got up to let her in. The older woman looked tired and strained. They were all affected. The end for many things was in sight.

Looking at Alexandra, Ebba shook her head. "Child, you need more rest. You're plum tuckered out. Better get some sleep. I can sit with Miss Eleanor."

"Thank you, Ebba, but I want to be with her."

"I understand, sugar, but you'd better eat something now. That'll make you feel better."

"I don't feel very hungry, but thank you."

Ebba moved slowly, tiredly across the room and set the tray down, then walked back toward the door. "It's a sad day, child, sad. I'm just glad that Eleanor and Mister Jarmon can't see what's happening to their home. Now, I'll just take Mister Jarmon's tray to him and see if he'll eat. Mister Giles is eating in the dining room. When I'm done, I'll come back to you."

"I'll try to get Eleanor to eat."

"You do that, sugar, you just do that," Ebba said softly as she shut the door behind her.

Alexandra sighed as she stood up and went to Eleanor's side. She whispered her name several times then spoke more loudly, but Eleanor slept on. She did not want to disturb her since it was the first time she'd not been kept awake with the dreadful coughs. Walking away, she went over to the tray. She picked up the bowl of thick soup and a piece of cornbread, and forced herself to eat.

Suddenly a horrible scream tore through the mansion. Alexandra jumped up, setting her bowl of soup down quickly. She had recognized Ebba's voice coming from the direction of Mister Jarmon's bedroom. She tried to still her suspicions about Ebba's scream as she leaned over Eleanor. She slept on. Alexandra ran out of the room, meeting Giles in the hall, a look of surprise and worry on his handsome face. Together they hurried to the old man's bedroom.

Ebba was sitting in a rocker by his bed, wailing softly to herself. The spilled tray was all over the floor where she'd dropped it.

Mister Jarmon lay in bed, his face white and pinched, dead.

Alexandra sank down into the nearest chair, and watched Giles walk across the room to his grandfather.

Giles was speaking to her.

She realized it from far away. How long had she been sitting there? She didn't know. Nothing seemed quite real anymore. Ebba still sat rock-

ing, crooning to herself.

"Alexandra."

She looked up. Giles was standing beside her. He no longer looked tired. He smiled, triumph written in every line of his handsome face. His eyes were hard points of light piercing into her.

"He's dead, Alexandra. We'll bury him tomorrow. We can't wait any longer in this heat and humidity. Anyway, there are no friends or relatives to invite. They're all dead. He was the last to hold out, but he was mortal, too, in the end. We're *free* at last. *I'm* free."

Alexandra looked closely at Giles, puzzled. Free? Had Giles thought himself trapped on a plantation that he disliked by a grandfather he felt nothing for? Perhaps Giles was a Southerner who would survive because he felt no reverence, no desire for what the South had been. Perhaps only those who clung to the past died with it. She did not know. It was a way of life and thinking that she could not understand, and did not want to. She had done all she could for Mister Jarmon. They would bury him, as they had the South, and it would be over. There would be no traces left, nothing to ever really define the essence of a way of life and the people who had created it.

"You can't know what it was like to be stuck out here, waiting to begin your life. There was nothing left for me, but I couldn't leave until it was all mine. It's done now, all over. Ebba can

261

get him ready. We'll bury him tomorrow in the family plot. I'll dig the graves in the morning."

"Graves?" Alexandra asked, chills running over her body.

"Of course. While I'm at it, I might as well complete the job. Eleanor can't last long."

"Oh, *no* Giles. Please don't dig her grave before she's gone. Surely that's tempting fate."

"Hell! I'll dig them both together. It won't be long now."

Alexandra rose unsteadily, not wanting to be with Giles a moment longer. How could he be so cold, so calculating, so unfeeling? He had lost his grandfather and he was relieved. Now he was anxious for Eleanor's death.

She walked away from him and went to stand beside Ebba. "Ebba, I'm going to sit with Eleanor, unless you need my help. She may need me and I can't do any more here."

"That's right, child. Go sit with her. See that she doesn't meet her end too soon."

Alexandra raised her brows. "I don't understand?"

Ebba shook her head and glanced over at Giles who watched them closely. "You go on, child, and try to rest. It's about all over now."

Not wanting to acknowledge the import of Ebba's words, Alexandra pushed everything from her mind as she left the room.

As the night wore slowly on, she dozed fitfully, waking frequently to hear the strange creakings of the old house and the frequent noise made by Ebba and Giles as they went about their business. But Eleanor slept on, almost the sleep of death, and frequently Alexandra would feel her pulse to see if she still lived. And so the night went on, almost dream-like as she awaited the dawn to make everything better in its clear light and warmth.

But as the dawn came, pink and moist, through the open windows, Alexandra's fears increased, for with the revealing light, the room looked even shabbier and more worn than before and Eleanor's face seemed even whiter and more pinched. And the heat came too, emphasizing the stifling mugginess of the day. She stood up, stretching her stiff limbs and wandered about the room, unable to sit still any longer, feeling as if something was about to happen.

"Alexandra. Alexandra," Eleanor's voice came softly, clearly to her.

She turned and quickly crossed the room to the weak woman who watched her with intense, burning eyes in a face almost masklike with its white skin stretched over protruding bones. Alexandra caught the thin, hot hand in hers, and bent forward to catch the barely spoken words.

"Alexandra, I've loved you like a daughter. I've not long left."

"No, Eleanor."

"Shh. I won't be in this world much longer. I have a request. I know it's a lot to ask."

"Anything, Eleanor. Anything."

"I, I—" she started to say, but succumbed to the wracking coughs that tore through her weak body.

Alexandra pressed the heavy cotton handkerchief to her friend's lips. Eleanor was too weak to help herself any longer. When finally it eased, Eleanor leaned back, even whiter than before, and Alexandra hastily hid the blood soaked cloth from her eyes.

"Please, Alexandra, will you go to my son? Go to Jacob in Texas. He's with his uncle, Lamar Jarmon, on the Bar J Ranch in south Texas, somewhere close to Corpus Christi." She paused, almost panting, then continued. "I want you two to know each other, and I want you to tell him that my last days were happy ones with you and that I died in peace. You shouldn't be alone. A woman shouldn't live alone. I know that—how I know that. And a man shouldn't either. My son, dear Jacob, shouldn't be alone."

"Oh, Eleanor. I'll go. Of course I'll go to Texas, but I can't promise what will happen."

Eleanor smiled weakly. "I know, my dear, love is such a mystery, but yet I feel that fate has brought you here to me—and to Jacob. Go to him. You will be safe with him and you cannot live alone. It is a hard, harsh world, Alexandra. If it does not work out, I will understand, but go for me and for the two of you." She stopped, closed her eyes tightly as her body shook in spasms of unreleased coughs. Finally, she gained control, sweat beading her forehead. "I want him to know that I loved him as always and that his grandfather did, too. I want him to know that he was never forsaken by his family, and that his Norwegian blood is strong in his veins, perhaps stronger than his Southern heritage."

"I'll go, Eleanor. He'll know all this and if I can help him in any way, I will. I promise you this."

Eleanor smiled, her face relaxing in happiness. "I can die happy now, Alexandra."

"Eleanor, don't leave us, please. We will go to Texas together."

"No, my dear, time has run out for me."

Alexandra looked on helplessly. As the two women cheated death a while longer, the door opened, and Giles and Ebba entered.

Eleanor watched the three people beside her, then nodded. "Ebba, you know my jewel box. Would you bring it to me?"

"Oh, Miss Eleanor, you know I'd do anything for you," Ebba said, before turning to leave the room.

Eleanor smiled wanly. "I've not much longer, Giles, and I'd like to thank you for what you've done for me in all the years we've been together. I've loved you like a second son, and if you ever need help, go to your uncle and brother in Texas. They'll gladly accept you and help you."

Giles smiled, a frozen movement across his

265

face, but his eyes remained black and hard. "Thank you, Eleanor, but I'll not need their help. I appreciate all that you've done for me, and I'm truly sorry that you can't join your son in Texas. We'll all miss you, of course."

Eleanor shut her eyes. She knew Giles well, better than most. He was a Creole, a Southerner, unlike her and her son. He would survive somehow, she knew that, but she wondered just how many people he would hurt on the way. But she pushed that thought from her mind. He was no longer her concern. She must think of Alexandra and Jacob.

The bedroom door opened and shut, then there was a flurry of movement as Ebba approached the bed. "Here you are, Miss Eleanor. There's not much left, you remember. We done sold most of it to eat."

"Thank you, Ebba. I know. Will you take out what's there. I've saved two pieces, not for value as much as for sentiment. Yes, there they are. I want you to have the brooch, Ebba. It belonged to my mother. You have been good and faithful all these years. I want you to have it. It is a family heirloom—from my family."

"Oh no, Miss Eleanor, I couldn't. I—"

"No, don't argue, Ebba. Please, take it with my blessings."

"Thank you, Miss Eleanor, thank you. I'll never part with it," Ebba said as she stumbled away from the bed, the brooch clutched tightly to her bosom.

"Now, Alexandra, this is very special. It is from my father's family. You see, the design is Norwegian. I want you to have it. You were his granddaughter, and my daughter. He would want you to have it. *I* want you to have it."

"But Eleanor, shouldn't Jacob's wife—"

Eleanor smiled. "I believe fate will take care of that, my dear Alexandra."

"Thank you, Eleanor. I will treasure it always."

"Now, I must rest. All of this has exhausted me. Go on about your duties, I will be all right here alone," Eleanor said, her breath growing ragged as her eyes shut, then suddenly she sat up, coughing violently.

Alexandra grabbed the cloth, but Eleanor jerked it away from her, pressing it to the blood that had begun to flow from her mouth. She glanced wildly around the room, not seeing what was there as the coughs wracked her body in one final spasm. She fell back against the white pillows, the blood stained handkerchief clutched desperately in her thin, white hand. And so she died.

Chapter Sixteen

The late afternoon air was heavy and damp as gray clouds gathered over the small party under the old moss laden tree in the Jarmon cemetery. There was no wind on the hill, no noise save that of the dull thuds as dirt fell, covering the plain wooden boxes; and there were no smiles on the faces of the three who stood vigil over the two fresh graves.

Giles was filling in the last dirt of Eleanor's grave. Mister Jarmon's grave was already finished for Giles had not taken the trouble to dig either grave very deeply. He hadn't deemed it necessary. Ebba stood over Eleanor's grave, tears running down her cheeks as she silently mourned her friend of many years.

The thuds finally stopped. Giles straightened up, threw the shovel to one side, then glanced at Alexandra. Kneeling, she placed a small bouquet of spring flowers in the soft, moist earth of each grave, then opened the small family Bible she'd found in Mr. Jarmon's study. Ebba and Giles bowed their heads as she began reading from the book.

Giles left Alexandra no time for mourning. When she'd finished reading from the Bible, he took her arm and led her toward the wrought iron fence that surrounded the family cemetery. Now that it was over, she felt devoid of emotion as well as strength and allowed him to lead her away. But at the gate, she stopped and turned back. Ebba was watching them with a worried expression on her face.

"Ebba, are you coming?" Alexandra called to her, sensing the woman's concern.

"No, child, I've got my own peace to make here. You go ahead. I'll be up to the house a little later."

Alexandra nodded and turned back to Giles. The lamenting tones of a song Ebba sang filled the air and swirled around them. It was a strange sound with words that Alexandra couldn't understand and she knew it must be something out of Ebba's mysterious African past. It must be a song for the dead.

Giles' hand was firm on her arm as he guided her through the thick grass and the maze of tree branches drooping low with the soft, gray, dead-looking moss. It all seemed to reach out at her as if to catch her in its clutches and hold her locked in the plantation's past. She tried to knock it away, hating the soft, almost sticky touch of the clinging moss, but it seemed to be everywhere, thriving in the warm, humid climate.

Now that it was all over, she wanted to hurry away. There was nothing left for her here. She had to leave, but she'd made no plans. She had been unable to do that while Eleanor still lived and now—now she couldn't seem to think. But she had to think, to plan. Eleanor had asked her to go to Texas and she'd promised, but Texas was so big, so wild, so untamed, so far away. Still, she had promised and perhaps she could lose herself in its vastness, hiding there from both Stan and Giles.

Giles. She stole a quick glance at his handsome profile. His face was as inscrutable as usual and his dark eyes seemed focused on some point in the distance. She had to get away from him, but how? He was so powerful, so determined.

As they approached the almost empty, barren mansion, his hand tightened around her arm as if he had sensed her thoughts. She turned cold with dread, looking nervously around as if some way of escape would suddenly materialize. He led her relentlessly on toward the house. She didn't want to return to it. She didn't want to face the ghosts there. She dreaded it almost as much as she did Giles.

Soon they were at the back door. "I don't want to go back into the house, Giles," she said.

"We're going in, *chérie*. We must pack our few things. We're leaving in the morning."

"No. I can't spend another night in there."

"Really, Alexandra, you're being quite foolish." And his dark eyes turned hard as he dragged her into the mansion.

He led her up the stairs, heedless of her desperate attempt to get free. She wanted to scream out, but there was no one to hear, no one to help. It was so quiet on the second floor, so deathly quiet, broken only by their hurrying footsteps.

She felt smothered by the oppressive atmosphere of the house and by the restraint of Giles' hand. As he paused momentarily before his bedroom door, she flayed out against him in an attempt to escape him before it was too late. But he merely chuckled demonically and opened the door.

He quickly crossed the room to a massive bed and threw her onto its soft, enveloping center. Then he locked the door. She looked up at the sound, fear catching at her heart, and saw him standing there, a soft, knowing smile on his lips.

Looking for escape, she glanced quickly around the room, hating on sight the heavy, masculine furniture. The windows were covered with thick, velvet drapes closed tightly to keep out the sun and air. The room was stuffy, humid and no breeze found its way inside. There was no movement anywhere in the house, only the two people caught together, staring at each other across the the room.

"Chérie, how alluring you look on my bed," Giles said, breaking the silence. "I would have enjoyed seeing you there sooner, but you've not been very obliging since New Orleans. I've been patient, have I not?" Slowly he moved toward her.

She shrank back in the bed, watching his intense black eyes. "No! No, Giles. You can't mean to—"

He kept coming closer.

"I, I'm not well. I must rest. The funeral—"

"Not well, *chérie?* Then I have just the thing for you."

He tuned abruptly and went to a sideboard. He picked up a decanter and poured a small amount of the amber liquid in a crystal glass, then added a white powder.

"Oh no, Giles. I'm not forgetting the brothel. I don't want it."

"It's not what you had before, Alexandra. This will be good for you. You'll like it."

"No! Put it away."

"You must remember to do as you're told," he said as he sat down on the edge of the bed and jerked her to him.

"No! Let me go!" she screamed, pushing against him, but he forced her mouth open and poured the liquid down her throat. She choked, gasped, then finally swallowed the drink.

"There. In a moment you'll feel quite well, Alexandra," Giles said as he let her up. He walked back across the room to pour himself a drink. He downed it with a quick flick of his wrist as his eyes roamed greedily over her reclining body.

She huddled back in the bed and felt a warm languidness begin to spread through her. Her arms and legs felt heavy, relaxed, like liquid. She leaned back against the soft pillows and watched Giles as he took off his coat, then began to undress. She smiled, thinking that she wasn't upset any longer. She didn't feel anything except a kind of euphoria creeping over her. It felt good. Nothing really mattered anymore.

Giles was walking toward her, his lean, hard body proudly displayed for her. He was a strikingly handsome man with a smooth body that was perfectly proportioned. He was closer now and there seemed to be a rosy hue to the room, to him, to everything. He was stretching his arms toward her and she didn't move away. She just lay still, not caring.

"Alexandra, my love," he whispered as his hands expertly undid her bodice, then continued with the rest of her clothing. "You are so perfectly beautiful. Our bodies are so perfect together. How can you not want to see them joined?"

He slipped the gown from her and gazed at her body barely shielded from him by her chemise. "I've never seen such perfect beauty." He pulled the chemise from her, the stockings, and

273

she lay naked before him, her breasts full, firm, her curls red-gold in the soft light. He pulled the pins from her hair, letting it cascade down around her body. "So beautiful, so very beautiful," he murmured, making no move to touch her.

She lay still, feeling herself lost in a rosy euphoria in which nothing, no one, could ever touch her, or hurt her again. And the young, dark god before her seemed a natural part of her dream. She moved slowly, stretching her limbs in abandon, letting her legs fall apart.

"You are so very beautiful, Alexandra. I have not had the chance to fully appreciate your beauty before. This time will be perfect. You know that you belong to me now, that I am your master in every way."

She smiled, stretching lazily like a cat. She hardly heard what he said, and it didn't matter anyway. Let the young god talk if it pleased him. But she wondered vaguely somewhere in her mind why he didn't touch her. Men always had before. But that was unimportant, too. It just felt delicious to be lying, without any confining clothes, on a soft, comfortable bed.

"You know, growing up on a plantation a boy has a chance to indulge in women early. I was not yet in my teens when I began, but there is a problem. Early on, a boy realizes that sex can become boring, no matter how beautiful the woman, if there is not more to stimulate him.

274

Look now at me. You cannot excite me by simply lying there, no matter how perfect you are. It takes more for me, much more. I have trained many slave women to cater to my desires and I will train you, also, until there is nothing you cannot, or will not do for me."

She focused not on his words, but on his body, and was surprised not to see the hard, bulging member she'd expected. Was there something wrong with her, with him? No, he'd explained that. Well, no matter, she only wanted to lie there undisturbed.

"I don't suppose you dance, Alexandra, or know any of the exciting arts of seduction? Well, no matter, there will be time for that later. Now, let's see, what shall we do?"

She watched his frowning face, as if he pondered dinner, or what jacket to wear. Then he smiled, his decision made. He took her hand and began drawing her up to him. She let him ease her toward him and then he picked her up in his arms. She wondered vaguely where he was taking her, but it didn't matter and she was much more interested in the feel of his hard, warm flesh next to hers. His masculine body reminded her of someone else. *Jake*. But no, she must never think of him again. He was gone forever.

Giles opened a door to what appeared to be a closet, but it was longer and he walked into it, shutting the door behind them. There was a dim light inside and she watched him as he reached up to the ceiling and pulled down a contraption. He pulled her arms high up over her head, then tied her wrists in the thing. What was he doing? She was suddenly almost afraid.

"Giles? What are you—"

"Shh. You must learn to enjoy the more exquisite pleasure of sex—pain."

She couldn't understand, but felt herself being pulled higher toward the ceiling. Her arms ached and she felt as if they were being torn from their sockets. Her feet no longer touched the floor and she hung there completely helpless. But she didn't really feel the pain. Then Giles advanced on her, a long, black whip in his hands.

"What are you doing, Giles?"

"We used these on the slaves. There are many ways to use a whip. I know them all. I won't mark you, Alexandra, you'll see. And soon you'll find this as much pleasure as I do. You'll learn to use it on me, too."

"Whip?" she muttered, wishing she could think more clearly, knowing somehow that this was wrong, that Giles must be mad, but she could not think through the languidness that had taken control of her mind and body.

He turned her around so that her smooth back, firm hips, and long legs were exposed to him, completely vulnerable and at his mercy. Sweat beaded his forehead as he snapped the whip in the air, then sent it reeling toward her

276

back. It contacted, cracking against her bare skin. He felt the first flush of excitement start in his loins. It had been so long. Nothing could satisfy him quite like this. Yes, Alexandra would be fine, just fine, he thought, as the whip bore down on her again. He must not strike too hard; he didn't want to mar her beautiful body, the body that strained now, sweat glistening, as it writhed away from the whip's terrible embrace. But the burning in him was growing, spreading, demanding release.

Excited now almost beyond control, he let the whip come down again and again across her shoulders, her back, her hips. Sweat glistened on his body and he wanted to feel her under him, but more he wanted to feel the sting of the whip on himself. He knew it couldn't be this first time, but soon, soon he would teach her how to be his perfect slave. Finally, the needs of his body became too great. He threw down the whip and approached her. He let his hands run across her blood drenched back, then twisted her around to him. She gazed glassy-eyed at him, not seeing or comprehending, but he didn't care. He had to ease the ache in his loins. He lowered her slightly, letting her fall into his arms as he released her wrists.

Catching his prize to him, he rushed back into the bedroom and threw her on the bed. He had no more thoughts for her now as his passion drove him on. He pulled her up toward him, bracing his knees inside her thighs, his manhood bulging, throbbing. Then he plunged inside her softness. He thrust hard, deep in his frenzy of passion until at last he reached the zenith of his desire. Then, satisfied, he rolled over, away from her, and fell into a heavy sleep.

Pain and agony seeped into Alexandra's stunned mind. She could not quite combat the effects of the drug, but she knew what had happened and she knew that she had to escape before Giles awoke. But moving was sheer agony, for her back burned and stung almost beyond endurance. Still, she forced herself to slip from the bed. She could hardly stand and held onto pieces of furniture as she made her stumbling way across the room. At the door, she glanced back at Giles, but he slept on, peaceful and sated. She turned the lock, the click seemed to echo endlessly in the silent room, but he did not move. She opened the door, shuddering at the creak it made, then tightly shut it behind her.

She took a deep breath, fighting the overpowering pain. She had to get away, escape the mansion. Stumbling repeatedly, falling and dragging herself up, she finally made her way to her own room. Hopelessly aware of her bloodied, nude body, she thrust the door open and fell into the arms of Ebba.

"Oh, child, child. That monster done hurt you bad. Oh, the women he's ruined. Oh, sugar, we've got to get you out of here. I was afraid so

I waited, but I never dreamed he'd go so far with you. Oh, child!"

She helped Alexandra to the bed, shaking her head and mumbling to herself.

"He's asleep, Ebba. We don't have much time."

"I've got to get you cleaned up first, child. Put salve on your back. You're not cut deep, but it's got to be tended."

"Hurry, Ebba, I'm afraid he'll awake. Are there horses?"

"There's a horse and carriage, but they belong to Mister Giles."

"Well, they belong to us now. And Ebba, you can't stay here any longer either."

"I'm going with you, sugar, you can be sure of that. Now, I'll just get the salve and be right back."

Alexandra took out her valise, stuffing stockings, a chemise, and one gown into it. She picked up the Norwegian medallion from her dresser and carefully tucked it into the valise. It was now her most important possession.

There was a sound at the door and she whirled around to see Ebba hurrying inside. She was relieved to see her friend for she was haunted by Giles' presence down the hall. He could easily wake up and find them in her bedroom.

Ebba quickly spread the noxious smelling salve all over Alexandra's sore back, then wrapped the

279

clean cloth all around her. Ebba slipped the gown carefully over Alexandra's head, pulling it down gently over her body.

Alexandra hurriedly picked up her valise and they stepped into the hall, looking carefully toward Giles' bedroom before rushing down the stairs. At the back door, they paused, breathlessly, to listen for any sound of him, but all was quiet.

Outside, the cool night air felt good against Alexandra's face and her head began to clear as the drug lost its effect. She would not think of what she had just been through, not now, she couldn't. She had to think of escaping from the plantation before he discovered her missing.

They hurried across the lawn to the kitchen. Once inside, Ebba grabbed her large, worn valise. It was stuffed with all her possessions.

"You were already packed, Ebba?" Alexandra asked, surprised.

"I knew Miss Eleanor was going, child, and I knew that I'd be going when that happened, too. This is all I have. Now, let's pack some food. I've baked cornbread and there's some meat to take. Hurry, child."

"Ebba, you pack the food while I harness the horse, unless you know how."

Ebba's eyes grew large. "Sugar, I'm afraid of those animals and I ain't never harnessed one."

"Well, I haven't either, but I've seen it done. I'll do my best. Is that the stable over there?"

"Yes, but hurry. He might wake up at any moment, and he'd kill us both sure as the world."

"I'm going, Ebba. You hurry, too."

She left the kitchen for the stable. How she would harness the horse she didn't know, but she was determined to use her last ounce of strength to escape Giles. Knocking aside the clinging moss and limbs of trees, she ran determinedly on, growing more angry by the second. The pain that riddled her body only served to intensify her determination to escape Jarmon Plantation.

She stopped outside the stable, standing there a moment as she took great gulps of air to catch her breath. When she flung the stable door open and stepped inside, she gasped. The horse had never been unhitched from his harness or the carriage! She wouldn't have to do it! But how completely cruel of Giles Jarmon. The poor animal. She hurried over to the dejected beast whose head hung down wearily. He eyed her suspiciously, as if expecting more punishment. There were old welts on his sides where Giles had whipped him frequently.

She threw her valise into the carriage and firmly took the reins as she pulled at the reluctant animal. The carriage jangled, creaked, and groaned as it rolled out of the stable. She gritted her teeth. The noise was enough to wake the dead, much less the sleeping Giles, but there was nothing that could be done about it. They *had* to have the horse and carriage. She led the horse, walking beside him to keep him quiet and reassured, speaking to him all the way toward the kitchen. They had to go around the mansion to the front yard to gain the main road. They weren't nearly free yet.

Suddenly a dark figure approached her. She gasped, biting her lip to keep from crying out and jerking the horse to a stop. Then her breath came out in a sigh of relief as she realized it was Ebba moving up to the carriage.

"Glad you got it, sugar. Ready to go?"

"Yes, Ebba. Giles had left the horse like this. But hurry, hurry. Get inside. You've got everything?"

Ebba nodded as she threw her things into the carriage, then hoisted herself inside.

Now, Alexandra thought, if we can just make it to the front of the house and down the drive without him hearing and coming after us.

She pulled at the horse. He was reluctant. She pulled again, straining her sore muscles, and he followed. The pain in her back was a constant red haze that drove her on, demanding that she not be subjected to Giles' brutal treatment again. Moss hit her face, blinding her as she strove to find her around the house. Finally, she was at the side of the huge mansion, then on the circular drive. At last, she could reach the one road leading away from Jarmon Plantation.

She stopped the horse and threw the reins inside. Before stepping into the carriage, she turned around. She wanted one last look at the mansion that had bred a person like Giles, but to her horror she saw the dark shape of a man on the veranda. Then he began to move, taking the stairs two at a time. Giles hit the ground and was running, running toward her!

She froze, unable to move. Every horror that had ever haunted her was embodied in the dark, sinister figure running toward her. But still she couldn't move and he was getting closer, and closer.

"Hurry!" Ebba hissed, and the familiar voice broke Alexandra's dreamlike stupor.

She got into the carriage, and grabbing the reins in both hands, she flicked them harshly over the poor animal's back. He jerked forward in surprise, then quickened his pace as she urged him on, but he was not quick enough. Giles was upon them. He grabbed Alexandra's arm, pulling, holding on as the horse gathered speed.

Desperate, Alexandra forgot her fright, her pain, as her hand came down on the whip Giles had left in the seat. Her fingers curled around it and as she raised it, she looked hard into his dark, furious eyes. Her eyes glinted like bits of green glass as she brought the whip down viciously across his face, striking again and again until his blood ran red and his face contorted in pain and rage. Still he hung on as the animal raced down the drive away from the mansion. She clung to the reins of the wildly running horse with one hand and plied the whip with the other. Then she saw her chance. There was a bend in the road with the branches of the trees hanging low along the side. She urged the horse on, then turned to Giles as the trees came close. She lashed out at him once more before the branches caught him, scraping his body away from her and the carriage.

Alexandra's triumphant laughter rang out in the quiet, still country night.

Part Three

The Eyes of Texas

Chapter Seventeen

Texas! Was it as endless as it seemed? Alexandra shaded her eyes as she looked far into the distance, wishing that she wore a more appropriate hat than the small fashionable one perched atop her curls. No matter how far they traveled, or how far her eyes could see, it was still a land of endless proportions—a flat, dry, dusty country filled with gamma grass, brush, and mesquite. There was no resemblance here to anything she'd known before. And surprisingly, many small animals as well as the large herds of wild longhorns and mustangs lived in this desolate country, thriving in the hot, dry climate.

Even the fine horse and comfortable sidesaddle could not keep the muscles of her body from aching as they rode deeper and deeper into south Texas toward the Bar J Ranch. Alexandra glanced over at her companions. They sat their horses well, seemingly tireless, but then they were United States Cavalrymen and were used to long hours in the saddle. Alexandra was not! And her healing back did not help matters.

Four soldiers were escorting her to the Bar J Ranch: Lieutenant Blake, his sergeant, and two enlisted men. She had been fortunate to attain their protection in Corpus Christi, the port where she had debarked from the boat she'd boarded in New Orleans. The thought of Louisiana brought memories flooding back.

She remembered how she had not slowed the poor horse down until Ebba and she were far away from Giles and the Jarmon Plantation; after the pace had slowed she had walked the exhausted animal much of the way to New Orleans. It had been a long, painful trip, but after stopping to rest several times, they had finally arrived just as dawn was breaking over the city.

Fortunately, Ebba knew her way around New Orleans and had insisted that she and Alexandra stay with some people she knew in the Negro section. They would be safer there; Giles would be less likely to find them. It was a small overcrowded house, but to Alexandra it had seemed like paradise.

As soon as the local banks had opened, she had reluctantly wired to New York for money. Now Stan Lewis was sure to look for her. She only hoped that once she was out of New Orleans, Stan Lewis and Giles Jarmon would not be able to find her in the vastness of Texas.

So she'd taken the chance, gotten the money, then had set about finding passage to Corpus Christi, the closest port to the Bar J Ranch in south Texas. She had been lucky. A schooner was sailing in three days; her money would arrive in time.

Before leaving, she had given Ebba cash to go out and purchase whatever clothes for her she could, with a special request to get a riding habit and boots. She did not dare shop for herself, too afraid that Giles or Madame LeBlanc would find her.

Ebba had been gone all afternoon, but had finally returned carrying many packages and boxes. Either she had been unable to buy or had chosen not to buy, any simple gowns. The ones she had purchased were luxurious and expensive. But there was no time left to shop again so she had thanked Ebba, grateful for anything at all to take along on her escape.

She had given the horse and carriage to the Negro family who had helped them, and also a substantial sum of money to Ebba to help her when she got up North.

She had enjoyed the interlude on the ship; it had proven pleasant and restful, the clean salt air flushing the humid rot of the dying South from her spirit, healing her. She'd shared a cabin with several Northern women who were going to join their husbands in Texas, soldiers stationed at the fort in Brownsville. Since an escort of soldiers would be waiting in Corpus Christi to meet the women, they had assured Alexandra that she would be welcome to travel with them for it would be much safer than trying to hire an unreliable escort.

So, by the time they had arrived in Corpus Christi, she had felt happier, more secure, more like her old self, and was looking forward to completing her promise to Olaf and Eleanor. The soldiers had been waiting, as expected, to escort the women and were more than happy to include Alexandra in their party. There had been wagons for the women to ride in and room for their trunks and the other military supplies which had also arrived on the schooner. She'd felt quite safe as they had ridden inland and then south towards Brownsville on the tip of Texas and near the Mexican border. The major had assured her that even though they would not go by the Bar J Ranch, he would send an escort with her over to the ranch.

The four days they had traveled to get there had been long, hot, and dusty, but she had enjoyed the company of the other women and the obvious admiration of the soldiers. One man in particular had been most attentive — Lieutenant Blake. He had always been there to help her, making sure she was comfortable. The major had even let him escort her to the Bar J Ranch, and she'd felt quite safe in his presence.

Suddenly, her thoughts were jerked back to the present as she saw an adobe building in the distance. Could that at last be the Bar J Ranch? The flat, prairie lands all looked alike to her.

"That's the Bar J hacienda, Miss Alexandra," Lieutenant Blake said, glancing at the beauty riding beside him. He was sorry she would not be going on to Brownsville with the rest of the party. But he didn't think a woman like this one would stay long in desolate south Texas. There was nothing here but a lot of half starving Rebels who'd fled the dying South after the war, and thousands of wild cattle and mustangs. No, it was certainly not the place for a fine Northern lady like Miss Alexandra Clarke, but she'd been adamant about coming. At least they had gotten her there safely, but if she didn't want to stay, he'd be only too happy to take her back to the others.

"It's like nothing I've ever seen before," Alexandra said, studying the adobe structure. At least it wasn't a one room shack, but still it was hardly a mansion. The structure was Spanish in architecture with a flat roof and a rounded archway in front. It seemed to fit the countryside, blending in with the colors and the stark, flat land. The sun was intense and it was already hot, much too hot for May. She wondered if it ever got really cold in the winter.

"No, ma'am, I doubt if it is. You'd be used to something much finer," Lieutenant Blake said.

"Finer, perhaps, but not as appropriate," Alexandra said thoughtfully.

Lieutenant Blake grunted, thinking that she didn't have any idea of what she was getting into. The Indians were about tamed, but the men of Texas were wild and almost impossible to control. The fort at Brownsville was supposed to keep things in order, but in this wide expanse of land, there was little they could do. Miss Alexandra was just too innocent a young woman to understand what she was getting into, and she wasn't strong enough to last through the hardships that were innate to the country. But she was stubborn as well as beautiful and was determined to see for herself, he thought. Well, give her a month, then she'd be begging for someone to take her away—to anywhere that was civilized.

Stopping in front of the entrance to the hacienda, Lieutenant Blake put his large hand over Alexandra's gloved ones. "Remember to come to me if you need help, Miss Alexandra. You will have friends in Brownsville when we get there. Remember that, *please.*"

She turned her bright eyes up to his face, looking at the strong jawline, the intense brown eyes. "Thank you for your interest, Lieutenant Blake, and for bringing me here safely. If I, indeed, need help or want to leave the Bar J Ranch, I will certainly think of my friends at Brownsville."

"Well, what brings you folks this way?" a voice hailed them, as a man walked slowly toward them from the hacienda.

Alexandra watched him closely, realizing that her time had come. She looked over at the lieutenant. He quickly dismounted and came over to her horse. He helped her down, his hands lingering on her small waist longer than was necessary, but she didn't notice, her attention caught up with the man who approached them.

"What have we got that the army needs now?" the man drawled as he stopped beside Alexandra and Lieutenant Blake, his eyes squinting in the sunlight as he eyed the group of soldiers unfavorably.

"We've come for nothing of yours, sir," Lieutenant Blake said smartly. "We've brought Miss Alexandra Clarke to you."

"Oh?" the man said slowly, his attention focusing on Alexandra. A beautiful woman, a rare beauty, he thought, as his eyes quickly looked her over. But what was she doing here?

Alexandra stared at the man, forgetting her manners completely. There was a feeling of aristocracy about him even though he was dressed so strangely in tight fitting pants, an open necked shirt, high boots with very high heels and a red scarf tied around his neck. There was an extremely large hat planted securely on his head, but she could see the sharp black eyes under it appraising her. And there was something familiar in his features.

"Well?" he asked, still watching Alexandra.

"I've come to see Jacob Jarmon and his uncle, Lamar Jarmon."

The man's expression didn't change, but there was a slight twitch to his lips. "Well, now, what would bring a fine Yankee lady all the way out here to see two hombres like that?"

Alexandra felt her face turning red. "I am Alexandra Clarke. I have just come from the Jarmon Plantation in Louisiana."

The man's mouth tightened, but not in friendship or pleasure. "So?"

This was not proving to be easy. Why had she ever thought they would welcome her with open arms? But she plunged on. She'd come too far not to continue. "Eleanor—"

"Eleanor?" the man asked quickly, his face softening for a moment before the hard mask came down again.

"She sent me to see her son and his uncle. She's dead."

The man uttered several strong oaths as he turned quickly away from them and paced the hard packed dirt in front of the hacienda. His hands clenched and unclenched as if it took great effort to control himself. In a moment he came back, then pushed his hat back on his head. "Welcome to the Bar J, Miss Clarke. If you're a friend of Eleanor's, then you're our friend, too. I'm Lamar Jarmon. You can call me Lamar, everyone does. Her son is here. You can meet him later."

Alexandra smiled back, her heart giving a tiny jump in relief. She'd been accepted!

"You'll be staying then, Miss Alexandra?" Lieutenant Blake asked discouragingly.

She looked at him, then back at Lamar Jarmon. "Yes, I'll be staying—if I'm welcome."

Lamar nodded. "You're welcome, but I must warn you right now that anyone staying at the Bar J has to pull their own weight. It's not a woman's world. You won't like it here."

"Yes, I understand. I'll do whatever is necessary, but you see, Eleanor asked me on her deathbed to come here. There are things I must tell you and then, I want to stay a while, just a while," she said gently, imploringly, her green eyes soft and moist.

"If Eleanor sent you and you're determined to stay after having traveled this far into Texas, then you know what you're getting into. But I'll warn you again, Texas is no place for a woman—not a woman like you."

Alexandra flushed again, but this time in anger. "Mister Jarmon, I am not a child. I know what I'm getting into. I made a promise to Eleanor and I never break my promises."

Lamar smiled slightly, thinking that perhaps

he'd judged the lady wrong, perhaps she was tough enough for Texas, at least she had a temper and was no mewling girl that would demand attention and pampering. Well, they'd see, but he knew one man who'd be mad as hell to have this little slip of a woman around the place. No, Eleanor's son wouldn't be glad to see the lady she'd sent here. Hell, he'd been so crabby and mean since he came back from New Orleans that hardly a man dared approach him. He'd always had a bad temper, but now it was almost always aflame. Well, at least things would be lively for a while. Of course, they'd have to send her away before they made the cattle drive to Kansas, but they'd cross that bridge when they came to it. He never worried in advance; it just made a man old before his time.

"Well, Miss Clarke, if you're as determined as you seem to be, perhaps you'll make it on the Bar J after all. Are those your bags on the pack horse?"

Alexandra grinned at him, showing her lovely white teeth and he caught his breath for an instant. The Bar J hands would never be the same after seeing her. There was no doubt about that, he thought.

"Yes, they're mine. I didn't bring much. I didn't know what I'd need."

He nodded, thinking that women never traveled light even when they thought they did.

"You can unload, men," Lieutenant Blake said, eyeing Lamar Jarmon uneasily. He turned toward Alexandra. "You realize there won't be any women here, except a Mexican or Indian perhaps. Are you sure you want to stay?"

She glanced at him, her eyes darkening. "Yes, I'm sure."

She was more determined than ever since these men were so sure she couldn't survive. After what she'd been through and what she'd learned, she could do just as well as any man. Texas, a place for men only! She'd show them!

She watched silently as the soldiers dismounted. There were only two large valises and one smaller one, but all three men assisted. They carried the bags up to the hacienda. There they waited, obviously unsure if they were welcome to enter a former Rebel home.

Lieutenant Blake noticed their hesitancy, understood it, and cursed to himself. The damn Rebels were so proud, as if they were better than the Northerners. Well, the North had won the war and proved just who was supreme, but the South couldn't seem to understand or accept that fact.

"Take them in, men, out of the sun," Lieutenant Blake commanded sharply as he looked straight at Lamar Jarmon, daring him to object.

Lamar simply smiled insolently. "Surely you and your men would like a cool drink be-

297

fore continuing."

Lieutenant Blake would have liked to have refused, but he knew that the day would be long, hot, and thirsty. For his men's sake, he couldn't turn down the invitation. "Indeed, yes. Thank you."

Alexandra preceded the two men, noticing the difference between this country and the plantation she'd left behind. It was clean here and the heat seemed to sanitize everything so that it was continually fresh. She liked the dry air much better than the humid, sweltering heat of Louisiana. She passed under the high arch that formed a gate in the long adobe fence surrounding the hacienda.

Inside, she was surprised to find that it was quite cool. The adobe seemed to keep out the heat, as well as the intense sunlight. The main room they entered was large and furnished sparsely with dark, massive furniture, elaborately carved in the Spanish style. There were brightly colored rugs and wall hangings on the floors and walls which she decided must be Mexican and Indian. She was fascinated as she looked about for it was all in such great contrast to her New York mansion, or the plantation. Everything that filled the room was utilitarian and a part of Texas culture. It was a man's home, a man's world. But she liked it.

"Please sit down, Alexandra, gentlemen," Lamar said graciously, waving in the direction of the chairs.

His use of her first name startled Alexandra but she did not object; it made her feel more welcome.

"No, thank you. We don't have the time," Lieutenant Blake said stiffly. "We must rejoin our company immediately."

"Of course. I understand. One moment, please."

Presently Lamar returned, carrying a tray with glasses and bottles. "Help yourselves, gentlemen," he said as he set the tray down on a table. "I'll see that your horses are watered while you're drinking."

Lieutenant Blake brought Alexandra a glass of water. She quickly drained the glass, then smiled her appreciation. He drank thoughtfully as he watched her. If only he could be alone with her before leaving.

He turned abruptly to his soldiers. "Men, if you're through, go see to your horses. We must be on our way."

The surprised soldiers looked up quickly, downed their drinks, and left.

Turning to Alexandra, he smiled. "Stand up, Miss Alexandra."

She looked at him in wonder, then did as he bid, suddenly not understanding the young lieutenant at all.

"You won't forget me, will you?" he asked softly, taking her hands in his.

"Of course not, Lieutenant Blake," she said.

"Good. I could never forget you — Alexandra, never," he whispered as he drew her to him.

She turned pink with anger. He was actually thinking of kissing her. Did he want payment for his escort?

"Will you give a soldier who adores you a goodbye kiss?" he asked, his eyes beseeching as he pulled her into the circle of his arms.

She calmed her anger, as she once would not have been able to do, and smiled sweetly at him, letting herself go limp in his arms. Fighting would only make him more determined, she knew, as it had with the others. His kiss wouldn't last long, then he'd be gone from her life.

Lieutenant Blake couldn't believe his luck. He grew bold, pulling her body close to his so that he could feel her firm breasts against his chest. She was an absolute angel. He touched her lips softly, found them yielding, then unable to control himself any longer, crushed her to him, his mouth hard on hers. He forgot everything in his complete absorption with the tantalizing woman. He'd never held a lady he wanted so much. And she wanted him. He could feel it.

"Lieutenant!" a sharp, authoritative voice ripped through the silence of the room. "If you're through pawing the young lady, I suggest you leave. Your men are ready and Yankees aren't welcome on the Bar J."

Lieutenant Blake jerked away from Alexandra.

He turned around, frowning, and was surprised to hear the gasp that came from her and see the stunned look on the man facing them.

"No! Oh, no," Alexandra cried, her gaze caught by a hard blue stare. "Jake!"

"Indeed, Alex," he said, his face hard, his blue eyes turning slightly gray as they flicked over her quickly, then back to the lieutenant. "I must beg your pardon, sir. I didn't realize you were getting paid for escorting the woman here. I'll return when you're finished." Jake turned his back and began to walk from the room.

"Oh, no, *Jake*," Alexandra cried, starting to run after him, but the lieutenant caught her just as Jake turned around.

"You wanted something, Alex?"

"I, I, you don't understand."

"I understand what I saw. What I *don't* understand is what you're doing here at the Bar J."

"I'm here to see Jacob Jarmon. What are you doing here?"

The lieutenant looked from one to the other, confused. They seemed to know each other, but there was no liking between them, that was obvious. His hand tightened on Alexandra's waist possessively.

Jake threw back his head and laughed, a harsh, mocking sound, then looked at her again, his eyes raking her body insolently.

"See here, sir," Lieutenant Blake said, "You

301

can't treat a lady like Miss Alexandra this way."

"Lady! You call *her* a lady?" Jake asked, laughing derisively. "You two seem to be under a great delusion, but I've no intention of enlightening either one of you."

"Well, I'm not staying here if you work here," Alexandra said sharply. "I'll just leave with the lieutenant now."

"Oh?" Jake asked, his eyes turning opaque so that she could not read their expression. "But I thought you'd come to meet Jacob Jarmon?"

She frowned in concentration. "Well, yes I did, but I never dreamed that *you'd* be here. What *are* you doing here anyway?" she asked angrily, hating the smug, cold way he regarded her.

He grinned again, his eyes crinkling at the corners. "I live here, my dear Alexandra. I work here."

"I don't believe it. Where's Lamar Jarmon? He'll straighten this out. You'll just have to leave!"

"Me?" Jake laughed again.

"Did someone ask for me?" Lamar asked, stepping into the room. "I could hear your voices clear outside. What's going on? Your men are waiting, lieutenant."

"I know, but there seems to be some sort of confusion here. Alexandra may return with me."

"Oh?" Lamar asked. "What's the matter, Alexandra, the ranch too much already?"

She flushed angrily. "What's *that* man doing here?" she asked, pointing to Jake.

"Why, he lives here, of course."

"Well, I won't stay here with him. You'll just dismiss him. There must be plenty of good hands. And a sea captain can't be much good on a ranch, anyway."

"Dismiss Jake? Why?" Lamar asked quickly, looking at Jake's inscrutable face, then back at Alexandra. "What's going on here? You came all this way to see him and now you want him sent away. I don't understand." Women were always trouble, but this one was worse than most.

"I didn't come all the way to see *him*. I came to see Jacob Jarmon, Eleanor's son," Alexandra said angrily.

"But didn't he tell you? He *is* Jacob Jarmon."

Alexandra stood there stunned, the silence almost overwhelming as her eyes locked with Jake's hard, unrelenting blue ones. She felt suddenly weak. Jake was Jacob Jarmon. He'd been in New Orleans. He'd been to the plantation just before her. He'd been going to Texas. Of course, it all made sense *now*. How could she have been so blind, so stupid?

"I, I'll go," Alexandra said weakly. "I cannot stay here, not with him."

"Of course you'll go," Lieutenant Blake said comfortingly, both his arms supporting Alexandra now. "This is no place for a lady like you."

"Get your hands off her, lieutenant," Jake

303

said in a deadly quiet voice, drawing his gun.

He wouldn't let another man touch her. He couldn't, no matter how much he hated her. He wanted revenge and what better opportunity than now, with her here on the ranch? She wouldn't be used to this type of work, the little whore. And she'd even pawned herself off as a fine lady to this idiot lieutenant. But if the lieutenant touched her one second longer, he'd kill the man, Jake thought irrationally. Where this woman was concerned, he always lost his head and he was doing it once more. He was a fool and knew he was a fool, but still he wouldn't let another man touch her. He wouldn't let her go! No matter what she'd done, he wanted her just as badly as he had before. Damn her cheating little soul, he still wanted her.

"Get out of here quickly, lieutenant, and don't ever come back. The lady came to us and she'll stay." Jake held his pistol steady.

Lieutenant Blake hesitated. He wanted Alexandra, but life was dear. He could read the deadly cold look on Jake's face; he knew the man would kill him if he didn't go. He would leave Alexandra now, but he'd not forget her, or this Jarmon quickly. Brownsville wasn't *that* far away.

The lieutenant stepped away from Alexandra, disentangling the hands that now clutched at him. He looked down into her desperate eyes. "The man's got a gun on me, Miss Alexandra. I can't take you with me."

"But I don't want to stay. You can't just leave me."

"I can't take you and the others can't come back for you. The men will never leave their wives for one young lady who's changed her mind."

"I'm going back with you. I won't stay!"

"Step back, lieutenant," Jake said dangerously, keeping his pistol trained on Lieutenant Blake as he walked over to Alexandra. Slipping his arm around her, he jerked her to his side. He hurt her and he knew it. He intended to hurt her and it wasn't the last pain she would feel from him either, he thought grimly. Her nearness brought back the familiar tightening in his loins. How could she have such a strong effect on him? He cursed his weakness.

"Let me go, Jake," Alexandra hissed at the man who held her so tightly to him, so possessively. "I'll leave. I won't ever come back. Just let me go."

"No," Jake said firmly, looking at the lieutenant as he motioned toward the door with his head, the gun firm in his hand.

Alexandra struggled against his hard body, trying to break free. She had to escape! She couldn't stay here with this man—in the same house. "Let me go!" she hissed.

Jake laughed shortly. "Be still, Alex, or I'll shoot the lieutenant *now*. Would you like that?"

She stopped squirming instantly and looked up at his face in alarm. He meant what he said. She could feel it in his taut body. He *wanted* to shoot Lieutenant Blake. No, she couldn't be the cause of the luckless lieutenant's death. She became limp against Jake, determined to do nothing to anger him.

"Now, get on your horse and ride out of here, lieutenant, and don't even *think* of returning for Alexandra. She belongs to me and I'll kill any man who tries to take her away."

"All right, Jarmon, you've got me now, but don't think this is over."

"No. It's all right, Lieutenant Blake. Don't return for me, or try to help. I don't want to see you killed. He'd do it. I know," Alexandra said softly.

"I can take care of myself, Miss Alexandra, don't you worry," Lieutenant Blake said, thinking that she really did care for him if she was willing to brave Jarmon to keep him alive. What was the story with these people? He'd give a lot to know.

"Lieutenant," Lamar finally said, "please believe me that the lady will be all right. She is a relative of ours and Jake has always considered it his right to protect her. They've had frequent quarrels. But it's all in the family, you see. Please, believe me."

Lieutenant Blake looked from one face to the other. He didn't know what to believe now.

Alexandra had originally said that she'd come to see Jacob Jarmon, but she'd not known him as this Jake and she'd not known this so-called uncle. They didn't look like gentlemen and the story was too confusing for his mind. He'd never encountered such a volatile family before. Well, he'd better get out of it now while he could.

"I don't know what to believe, but I'm going. I've got no choice. But remember what I told you, Miss Alexandra," he said as he turned to leave.

"Lieutenant," Jake said, his voice even softer, "remember what *I* told *you*."

Chapter Eighteen

"Have them followed. I want them off Bar J land," Jake said.

Lamar nodded at him, then strode quickly from the room.

Alexandra wished Lamar had not left her alone with Jake.

"Do you always pay in kind for what you get, Alex?"

"I don't know what you mean."

"You don't need to carry money with you, do you, sweet?'

"I have money. Jake."

"Sure you do *now*. The money you got from the cat houses in New Orleans. You must have made a nice sum there."

Alexandra bit her lip. He had believed what Captain Sully had said about her. "You don't know that, Jake. You've jumped to the wrong conclusions. I was with Eleanor Jarmon."

"Don't bring my mother into this," Jake said angrily.

"But Jake, that's why I came here. She sent me."

"You lying bitch," he said hoarsely as he pushed her from him.

She couldn't stop herself as she lost her balance and fell hard against the wall. She slid down to the floor. She felt slightly stunned and watched him apprehensively as he approached, then stopped, his feet wide apart. In her daze she studied him. He looked different. He was dressed like a cowboy now and he looked the part—rough, mean, tough. Could he be as cruel as he looked? He hadn't been on the ship, but this hard man she didn't know. And she was afraid of him.

"Don't mention my mother again. I don't want her name to cross your lips. Do you hear me?" Jake spat at her as one hand came down toward her, the other reholstering his gun.

She shrank back, expecting him to hit her, but instead he jerked her up. She fell against him heavily. She could smell the masculine odor of him, feel the heat from his body. She remembered, though she tried hard to forget, that he had always made her weak and willing in his arms. She looked up at him, their faces close.

Jake's arms came about her slowly, almost hesitantly, pulling her closer. His blue eyes were still hard, but there was almost doubt in them now. His face moved closer to hers, and she forgot all that had come before as his mouth touched hers in a fiery, demanding kiss. She could not help herself. Her arms moved up around his neck, feeling his hair, his hard muscles, as his tongue plunged deeply into her mouth. He instantly awakened all the sleeping fires in her and she responded, kissing him back with all the denied passion that had built up since she had run away from his ship.

Suddenly he stopped, pushing her back from him, his brows drawn together in an angry scowl.

"Jake," she breathed, feeling as if she would fall if he made her stand alone.

"You damn whore. You know all the tricks, don't you?"

Her eyes widened in alarm.

"You think I won't hurt you if you give me what I want from you, what I've always wanted from you. It's the way you work, isn't it?"

She shook her head in silent, sad denial.

"You've used me from the first, haven't you? You started with that story about a man raping you to make you marry him so I wouldn't be angry when I discovered you weren't a virgin. And Sully, you paid him for the trip with your body, didn't you? And me, you paid me, too, for the trip to New Orleans, didn't you? But you didn't want to come with me here to Texas, not then. You wanted to make money in New Orleans, selling your body to men, and you did!"

"No! No Jake, it's not true!"

"Sure it's true. I just want to know why you prefer all the others. Even that kid lieutenant was going to get his for bringing you safely here. But me, when it comes to me, you fight, you always fight. Why, Alex, why?"

"No, Jake. You don't understand," she cried desperately as his frown deepened and his fists clenched. "I never did any of that. I'm not a whore!"

"Hell if you aren't. I saw you myself at Bella's in bed with my half-brother. You let my brother have you, begged him to take you. I *saw* you. Do you hear me? I *saw* you in bed with my brother," Jake hissed, his voice low and insistent.

"Oh, no," Alexandra groaned, covering her ears with her hands. He'd never believe her now. That was it. That's what Madame LeBlanc had wanted. It was all too horrible. Jake hated her. She knew it now, and why. She wanted to faint, anything to make his burning, accusing eyes go away.

Suddenly he grabbed her, pulling her roughly against his chest.

"This is one time you're going to share your charms with me, Alexandra, and you're not going to fight me, you're not going to turn away from me. I know you for what you are and you can't pretend innocence and shyness any longer. I'm a man and I want you. You know what

311

that means. A whore knows only too well what that means."

"No, Jake. Don't do this to me. Please," Alexandra pleaded as he dragged her down a long hall, then kicked open a door.

He strode into the room, locking the door behind him. He pushed her to the bed. "Get your clothes off, Alex. I want to see you as all those other men have seen you." He began removing his own clothes.

She cowered on the bed. Jake frightened her. He was like a madman. He hated her so much he might really kill her. Perhaps he *would* kill her if she didn't do what he said. No one would ever find her body. She was alone in Texas and no one knew where she was. This seemed worse than anything that had ever happened to her before. Jake was like flint, unbending, unfeeling, only determined to take what he wanted. Well, all right, if he wanted her to play the whore, she would. It didn't matter any more; nothing mattered any more. She had lost too much.

Calmly, she got off the bed. She began by taking the pins out of her hair. Jake stopped, stilled like an animal with a scent, his hands on the buckle of his belt, his hard, bronzed chest bared before her, as his blue, too blue, eyes watched her suspiciously, yet with complete absorption. Slowly, watching him, she pulled out the last pin and felt her hair tumble down all around her. She could feel his desire like a tangible force in the room.

Next came her jacket, revealing her sheer silk blouse. She hesitated.

"I don't believe the time to stop is now, my dear," Jake said dryly.

She flushed with anger, then continued. She unbuttoned the blouse, slipped it off. Only her thin chemise covered her breasts and she saw his eyes narrow as he watched her movements. The skirt and petticoats were then unhooked, sliding off her almost of their own accord. She stood before him in her sheer chemise and her high boots. What a ridiculous sight, she thought.

Jake smiled coldly, then advanced toward her. "I believe we really should remove the boots, Alex."

He wasn't making it easy for her, she thought, but then he believed the worst of her. He pushed her back against the bed, grabbed one foot, pulled the boot off and then the other. Now she wore nothing except the chemise which concealed very little.

"I see my memory wasn't as good as I thought," he said thoughtfully as his eyes raked her body.

She glared at him, hating his insolence yet feeling her heart beat fast. Could she still want him?

"You are more beautiful, more sensuous than

a man *could* remember and not go crazy wanting you. It must be worth quite a lot to you."

She flushed angrily. "I don't sell my body, Jake. I've never even given it willingly."

He laughed harshly. "You're giving it to me now, aren't you?"

She didn't answer, trying to control her growing temper. Yes, she still wanted him. And she had to admit that she had given herself to him willingly before. And she might again. Only she wouldn't tell him. He already had too much power over her.

"Aren't you?"

"No. Yes. Whatever you want to think. I don't care."

"There's no need to pout just because I won't pay for your services, Alexandra. Now, come over here and finish undressing me."

"What?" she asked, her eyes flashing dangerously. He was about to push her too far.

"Come here. You know what to do."

She walked slowly over to him, reached out, not touching his skin, unbuckled his belt, then unbuttoned his trousers. They slid to the floor. Backing away, she saw the object that was to claim her; it was erect and pulsating with need. She hesitated as he walked toward her.

"I, I—no, Jake, please." She was afraid that if he touched her in desire she would be lost to her own building passion.

"Are you still playing the innocent? Don't! It

314

doesn't fit anymore. I know what you are. Now, be the whore with me, or—"

She looked at his proud, handsome, angry face. Why was she fighting him? Her body didn't care about the insults or the anger. But her mind did and it was losing the battle. For she knew, above all else, that he wanted her. Desperately.

Hesitantly she extended her hands toward his chest, but he caught them and twined them around his hot, throbbing member. She moaned low in her throat as his hands covered hers, moving with hers, teaching her the rhythm.

She heard a groan and looked up. Jake's face was tight, his eyes dark. He looked at her in almost pain. "Damn, Alexandra. What you do to a man should be outlawed. No wonder you can make your way with it." He picked her up and carried her to the bed.

She looked toward the door, thinking of escape as she tried to push her feelings down.

"No. Alex. Don't even think it."

Silently cursing her treacherous flesh, she let him gently place her on the bed, then stretch out beside her.

"Now, show me how a whore treats a man. But first, take off your chemise."

"I'm not a harlot."

"Stop playing your coy games. You know what I want from you."

She hesitated, then sighed. Closing her eyes,

she pulled the chemise up and off her body, flinging it away. Tentatively, she leaned over him, not touching his body. His arms came around her and he crushed her lips to his. They were warm, firm, and something stirred deep within her, memories returned, unbidden, and she parted her lips. She slipped her tongue into his waiting mouth almost hesitantly, and was met by his swiftly attacking tongue. She moaned, ready to retreat, but her head was caught by his hand and her mouth molded against his own. His kisses sent shivers over her, causing a burning to start in her depths. She moaned again, remembering how he'd affected her before. She'd not felt it since they'd parted.

Jake could not wait for her slow feminine tricks. His desire was quick, hot, and had to be satisfied. What did this woman have that made him forget all others? He had vowed never to look for her after he'd seen her in the arms of Giles, but here he was with her. He couldn't help himself. He rolled over on top of her, reveling in the feel of her soft flesh under his body, her soft hair entwined in his hands as he tasted her sweet mouth. Damn, but he'd missed her, needed her, wanted her. No matter that she was a cheat, a whore, a liar. He wanted her! He could not deny that; no matter what she was, he couldn't stay away from her.

He whispered words in her ears, words in French and Spanish that she couldn't understand, but it didn't matter. All that mattered to Alexandra was the feel of his body on hers, his lips traveling over her face, covering her in kisses, his hands moving over her body, searing her bare flesh wherever they touched. Her body ached all over for him, she wanted to feel him inside her, she needed him as she'd never needed anything before. What was wrong with her? He was treating her like a whore and still she wanted him, anything so long as he satisfied the burning deep within her.

Moving down her body, his lips nibbled her soft flesh and he could feel her surrender to him. He captured one taut pink nipple with his mouth, plying it with his tongue until it stood up hard, demanding more. He caressed the other, too, before moving lower. He had to control himself not to take her quickly, harshly. He wanted her to feel what he did. He wanted her to respond to him as he'd seen her respond to Giles. He wanted to burn out every other man who'd gone before him.

Moving still lower, he parted her legs, exposing the soft warm pinkness that he knew awaited him. He heard her moan, but she didn't fight him this time, or struggle. Instead, he felt her hands in his hair, pulling, almost beseeching. Not yet, he thought, not yet. Hungrily, he plunged his tongue into her softness. He felt her arch up against him and cry out softly. He moved inside her swiftly, quickly, carrying her along to what he knew she could experience. She moaned louder, tugging at his hair.

He couldn't get enough.

She couldn't get enough.

She tasted of all the delights he could imagine and his tongue darted swiftly, expertly bringing her to ecstasy and back again. Then he positioned himself between her thighs, almost unable to wait any longer.

"Jake. *Jake*," she moaned softly, weak and pliant, wanting more of what only he could give her.

"Yes, Alex, now. Now," he said as he let his throbbing member press gently against her, making her want him. Then he pushed into her, slipping in easily for she was ready, anxious for him. He smiled to himself. She wasn't fighting him. No, she welcomed him—as she had others. Others! He thrust harder. She cried out, her eyes fluttering open, then closing as his mouth came down hard on hers. He drove harder into her, feeling her softness catch him, caress him, hold him inside. He groaned, knowing that he should stop, not give her the pleasure that she wanted now, begged for, but there was no way he could stop, no way he could leave her unsatisfied. He moved swiftly in and out, in and out, and she held him to her, murmuring his name over and over, returning his kisses with all the passion he knew she was ca-

318

pable of. Damn! She kissed like a whore, made love like one, demanded like one. How could he ever have thought she was a lady? A lady didn't make love like this. But all thoughts were driven from his mind as he moved deeply into her, driving everything from their minds except the ultimate peak of pleasure they shared together.

Slowly, their satisfied bodies relaxed. Jake continued to hold her to him, murmuring soft words. But she stirred under him and he rolled off, complete reality returning to him. She'd done it to him again; made him forget his anger, his frustration, how much he hated her. It was her whore's tricks that made him want her so much. She was an expert, that's what she was.

Alexandra lay there, trying to regain her composure. How could this man who treated her so badly, who seemed to hate her, take her to the brink of complete forgetfulness and beyond? Why was he the only man she responded to? With Jake, she cared for nothing else except to be in his arms, held close to him. No, she mustn't let herself feel this way. He had used her, no matter what else. He had insulted her. He believed her to be a whore. But for the moment she didn't want to do anything to break their peace. She *knew* it wouldn't last long and she didn't want to feel the usual fury that consumed her in his presence. Why was there so much anger between them?

"You shouldn't have come, Alex. You know I can't keep away from you. It's no good, you being what you are, but I won't let you go now that you're here, not until I can get you out of my blood," Jake said, his voice distant again.

She felt her body tighten. "I didn't know who you were. How was I to know you were Jacob Jarmon? How could I possibly know?"

"I don't want to hear your lies. I know what you are. You found out about my family from Giles and from Bella, too, probably, but what game you're playing with me won't work."

"It's no game, Jake. Why won't you listen to me? Why must you just always use me?"

"Use *you?* Hell! I'm the one who keeps getting used, but you won't do it anymore," he said, his body tense, his voice hard and cold.

"I don't want to. I just want to leave. You believe the worst of me so let me go."

He grinned suddenly and turned to look at her, running a finger down her naked body. "Let you go? My dear, do you have any idea how scarce beautiful women are in Texas? And you're exceptional. I'd be a fool to let you go, and I'm no fool, at least not that kind."

She looked away from him, feeling horribly trapped. What would he do with her now?

"You'll stay here, Alexandra, to serve me for a change, and I'd better not catch you with any other man or I'll horsewhip you."

She turned pale, her eyes dilating with fear as

she remembered Giles and his whip. "You wouldn't, you wouldn't do that, would you, Jake?"

He frowned, looking at her closely, surprised by her reaction. What would she know of a whip? It was just a threat. He'd never mar her body. Still, it was strange. She watched him now as if she was truly afraid. He stroked her cheek gently, then said, "What do you know about whips, Alex?"

Her color mounted. She'd never tell him. "Nothing. *Nothing.* It sounds dreadful, that's all."

She looked away from his blue eyes. Sometimes she could get lost in them, lost in their blueness, but now they were hard, closed to her. She felt alone and helpless, trapped by him and by her own body.

"You're going to work as you never have before. And it won't be on your back this time. Don't cross me and we'll get on fine. But if you do—" He laughed coldly. "You see, my dear, you belong to me now. Only to me."

Chapter Nineteen

Banging noisily around the dirty kitchen, Alexandra mumbled furiously under her breath. Not that there was anyone to hear her. They'd all gone, leaving her completely alone in the hacienda. Jake had made her get right out of bed after they'd finished. She'd dressed hurriedly again in her riding habit since he hadn't given her time to find something more suitable in her bags.

And, on top of everything else, he'd had the nerve to move her valises into his room. She was so embarrassed. How would she ever explain the situation to his uncle? How could he treat her so badly? He'd quickly shown her the kitchen, then how to cook beans. Beans! She'd learned a little about cooking on the plantation, but the food here was entirely different. And he'd had the nerve to tell her that she was taking the place of Rosa, a Mexican woman who had worked here before. She supposed he'd used this Rosa in his bed, too!

She stirred the beans slowly, mechanically as they came to a boil, then decided that she could do nothing more for them. The kitchen would have to be cleaned, but not in her riding habit. It was the only one she had. She would simply have to change to something more suitable.

Going back to Jake's bedroom, her bedroom now, she opened her bags and looked through the assortment of gowns. They all seemed heavy, hot, and completely inappropriate for cleaning a kitchen. They even seemed wrong to wear in the hacienda. She would undoubtedly ruin them in no time cleaning. Well, there was nothing to be done, unless—

She slipped out of her riding habit, then folded it carefully before laying it on top of one of the bags. She stood there in her sheer chemise, reveling in the coolness without the hot clothing. She would simply not put anything else on. The men wouldn't be back until late and no one would see her. She'd have time to take a bath and dress before anyone returned. Pleased with her plan, she padded, barefoot, back to the kitchen.

Men, she thought as she looked around herself, had no conception of what a kitchen was supposed to be like. Not that she'd had that much experience, but she'd learned a lot from Ebba. She began sorting the food, putting it away after she'd scrubbed the shelves. It was hard, dirty work, but there was satisfaction in the job, too. The beans were finally getting soft, and she decided to put another large pot of water on to boil, planning to bathe when she finished the kitchen.

Looking up later, she realized that the day was getting on — soon it would be sundown. She thought she heard something outside, but it was too early for Jake and Lamar. She hesitated, listening, but when there was no other noise, she turned back to survey the room. It was sparkling clean. Pushing a strand of hair back from her hot, sweaty face, she looked up at the open door.

She froze. A man stood there watching her, showing white teeth against a dark, swarthy face as he grinned, his eyes appraising her almost nude body. He was a slight man dressed in dark trousers, high boots, a dark red shirt, and a blue bandanna tied loosely around his neck. His face was shadowed by a huge, wide brimmed sombrero. His eyes were beady and black, and they raked her insolently as he leaned against the doorjamb, his right hand hovering near the six gun slung low on his hip.

There was only one word for him — deadly. She shuddered, wishing for the first time that Jake had not left her alone. This Mexican was terrifying.

"I've no plan to harm you, *chica*. Heard about the cavalry patrol and the fine lady they

324

escorted here. Gets a man's curiosity up. You're a pretty *gringa,* aren't you? Jake's had a change in taste, I see."

"I don't know what you're talking about. I'm here to visit his uncle, Lamar Jarmon."

The hard black eyes swept over her again, then back to her pale face, with chin held high. "Maybe, little one, maybe, but I know this *hombre.* You're Jake's woman."

Alexandra flushed vividly red, only too aware of her lack of clothing and this man's leering eyes. "If you don't mind, I'd like to change. Jake and Lamar will return shortly and if you'd care to wait—"

"I'm not here to see them, señorita. I'm here to see you, and you've made that easy."

"Well you've seen all you're going to see. Now leave!" Alexandra hissed, forgetting his pistol in her growing anger.

"Temper? Nice. I like you. Jake won't mind sharing you with me. After all, I shared Rosa with him until he kicked her out."

"Rosa?" Alexandra asked, a cold feeling beginning to grow in the pit of her stomach.

"Sure, my intended, Rosa. She worked here as a cook, a housekeeper. She was Jake's woman for a while—until he got tired of her."

"Well, I know nothing about that. It happened before I came and doesn't concern me in the least."

325

"It concerns you now, *chica*. Jake took my woman. I take his. Then we're even. *Si?*"

"No!"

"You talk too much, little one," he said, beginning to move toward her.

She stepped back, watching him warily, then screamed before turning to run out of the kitchen. She could hear his spurs jangling as he came after her. Suddenly, she slipped on one of the rugs and fell heavily to the hard floor of the main room. Groaning, she tried to get up again, but he was on her immediately, grabbing her hands and pulling them up high over her head as he straddled her legs, pinning her to the floor. She screamed and screamed. Someone had to hear her!

Cursing a long string of oaths in Mexican and English, the man slapped her hard across her face.

With his free hand, he felt of her body, barely covered by the sheer chemise, with quick, experienced movements. She twisted in his grip, trying to free herself. He strengthened his hold, hurting her painfully as she struggled against him, trying to kick, bite, scratch, but he held her pinned to the floor.

"You're a wildcat, aren't you, *chica?*" he asked hoarsely as his hand reached for the buckle of his belt and began to unfasten it. His black gaze held her wide, green one, filled with hate and loathing. "That's all the better. I like

326

that. I only wish my Rosa had fought so well."

Suddenly soft, measured footsteps sounded in the room, but before the Mexican could react, Jake said in a low, controlled voice, "I wouldn't move, Pecos, if I were you."

The man over Alexandra tensed, his mouth tightening, but not a muscle moved. He obviously knew how close to death he was as he looked up into Jake's cold blue eyes and the dark muzzle of the drawn forty-five.

"That's my woman you're straddling. Finish only if you don't want to walk out of here alive."

Alexandra had never before heard such deadly calm in anyone's voice. She didn't move either, afraid he'd shoot her, too, if given half a chance. She could see the difference in the man over her. He wasn't quite so sure anymore, even though she could feel the anger seething in him.

"I've no desire to be a dead man, *gringo*. I only do what is right."

"Hell if you do. Now, very slowly, very easy, throw your gun over here, and don't get smart."

Alexandra lay there, watching the man almost in disbelief. Could this be happening? Did men really go about solving their differences with guns? Where was the law? But the man slowly, carefully removed the pistol from his gunbelt, then flung it toward Jake's feet.

"Good. That's good, Pecos. Now carefully, remember I'd just as soon shoot you as look at you, the knife. The one you wear in your right boot."

The Mexican scowled, but began to move his free hand down toward his boot. Could the man really be armed with a knife as well as a gun? Alexandra could hardly believe the savagery of this land. But soon the silver blade gleamed for a moment over her face before it was thrown beside the gun.

"That's right. I may yet let you live, Pecos. Slowly, very slowly, get up. Be careful not to touch my woman any more. I don't like my woman touched by another."

"Neither do I," the Mexican muttered as he slowly raised himself from Alexandra.

"Don't move, Alex, until I tell you to," Jake commanded. He knew the Mexican was a dangerous and clever hombre. He didn't want him grabbing Alexandra in defense. It could lead to her death. "For your information, Pecos, Rosa came here wanting work and wanting to get in my bed. I merely obliged."

"Sure, *gringo,* and you're calling her a—"

"I'm calling her nothing. I'm telling you the facts. She's gone back to her family. Let that end it. It's finished here. As you can see, I've got another woman. Rosa's yours. Leave it at that."

"It may be easy for you to forget, *hombre,* but I am a man and she is my intended."

"Get out, Pecos, and don't let me see your

face or the faces of your *amigos* on the Bar J again. I want an end to all this. Rosa is nothing to me. She's yours. If I kill you, you won't be able to enjoy all her little delights."

The Mexican flushed darkly, barely holding his temper in check as he walked slowly from the room. At the door, he turned back, glanced at Alexandra, then back to Jake.

"It's not over, *gringo*. You've dishonored Rosa. We don't forget that. You'll be hearing from us."

Then he was gone, slipping away as quickly as he'd come.

Jake hurried to the door and watched him ride away while Alexandra cautiously got up from the floor and draped an Indian blanket carefully around herself. When the sounds of the retreating horse died away, Jake holstered his pistol, and walked slowly back to Alexandra, his blue eyes hard. He stopped in front of her, then jerked the blanket from around her shoulders and tossed it aside. She still wore only the chemise and was marked with dirt and grime from her afternoon cleaning, but she lifted her chin in defiance.

"That's all you were wearing, Alex?" Jake asked.

"It was hot. I was cleaning," she said, her anger growing now that the danger was past. "You said I'd be alone. That man was going to rape me!"

He laughed shortly, a harsh sound. "Once a whore, always a whore. You may be able to live without clothes in a brothel, but my dear, in my home you will clothe yourself properly."

"Well, this was appropriate for cleaning. I could hardly wear satins and silks, now could I? You seem to have forgotten that I didn't expect to take the place of Rosa, that Mexican bitch. I'm no whore—"

Jake slapped her, the crack sounding like a shot in the room as his pent up fury finally broke. "Rosa was no bitch. You're the only damn bitch around here, and you're trouble, nothing but trouble."

She tried to rake his face with her nails, fury pounding in her brain, making everything red and hot. She wanted to hurt him as he'd hurt her, as he was always hurting her. But he was swift and grabbed her wrists, twisting her arms behind her, forcing her body against his so that her breasts strained against his chest.

"You'll do as I say, Alexandra. You belong to me," he said gruffly, feeling himself responding to the soft body quivering against him.

"No! I'll never belong to you, you brute!" Alexandra cried, kicking out at him.

Cursing, he lifted her up into his arms and strode out of the room. Carrying her into his bedroom, he kicked the door shut behind them, then crossed the room to the bed.

He threw her down on it. "You're mine and

you know it, Alex. I'll prove it once again since you seem to have such a short memory."

"No! No, Jake." She struggled as his powerful hands reached out and tore the chemise from her body.

Quickly joining her on the bed, he pulled her legs apart, then pushed his knees up between her thighs. His own anger with Pecos lent fury to his actions and he undid his trousers with no thought to Alexandra's own feelings.

Seeing his bulging manhood so ready to take her, she cried out again, "No! Not like this, Jake." She couldn't bear for him to touch her in anger and revenge.

She struggled, fighting him, but he quickly wrenched her arms behind her back, then grabbed her hips in his hands to pull her toward him, her softness completely exposed to his desires.

Could he never feel that Alexandra was really his? The only time she seemed to respond to him was in bed, when he had pushed her beyond all control. At no other time could he believe that she was completely his, that all the other men were blotted from her mind, her body. Even here in his own home, a man had come and would have taken her. And how much would she have protested?

Furiously he thrust into her, knowing he was hurting her for she was dry, unready, but he wanted it that way. He wanted to hurt her for

all the other men, for his inability to conquer
her, and so he drove deeper, hearing her cry out
in anguish. Then he forgot his reasons, his motives as his flaming desires took over. Blood
pounded in his head. He couldn't think. He
could only focus on the point of fiery hunger
that he drove over and over into her, determined to blot out the others once and for all.
And make her belong to him.

Then he could feel the difference in her. She
wasn't fighting him anymore, but instead was
holding him to her in the same urgency that he
held her. She was soft and moist inside, letting
him slide easily in and out. He covered her lips
with his own, plunging his tongue into her
mouth as his staff plunged into her softness.
She was his! She belonged to him. She wanted
him, too. He knew, he could feel her surrender,
her acceptance of him. He moved harder, faster,
bringing them both to the peak that blotted out
reality, leaving only a clear, clean union of their
two bodies.

As he withdrew from her, she moaned, clinging to him, and all his memories suddenly returned. Cursing her as well as himself for his
need of her body, he jerked away, sitting up
quickly. He had to catch his breath, but he
didn't look at her again until he got up, fastening his trousers, for he knew if he saw her soft,
yielding body, he wouldn't leave. No matter
how he intended to hurt her, it was he that

seemed to die a little each time he buried himself deep within her. What was happening to him? He'd never been this hungry for a woman before.

"Get up, Alex, and get dressed. It's time for dinner. I'd like to see how well you cook. Somehow, I imagine that the kitchen is not as familiar to you as the bedroom."

He chuckled at the fury in her face, then quickly left the room before she had time to answer him.

She flounced off the bed. She'd show him she was no pampered harlot. She'd learn to cook. It couldn't be too hard. Lots of women did it. So she'd just learn and prove him wrong. Of course, if her body wouldn't turn traitor in his arms, he'd think her less the whore. But when he touched her, she was lost!

Sighing, she walked over to the dresser. Fortunately, she'd brought a clean pail of water into the room earlier, for now she'd never get the desired bath. After quickly washing herself all over, she began hunting through her valises for something to wear. Nothing was at all appropriate. She finally decided on the coolest looking gown—a low cut, soft green silk with a matching chemise. She slipped these on, hardly aware of how they emphasized her beauty. She put her hair up loosely and decided she was ready. It was the best she could do.

She went into the kitchen. She didn't know what to serve with the beans since she didn't have the right ingredients to make cornbread, the one bread she knew how to make since Ebba had taught her. She knew how to make coffee and after starting that, she decided to serve some dried beef she found.

While the coffee was brewing, she went out into the main room and began setting the table. As she worked, Lamar walked into the room, dressed in dark trousers and a loose blue shirt. He looked much more the Southern gentleman now, except for his weathered face and hands.

"Good evening, Alexandra," he said, coming toward her, a smile of pleasure transforming his face.

"Hello, Lamar," she said hesitantly.

He stood there, continuing to smile at her, unable to keep his eyes from her perfect body so tantalizingly revealed by the gown. No wonder Jake was so wild about her—she was indeed a rare beauty. Her cheeks were flushed and he could see the difference in her eyes. They were languid looking and her movements were slow, almost dreamy. Jake had taken her again. He shook his head, thinking that the young woman would hardly survive if his nephew continued to take her to his bed constantly. But she didn't seem so unhappy now. How did she really feel about Jake? He couldn't tell, but he could read the signs of fulfilled sex in her lovely face. But

334

then, women had never accused Jake of lacking virility.

"I don't know about dinner," Alexandra said, interrupting Lamar's thoughts.

"What, my dear?"

"Dinner. Jake told me to cook it, but I can't find enough of anything. Anyway, I've never cooked much, but Jake insisted so —"

"I'm sure it'll be fine. We're used to almost anything out here. A Mexican woman worked in the kitchen, but she left after Jake came back from New Orleans." He suddenly realized the implications. Jake had been sleeping with Rosa, but when he returned he was so mean he drove her off. The hacienda had been a mess ever since, but they hadn't had the time or inclination to do anything about it.

"You mean Rosa?"

Lamar nodded uneasily.

"I suppose Jake told you about that Mexican, Pecos, coming by."

"Yes, he did."

"Well, it wasn't my fault," she said defensively.

"Of course not. There has been bad blood between our cowboys and Pecos' banditos before. They can't seem to resist our cattle, or our women now. But don't let it worry you, Alexandra. We can handle Pecos and his *hombres.*"

"All right, Lamar. I won't."

335

"Good. Jake will be here in a minute. You can go ahead and serve if you like. He was just rinsing off when I left him outside."

"Fine," Alexandra said, then went back to the kitchen. She put the beans in a big bowl, then carried them in to the table. She put the dried beef out, too, and mugs of coffee. Just as she was finishing, Jake strode into the room.

He looked her up and down, then grinned. "Wouldn't that gown be more appropriate in the parlor of a house in New Orleans? But then, you came prepared to entertain, not work, didn't you?"

She flushed darkly.

"If that's the best you have to wear around here, we'd better find you something more appropriate."

She turned her back on him, determined not to let him anger her again.

"Eat the beans, Jake," Lamar said. "Arguments will ruin our digestion."

The beans were passed and both men looked questioningly at Alexandra as they took their first mouthful. Immediately their eyes met and they grimaced. She could hear strange crunching sounds as they chewed. She looked at them, puzzled.

Suddenly, they both jumped up and ran outside. In just a little while they both returned, laughing heartily. She looked from one to the other, even more puzzled. What had happened?

Lamar spoke first, after taking a big swig of coffee and swishing it around in his mouth. "Uh, did you wash the beans, Alexandra? Did you remove the rocks and bits of dirt?"

She looked at him in surprise. "No. Jake told me to put them into water and boil them for a long time, so that's what I did."

"Well, I never dreamed you'd be idiot enough not to wash them. Don't you have any sense?" Jake asked hotly, then began laughing again. Lamar joined in his laughter.

It was all too much! Alexandra looked at both men, growing angrier by the second, then stood up. Her eyes were a brilliant green as she glared at Jake. "I don't know anything about cooking and you know it. I'll learn, but I can't without a teacher. Now, if you want a decent meal, you'd better get someone who knows how to cook. I, I —" her voice broke, but she steadied it again, "I don't know how and you know it. I'm going to bed. You can do what you want with this mess," she finished, and started out.

"Alexandra," Jake said, his cold, deadly voice stopping her.

She hesitated, then turned back. His eyes were hard blue stones in his darkly tanned face. She glared at him, her anger boiling inside. She'd seen him like this with the Mexican today. He would be absolutely ruthless.

"What?" she asked stonily.

337

"Throw the beans out. Wash some more, then put them on to cook. We'll need something to eat tomorrow. We'll chew on the beef tonight. And put some salt and dried beef in with the beans."

"Oh, Jake, I'm tired. I don't care about food. I just want to be left alone," Alexandra said unhappily, knowing even as she spoke that she couldn't disobey him. He'd force her to do what he wanted. He was so much stronger. How she hated his strength!

"Do what I say, Alex," he said, his voice hard and cold.

Not looking at either of the men, she tiredly began picking up the bowls, trying to keep her lovely gown clean. She made several trips back and forth to the kitchen, clearing the table as the men left to sit in the big chairs and drink whiskey. It wasn't fair, it just wasn't fair that he should make her work so hard, she thought as she began washing the beans, careful to clean them thoroughly. But she *would* learn to cook!

In the next room, Lamar tried to understand what was happening with Jake, but he could not get far.

"Don't you think you were a little rough on her, Jake?"

"Stay out of it, Lamar. Alex is my affair."

"Maybe, but—"

"I don't want to discuss it. When do you think we'll have a big enough herd to leave?"

"Well, I'm thinking in about three weeks, or under. We should have about two thousand head by then. We can't handle much more than that and it'll be a long drive, the longest ever."

"Yes. This McCoy in Abilene had better be on the level. Said a cordial welcome awaited all trail herds at a place in Kansas called Abilene and his agent had better have meant it," Jake said menacingly.

"He's on the level. After all, he's the man who got the Kansas Pacific railroad to extend its line further west to that place called Abilene. And if we can get our herd up the Chisholm Trail, we'll have a good market for our cattle this year, as well as in the years to come."

"We've got to make it. These longhorns are as thick as grass and ours for the taking. We could sell them in San Antonio for three dollars a head, but why not make the drive to Abilene and get forty?"

"No reason at all. The time's right. The North needs beef. And if the Chisholm Trail works out, then we've got it made. We'll have the money to make this a damned fine ranch."

"We've got the best cowboys around — experienced, sure, ready to go. Our remuda of mustangs could be better, but they'll just have to learn on the drive."

"You figure ten to fifteen miles a day for the herd. If we can leave by the first part of June, we should be there by September."

339

"No reason we can't leave by then. *I'll* sure be ready."

"What are you going to do about Alex? She can't make the drive with. us. She'd never survive and you don't know what we'll run into — Indians, rustlers, who knows what else."

"Leave that to me. I'll see to her when the time comes," Jake said irritably, then got up. "I'm going to bed. It's been a long day."

"Jake?"

"Yes."

"About Pecos. You think he'll cause any more trouble?"

"He'd better not, the fool."

"Nevertheless, I'd watch Alexandra a little more closely."

"Could be you're right," Jake said, nodded at Lamar, then walked back toward the kitchen.

His thoughts were all for her now. She was the only thing that could make him forget the ranch — and the all-important cattle drive. He looked into the kitchen and his face softened. She was sitting on a low stool, her head in her lap, asleep, in front of the beans. She was still wearing the ridiculous gown. He stoked down the fire and put more water on the beans. He lifted her up into his arms and she didn't awaken. She was so small and light that momentarily he wished he hadn't been so hard on her. She wasn't used to this type of life, didn't

340

even want it, but he hardened his heart against her, remembering what she was.

He carried her into his room, shutting the door behind them quietly, then placed her gently down on the bed. He undid her clothes, thinking that he'd have to get her something else to wear, and as he removed them, she groaned, waking slightly, and smiled softly, then curled into a ball as he tucked her under the covers. He hastily shucked his own clothes and got in beside her, pulling her small, warm body close to him. He felt the familiar tightening in his loins, but didn't try to awaken her. He simply curled his body up to hers, smelling her sweet scent as slumber quickly overtook him.

Chapter Twenty

Jake awoke just as the sun was rising. He cursed himself for oversleeping. There was too much to do—he had to get those cattle ready for the drive. He got out of bed, and swiftly put on his clothes. Lamar was waiting for him in the main room, already dressed and ready.

"Morning, Jake," Lamar said, noticing his hastily donned clothes and sleepy expression. Jake hadn't slept late in he couldn't remember when. Alexandra made her presence felt even when she slept. It was interesting, he thought, watching Jake closely. He'd never seen Jake so affected by a woman and wondered if it would change him.

"Let's eat down at the chuck wagon," Jake said as he buckled on his pistol and grabbed his hat.

"What about Alexandra?"

"She can come down later so Cookie can teach her something about cooking."

Lamar nodded. "Why don't I wait here

awhile? There are some things I could do, and then I could bring her down. She'll awaken soon, I imagine."

"All right. That suits me. By the way, did Rosa leave any of her things around here? Alex is going to need some clothes to wear."

"I'll see what I can find."

"Good." Jake put on his hat and walked out.

Sun was flooding the room when Alexandra awoke from her deep sleep. She was instantly alert and apprehensive. Her memories of the day before came flooding back and she cautiously turned in the bed. Jake was gone! She felt a strange emptiness at his absence. She got up. He'd be somewhere about, waiting to give her orders for the day so she might as well be dressed and ready when he came back for her.

Hurriedly, she splashed water on her face, and put on the riding habit and boots. Even if it were hot, her body was completely concealed, and in Jake's presence that was certainly necessary.

The house was strangely quiet and she wandered out of her room, curious. She went to the kitchen. Someone had taken the beans off the fire. They looked good. She suddenly felt hunger gnaw at her stomach. Grabbing up a bowl and spoon, she helped herself generously to the beans and began eating. Surprisingly, they were good, or else she was so hungry anything would have tasted delicious.

There was a sound near her and she looked up to see Lamar coming toward her. Surprisingly, he looked a great deal like Giles and she felt herself stiffen automatically. Was Giles looking for her now, and Stan, too? She couldn't let them find her, but was being Jake's harlot any better than what they offered? She shook her head, her green eyes troubled as she tried to cast the men from her mind. Thinking of her situation only made her unhappy and confused.

"You're looking very rested this morning, Alexandra," Lamar said as he approached her, bearing something in his hands.

She smiled at him. "I slept well. What do you have there?"

"I think these might fit. Rosa left them. It's what the peasant women wear and it's appropriate to the heat here. Jake and I thought you might be more comfortable in them around the hacienda."

"Oh?" Alexandra asked, immediately interested. So this is what Rosa wore.

She shook out the bundle to discover a white peasant blouse and a brightly patterned skirt. It was perfect, no matter that it wasn't what she was accustomed to, or that they had belonged to Rosa. She could cook and clean in them without being hot or encumbered. In fact, she looked forward to wearing something so comfortable and uninhibited. Looking up at Lamar, she smiled her rare, sweet smile and was rewarded by an answering smile from him.

"It's just perfect, thank you. I'll change right now."

"I wouldn't change just yet," Lamar said, halting her movement.

"Why not? Aren't I supposed to clean the rest of the hacienda? It certainly needs it."

He shook his head. "Jake wants you down at the roundup. Cookie's there. He wants you to learn how to cook first of all."

"Cookie? Roundup?"

"I'll tell you on the way," Lamar said. "Just come as you are. You'll be riding and that'll be best."

Outside, Alexandra dubiously regarded the horse Lamar had chosen for her.

"This is a mustang," Lamar explained. "They roam wild over Texas, but this mare has been trained. I think you'll like her since she's small and sturdy. I'm sorry we don't have a sidesaddle."

"I can manage if we don't have to go too far."

"Good."

Lamar helped her up and soon they were on their way. There was a majestic beauty about the land—so free and open. She found herself liking it even more and more as they rode along. Lamar didn't seem to be in a hurry and they rode side by side, the horses walking. The sun was warm on her face and the air was

345

clean and fresh. She knew a person could feel free here. Except that she wasn't, not really.

"Alexandra, I know this all must be very strange to you, especially the situation with Jake. I'm even more confused than you are, and I'd like to say that I don't approve of the way Jake is treating you. But you are both grown and I haven't felt that I could interfere. But I am curious about you. Would you like to tell me how you came to be here and what you know about Jake's mother?"

She sighed. "My tale is a little unusual, but you should know, I believe." And then she told him her story, leaving out those incidents that would embarrass them both.

When she finished, Lamar understood some things much better; other things were more unclear. If what she'd said was true, she was a wealthy woman of a fine family. Then why the hell was Jake treating her like a harlot?

"I'm glad you came, Alexandra, and I know that when Jake cools off, he'd like to hear all this from you."

"I hope so. His mother wanted him to know. And something else. Mister Jarmon, your father, died the same day. They're both buried in the family cemetery."

"So he finally gave up," Lamar said, his jaw tightening. "There was no love lost between us. He'll be happier. He couldn't have lived with the defeat of the South."

346

"Giles is closing the plantation and moving some of the furniture into a townhouse in New Orleans."

Lamar laughed shortly. "That sounds like Giles. He always did prefer the city life. Well, fortunately, it's no concern of mine now."

"There's not much left there anymore."

"Do you have any proof of this story?"

Alexandra frowned. "You don't believe me?"

"It's not that. The story's too incredible for you to have made it up, but Jake may not."

"I have the medallion Eleanor gave me. The Norwegian one. She wanted me to have it."

Lamar whistled. "Eleanor gave you that? She prized it more than anything. It was all she had left of her father."

"I know, but she looked on me as her daughter."

"Yes, I can see why. I'm glad you were with her at the end. You might show it to Jake when you tell him."

"I will." She paused, then hesitantly continued. "Lamar, could you help me leave? I think Jake must hate me. Once I've told him what his mother said, there's no more reason for me to stay. I could go to Brownsville where I have friends."

Lamar looked at her kindly. "Of course I'll help. But I don't believe Jake hates you. Far from it. He's obsessed. It makes him feel hogtied. He's fighting the ropes now, but if you give him time—"

"No! I mean, perhaps I shouldn't wait." Her heart beat fast. Could Jake really feel that strongly about her? No, she mustn't get caught up in the emotions he made her feel in bed. She couldn't trust him.

"We're building a herd to take to Kansas. We'll be driving it to San Antonio in about three weeks. If you'll stay with us that long, we can leave you safely in San Antonio. I have friends there who'll see you get to Brownsville."

"Thank you. I think I can wait." In fact, she might be safer if she stayed at the Bar J longer. Surely neither Stan nor Giles would think to look for her here. She glanced around the sprawling ranch. Perhaps she didn't want to leave yet. Maybe she wanted to wait and see if what Lamar had said about Jake were true. Obsession. She wasn't immune herself.

They rode in silence for a while longer, and soon they reached the camp. "Oh!" Alexandra exclaimed. "There are so many cows."

Lamar smiled. "We're rounding up all we can, then bringing them in here to be branded for the road."

Lamar guided her away from the cattle and toward the chuck wagon. The wagon was a covered affair with several drawers on the back side which contained the cook's supplies and food.

Cookie looked up as they approached. He stepped forward, wiping his hands on the big

348

white apron he wore.

"So, this is the little lady Jake told me about. He didn't tell me you'd be so pretty. Welcome, miss. You can call me Cookie. I hear you want to learn to cook so I guess I'll be teachin' you."

Alexandra liked him right away. He was an older man with a full set of shaggy gray whiskers, and his brown eyes twinkled merrily. She smiled back at him and he beamed even broader. She felt instantly that he was a friend and warmed to him.

"Thank you, Cookie, and please call me Alexandra."

"Ain't much to it. On a drive, don't cook much more than coffee, beef, and sourdough biscuits. Today, I'm making a stew. That's always a special treat. I'll show you how. Ain't hard. Ain't hard at all."

"Thank you," Alexandra said graciously, beginning to push up her sleeves.

"I'll be leaving you now, Alexandra. You'll be in good hands with Cookie," Lamar said, then touched his hand to his hat before quickly walking away.

The morning sped by as Cookie showed Alexandra how to cook. She was an apt pupil and enjoyed his company as he regaled her with tales of the trail and the cowboys.

He explained that everything a cowboy wore was necessary to his trade. He might look like he was dressed in a strange get-up to a tenderfoot, but it was all necessary to droving. The tall, broad brimmed sombrero protected him from the sun and rain, the lariat was for roping, his gun protected him from Indians, rustlers, rattlesnakes and numerous other enemies, the chaps protected his legs when on horseback, which was most of the time, gauntlets were necessary to protect his hands and wrists from rope burns, and his high top boots with high heels protected him against rattlesnake bites and held him in the stirrups.

Alexandra found it all fascinating, and she began to long for a closer look at these men and their activities.

When the cooking was finished, she glanced around. "Do you suppose I could go over to the corrals and have a look? I wouldn't get in the way."

"Don't know why not, Miss Alexandra."

She smiled. "Thank you for everything, Cookie. You've been a gold mine of information. I'll go back to the hacienda soon and try out what you've taught me."

Cookie smiled back at her, then turned to resume his chores. She walked away from him, adjusting her small hat, wishing it would give her skin more protection from the glaring sun. She should use a sombrero or she'd soon be as dark as the cowboys. She walked back to her pony. It was still waiting, languid in the hot Texas sun. She struggled to mount, accustomed to help, then finally made it up. The saddle was uncomfortable, but soon she would be used to it.

Trotting her mustang over toward the corrals, she found the one Cookie had pointed out. Several cowboys were standing around. She got down, then approached the wooden fence. The cowboys stopped their activities, staring at her.

"What's happening in there?" she asked as she came up to the corral.

"Bronc busting, miss," one told her.

She scarcely heard his words as she realized that it was Jake on the bucking, twisting wild pony's back. She couldn't believe what she saw. He held on to a single rope, one hand flung out as the animal moved in impossible contortions around the corral. She leaned closer, feeling the rough wood against her hands and the sun hot on her body. She'd never felt so alive, watching the man and animal joined as one and yet fighting each other to gain supremacy. It was superb and she felt something stirring within her, a deep, purely animal pleasure in what she watched. Jake looked so completely masculine, so determined, so strong, and the animal was beautiful, also determined to be strong and free. Her breath came more quickly, nothing seemed to exist for her except the battle between the two wild things before her. She wanted to become a part of the scene, share the complete abandon of nature. As she watched the struggle, she began to see the change. The wild mustang slowed, still trying to throw his rider, but his strength was spent and slowly his bucking, twisting movements ceased, until Jake rode him quietly around the corral.

Only then did he see Alexandra. The horse had been a hard one. None of the others had been able to break the mustang, but Jake's foul humor had enabled him to ride the horse into submission. Alexandra had been in his mind as he'd ridden; he'd imagined that he was breaking her to his will. And then, when the mustang finally had been broken, he'd looked up to see her standing there: her crazy hat off to one side, her hands gripping the wooden rail, and her eyes burning like green fire.

He wanted her in that moment more than he had ever wanted her before. He had to make her his own, just as he'd made the horse his own. Tossing the rope to one of the cowboys, he got off, hardly feeling the strained muscles in his body as he bent low to crawl between the railings to her. His eyes never left her and as he stood beside her, he could smell her warm, sweet fragrance. He took her hands, their gaze caught, and led her away.

They rode back to the hacienda in silence. No words were necessary. Alexandra knew what he wanted and she admitted to herself that she wanted the same thing.

Jake helped her dismount, his hands never

leaving her waist as he guided her into the house, to the bedroom. He turned toward her. She still watched him with her wide, hungry green eyes. He'd never seen her look at him like this and it excited him beyond control.

As he began to undo her riding habit, she didn't move, but stared at him as if she'd never seen him before. He quickly removed his own clothing. When he looked back, she was in the bed, a strange, haunted look in her soft green eyes. Soft. Yes, they were soft, dark, like moss on a river bank.

He slid into bed, and pulled her to him. This time she didn't fight as the fire between them burst into a raging inferno.

Chapter Twenty-one

Alexandra threw a few more ingredients into the bubbling water in the iron kettle. She was angry, furious with herself. How pliable she was. How weak! She should have known that Jake's regard for her couldn't change. So he had taken her with more tenderness than usual, and she had let him—invited him, really. But then, as soon as he had used her, he was up and dressed, dismissing her as he would a common harlot. She was a fool for caring!

She had her hands in the middle of a bucket of water, rinsing out a rag to clean the kitchen when she heard a horse neigh. She looked out and saw a mustang tied outside. She walked into the main room.

Standing in the center of the room was a pretty young Mexican woman with her hands on her hips. She wore peasant clothing similar to Alexandra's, and her full young breasts strained against her white blouse, the nipples dark shadows against the thin cloth. The Mexican regarded her haughtily.

Alexandra, in confusion, took a few more steps into the room, then stopped. "May I help you? Are you looking for someone?"

The woman's face twisted viciously. "I found who I'm looking for, *gringa* bitch!"

"Oh, I see," Alexandra said, smiling softly, "You must be Rosa."

"I suppose *he* told you about me."

"Well, Pecos—"

"Pecos! I don't mean that fool. I mean Jake."

Alexandra raised her brows, her eyes glowing slightly. "Jake?"

"Yes, my man, you bitch. I came to see you. Pecos said you were here."

"I'm not surprised. He *did* try to rape me, you know. I believe it had something to do with you."

"*Rape* you? Ha! He wouldn't want a skinny little *gringa* like you. Neither would Jake. You've bewitched him, haven't you?" she asked, her eyes narrowing as she stepped closer.

"Bewitched? Really, Rosa, don't be silly." Alexandra's attitude was amusement at the Mexican woman's rage, and it only served to further infuriate Rosa.

"Then why would they want you?"

Alexandra shrugged. She had little interest in discussing these two men with Rosa. Still, it was interesting to see another of Jake's previous

355

women. This one was pretty, voluptuous, and young, perhaps sixteen. He had good taste, she had to admit, remembering the beautiful Madame LeBlanc and the seductive Caroline.

"Look," Rosa said, stepping closer, "Jake belongs to me, *Rosa*. We had an argument. I left and took Pecos as my new man, but it was only to make Jake jealous. He's *my* man. You understand?"

Alexandra shrugged. "So?"

"So! I want you gone. Leave. Go! Get out of Texas before I scratch out your eyes!"

Alexandra laughed, a patronizing sound. "Listen to me, Rosa," she said softly. "I'm here and I'm going to stay as long as I want. Not you nor anyone is going to tell me what to do. And another thing, Jake's not *your* man any longer."

Rosa's eyes grew wide with rage. Without warning, she leaped on Alexandra, pulling at her hair, trying to scratch, kick, claw. But Alexandra had had a little experience in New Orleans, and she had some tricks of her own.

They rolled over and over on the floor, hitting furniture, slipping on rugs as they fought, tearing at each other's clothing. Rosa fought like a shecat, bent on revenge, determined to mar Alexandra, and so ruin the appeal she had for the man she wanted. She savagely dug her hands into Alexandra's long golden red hair, pulling until Alexandra slapped her across the face.

Rosa got up on her knees, her black eyes flashing. "So, the *gringa* can fight. I'm surprised, but it's no matter. I'll see you dead for this. *Dead,* do you hear?"

"I hear, you little bitch, but if I catch you around here again, I'll finish you myself. And if you *ever* go near Jake again, I'll mark your face so that *no* man will want to look at you again," Alexandra hissed, her breasts heaving.

Rosa was holding her blouse together in front as she gasped for air. Then, suddenly, she dropped the torn cloth, exposing her round swelling breasts, the dark nipples hard. She ran past Alexandra to the door.

Alexandra turned around to see Rosa throw herself against Jake, sobbing, clutching at him.

Alexandra met Jake's eyes, turning crimson as he regarded her with amusement. Lamar stood away from the group, reluctant to join the fight.

"Do your words mean you're not willing to share me, Alex?" Jake asked as he pushed Rosa from him.

"Oh, no!" Alexandra cried, furious that he should have heard her threat, and embarrassed as well.

Rosa fought Jake's strong hands to regain her position against his chest, pushing her bare breasts toward him, tempting him, begging him to take her.

"Jake, Jake, this woman has hurt me. Just

357

look what she has done to my blouse," Rosa said, her head back, to better reveal her full breasts.

"Yes, I see," Jake said wryly, looking down at the two twin mounds arched towards him. "You do seem to have a problem, Rosa." And he pulled the torn fabric over her breasts.

"Jake, Jake, send her away. You don't need that *gringa* woman. I'm warm. I'm yours. You wanted me before. Take me again."

Jake looked down at her, then back at Alexandra, as if making a choice. Watching Alexandra's rising fury, he smiled, his teeth a startling white against his tanned face. He raised his hand and cupped Rosa's chin, gazing down at her pleading face.

"Leave, Rosa. I suppose *I* belong to the victor and *Alex* appears to be the winner."

Broiling with rage, Rosa stormed out of the hacienda, and Alexandra, humiliated and herself enraged, followed her out of the room and locked herself in her bedroom.

In the days that followed, Jake did not let Alexandra forget the incident for he found it amusing, especially since it was sure to raise her temper. He told her many times how she had to take good care of him since she'd won him in a fight and promised to mar any woman who tried to steal him. Alexandra had no retort for this. She still could not believe she had been wild enough to say those words. But for some

358

reason that she couldn't understand, it had helped make Jake and her closer.

He was even teaching her to shoot, for as he'd told her one day, "As often as you need to defend yourself, Alex, I'd better teach you how to shoot. Someday I might not be around to save you from the lusts of *other* men."

He also thought that was funny, but after the incident with Pecos, he always made sure that at least one cowboy was near the hacienda when he was away. Even that was cause for his humor and teasing. He told her that all the cowboys could hardly work for pining over the beautiful Alexandra. It was true that whichever cowboy was left at the hacienda was forever trying to help her in the kitchen, or with the washing or cleaning. Of course, they were more trouble than help, but they did it with such good humor and delight that she'd usually let them haul water or bring firewood in for her. And Jake didn't seem to be so jealous of them, although he kept a close eye on her and her attitude with them. It was all perfectly innocent and they treated her like a great lady.

The days slipped by easily, one into the other, until she realized that it had been three weeks since she'd arrived in Texas. She was made very aware of the time by something she could not ignore. She could no longer deny the fact that she was pregnant.

Her time had come and gone, over a month since New Orleans. She knew the child was Jake's. Should she tell him? What would he do? Oh, why did it have to happen now of all times? But it wasn't her fault. Jake continued to seduce her every night, as if it were his due. But perhaps she shouldn't put all the blame on him. She wanted him as much as he wanted her. Yet it was strictly physical desire. No words of love had passed between them. She had kept her emotions under control until now.

She paced, trying to think, trying to reason. The baby should have a father. She couldn't give birth to an illegitimate child. That wouldn't be fair to the helpless baby. If Jake loved her it would be different, but he didn't. He didn't seem to hate her any more and he had even questioned her about her past, wanting to know everything, especially about New Orleans, but she'd been stubborn. After he'd rejected her story originally, she'd not told him another word. Not even about his mother. Now she wished she hadn't been so proud.

There was a sound in the house. She looked up to see Jake walking toward her, a frown puckering his forehead. She caught her breath. It was mid-morning, and he was *never* home at this time of day.

"Jake?"

"Everything's all right. I came back to talk with you. Can I sit a minute?"

She looked at him, concerned. She rarely saw him this serious.

He turned a chair around, pushed his sombrero back, then stared at her with intense blue eyes.

He reminded her of the time in the cabin of *The Flying J* when she'd first talked with him, not knowing what to expect. She felt that same way now.

"What am I going to do with you, Alex?" he asked slowly.

"What do you mean?"

"The herd will be ready to leave for San Antonio in two days."

"I'm glad. I know that's what you want," she said, trying to keep her fears from her eyes. "Jake, before you go on, there's something I'd like to tell you."

His eyes grew more intense, focusing on her fully. "Go ahead."

"Well, I've been stubborn. I want you to know about me. I should have told you before — when you asked."

"It's been up to you, Alex. I *am* curious. You just don't act much like a whore. I can't figure you."

"Oh, Jake, I'm no harlot. You see, the men, well, it really *wasn't* my fault. I was raped that first time just as I told you."

"I don't want to know about the men."

"Yes, damn you, you're going to hear. You've

been condemning me ever since we met. Well, now you're going to hear the facts. I'm truly Alexandra Clarke. Your grandfather in New York City was my guardian. He raised me after my parents died, after you and your mother left him. Before he died, he asked me to find you and Eleanor in New Orleans. So I hired Captain Sully and his schooner. He wanted to rape me and was going to let his crew have me. I jumped overboard. You saved me."

"Alex! Stop this."

"No, I *want* you to hear it, *all* of it. You took me to New Orleans. You frightened me. Our, our lovemaking frightened me. I was so inexperienced. I escaped. I, I somehow got on to Gallatin Street."

"Damn, Alexandra," Jake cried, standing up and pacing as he ran his fingers through his hair in agitation.

"Yes, Gallatin. Rather stupid of me, but I didn't know—not at first."

"I don't want to hear any more." Jake sat down, his blue eyes dark with pain.

"I was desperate. I walked the street, trying to get out, but a man pulled me into a dance-house."

"Oh, no!" Jake moaned, hunched over, his face in his hands. "If I'd only known."

"The next day I was sent to Madame LeBlanc. I only sang and played the piano there, Jake, please believe me. That last night

362

they gave me something in the champagne and Giles took me. It was the only way he could get me."

"And to think what I believed! That damned Bella and her tricks. She set it up, and Giles, too. I see it all now." He paused, staring at her intently. "I'm sorry, Alex, can you ever forgive me?" he said in a pain-filled voice.

She looked deeply into his eyes. He *did* believe her. She smiled. "Yes, Jake, I can. They fooled us both. I suppose they were jealous, and then they wanted the money."

"Money?"

"I, I'm an heiress, Jake."

He laughed. "You mean I'm breaking my back over these damned longhorns when you've got a fortune?"

She let her long lashes cover her eyes. "You'd want my money?"

"Hell, you know me better than that. I don't give a damn about your money. It's yours. Keep it. A lot of good it's done you so far."

She opened her eyes wide, the green depths softening. "Giles took me to the plantation. I stayed with Eleanor until she died. It was her lungs. She didn't want you to stay with her."

Jake got up again and paced. "I knew she'd been sick, but she should have told me. I'd have stayed. The ranch could have waited."

"She knew that, but she wanted you to go on with your life. She loved you very much."

"It all could have waited."

"She wanted me to tell you that she loved you and that she was happy at the last to have me with her and to know that her father had loved and forgiven her, as well as you. That's partly why he sent me—to tell you that he loved you and that he'd been a stupid old man."

Jake smiled. "I wish I could have known him better. I wish Mother had stayed with him."

"Eleanor gave me this," she said, pulling the medallion out of her blouse and up over her head to show him. She held it out. "I believe it really belongs to you."

He crossed over to her, then looked down at the medallion. "She gave that to you?"

"Yes, she looked upon me as her daughter."

"Keep it. If she wanted you to have it, then it's yours," he said, closing her fingers over it. He sat back down and watched her, his blue eyes hard.

"After your mother died I came here because I'd promised her I would and also because Giles was trying to force me to marry him. I thought I would be safer here. Ebba left the plantation with me, but she went up north when I came here.

"I'm no harlot, Jake."

His eyes held hers for a long moment. "No, you're not, but damnit, Alex, in bed you're sure no lady."

364

Her eyes widened, then she laughed. He looked at her in surprise, then they both laughed together.

"Well, damn it, Jake, in bed you're no gentleman."

He shook his head. "I don't know. You've got me in such a lather. Do you want to go home? Do you want to stay in San Antonio? I can't take you on the trail drive. It would be impossible."

"Then, when you go, you'll leave me somewhere," she said coldly, her heart beating faster as she waited for his reply. Had it all been for nothing?

"All right, if that's the way you want it, Alex," he said just as coldly.

Alexandra stood up, knowing that he couldn't send her away if he loved her. She could never tell him about their child now. She wouldn't take charity for love. She hid her emotions behind a frozen mask, but her face felt strained.

"Very well, Jake. My promises to Olaf and Eleanor have been completed so nothing holds me here any longer. I'll go with you as far as San Antonio, then we'll part company."

She looked at him quickly, then stepped around him and through the door.

"Alex?" he called, but it was too late.

She had grabbed her hat and hurried outside. She heard him calling, but ignored him as she quickly mounted her horse and struck out on her own, riding hard and fast away from the hacienda, away from Jake.

Jake! Jake! her heart cried out as she rode. Now that the cattle were ready to drive, he was willing to throw her away, discard her. How could she ever have thought that she could win his heart. She was a fool! She would leave him and never return. And he would never know about his child. *Never!* Once they parted ways in San Antonio, he'd never see her again.

Chapter Twenty-two

Alexandra continued to ride away from the hacienda, determined to outdistance her anger, her hurt, her discontent, and slowed only when her mustang began to tire.

Soon the coolness of sunset descended and as the wind whipped against her face, she pushed her hat back so that it was held only by the leather thong around her neck. She felt exhilarated with the wind in her hair and the strong mustang beneath her.

She found that she'd grown to feel a part of Texas in the weeks she'd lived there and no matter how furious she was with Jake, she still loved the Bar J, the life on a ranch. She would almost hate to leave it, but leave it she must no matter the pain in her heart. Jake no longer wanted her and so she had to make a life for herself and her child somewhere else.

Suddenly, her horse snorted, shying. She looked up, alarmed. She'd come to depend on the instincts of her mustang. Not far away was a group of men riding toward the Bar J herd. Rustlers? Had they seen her? She pulled her mount quickly to a stop and watched the riders.

They hadn't seen her for they rode straight ahead, intent on their destination. She could see them start to round up the herd. No matter how she felt about Jake, she wouldn't let anything happen to the ranch and the cowboys if she could help it.

Jerking the mustang around, she flicked her lightly with the reins. She had to warn Jake and Lamar. Her horse seemed to understand the urgency and was soon running swiftly back toward the hacienda. She held on tightly, urging her mount, unaware of the brush and mesquite that tore at her clothing in her desperation to warn the Bar J.

At last, the hacienda was in sight and she pulled the heavily breathing mustang to a quick stop in front of it, her own breath coming in gasps, her hair blown loose and billowing out around her like golden fire with the last rays of the sun striking it, her clothes torn and her body scratched from the brush.

Before she could jump down, Jake was beside her, helping her down.

"Jake! Rustlers! A group of men riding for the herd. They aren't far away. I saw—"

"Hell! You're sure, Alex?"

She nodded at Jake, then noticed the saddled horses in front of the hacienda. Several cowboys stood with Lamar, worried frowns on their faces.

"I'm sure, but what's going on here?"

Jake grinned sheepishly. "We were about to go in search of you. I told Lamar that we'd wait until sundown and if you weren't back by then —"

"I can take care of myself, Jake. I always have," Alexandra said, cutting him off coldly before turning toward Lamar. "What can we do?"

Lamar had motioned to the cowboys the instant he'd heard the news. They now stood close by, ready for orders.

"Jake?" he asked, anxious to move.

"Got to head them off. If they stampede the herd, we're lost. Lamar, you warn the cowboys on watch. Have them ready in case we can't head off the rustlers. I'll take these men and try to stop them. Take Alexandra with you. I don't want her left here alone."

"No! I want to be in on it. I can use a gun," she said stubbornly, determined not to be left out.

"Damn it, Alex. Go with Lamar. I'm not going to have you along."

"Well, I'm going," she said, climbing back on her mustang.

Jake glared at her, but he didn't have time to argue.

In a few minutes, they neared the herd. They all stopped their mounts. The animals shied, sensing the impending danger. Alexandra held her horse close to Jake's. These men wouldn't get off lightly if they dared to test Jake, she thought, glancing up at his stern, hard profile.

She looked back toward the rustlers, coming closer now. They were galloping, having seen Jake waiting for them. When they were close, she instantly recognized their leader — Pecos! Revenge? Hate? The banditos brought their horses to a halt a few feet from Jake's group of cowboys, then Pecos walked his mustang closer.

"Gringo, you have come to welcome us?"

"What are you doing on the Bar J, Pecos? I thought I told you to stay away."

"There's a little matter unsettled between us," he said as his black eyes flicked over Alexandra insolently.

"There's nothing to settle between us."

"No? Your herd. It is very fine. It is ready for the drive. The cattle are nervous, *verdad?* They are ready to move. If a sudden sound or an accidental shot was fired into the herd — "

"Don't threaten me, Pecos," Jake said, his voice hard.

"Threaten? Me?" Pecos asked innocently, his palms turned up as he expressed his innocence.

"Take your boys, Pecos, and get off Bar J land now! Don't come back, or you won't get off so easily next time."

"Gladly. We came only for the pretty señorita. We would have her for a time to settle old scores, then she would be returned, only a little used," he said, chuckling deep in his throat. His men laughed behind him, their rough, loud voices harsh in the evening air.

Alexandra sat very still, her face a mask revealing nothing. She would not show fear, whatever Jake did, whatever happened to her. She had lived through a lot and she would survive this night, too.

"You're beginning to anger me, Pecos," Jake drawled, his hand lowering to his gun.

"Am I? I cannot understand this, *gringo*. I merely came for the woman," Pecos said, his own hand dropping toward his pistol.

"The woman's mine, Pecos."

"So, you will have the fight, *hombre?*"

And then the world seemed to explode into a horror of belching guns, cursing men, and plunging horses. Alexandra heard Jake holler, "Get to Lamar, Alex. Warn the others!"

She wheeled her horse as she saw several men fall from their mustangs, only to begin fighting on foot for the two groups had merged into one struggling, panting, fighting mass of desperation. She could not discern Jake from the others and she couldn't tell how many were dead, or wounded. She pushed her horse on, away from the scene of death and blood and toward the restless herd, toward the others who must be warned.

She galloped furiously up to the chuck wagon, pulling her mustang to an abrupt stop in front.

Cookie rushed out, a rifle in his hands. "Lord, Miss Alexandra, thought you were the rustlers. Almost shot you."

"Cookie, where's Lamar?"

"Out with the herd."

"I must warn the others. It's Pecos and his banditos. They're fighting with Jake and the cowboys. I don't know what—oh no! Look! The barns are on fire. Oh, Cookie!"

The dark night had suddenly exploded into bright lights and leaping flames coming from the direction of the hacienda. Alexandra felt a small fury grow in her breast. So—Pecos had brought two groups: one for the hacienda and one for the herd!

"What will we do, Cookie?"

"Look, miss, Jake'll take care of those banditos. You warn Lamar and I'll come with you. Then we'll see if we can save the hacienda, if it ain't already too late."

Alexandra and Cookie told Lamar what was happening, then they rode as close to the hacienda as they dared. Cookie checked the pistol on his hip, then jerked his rifle from its

372

saddle sheath. He nodded at Alexandra and they ran, crouching low, toward the hacienda. The barn, bunkhouse, and outbuildings were already ablaze, but Alexandra was relieved to see that the hacienda was as yet undamaged. They ran on until they were close to the hacienda. Loud voices came from inside and she leaped forward, determined to stop the banditos, but Cookie grabbed her roughly and pulled her back into the shadows.

"You can't run in there, Miss Alexandra," he hissed in her ear. "They'd shoot you down. Look, there's only three mustangs tied out front so there's probably only three inside. That's the Bar J buckboard they've got, too — planning to stow the loot in it, I bet. They weren't figuring on much trouble up here. Thing to do is wait them out. Can't go storming inside. Can you handle a rifle?"

"Yes," Alexandra whispered, taking it in her hand.

"Good. Now, I'll cover the front door. You take the kitchen door. When they come out we'll get them."

Alexandra ran around to the back of the hacienda, after seeing Cookie take his position behind the buckboard near the front door. There was no cover near the kitchen door except for the old waterwell. She crouched down behind it, bracing the rifle on the well, aiming it and with all her senses on the kitchen door.

Suddenly she heard the sharp click of a hammer being drawn back into firing position. The sound was close to her left ear—too close. The cold steel of a rifle barrel touched her cheek and she heard a heavy voice say, "You should not play with guns, *chica*. Someday they might hurt you bad. Throw your gun down the well, won't you please? For Jose?" Then his voice lost its humor and became hard and deadly as he added one final word, "Now."

Alexandra had no choice. She slowly edged the gun forward until it toppled into the well. It clattered downward and she heard a splash.

"Thank you, señorita. Now stand up and walk slowly ahead of me to the kitchen door," he ordered. She did. Once there he tapped softly on the window and soon the door was opened from the inside by another grinning Mexican.

He pulled her inside, letting his rough hands run up and down her arms. She tried to shrug him off, but he only tightened his grip as he dragged her into the main room. Another man awaited them there. He walked up to her while one bandito kept the gun on her and the other held her to him, his hands moving up her shoulders, finding the bare skin exposed by the low cut blouse.

She was determined to show no fear and looked boldly back at the bandito who stood before her. She could smell his body heat and the stench of many weeks without soap and water. Grinning, he swept off his wide sombrero, revealing oily black hair.

His two coal-like eyes raked her body. "We are glad you have joined us, señorita. And now, should you not call to your old friend outside to throw down his gun and come on in to our little party? Eh?"

"Never!" Alexandra clenched her fists.

"Oh? Then you would see him die?"

Her mind whirled. But what choice did she have? And so she called out to Cookie who reluctantly threw down his sixshooter and walked inside, his hands reaching for the sky.

"Now, *muchachos,* we will have our fun," the leader said to his men as he grinned at Alexandra. "This is much trouble, *chica,* to get you for Pecos, and we should have a little reward, don't you think?"

"No! You're all madmen. And you'll all be dead as well. Jake and Lamar are on their way."

"I think not, pretty *gringa.* Pecos keeps them busy tonight."

"You're mistaken—" Alexandra started, but yelped in pain as the bandito holding her suddenly pinched her breast. Furious, she kicked out at him, striking his shin. He dropped her arms as she turned on him, pummeling him with her fists.

375

Cursing, the leader grabbed her, slapping her cruelly back and forth across the face. The heavy blows quickly subdued her and blood trickled from the corner of her mouth. Then he dragged her toward the table, calling out orders to his two men. They quickly tied up Cookie, leaving him so he could watch.

The leader swept everything off the table onto the floor, then threw Alexandra on top of it. She struggled, trying to get away, but the other two banditos were there to help. One grabbed her struggling hands, pulling them up over her head, while the other secured her ankles, pulling her legs apart. She screamed, writhing desperately on the hard tabletop as her captors grinned at her, showing tobacco stained teeth. She shuddered in revulsion and screamed again. Surely someone would hear her cries for help.

The leader slapped her again, causing more blood to run from her swollen, bruised lips. She could feel the salty taste of her own blood as it ran into her mouth. But she didn't scream out any more for her throat was raw. She struggled against the hands holding her down, but her efforts were feeble now.

The leader got onto the table. His friends urged him on as he leaned over her with his large knife and cut open her blouse, exposing her white breasts, the nipples an inviting pink in the soft lamplight. He covered her breasts with filthy hands and squeezed, causing her to writhe in pain and revulsion. He laughed cruelly, then stepped between her parted legs. Brandishing his knife again, he cut her skirt from hem to waist. He tossed the fabric apart, then fell to his knees between her thighs. The other two banditos held her down as she struggled.

Suddenly the cold, deadly voice of Jake called out, "You're a dead man, *hombre*."

It all happened fast. The leader jumped up from Alexandra, going for his pistol as the other two banditos ran from the room toward the kitchen. There was an explosion of firing guns and the leader fell back onto Alexandra, spilling his warm blood down her nearly naked body. She looked at him, horrified, as Jake and Lamar ran from the room after the two other men. There were sounds outside: guns banging loudly, horses neighing, then the sound of pounding hoofs, retreating further and further away.

Alexandra pushed the dead bandito to the floor, then sat up to pull her clothes around her as best she could.

Jake and Lamar hurried back inside. As Lamar drug the bandito outside, Jake turned to Alexandra. He hugged her close, then followed Lamar to finish what they had started.

By the time they returned, Alexandra had hastily wrapped an Indian blanket around herself. She was trying to untie Cookie, who watched her with a crooked smile. She was bloody, cut, bleeding, scratched, and her hair was matted. But she was oblivious to everything as she struggled with the hard knots.

Jake walked over to her, his face set in hard, unrelenting lines. He was dirty, too, his clothes torn, and blood trickled down from a cut on his face. But he was unaware of all this as he stood over Alexandra, determined to give her comfort but not knowing quite how.

Lamar moved more quickly, pushing away Alexandra's hands as he began untying Cookie. Jake touched her arms, drawing her to him, his eyes a soft, concerned blue.

She looked up at him, then jerked away.

He was surprised, his face questioning. "Alexandra? It's over. The banditos are all gone."

"Thanks, I'm glad," she said coldly, moving away from him.

Jake let his hands drop to his sides, watching her, confusion evident on his face.

"Let the others that got away be, Jake. They didn't harm me."

"They didn't, didn't —"

"You got here in time."

"I was afraid we'd be too late, Alexandra," Lamar said, his voice troubled.

"It's all right now. The herd?"

"We stopped the banditos. They got close,

but we killed some, ran the others off. They won't be back soon," he said drily, "not after that licking."

"Good," she said, smiling softly at Lamar and Cookie. "Some of the cowboys must be hurt. Bring them up here and I'll see to them. Cookie can help me."

"You bet, Miss Alexandra. You get dressed and I'll start in the kitchen," he said as he got up and walked away.

Alexandra turned toward Jake. "I'd better start with you."

"Take care of yourself, Alex." He looked at her closely. "You need some help, too."

"I guess you're right," she agreed reluctantly. "Do we have anything to use for bandages.

"Sheets will do," Lamar said. "Look, I'll go back for the men and send them here in relays." The strain between Jake and Alexandra was obvious and he wondered what had happened. He'd expected to see her throw herself into his arms after he had rescued her. Instead, she seemed cooler than ever.

"I'm going with you," Jake said. "I'll help there while the others come in."

Alexandra turned away, feeling a hard knot constrict her chest. She walked quickly to their bedroom, and washed off the blood and dirt from her body. The cuts and scratches burned, but they weren't deep and would heal soon enough. She put on her riding habit, glad that it covered her wounds completely, then pulled on her boots. Although the night was warm, she felt chilled and was glad for the heavy clothing. She began brushing her hair, trying to get the tangles and weeds out. It was hopeless. Finally, she plaited it, then threw it over her shoulder. She didn't have time to worry with her hair. She scrubbed her face in a basin of water, but it didn't help her puffy, discolored lips. Sighing as she took a last look at herself, she hurried out of the room.

She quickly got out the sheets and began tearing them into strips. When this was done, she joined Cookie in the kitchen. He had a kettle of water boiling and in another kettle, he was busily making a stew. Coffee was also brewing and he'd gotten out a bottle of tequila.

He grinned at her when she entered. "You look a sight better, Miss Alexandra. Those cowboys sure arrived just in time. Sorry I wasn't more help to you."

She patted his arm gently. "No one could have done more, Cookie. It's all ended well. We just have to get those cowboys repaired so they can make the drive."

The first relay of cowboys came in, at first sheepishly showing their wounds, then with more abandon as they realized the attention they got from Miss Alexandra with each wound. They'd never fought so well, or so hard, or had such *bad* wounds. She was regaled with stories of their daring. They'd never enjoyed the aftermath of a fight more. She soon had them bandaged, fed, and tequila and coffee poured down them. They were ready for another fight.

About dawn, Alexandra and Cookie sat down at the table to rest and eat. Both showed the ravages of the night before, but still they were both lighthearted for they had helped save the Bar J. They heard more horses outside and in a moment Jake and Lamar entered, looking exhausted.

Jake smiled tentatively at Alexandra as he walked in, his hat in his hand, cursing himself inwardly for feeling like a young school boy with his first girl. There was something wrong with Alexandra, but he couldn't figure it out. He wanted to part friends. He liked her spunk and she'd helped to save the ranch last night, even endangering her own life. Of course, in a way she'd been the cause of it, too. He knew he'd be better off when she was out of his life and he wished he could be more pleased about their parting in San Antonio. But he wasn't. He didn't want to let her go.

Looking from Alexandra to Cookie, Jake said, "The herd's okay. We'll point them toward San Antonio tomorrow at first light."

Cookie grinned. "Great. I'll be ready. Soon as you two are fed, I'll get back down to the outfit. Those boys will be hungry again in no time."

Alexandra stood up. "Let me fix those wounds for you, Jake."

She began to wash Jake's face. She tried not to notice the hard lines etched there that had become so familiar to her, or the blond hair that had formed a stubble of beard. Fortunately, the cut was not deep and would leave no scar, she thought, then turned her thoughts away from his future. She'd never see the wound healed.

"Take off your shirt," she said softly, trying to still her heart as it suddenly began beating faster. She touched his golden brown skin as she washed the dried blood away from the cuts. He caught his breath, his muscles tightening, and she knew it was painful for him. She wrapped white cloth around the wounds to protect them from dirt.

"That's the most I can do. You'll be fine."

And before she'd had time to move away from him, he put his large strong hand on her arm. "Thanks, Alex. You proved you're a true Texan last night."

She jerked away from him and stood up. "I'm from New York and I'd have done as much for anyone who needed help," she said abruptly, then turned and left the room, so he could not see her eyes glistening with unshed tears.

No matter what, she'd never let him see how much he'd hurt her. But pride was a cold and lonely feeling compared to passion. And love.

Chapter Twenty-three

Later that morning there was a furious clatter of horsehoofs that came to an abrupt stop just outside the hacienda.

Alexandra was instantly alert. She knew it couldn't be anyone from the Bar J. They were all down with the herd.

In the main room she grabbed up a rifle, checked to make sure it was loaded, then calmly walked outside. The rider still sat on his horse and the sight that approached him did not make him anxious to get down. He almost didn't recognize Alexandra as she walked toward him, the gun aimed and handled surely. Her face was tanned and her green eyes were hard, sharp in the morning sun.

As their eyes met over the muzzle of her gun, he smiled shyly. "Surely you're not going to shoot *me*, Miss Alexandra, not when I've come to rescue you."

"Lieutenant Blake!" she said, recognizing him.

"Now what is this about rescuing me?" She lowered the rifle.

He got off his horse and strode over to her. "Miss Alexandra, you surely don't believe that I could have forgotten you and your plight here. I returned as quickly as I could after explaining the problem to the major."

"Thank you, lieutenant, but I've been all right, truly."

"You do want to leave, though, don't you?"

She felt her heart pound hard, knowing the answer she must give. "Yes, I want to leave," she whispered.

"Good! I'm mighty glad. I'll take good care of you. I'll treat you like the lady you are," the lieutenant said happily.

"Thank you, Lieutenant Blake. I'm sure I can depend on you to be a gentleman."

"That you can, Miss Alexandra. But we'd better go. They're down with the herd and if we leave now we'll get a good day's start on them if they decide to follow you."

"Oh, I don't believe they will, lieutenant. You see, they're due to point the herd for San Antonio tomorrow morning. Nothing would make Jake Jarmon abandon that herd. We'll be quite safe."

"Nevertheless, I'd feel better—"

"Very well. Why don't you water your horse while I get my things."

Lieutenant Blake watched her a moment as

385

she turned and walked back toward the hacienda. She sure had changed, he thought. It must have been mighty rough on her, a lady so gently bred. Well, he'd take her out of all this. Take her back to civilization where she belonged and then court her, make her love him.

Alexandra did not linger in the hacienda. Her mind was made up and there was no turning back. She would rather leave Jake now than have him leave her in San Antonio. Besides, here was the lieutenant, a handsome man, anxious to protect her. She would get him to marry her, be the father of her child. And he would never give her any trouble. She could control him. So, her problems were all solved by the timely arrival of Lieutenant Blake. Why, then, did she still feel the hard knot in the pit of her stomach and why did her heart ache so? She refused to answer that question.

She hurried into the bedroom she shared with Jake where she splashed cool water on her face and replaited her hair. She would have room for none of her clothing. The riding habit she wore would be fine for the trip. All she needed was some money which she took out of her valise and slipped into the pocket of her riding skirt. Lovingly, she picked up the Norwegian medallion and slipped it around her neck, tucking it safely inside. Everything else she would leave. Picking up her gloves and sombrero, she was ready to go.

She looked neither right nor left as she walked through the hacienda. It was over here and she wanted no memories.

The lieutenant helped her up into the saddle of her horse, and they were on their way.

Lieutenant Blake knew his way, guiding Alexandra away from the hacienda all morning, taking her constantly east. The route was similar to the one they'd taken coming from Corpus Christi the first time, but she didn't realize this for the mesquite country all looked similar to her. In her rides over the Bar J she had not come this far east. She wouldn't mind staying in Brownsville for a while. She would be safe from Giles and Stan with the cavalry and Lieutenant Blake. Eventually she would go back to New York, but for the moment she didn't want to leave Texas. She didn't know what hold the land had on her, but she felt as if they were kindred spirits.

The morning was long and she began to ache in her legs, her hips, her back as they continued to ride, always east away from the Bar J. She wasn't used to riding for such long periods and although she tried to keep up with the lieutenant who still sat his horse as if they were just beginning their ride, she finally could take no more.

"Lieutenant Blake, please, can we rest? I'm exhausted."

He glanced over at her, frowning slightly. "I

suppose so, Miss Alexandra, but we have a long way yet to go before we reach camp. I don't want to be caught by the Jarmons."

"I've told you, lieutenant. They aren't coming. We needn't rush so. Brownsville will still be there when we arrive."

He glanced at her closely, then shrugged before looking around them and heading his horse to a clump of mesquite. He stopped, then got down to help her off her horse. Her legs gave under her and she fell against him. He picked her up in his arms and carried her over to the slight shade and set her down, his face set in worried lines.

"Why didn't you say something sooner, Miss Alexandra? I didn't know. I'm so used to riding."

"It's all right."

"You just rest here and I'll get some water and dried beef. That's all I brought."

"That's fine," Alexandra said as she reached down to rub her legs.

"You sure you can go on?" the lieutenant asked when Alexandra had finished eating.

She smiled at him. "Yes, I'm better now."

They rode on and on, ever further from the Bar J. Alexandra was so tired she could hardly stay in the saddle.

"It's not far now, Miss Alexandra. I know you're tired, but you can rest this evening. Can you make it a little longer?"

She looked over at his face, the last rays of the sun showing his own tiredness mingled with his concern for her. She smiled unsteadily. "Yes. We've come this far. I'll make it, but you'll have to get me off my horse."

He laughed shortly. "I'll be happy to do that. And we'll take it easier from now on to Brownsville. I just wanted to be off Bar J property and have a good start on the Jarmons."

She smiled weakly, shaking her head. He just wouldn't believe that Jake would not come for her. It was over. The ache in her heart told her that.

Finally, when night covered the flat Texas prairie, they arrived at the camp Lieutenant Blake had so steadfastly led them toward all day. Alexandra could see the soldiers' campfire ahead and was grateful for the comfort it would offer in the great expanse of night. She would be only too glad to rest, eat, and sleep.

Lieutenant Blake slowed his horse so that she could ride in beside him. "We're here, Miss Alexandra. You'll be all right now. Some friends of yours have agreed to help us. I was lucky to meet up with them. They set up the camp, and they'll go back with us to Brownsville."

Alexandra opened her mouth to protest. She had no friends in Texas. But they were already within the camp. Two men stood up, then walked forward, the light of the campfire be-

389

hind them casting their bodies in shadows that loomed large and menacing.

Suddenly she felt apprehensive. There was something familiar about the forms that approached them. She jerked the mustang's reins, starting to turn around. But she was too slow. Four strong hands shot out, grabbing the horse's reins, pulling the animal back.

"Now, Alexandra, you wouldn't run away again, would you?" a smooth eastern voice chided her.

"Stan!"

"At your service, my dear."

"And would you run away from me also, *chérie?*" a slow melodious voice of the South beseeched her.

"Giles!"

"Only for you would I come so far, or endure so much."

"Oh, *no*. No!" Alexandra sobbed, her voice catching with emotion.

"Gentlemen, you've startled Miss Alexandra. I know it must be a shock for you, my dear, but then they wanted to surprise you, knowing how happy it would make you," Lieutenant Blake said.

"Happy? *Happy*, Lieutenant Blake?"

"Indeed. Now, gentlemen, we must let Miss Alexandra rest. She's not as strong as we are and it's been a long, hard day."

"Sure. Sure, Blake," Stan said, stepping back

from Alexandra's horse, and Giles also moved to the other side of her mount.

Lieutenant Blake got off his horse, then walked toward Alexandra. "I'll have you down in just a minute, Miss Alexandra. Then, you can—" he started to say, but his words were lost in the belching of a gun as it went off in his back. Puzzled, he looked up at her for a brief moment before he fell forward on his face, dead.

"No! Oh, Stan, no," Alexandra cried, watching Stan quickly pocket the pistol before kicking the lieutenant's body over to make sure he was dead.

Afterward, she thought that she should have known they were going to do something ugly when Stan stepped back and Giles moved to the side. If she hadn't been so tired, or if she hadn't forgotten just how ruthless they were, she might have warned Lieutenant Blake. Now it was too late. Oh, she should have suspected. The lieutenant hadn't known them as she did. She looked down at his handsome face, now smudged with dirt, a large red stain on his chest. Lieutenant Blake would never ride beside her again, protecting her in his kindly way.

"Come, Alexandra," Stan said as he reached up for her, "the man meant nothing to you."

"There was no need to kill him, Stan," she said, struggling against his hands as they encircled her waist to lift her down.

"Of course there was. He would have raised heaven and hell to get you back, and he was in the cavalry. Unfortunately, we needed him to bring you to us, or we'd not have bothered with him at all."

Growing impatient with her struggles, however feeble, he jerked her down and she fell weakly against him. He lifted her in his arms and strode into camp. He set her down near the fire where Giles was busily filling a plate of food. In a moment, he turned to Alexandra and handed the tin plate to her.

"Eat up, *ma chère*. You must be very tired and hungry."

He also handed her a strong cup of coffee laced with brandy. She wanted to refuse the food, the coffee, but she was starved, her stomach felt caved in, and if she didn't regain her strength, she'd never be able to figure out a way to escape. She simply had to eat and sleep in order to be able to flee.

Stan had taken the lieutenant's saddle and bridle off his horse and was now doing the same to Alexandra's mustang. She was glad he would let the horses rest, too. She watched him, her mind sleepily unconcerned, then suddenly gasped as she saw him hit each animal on the rump, sending them flying into the night.

She sat up in alarm. "What do you mean by running off my mustang?" she asked angrily, her eyes flashing a brilliant green in the fire-light.

"Now, we couldn't very well go about with a cavalry branded animal, now could we, my dear? And your mustang hardly suits us either."

"They were good horses," she said stubbornly.

"I'm sure they were, my dear," Stan said as he walked over to her, carrying a length of rope. "Now, if you'll hold out your hands, we'll be done here."

"What?"

"I'm going to tie your hands, Alexandra. You certainly don't expect me to trust you."

She scooted back, then tried to crawl away, but her body was weak, almost lifeless. He grabbed at her, but she kept moving her arms, her legs, jerking them out of his reach. Finally, exasperated, he called for Giles. Soon, they had her pinned down and Stan tied her hands roughly, tightly in front of her.

They stood up, satisfied. She pushed herself to a sitting position, her eyes glaring at them as they turned from her. She sat by the campfire helplessly. If only she could rest, then she could think, make plans, but at the moment her mind wouldn't work. She shut her eyes, too tired to even care what her captors were doing.

When she opened her eyes again, Giles and Stan stood above her. Giles knelt down and lifted her into his arms. She struggled against him, crying out, clubbing at him with her bound hands. But it did no good. Giles carried her away from the camp while Stan put out the fire. The horses were ready to travel, having rested all day long. They were strong, magnificent beasts, and the one Giles carried her to had a sidesaddle. As he lifted her up, helping her to straighten her garments, the full impact of their plans hit her. They were going to travel *all* night!

She groaned, her body rebelling at the thought of more hours in the saddle. "No, Giles," she said, "I can't ride any longer. I've got to rest."

"A Clarke saying she's tired. I don't believe it, Alexandra. You can sleep in the saddle," Stan said. "I'm going to lead your horse, even if it is slower. I'll never trust you again."

He picked up the reins to her horse and led it over to his own. She had to go with them. She had no choice. Her hands were bound, she was in the saddle, and Stan led her horse. There would be no Lieutenant Blake to rescue her. Jake would not come either.

They turned the horses in a northeasterly direction towards the port at Corpus Christi, taking Alexandra with them, their unwilling victim once more.

Chapter Twenty-four

Jake slid off his horse, then ran, crouching low, into the camp Giles and Stan had left behind. He couldn't be more than a couple of hours behind them now, he calculated, as he turned the still hot campfire ashes over. He'd originally been alerted to Alexandra's plight when he'd found the two horses further back on the trail. The mustang had started back to the Bar J and the cavalry horse had come along. He had them now, tied to his own mustang.

Jake had left the herd in late morning to check on Alexandra. He thought she'd be safe, but he didn't know about Pecos. He'd not killed the man and there had been the chance he'd return for Alexandra.

That had been his first thought when he'd found the hacienda empty and Alexandra gone. Still, it was strange that there had been no sign of a struggle and only one horse had left with her. He knew he couldn't let her be taken by

Pecos and what was left of his Mexican banditos so he'd written a quick note to Lamar, telling him that he'd gone after her and to go ahead with the drive. He'd try to catch up with them in San Antonio. He'd hated to leave the herd at such a critical time, but he knew Lamar and the cowboys could start the drive without him.

As the day had worn on, he had begun to doubt his first assumption. The trail led east and north towards the coast, not south toward Mexico. It made no sense.

After dark, he'd come upon the two horses and caught them, quickly examining their shoes. They were the two horses he'd been tracking all day, but now they wore no tack and were still hot and foamy from the long, hard day. When he'd seen the cavalry brand on the bigger horse, and recognized the other as his own mustang, he knew Alexandra had gone with the young lieutenant. Something dark and sinister had risen in his blood at this realization and he had glared into the dark night, determination to find the two blotting out all other thoughts.

But what had happened to them? Why would they have let their horses go? Finally the seething anger that had at first consumed him gave way to concern for Alexandra's safety. He'd hurried on, taking the two horses with him in case he'd need them later.

And the tracks had ended at this camp. He

realized from the ashes and scraps of food that two other men — judging from footprints — had waited here all day for the lieutenant and Alexandra. Jake found the blood stains in the dirt. He followed them to the mesquite thicket and found the lieutenant's body.

The picture was complete in his mind. Alexandra had told him she'd been pursued by Stan, a man from New York, and Giles. These two men must have joined forces to capture her. Banditos did not come this far east, and there was no herd here to tempt rustlers. It had to be Giles and Stan.

Grim determination set in. He'd be damned if he'd let Alexandra be carried off by two devious men set only to get her fortune. The herd could wait a little longer. He had to get to her before they reached Corpus Christi and sailed back to New Orleans.

He hastily threw the lieutenant's body over the saddle of the cavalry horse, tying it on securely. There was no point in letting the buzzards get the poor devil. He'd only wanted to help Alexandra and had gotten killed for his efforts.

He mounted his own mustang, leading the other horses behind him, then started out once more, determined to catch up with the party by morning.

Anger burned in him as he pushed the horses on, gaining steadily on the riders ahead of him.

They weren't used to the wild Texas land and he knew how to ride the country, getting the most from his horses. As he rode, he kept seeing Alexandra's green eyes, sometimes soft and laughing, sometimes cold and hard, but always with him. She was always with him no matter her moods, no matter what she did. He could almost feel her thick, soft hair in his hands, her soft, yet firm body beneath his own. That's really why he'd gone back to the hacienda. He was going to ask her to go with him on the trail drive, no matter how foolish or stupid it seemed. Where Alexandra was concerned, he couldn't think or act rationally. And he no longer cared.

All night he followed, tracking ever closer and closer to the three ahead of him. As day began to dawn, casting its pink light over the country, he smiled to himself. They would rest soon. They'd have to. They weren't as used to long hours in the saddle as was he. He'd have them then.

He knew he was close when he saw their trail change. The riders had stopped, as if considering what to do. He looked quickly around. Yes, he saw it, too. A clump of mesquite up ahead that would make a good campsite. That's what they'd done. Good. He'd be able to sneak up on them easily.

He rode in closer, then veered off to the north until he was out of sight of the camp.

He tied the three horses loosely to some low mesquite. Then he hurried, stealthily, toward the camp. When he could hear their voices, he dropped to his stomach. He would take no chances on being discovered.

He crawled the rest of the way into the mesquite thicket. The day was dawning hot and clear as he raised his head above the brush to assess the camp. His mouth tightened, his eyes narrowing dangerously as he saw Alexandra on the ground near the campfire, her hands bound in front of her. Giles was nearby, impeccably dressed in his dark riding clothes but nervous, pacing. The other man, lean and older, had to be the one called Stan. He sat on his heels, hunkered over the fire, drinking coffee, watching Alexandra.

Jake stood up and walked lithely, soundlessly into the camp, his gun drawn and ready.

Alexandra looked up, her eyes widening in disbelief as she saw Jake standing there, tall, rugged, and deadly.

Giles saw Alexandra start and spun around. Cursing, he grabbed for his pistol, fatally disregarding Jake's already drawn forty-five. Jake shot. The slug tore through Giles' chest, the force of the deadly projectile knocking him backward to the hard ground.

But, before the echoes of Jake's first shot had died away, before Jake could fire gain, Stan's gun was in his hand. He fired. Alexandra screamed as blood gushed from Jake's head. His pistol fired uselessly into the hard packed dirt. He staggered. And as he fell to his knees his gaze sought out Alexandra, locked onto her for a second, then his eyes closed as he crumpled to the ground, his gun still clutched in his hand.

Alexandra screamed again and again, the sound cutting mercilessly through the cool morning air.

She struggled to her feet, her eyes fastened upon Jake, more screams shattering the dawn.

Stan slapped her hard across the face. She fell back, blood dripping from her lips as she whimpered, her eyes still on Jake.

Then Stan leaned down and jerked her up by her raw, swollen wrists. Leaning close to her face, he rasped, "So much for your two fine heroes. My problems are entirely solved. You are mine now, Alexandra dear."

"No! No, Stan. I'll hate you forever!"

He laughed harshly, then dragged her to the waiting horses.

"There is no point in wasting any more time around here. Better things await us in New York."

"No, Stan. You can have the company. I don't care. Just leave me here." Alexandra moaned numbly, her eyes still frozen on the distant, motionless figure of Jake.

"I told you a long time ago that I intended

to have you, and have you I will. We're going to New York."

He lifted her up and dumped her sore body into the saddle. By late that night, he thought, they'd be in Corpus Christi where they could catch a schooner to New Orleans and once out of Texas, he had no worries. Let the buzzards do their work on those two. It served them right for trying to foil his plans. He quickly unsaddled Giles' horse, then hit it on the rump, sending it running. There would be no questions now.

Leaping into his own saddle, he looked back at Alexandra, a smile curving his thin, cruel lips. She was his at last.

Alexandra could barely keep herself in the saddle as Stan led her through the hot, dry land, pushing relentlessly on towards Corpus Christi. Her entire body ached, but it was nothing in comparison to her heart. In the moment that she'd seen Jake standing in the camp—so proud, so dauntless, so defiant—she'd realized her total and absolute love for him. She had wanted to rush into his arms and tell him she loved him, that she'd go anywhere with him as long as he'd let her. And then he was dead, lost to her forever. She knew she had loved him from the first, but her stubborn pride had not let her admit it. Oh, to be so foolishly late!

And he'd come for her. He'd left the herd and come for her. It could have meant only one thing. He'd realized, too, that he loved her. He'd come to rescue her and take her back with him to join the trail drive to Abilene. She'd have gone, gladly enduring any hardships, anything to have been by his side. But now he was dead. *Dead!* She felt lifeless, too. There was nothing left for her, nothing left of Jake.

No, there was her baby, *their* baby. Jake's child grew within her. She smiled softly to herself. If it had endured the past few days and nights, then it wanted to live. It was strong and courageous just like Jake had been, like Texas was. She would live to have their child. It was his legacy and she could live knowing that a part of him still lived.

Once more the day wore into night, but still they traveled, the horses now as tired and weary as their riders. Alexandra slumped forward in her saddle. She fought the sleep that strove to overtake her. She was afraid of falling from her horse and hurting the child which grew inside of her. And so she rode on, fighting the pain, the sleepiness, the painful memories.

Soon she could feel a difference in the air. She was near the ocean: Corpus Christi. She could smell the salt sea breeze, feel its moistness on her skin. How different, how very different from the dry, dusty air of south Texas.

Just outside the town, Stan stopped his horse and pulled Alexandra's up beside him.

"I'm going to untie you, but don't try to get

away or it'll be painful for you. Don't give me any trouble here. All right?"

She nodded mutely, her throat dry and rough.

He quickly cut the rope, throwing it on the ground. "Now, stay beside me when we ride in. It could be rough here. I'll get us a room. Don't say anything to anyone or I promise you, Alexandra, that anything you've experienced before will seem pleasant in comparison."

They moved forward again, entering the dusty streets of Corpus Christi. Stan rode steadily toward the one good hotel where they stopped. Inside, it was almost dark, only one lamp burned on the registration desk. Alexandra leaned against the counter for support. He rang the bell once. Waited. Then in irritation rang it several more times. Finally, the owner stumbled down the stairs, a scowl on his face.

"The lady is exhausted. She's been riding for hours. We need a room for the night," Stan said.

"Pay in advance and sign here," the man said as he swung the heavy, leather bound ledger around to Stan.

Alexandra watched him sign, "Mr. and Mrs. Smith." Always careful, even in Texas, she thought. He wanted no dead men rising to haunt him when he was back in New York City. It was just like Stan, just like the cautious, scheming Stan Lewis.

When money had exchanged hands, the regis-

403

ter signed satisfactorily, the man handed Stan a key, then went up the stairs ahead of them.

Once in the room, Stan said, "I'm going out to make plans for tomorrow, Alexandra. I trust you're tired enough not to make trouble for me." Then he turned and left the room, locking it from the outside.

Alexandra dimly heard the steps that receded from her room, down the hall, and away from her. But she was not really sure of anything as sleep engulfed her, carrying her into the deep oblivion she craved.

It was still dark outside when Stan leaned over her, holding a lamp above her head to look at her better. The light awoke her, as well as his presence, and she stirred, feeling as if she could never leave the bed again.

"Wake up. I've sold the horses and booked passage on a schooner going to New Orleans. It's the best I could do. You'll be staying in a cabin with several other women. You can rest on the way. Get up. We won't be delayed."

"Oh, Jake. I'm—"

Red stars exploded in her head as Stan slapped her across the face. She just lay there, shock almost taking over completely.

"Don't you ever, ever call me by *his* name again. Do you hear me, Alexandra?" he hissed fiercely, leaning over her prostrate body.

Then she remembered. She'd been dreaming of Jake, and she'd said his name automatically.

"Do you understand me?" he hissed again, grabbing her limp body and shaking it.

"Yes. Yes, *Stan*."

"Good. Now, get up. The skipper wants to leave at sunup and wants us on board now."

Alexandra felt as if a thousand pins were stuck in her body as she raised herself up, gently edging her legs over the side of the bed. Stan stood to one side watching her, then groaned in disgust. He grabbed up a bottle and a glass and came over to sit down beside her. He poured a generous portion into the glass, then held it up to her lips.

"Drink. Cheap whiskey ought to revive you. Drink it all."

She obediently took the glass, her hands shaking as she tried to hold it to her lips. He took the glass away and poured the whiskey down her throat. She choked on the fiery liquid as she swallowed. When she had drunk it all, Stan poured himself a drink and downed it quickly before setting the bottle and glass aside.

He came back to her and jerked her to her feet. The room swayed wildly for a moment, but she did feel better. She didn't ache so much any more for the whiskey on her empty stomach had gone straight to her head.

"That's better," Stan said, taking her arm and leading her toward the door. "Now, don't speak to the other passengers. Pretend you're sick or something. I don't want any trouble from you."

"All right, Stan," she said unsteadily, feeling her legs wobble as she followed him out of the room.

Downstairs, he flung the room key on the desk, and with a firm grip on Alexandra's arm, led her outside. He looked neither right nor left as he hurried her along. She wished he wouldn't walk so fast. She had trouble keeping up with him.

Finally, they reached the quay and what happened afterwards would always seem more like a nightmare than reality. Stan got her on board, then settled her in the room with three other women who were all asleep. They only grumbled as she bumped into their beds getting to her own. Then she sank down into her bunk, fully clothed, and fell into a deep, exhausted sleep that lasted the entire trip except for the brief moments of wakefulness when her queasy stomach demanded relief. She ate little; for the most part she slept.

Stan had to carry her off the schooner to the New Orleans dock. She was too weak to even lift her head. They went to the best hotel in New Orleans, and he carried her inside. She was embarrassed by her dirty, ragged condition in the magnificent lobby of the hotel, but after what she'd been through she was lucky to be alive. He carried her upstairs to a spacious, luxurious room and laid her gently on the bed. She looked around herself in wonder, surprised to realize that she had become completely unaccustomed to such luxury.

"I'm going out, Alexandra. There's much for me to do before we can leave. I'll have food and hot water sent up to you. I'll be back when I can. In the meantime, don't try to escape." He paused, and looked down at her white, pinched face and limp body. "In fact, for once I don't believe I'll even have to worry that you'll try to escape. I don't believe you can."

She merely looked at his satisfied face. She was beyond feeling, beyond comprehending. She only wished to lie still and perhaps the queasiness in her stomach would go away. She was only dimly aware when he left the room, locking the door behind him, as she drifted off into a deep sleep.

Later she was abruptly awakened when a maid entered, carrying a tray. Behind her more people brought hot water to fill her bath. The maid set the tray down, then came over to Alexandra and hesitantly asked, "Will that be all, ma'am?"

Alexandra slowly opened her eyes and looked at the young woman a long moment, before fully comprehending the situation.

"Oh, no. No, thank you. That'll be all."

The maid bobbed, then hurried out, the others following.

Surprisingly Alexandra felt better, not quite so sick. Her stomach felt almost back to normal.

And a long, hot bath would be wonderful.

She began slowly, carefully removing her torn, dust-coated riding habit. She pulled off her boots with great effort, then stood up and walked slowly across the room. Catching sight of herself in the full length mirror, she stopped, hardly recognizing herself.

She was thin, painfully thin, and her eyes seemed like enormous green orbs filling her face. Her hair was matted with dirt and grass. She was a shadow of her former beauty.

She pulled the tray of food over to the bath, then sank down into the soothing waters of the tub. And so alternately eating and bathing, she passed the time until the water had become cold and the food had been consumed.

She washed her hair, and wrapped it in a towel, not knowing what else to do with it until she had a brush. After drying herself all over, she walked back to the bed. Sleep soon eased the tension in her face, changing her again to the once innocent girl.

It was dark the next time she awakened and Stan was lighting the lamps.

"Feeling better, Alexandra?" Stan asked when he saw her eyes open.

"Yes."

He sat on the edge of the bed and she moved away from him, keeping the covers high around her neck.

"I managed to book passage for us on a

steamer leaving for New York City tomorrow morning."

"Tomorrow?" she asked in a whisper.

His gray eyes darkened. "There's no point in lingering here. You can recover on the ocean voyage. That's supposed to be good for people. And I want to get back to New York. I've been gone too long already. I bought clothes for us today, only a limited amount, of course. Can you dress yourself?"

Alexandra nodded.

"Good. I have a room of my own. We're traveling under our own names now and I don't want to hurt your reputation since your name will be henceforth linked with mine. Unfortunately," he said, letting his hand run over her bare arm, "it will seriously inhibit my desires. But I believe I can manage until we reach New York."

Alexandra looked up into his face. He was smiling cruelly, his gray wolf eyes greedy as they regarded her soft form outlined beneath the covers. He leaned forward, his eyes burning, but she put out a hand to ward him off. The thought of another man touching her after Jake was repulsive. She couldn't even stand the thought.

He leaned back, his eyes dark. "So that's how it is to be. All right, for the present, but your bed will be shared once we reach New York."

She looked away without speaking, and he

left the room, locking the door behind him.

She got up, looking through his purchases to find what she wanted — a brush. She began to work on her hair.

It took a while to restore her hair to its former luster, but when she was through she was rewarded by a recognizable Alexandra. The face looking back in the mirror was no longer soft and vulnerable. The green eyes were hard, determined, and knew about life. This Alexandra would get what she wanted. She would control her own fate. She would marry Stan when she was ready, giving Jake's child a name, then she would have her revenge.

Her mind set, she returned to bed to sleep the dreamless sleep of the untroubled mind.

She knew nothing more until Stan woke her the next morning. He was quite upset that she wasn't already dressed. He looked normal in the sober business attire of New York. After admonishing her, he left her to dress while he ordered breakfast downstairs.

She hurriedly began dressing, throwing on the undergarments he'd chosen for her, then slipped on the dark, plain gown. She pulled her hair back into a plain knot at her neck, then perched the simple hat on her head. She felt hot, stuffy and unattractive in the clothes he'd selected for her. Stuffing the extra garments in the valise, she left it on the bed, then went downstairs to join Stan for breakfast.

He'd chosen a small table by a window with sheer white curtains and was just being served when she arrived. He looked at her critically as he seated her, then nodded approvingly.

As she began heaping food on her plate, he watched her suspiciously. Then he smiled, his gray eyes glinting with pleasure.

"One would almost think you were eating for two," he said, his voice heavy with meaning.

She blushed and avoided his eyes.

"I wondered on the schooner coming from Corpus Christi. No one else except you was seasick. I thought it was because you were so exhausted, so tired, but now I have another thought. Is it Jake's child, Alexandra?"

Her hand shook violently as she picked up her cup of chocolate. "It does happen, you know," she muttered.

He nodded, a smile still on his face. "I couldn't be more pleased, although that might surprise you. You see, now you *must* marry me and of your own accord if you don't want your child to be a bastard. And we know about bastards, don't we? Another bastard in the fine Clarke family could hardly be tolerated, now could it?"

She looked into his cold gray eyes. He was playing right into her hands, while thinking that he was making the clever move, trapping her by her pregnancy.

"No, it could not."

"Then you'll marry me to give your child a name, if for no other reason?"

"Perhaps," she said, not wanting to appear eager.

"You must remember, Alexandra, that no other man of any respectability will marry you, knowing you carry another man's child."

She looked down, then back up at him, thinking how very sweet her revenge would be.

"Say you'll marry me."

"I don't love you, Stan."

"Hell! That has never mattered to me. It's completely unimportant. You need me. Yes, by God, *you* need *me* this time. You should be begging me to marry you. But I'm being nice. I'm asking you to marry me, Alexandra. Will you?"

She let out her breath, sighing, then said quite clearly, "Yes, I believe I will, Stan Lewis."

He smiled triumphantly at her, then picked up his fork. "Eat up. New York awaits us."

They finished their meal in silence, then he escorted her to the open carriage waiting outside, their luggage already brought there by the porter. Alexandra had her last look at New Orleans in the early morning light. It looked softer, more romantic than before. She was not hungry, or hunted this time, but somehow, she no longer had the spirit or optimism that had been hers before. Her youth had left her along the way.

Once at the quay, they were escorted with great ceremony to their cabins. She knew this journey would be entirely different from the original one. Stan left her in her cabin, a nice, clean room, and she sat down on the bunk, thinking that no matter how perfect this trip was, she didn't have Jake to look forward to. She'd met him on the first trip and nothing could ever make her forget him and what they'd shared together.

Love. Passion. And a child. She would make sure nothing ever hurt their child the way she had been hurt. And Jake would live always in her heart, in her mind, and to their child.

Part Four

The Sidewalks of New York

Chapter Twenty-five

The night breeze, which had cooled very little since the day, wafted into Alexandra's bedroom on the second story of her mansion, bringing with it the sounds of New York City in the summer. She walked across the room to the window and pulled back the drapes to look out onto the lighted street. The breeze was humid and did little more to improve her mood than the sounds of so much congested humanity.

She let the drapes fall back into place and went to regard herself in the full length mirror, thinking how different the hot, dry air of Texas, the wide open spaces, and the sound of nature, of cattle, of wild mustangs were from New York City. She had thought she might forget it, lose herself in New York again. After all, it was her home. But it hadn't happened. She couldn't forget the hacienda, the cowboys, the quality of life there. And, she couldn't forget Jake. He would always be with her. At nights, her body ached for his touch, his nearness, but she comforted herself with thoughts of their child, who grew steadily within her.

She looked at her stomach in the mirror. The baby didn't show yet. She had put on some weight since leaving New Orleans for there had been the long trip back in which she had rested and enjoyed the food served on the ship, and her breasts had grown larger, rounding her figure more. She knew she was desirable by the looks she caught in Stan's eyes, but she didn't feel alluring. Jake had made her feel sensual, alive, beautiful, and she'd wanted to be all those things for him. Now, it didn't matter.

The pale green satin gown she wore was cut low, revealing the soft curves of her ripening breasts, and fit tightly around her still small waist to flow gracefully to the floor. It was a beautiful gown and she'd decided to wear her mother's emeralds with it. Her hair had been styled beautifully, pulling the golden-red locks into curls and twists all over her head. Stan should be pleased.

He had insisted that she look especially beautiful tonight since it was to be her first real introduction to New York society. He was taking her to the opening of a new play at the theatre. He was using her as he would a new horse, or carriage — as an extension of himself to impress the important members of New York society. Well, let him, she thought, for it would help her child take his or her rightful place in New York City.

When she had returned with Stan two weeks ago, she had found little changed in her mansion, or with her family. Her housekeeper had been very efficient and all was in order. Her cousins had come to visit her, bringing their odious sons, all engaged now and bringing their simpering fiancées. She'd endured their presence patiently, graciously, and had even suffered Stan's possessive pride in her before the others. He had announced their engagement immediately, with the family's complete approval. She kept her thoughts to herself and played the docile female for them all, but deep inside her plans were unchanged. Stan would feel the double-edge of her revenge when her child had been safely born into the world.

Until then, she played her role. Stan pressed her for a quick marriage, but she kept putting him off. She could hardly bear the thought of having him in her home, sharing her bed. How could she stand his hands on her after Jake? But Stan kept telling her that if they didn't marry soon, her pregnancy would show, and how would they explain a baby that was born too early. He was right, of course, but it was so hard to accept Stan as her husband.

She still loved Jake with all her heart. He was the man who should have been her husband, the man to share her life. She just couldn't seem to reconcile herself to his death, no matter that she had seen Stan shoot him. She could still feel him, sense him. It was as if he lived and called to her. But no, it was not possible. He was dead. She had to accept that fact or she could not go on.

She glanced at herself once more. Her face had paled and her eyes had grown bright and soft with thoughts of Jake. She shook her head, willing the tears not to come. It did no good to think of him, want him, almost feel him with her. No! She had to stop thinking of him, or she would go mad.

She hurried from the room, trying to run away from the memories that haunted her every moment. Sometimes she would wake in the night, drenched with sweat, and the memory of Jake holding her in his arms would be so strong that she would reach out for him, call to him. She could not bear life without him. . . .

Stan was standing in the foyer when she came down the staircase. He looked up at her, his gray eyes suddenly softening. He walked toward her, and as she reached the last stair, he took her hands and pulled her softly against his chest. She suffered his light embrace, reminding herself that this was the man she would marry.

He tilted her chin up with his hand and looked down into her green eyes, now hard and cold.

"You are magnificent tonight. The gown is

superb and the emeralds—well, no other woman will be able to compare with your beauty."

"Thank you," Alexandra said stiffly, detaching herself from him and walking away.

He frowned, then followed her retreating form. She went into the parlor, looking pensively out the window. He stood back from her, watching. She'd been like this ever since the trip back. She was so distant, so cold. There was no fire in her as there had been before, no spirit. He wanted the other Alexandra back, even if she fought him all the way. This woman he could reach in no way. Nothing he said or did caused any reaction in her. It took all his will power not to ignore her cold, biting eyes and simply throw her on the floor and take her as he had the first time and prove that underneath her cold exterior she was still a warm, vital woman. But he was afraid of losing her so close to the wedding. He wasn't sure of her yet, perhaps even less sure than before for she had grown into a strong woman, a woman with no fears, no worries, simply a woman waiting the passage of time. If it had not been for the baby she carried, he wondered if he could have made her marry him. She was so withdrawn now, nothing reached her, nothing at all.

"Shall we go, Stan?" she finally asked.

"Yes, of course, dearest. I've timed our arrival perfectly. You'll be the most talked about woman in New York by tomorrow."

"How nice," Alexandra said dryly.

He helped her up into the elaborate open carriage, proud to display her in such a vehicle, but as he sat down beside her, he noticed that she merely gave the carriage a quick flick of her cold, piercing eyes. She was not impressed. Nothing he did, no matter how thoughtful, how expensive, how kind, impressed her. She even seemed to regard New York City as some overcrowded, dirty warehouse of people. It was the jewel of America! The rest of the country was barbarous in comparison. Hadn't he seen for himself the decay of the South, the wildness of Texas.

Leaning toward her still figure, he said lowly, so the driver couldn't hear, "Alexandra, I have found a lovely little chapel in New York. I believe you would like to be married there. We will want a quiet, quick wedding. Later, we can give a magnificent ball to introduce you to all the New York notables. I've taken the liberty of engaging it for one week from today."

"What?" she whispered, feeling her heart beat quicken.

"You've seemed unable to make a decision, my dearest, and you know we shouldn't wait much longer. The doctor—"

"I know. I know, but—"

"No buts, Alexandra. We're going to be married. There's no point in further delaying this. Will you have your gown ready in a week?"

She clenched her hands, the knuckles going white in her agitation. He was right. She had to marry him and soon. Jake was dead. He *was* dead. Oh, why couldn't she accept that?

"Alexandra?"

"Yes," she whispered.

"You agree — in one week?" he asked, relief in his voice.

"Yes," she said, more loudly. "In one week, Stan. You are right. We cannot wait longer. I *must* think of my child."

He covered her small hands with his large one. "You won't regret it. I'll be good to you. I will make you an excellent husband. I do love you, Alexandra," he said, wanting her to know that he wanted more than her fortune. "I know you don't believe that, but I do. How could I help loving you?"

Alexandra was still silent, gazing at the passing buildings. What more did he want of her than marriage?

"I hope that someday you will come to love me, too," he said, a hopeful note creeping into his voice.

Finally, she turned to him, trying to soften the expression she knew was set on her face. "It is much too soon for this, Stan. We'll be married, then we'll see."

He nodded. He had to accept what she would give him of herself, he finally realized. He could take her body by force, but not the essence of Alexandra. Only she was free to give this, or to withhold it.

They rode the rest of the way in silence, each lost in personal thoughts.

Soon the carriage came to a stop before a magnificent, lofty building. Alexandra looked at it curiously, almost laughing at the thought of how ridiculous it would look if plunked down in the middle of south Texas. And what of the richly, ornately dressed people? They would look even more absurd. Stan helped her down from the fine carriage and into the milling mass of people who gossiped and watched each other as they made their way slowly into the theatre.

Stan escorted her possessively and determinedly through the crowd, keeping a tight grip on her arm. He acknowledged acquaintances here and there, but was careful not to stop and chat. He wanted them to see Alexandra tonight and wonder. Tomorrow the newspapers would be full of her beauty and his triumph, but they would not meet her until after the wedding when he could present her as his wife in the sumptuous ballroom of their mansion. Then the first step toward his goal would be completed.

He was an ambitious man. He'd always been ambitious. Perhaps it was because of his birth, but he wanted more than money. He wanted a high place in society. And he wanted to enter politics. There he could gain the real power and money that he craved. With the beautiful Alexandra Clarke at his side, he could achieve all his dreams. And soon, very soon, she would be his—completely his.

Inside the theatre, the furnishings were ornate, gilded, and plush. Alexandra couldn't keep herself from comparing them with the simplicity and strictly functional furniture in Texas. Of course, perhaps one day Texas would succumb to the ease and comfort of money, but that had not happened yet. She could appreciate the beauty of the place as Stan guided her up an ornate staircase toward the box he'd secured for the performance that evening. It had cost him dearly, but he had to have the perfect setting for the jewel of Alexandra.

Once in their box, Stan looked around and down into the audience, satisfied when he saw the faces turned up to them. He smiled gently at Alexandra, taking her hand in his. He was very much aware of the portrait they made.

"Do you like your seat, dearest?" he asked softly.

She stared frostily at him. "The seats are excellent. I hope the play is as good, as if it really matters."

"I'm sure it will be."

Alexandra nodded, then turned her head to gaze back over the crowd. She had never felt more alone, more estranged, more unloved than at that moment as she sat in one of the best

425

seats in the theatre on the opening night of a new play in New York City. She wore a fortune in emeralds around her neck, her gown was a designer's dream, she was more beautiful than ever. But she didn't appreciate her beauty, her wealth, or the theatre, not at that moment. For she saw the wealth that was worn on the people that filled the theatre as a contrast to the poverty of the South and Texas. She found that she no longer belonged with these people. Her heart was with the people of Texas, those men and women struggling to exist. Texans were alive, vibrantly alive. When she thought of their struggles against nature, against Indians, rustlers, she was not impressed by the people around her dressed in all their finery.

Their faces weren't tanned, their muscles weren't hard, and their instincts weren't sharp — if a man and a woman hadn't these qualities in Texas, they were dead. Here, they could live in luxury yet not be alive. For what did they feel sitting here, waiting to be entertained by others? In Texas, at the ranch, on the trail, with the cattle and the mustangs, people knew they were alive by the sheer energy they exerted every day to survive. And entertainment? They entertained themselves. People lived there by their wits, their own strength, and their own determination. Here, someone could exist on inherited money or a spouse's wealth or perhaps by fleecing those less fortunate. She knew she didn't want to live in New York City anymore. Right now, she didn't belong. She didn't want to belong.

The curtains rose and the play began. Alexandra tried to concentrate, but soon she turned her thoughts away for it was not real to her. During intermission, Stan kept her in the box. Once the play was over, he hurried her out and into the lobby. He waved, smiled, and nodded to many people, but made no attempt to stop and introduce her.

The moon was just a pale sliver, the street dark except in patches where a streetlamp shed its pale, ineffectual glow, but Alexandra was glad for the darkness. It offered an escape from Stan's unwavering gaze as they rode toward her mansion.

The carriage was going unusually fast as an older woman stepped off the street. Alexandra screamed. The carriage swerved—but not in time. It struck the woman, knocking her back against the curb.

"Stan! Stan, stop the carriage. We've hit someone," Alexandra cried, concern in her voice. "Didn't you see? We must go back."

"The night watchman will take care of it. There's no reason for us to get involved. Anyway, decent people aren't out on foot at this time of night. Probably some drunk."

"Stan, we *must* go back," she said more firmly, not surprised at his callousness.

"But, Alexandra —"

"Please, for me," she said, her face close to his, her hands gripping his arm.

"Yes, all right. We'll see about it," he said, unable to deny her the request when she was so close that he could smell her sweet scent and feel her soft hands beseeching him. He always lost some of his control when he was this near her.

He called out to the driver and soon they were by the older woman. She lay exactly where she'd fallen, a crumpled heap of humanity in tattered rags. Alexandra started to get out of the carriage.

"What are you doing?" Stan asked, putting a restraining hand on her arm.

"I want to see if she's alive or needs a doctor."

Groaning inwardly, Stan ordered the driver down. He went over to the limp form on the street, picked up the woman, and carried her back to the carriage. He placed her on the seat opposite Stan and Alexandra, then resumed the driver's seat.

"You can drive on," Stan said after a moment.

When they'd started moving again, Alexandra leaned over the inert form, felt the pulse, then looked back at Stan in triumph.

"She's still alive. We'll take her home. It's the only thing to do. Then I'll send for the doctor.

We can't just leave her somewhere."

Stan looked at Alexandra in hurt bewilderment for a moment, then decided that it had to do with her pregnancy. She would probably mother any hurt thing, any stray animal. He would certainly be glad when she had the child.

"All right," he said wearily, "but she's your responsibility."

"Good. That suits me fine."

They rode back to the mansion in silence. Alexandra watched the woman's form anxiously while Stan thought it was a bad ending to his perfect evening. He had envisioned himself in Alexandra's bed, not playing servant to some vagrant. Well, if it kept her happy, he'd have to live with it. He couldn't afford to displease her.

Once in the house, Alexandra quickly rang for her maid. When she appeared, Alexandra instructed her to put their guest in the room next to her own suite, then remove her clothing, bathe her, and find some fresh clothes for her.

The maid led the driver, still carrying the unconscious woman, up the stairs.

Stan had to restrain Alexandra from following the two upstairs. He pulled her into the parlor. "Dearest, you must not concern yourself so. Your maid is a good woman and will take care of the lady. I'll go now and send for the doctor. You'll see that the woman was not badly hurt."

Alexandra nodded, her thoughts with those upstairs. She was anxious for Stan to leave.

429

"Now, come give me a kiss good night."

And hardly thinking, Alexandra went into his arms, raising her soft lips to him. She just wanted to be rid of him.

She was startled to discover his lips parted and his tongue thrust against her mouth. She twisted away, protesting, but his arms closed like iron bands around her, his hands moving rapidly all over her body as he pressed against her, his hips grinding his hard manhood against her stomach. She pushed against his chest, groaning under his fierce demands.

Finally, when Stan knew he was almost beyond control, he dropped his hands and backed away, his blood pounding in his head, his eyes a dark, opaque gray. He could hardly think. She took away any thoughts except those of her soft body and his need to penetrate it, take it, make it the special vessel for his needs.

After he had himself more under control, he looked into her burning green eyes. "I'm sorry. I can't help myself with you."

Her expression was cold, inscrutable. "I'm going upstairs now. Please see to the doctor."

Alexandra hurried up the stairs to the injured woman's room. She stepped inside.

"Only her head seems to be hurt," the maid said.

"Good. Maybe it's not bad." Alexandra walked to the bed. The woman they had hit lay still. She had dark skin and gray hair and her thin body suggested she hadn't eaten well in a long time.

Alexandra looked at her maid. "You can go now. Send the doctor up as soon as he arrives."

She picked up a lamp and carried it with her to a chair by the bed. She held the light over the woman.

She gasped, almost dropping the lamp. "Ebba?" she whispered hesitantly, setting the lamp on a nearby table. "Ebba," she repeated with more conviction, taking the limp hand in hers. "It's Alexandra, Ebba. You're with me. You're safe now. Can you hear me, Ebba?"

Slowly the woman's eyelids fluttered, then they opened, revealing large dark eyes filled with pain and suffering. They focused on Alexandra in confusion. A slight frown appeared in her smooth forehead, then a soft, hesitant voice said, "Miss Alexandra? That you, child?"

"Yes, oh yes, Ebba. It's me, Alexandra. It's me," she said, laughing as tears ran swiftly down her cheeks. She was so happy she couldn't believe it. She was no longer alone. Here was someone she loved. Someone who could share her life.

Tears began to run down the old woman's cheeks, too. "I'm sure glad to see you, sugar," she said, her voice strengthening. "I'd about given up on this old world."

"Oh, no, Ebba, you're safe now. You're here

431

with me in my home. You need never worry about anything again."

"You mean that, Miss Alexandra? I can't go back on the street again. I just can't."

"Oh, no. You'll stay here with me. I need you, Ebba. I need you desperately. Do you hear me? You *must* get well."

"You need *me,* child? I thought no one needed old Ebba anymore. I couldn't see no reason for living. No more friends, no more family—"

"You stepped out in front of the carriage on purpose?" Alexandra asked in amazement.

A sheepish look came over Ebba's face. "And I'm ashamed of it, too, sugar, but you see when you left me in New Orleans, I caught that ship. I made it fine until I got to this here city. Before I'd even gotten to my friends, I'd been robbed, beaten, everything I had taken. This is a frightful place, child. It ain't good to us from the South. Supposed to be a place for us here, but there ain't. We'd be better off back in the South. At least we knew what was what there. My friends were as bad off as me. Couldn't get no work, couldn't get no help. Had to live any way they could. They're dying here, child. There's no place for them and in the winter, the cold gets them. I couldn't take it no more. My friends were giving me *their* food. I couldn't do that. Weren't right. There just was no more reason for living."

432

Alexandra leaned over Ebba, stroking her face lovingly. "Listen to me, Ebba. I've sent for the doctor. He'll be here soon. You just can't die. I have no one else. Do you hear me? You're the only family I have left. Listen, Ebba, I carry Jake, Jacob Jarmon's, child in me. His child needs you. *I* need you."

"What's that you say, child?" Ebba asked, her black eyes intent.

"I'm carrying Jake's child."

"Thank the Lord. There's going to be another Jarmon. Oh, sugar, nothing could make me happier," Ebba said, looking into Alexandra's face happily. "And nothing could kill me now. Got to get up out of this bed and take care of you. Got lots to do. You made any baby clothes yet?"

Alexandra shook her head negatively, laughing.

"No! You young things just don't understand. Those babies come quicker than you realize. A Jarmon," she said, beaming. "You and that Jacob. Now, he was always the man in my books. What a fine child you two will have."

Alexandra smiled, thrilled to see the light back in Ebba's eyes.

"But where's that scoundrel? That Jacob? Didn't that boy marry you?" Ebba asked sternly.

Alexandra stood up quickly, walked across the room, then came back to Ebba. Her voice was very quiet when she said, "He's dead, Ebba. I saw him killed."

"Good Lord! Bless the poor boy's soul. Can you tell me about it, sugar?"

"Oh, Ebba," Alexandra cried, flinging herself into the chair, "I can't! It's still—"

"I understand, child. Ebba understands. You'll tell me when you can. Right now, we'll just take care of you. I don't need no doctor no more. You're medicine enough for me. See, I'm feeling fine now." Ebba grinned.

Alexandra dried her tears. "You're going to stay right in that bed until the doctor gets here, then you're going to have some broth—"

"Broth?" Ebba asked, groaning. "Oh, child, I've been starving long enough. I need some real food."

Alexandra laughed, feeling happy inside. "All right, providing the doctor approves, you'll have whatever you want."

"Oh, that sounds good, Miss Alexandra. I hope he gets here soon."

"Oh, he will, Ebba, then everything will be fine, just fine."

Chapter Twenty-six

A perfect day for a wedding, Alexandra thought grimly as Ebba adjusted her beautiful white wedding gown. The sun was shining and a cooling breeze blew in through the open window, but it didn't please her. She had, in fact, hoped it would rain. That would have suited her mood better.

"You sure this is right, child?" Ebba asked, watching Alexandra in concern. "Grieving for another man ain't much of a way to start a marriage."

"I know, Ebba, but my baby must have a name."

"There's something about that man—"

"He's all I've got," Alexandra broke in.

They had spent a busy week shopping for the wedding and the baby. They had both indulged in all kinds of delectable foods and regaled each other with all the events that had transpired after they had parted in New Orleans. They had spoken little of the future, and when they had, it had centered around the baby — their one tie with the past.

"Well, I still wish you were happier, sugar. But time will heal. It always does," Ebba said, nodding in satisfaction at Alexandra's image in the mirror.

"I hope so, Ebba, I hope so."

"It's time, child. If you're set on this course, then we might as well get it over with. That baby won't wait for no minister when it's ready to come into this world."

Alexandra laughed. "No, I'll bet my child won't."

She took a deep breath, then walked across her bedroom toward the door. Ebba followed, her heavy silk skirts rustling.

Downstairs, Stan awaited them in the parlor, dressed as befitted the occasion. Now that the wedding was at hand, he had become nervous. What if Alexandra decided not to go through with it? What if she became sick? What if something unforeseen happened? He'd waited so long for this moment that he simply wanted to grab her by the hair, drag her to the altar and have done with it. If there needed to be niceties, they could have them later. All the preparations had made him anxious, and Alexandra had been even more remote since Ebba had joined her. That was one woman he'd get rid of immediately after they were married, he told himself as he paced the room.

He looked up to see Alexandra walking toward him, Ebba behind her. He forgot all the waiting, all the nervousness in her presence. He didn't think he'd ever seen her so lovely, but then he always thought that each time he saw her anew.

He walked over to her, and kissed her hand. She was cold. He sensed her nervousness and complete withdrawal. Well, no matter. She was going to marry him one way or another. He'd gone through too much, killed too many men to lose her at this point. She was merely frightened by the thought of marriage. He'd take care of that. He would give her no more time to think.

"Come, Alexandra, it's time," he said, extending his arm, and they were on their way.

The carriage moved swiftly down the street, carrying the trio rapidly toward the chapel. Somehow it didn't seem quite real to Alexandra, even though she could feel Stan's hands heavy on her own. The streets were crowded with people bustling around, absorbed with their own business. They could not know, or even care, that she was on her way to be married to a man she didn't love, or that her heart was breaking for love of a man who was dead, killed by her own fiancé. But she cared—desperately! Oh, Jake, why couldn't it be you by my side?

The carriage moved relentlessly on, pulling closer and closer to the chapel. It would not

wait. Stan would not wait. Only Alexandra
wanted to stop the quickly approaching moment
when she would stand by Stan Lewis in front of
the altar. And as she sat there, her mind
searching for escape like a butterfly fluttering
against a windowpane, the carriage rolled to a
stop in front of a small stone building near a
large, magnificent church.

Stan turned to her, smiling.

Unable to face his triumphant expression, she
looked away, down the street. Her tormented
green eyes widened, softening, as she stared at a
solitary male figure some distance away. Her
heart seemed to catch, then began pounding
rapidly and with each beat one word reverber-
ated in her mind — Jake, Jake, Jake.

Her hand automatically covered her mouth to
stifle the word that wanted to burst forth.
There was no Jake. He was dead. There was
only Stan Lewis!

She jerked her head around, her eyes bright
with tears and pain, her heart close to bursting.
She could not breathe.

"Alexandra, are you coming?" Stan asked impatiently.

She tried to stop her reeling mind. Stan stood
on the ground, his arms extended toward her. It
was time. She had to go to him. She willed
herself not to look back at the lone man watching her, his legs spread wide, his arms at his
sides. Jake *was* dead.

"Alexandra."

"Yes. Yes, I'm coming, Stan," she whispered.

She felt Stan take her arm. If she turned around, would the man still be there watching her? She must not look. She must not!

The high, elaborately carved, double doors to the chapel opened, and Stan led her inside. It was cool here, and intimate. It was all smooth woods and deep, rich velvets. They walked side by side down the aisle, Ebba behind them. An aisle had never seemed so short.

The minister and his wife were happy, smiling, gray-haired people, who nodded encouragingly as they came closer. Flowers appeared. Alexandra could smell them as she held the delicate blossoms in her hands. How long would they live?

They spoke in whispers. She couldn't seem to hear their words. Was the solitary man still outside?

Stan held her hand. His was hot. Hers was cold. She could feel Ebba's nearness on her right. She could not feel Stan on her left. He did not exist for her. The minister's wife was smiling at them, her eyes warm. The minister had opened his Bible. He was speaking. What did he say? She couldn't seem to hear him.

There was a noise behind them. The doors opened. Steps rang out momentarily in the chapel. Her heart gave a tiny leap. She forced herself to look at the minister.

He was looking past them toward the back of the chapel. His face was confused. He frowned slightly before turning back to his Bible. He cleared his throat, then began reading again.

"And if there be any man present who knows a reason why this man and this woman should not be joined in holy matrimony, let them speak now, or forever hold their peace."

Silence.

Her heart beat faster. The chapel was quiet. Let there be a reason, please. There is a reason, many reasons. I cannot marry this man. He killed my love. How can I marry him? Will no one speak?

Silence.

The minister cleared his throat, glanced to the back of the chapel, waited, then resumed speaking.

"Alexandra?"

Her name. The minister had stopped speaking. She looked at him. What did he want?

"Do you take this man—"

That was it. Her answer. She must agree. It was only two words. Two short words to bind her to Stan Lewis forever. Two small words to make her Stan's wife.

"Alexandra?"

The minister was looking at her. Stan was looking at her. She opened her mouth. What were the words?

"I—I—"

"She doesn't!" boomed a familiar voice from the back of the chapel.

"Jake!" Alexandra cried, her heart almost bursting with happiness.

But as she whirled to see her love, Stan reached inside his jacket. He had come prepared. As he drew his pistol, he swiveled around. The minister saw him and reached out to stop him, the movement prematurely jerking Stan's finger against the trigger.

The pistol fired. A bullet tore through the minister's arm, spraying bright red blood over Alexandra's white gown. The minister's wife screamed and reached for her falling husband.

Stan ignored the wounded man and continued to spin, his gun still smoking, holding Jake's life in its next chamber.

But Jake was ready.

His hand was steady, his eyes hard as he squeezed off his shot, the only shot he would need. Jake's bullet smashed into Stan's chest, hurling him backward across the altar where he remained motionless as his life gushed out. His gray eyes were bewildered, then glazed over and saw nothing more.

Alexandra flew to Jake, flinging herself into his arms as tears of happiness ran down her face.

Was it really true? Could he be real? She looked up into his hard, handsome face. A fresh pink scar was etched across his temple and she ran her fingers along it. He *was* real!

Jake crushed her to him. "I love you, Alexandra. I love you."

She eagerly pressed her lips to his.

Nothing could ever separate them again.